I0739141

Cover Design and Interior Format

THE SHADOW

THE ORIGINAL'S TRILOGY

CARA CRESCENT

DEDICATION

WE ALL KNOW THE FRIENDSHIP hierarchy, right? You've got your acquaintances, your girls, your bff, and, if you win life's lottery, your "person"—courtesy of Grey's Anatomy. Your person has been around a long time. She's seen you ugly cry. She's been there through births, deaths, litigation, surgery, marriage, divorce, you name it. She's the one that helps you up when you fall down—she's usually laughing so hard she's crying when she does, but, you know, she helps you up and that's what matters. She's probably used your PIN at some point. Her name is on legal documents somewhere in your home. If you've ever done something a bit dodgy…your person was there. She helps herself to items in your fridge and if she discovers she took something you wanted, she begins to eat with relish, smacking her lips and moaning in pleasure. Your person may even have bitched for a two hour car ride because you gave her catch phrase to the hero instead of the heroine—all right, maybe yours doesn't do that, but mine does. And you put up with it because your person "sees" you—the real you without your social polish. She sees you and she still chooses to be your friend. Not only that, but she allows you to see the real her and that's a blessing because then you know you're not the only crazy person in the world.

I've never been too lucky in most things, but I did win life's lottery.

To Yelena Stock—my person.
"It's all about perspective."

When the Original is no longer cursed
She'll come to thee as three.
All as humans first,
Then as daemons are set free:
The Beacon burning bright,
The Shadow hidden from sight,
The blighted, damned Knight.

—The Black Book of Daemonology

CHAPTER I

London, England

DUNCAN SINCLAIR WASN'T A FIRM believer in rules—they tended to complicate the hell out of life—but he did have three. Three rules and a vague sense that he'd landed himself here because he'd broken them.

Rule one: Never let true emotions show. With his hands stacked behind his neck, he leaned back into the head of the Vampiric Council's chair, propped his booted feet on the table, and whistled the "Arsenal Anthem." With a little luck, he looked like a male without a care in the world. A far better state than the turmoil crawling beneath his flesh.

He sat alone in the cavernous chamber where the Vampiric Council held court far below London's streets. Thirteen high-backed leather chairs surrounded the table, one for each Council member. The room was a mix-match of modern-technology and gothic-vampire-chic with flaming wall sconces situated between vast displays of monitors—telly, computer, security, and infrared. From the look of things, the Vampiric Council appeared intent on staying in the know and that made his ass clench.

An ignorant Council could be a dangerous thing, but a well-advised Council was the stuff of nightmares.

He'd always done his best to avoid the barmy bastards even while being indelibly attached to them. It was a shitty position to be in. Akin to being chained to a rabid lion, dragging him along in the wake of its destruction. And while he couldn't outright beat the system, he did fuck with it behind their backs, making his own decisions when the Council's directives didn't mesh with his ethics.

He hadn't had cause to enter this room in almost five years because he'd followed his bloody rules and stayed off the Council's radar. Guardians never came to the Council—not unless they'd fucked up or were owed a favor. Which brought him to Rule Two: Do the job and do it well. He did his job, assassinated those on his kill orders and kept his damn emotions to himself.

Well, most of the time. He'd mucked up the last job Leopold had sent him on. Leopold, the head of the Vampiric Council, had called in a favor five years ago. Duncan had taken the job, didn't have much option not to but when he'd discovered his target was a fourteen-year-old lad with the same coloring as his own son, he'd allowed his emotions to guide him. He'd saved the lad instead of ashing him. Recently, he'd begun to realize he'd gotten as attached to the lad as his own son. God knew he'd tried not to. Love was a messy, thankless emotion which is why Rule Three was simple: Never love.

Not surprising to his mind, then, that he'd ended up here, the last place he wanted to be. That's what he got for breaking every last damn rule for that ungrateful little shite.

Unfortunately, in Harry's case—the lad he'd been sent to dust—his rules had conflicted with a vow he'd made centuries ago to his own son. He'd promised to never again walk away from a problem just because it was easier.

So, he'd helped Harry . . . was still helping Harry. And now he had a sneaking suspicion the Council had sussed out their secret and intended to make him redundant in a permanent way.

The sharp raps of footsteps on stone echoed in the chamber as some-one approached. Duncan forced himself to remain still, even closed his eyes, as if he might be napping. With his hands stacked behind his neck, his fingertips brushed the hilt of the knife holstered between his shoulder blades. He was prepared to fight his way out of the room should things go south.

Only one set of footsteps approached, coming around to stop in front of him. "You know, they say that table was made from the scale of a dragon."

Well, shite. Leo himself had come up. Duncan sighed and opened his eyes to scan the iridescent surface he'd propped his boots on. The table *was* beautiful: The dark surface changed color—blue, green, purple, pink—as he tipped his head this way and that. He'd always been partial to the thing. "Been 'round three-hundred years and never seen the like. I'm more apt to believe it came from a mutated abalone shell than some fancy dragon," he muttered.

He turned his attention to Leo. The head of the Vampiric Council had been transformed at a young age. He couldn't have been more than twenty with his slight frame and soft hands. In contrast to his youthful appearance, his hair was as white as the handkerchief sticking out of the pocket of his dark blue suit.

The corner of Leo's mouth tipped up. His hand shot out, knocking Duncan's feet to the ground. "Show a little respect, Sinclair."

Slowly, with an amused twist to his lips, he unfolded himself and stood. He'd always been a big brute of a man—a fighter in his human life—with a mug to match. He'd learned from experience people rarely found him approachable at first glance—his jaw was too square, his forehead too high, his neck too thick. He canted his face down to look Leo in the eye. "You all right, Leopold?"

"I'm well." Leo crossed his arms. "You?"

"Good as gold, luv." An old Cockney expression that had more to do with his state of being than his general health—*Don't fuck with me, guv, I'm the genuine article. No fakery here.*

Leo's lips quirked in an expression that could indicate irritation as easily as humor. He'd much prefer Leo's annoyance. He was a sick bastard, so anything he found amusing was likely right dodgy.

"I suppose you're anxious to know why you're here."

Duncan stuffed his hands in his pockets, rocking back on his heels. "Thought maybe you missed me."

"Funny. You always were." Not even the corner of his lips curved. His expression remained flat. "I have a job for you."

He froze for half a second. This wasn't what he'd expected. He'd been set for a row—the kind only one body walked away from. "Go on."

"I need a woman killed."

Duncan didn't so much as blink. As an assassin, he didn't have the option to be picky in his targets, but this was unusual. "A woman. Not a female?" He'd never been asked to kill a human before.

"There are two." Leo waved his hand in a dismissive gesture. "I don't think it matters which one you kill."

This time, he couldn't help it when his brows drew down and his nose wrinkled. "Usually, when someone orders a hit, guv, they're a bit more specific. Do I pick a woman at random?"

"Don't be an idiot." Leopold started pacing.

When he brushed his hair from his forehead, his hand shook. Interesting.

"There are two women in Washington—the state, not the Capitol. My secretary will give you their last known address."

"How old is your information?"

"Twenty-four hours."

"Who's your informant?"

"Julius Crowley."

"Fuck's sake." Duncan snorted. He wouldn't trust that slick git any more than he'd trust a card sharp holding all the aces.

Leopold whipped around, pinning Duncan with his stare. "Did I ask your opinion?" He turned, his long white hair whirling around his shoulders. "You know, it's odd. I knew the Watchers would send someone, but I'm curious why they chose you."

Lovely. This just kept getting better. The Watchers—the two-hundred angels fallen from grace—gave the Guardians—assassins like him—their orders. They saw and heard everything, everywhere, and punishment for failure was swift and irrevocable, making it impossible to duck their orders. The reason he'd gotten away with helping Harry was because that kill order had come from Leopold, not the Watchers.

In the grand scheme of things, while the Vampiric Council rode herd on the Guardian, Duncan and the others had no problem skiving their more . . . questionable orders. The Watchers on the other hand, no one disobeyed. That put him in a precarious position. He wasn't allowed to kill humans, yet here they were ordering him to do so. This whole thing was sketchy.

"The Watchers've been giving me plenty of work." He shrugged. "Me feelings won't be hurt if you'd rather send someone else." In all honesty, he'd prefer it.

"I suppose they have their reasons." Leo narrowed his eyes. "I'm surprised they chose you, is all." His cold green stare raked over him.

You. A Cockney bastard who's IQ had always been measured on looks and quality of speech.

Duncan jerked his head to the side to crack his neck.

"I suppose after what you did to your family . . . ." Leo sniffed. "This should be routine."

Adrenaline spiked through Duncan's veins as the urge to destroy the little fuck almost overwhelmed his common sense. He needed every ounce of discipline to keep his temper in check. Like everyone else, Leo had made an assumption based on his looks. No one ever bothered to ask for the facts. "Anything else?"

"The women are under the protection of a Guardian gone rogue."

Yeah, right. Guardians didn't go rogue. He damned near rolled his eyes before he remembered sarcasm wouldn't help the situation.

"It's the women affecting him, I'm sure." Leopold waved his own spurious reasoning aside. "Kill one. Bring the other to me. If the Guardian gets in the way, dust him, too."

"Who is he?"

"James Pasquino."

Yeah, Leopold was feeding him a load of bollocks. Though he'd never met him, Pasquino was the one Guardian the Vampiric Council had always held up as an example to all the rest.

This was like the situation with Harry all over again. The Council must have bunked something up and they were using him to sweep the evidence under the rug. But he hadn't cleaned up the last mess. He'd taken Harry home.

And the Watchers bloody well knew that. They knew *everything*. So, why'd they pick him? If they'd wanted to punish him for disobeying Leopold and hiding Harry, they could've tipped off the Council ages ago, having both him *and* the lad dusted. But the Watchers hadn't.

He pursed his lips, kissing his teeth. More likely they chose him because they knew he'd protect the innocent. Damn, things must be bad if even the Watchers were plotting against the Council. "You know, I think I got the gist of the job now."

Leo tipped his head to the side, studying him. "Maybe you're not the right Guardian for this job. I need to think. I should ask for confirmation. I may have misinterpreted their message."

Duncan opened his mouth to argue, but before he could reply, the electronics in the room came alive, beeping and humming. All the screens read: Duncan Sinclair. Some flashed his name, others ticked the letters across the bottom of the screen. The Watchers had their minds set.

Leo turned a slow circle, taking it all in before his glare returned to Duncan.

He smiled. Shrugged.

"You have three days, Sinclair."

Duncan turned on his heel, moseying out of the room, whistling as he went.

Nobody disobeyed the Watchers.

Not even Leopold.

LEOPOLD CLOSED HIS EYES, PULLING his consciousness back into his real body. His doppelgänger—the projection of himself—still stood in the Council chambers ready to respond with rote answers should anyone come upon him.

He opened his real eyes. His body sat in the same position he'd left it in, seated in the chair next to where he'd left his mate sleeping. She'd been up for some time, though.

Evelyn stared back with one clear eye. The lid sagged over the left. She smiled, but only the right side of her mouth curved up. A thin line of clear spittle ran from the other corner of her mouth, down to pool on the rise of her breast.

She'd been trying to dress herself again. She wanted so much to be as strong on the outside as she was on the inside.

He swallowed past the sudden lump in his throat. "I see we've been busy, dearest." He leaned forward in his chair, tugging the sides of her blouse closed; the material had been caught under her useless left arm. "Let me help."

She sighed. Her right hand fisted, but she didn't fight.

"I know. I can't imagine how difficult this is . . . all these years." He kept his gaze focused on hers while he buttoned the top. "But it won't be long. We'll have them soon. The ones who did this to you."

"C-c-c-" She swept her right hand out to the side. Started rotating her hand. She always did that when concentrating. "C-c-co. Co. Cov-Cove." She nodded, her one eye bright. "Coven."

He smiled. Corrected her pronunciation. "Coven." He grabbed a napkin off the nightstand and wiped away the spit leaking from her mouth. "Not the coven, but the Original. The two of them, the important ones, but we've got them this time."

"Bet-b-b-better."

"Yep. You're going to get better. They did this to you; they can damn well un-do it."

"Cro-o-o—"

"Crowley?" He shook his head. "The bastard disappeared again." Julius Crowley . . . well, the thing inside Crowley, excelled at fuckery. He must be planning to take the two women for himself. To use them to get free from his fleshy prison. Once free, the son of a bitch would be uncontrollable.

He refused to allow that to happen. Crowley hadn't upheld his end of their bargain yet. While Leopold couldn't force the issue, he could ensure the bastard didn't have access to the Original or her powers any time soon. "I sent Duncan to kill one of the women and bring the other to us."

Her eye widened. "Wh-wha?" She shook her head. "W-w-why?"

Because he didn't have a choice. The Watchers had taken an interest in his activities. While he wasn't sure whose side they were on, he didn't dare disobey them. "The Watchers insisted I send him, but they didn't oppose my orders." Perhaps they had their own reason for wanting the Original out of Crowley's grasp. He slipped his hand under the hem of her skirt where the prying eyes of the Watcher's couldn't see and squeezed her thigh, letting her know more was in the works than what he could say. "It's all part of the plan."

What he wasn't sure of is why Crowley—the thing inside Crowley—hadn't tried to stop him. Somehow, he had the sinking suspicion the bastard approved of his move. But why? Perhaps he didn't want to deal with the power of both women together, either.

CHAPTER 2

Carnation, Washington

EVERYTHING WAS GOING TO BE fine.

Trina Lopez stared into her mirror. She'd been doing so more often in recent years. She wasn't looking for signs of aging, nor admiring herself. She was checking to make sure she was still there.

When people had first started ignoring her, she'd thought everyone had discovered the crime she'd committed and were avoiding her. Eventually, she'd realized the truth: People no longer saw her unless she drew attention to herself. She could stand naked in the middle of a crowded stadium, and unless she shouted, "Hey, look at me!" no one would notice.

That wasn't a feeling. Nor a psychosis. It was a fact.

She'd learned to deal with it. Would make some smart-assed comment every time she walked into a room to gain people's notice. She'd say "Hi" as she passed friends in the halls. She went out of her way to be seen when it behooved her to be seen. The rest of the time . . . well, the rest of the time she disappeared altogether from their consciousness—out of sight, out of mind.

But now that she was home . . . Trina grinned. She wasn't invisible anymore. Why? She had no idea. As a child she'd hated Haven House. After Rowena had consigned her to the Navy at the age of seventeen, she'd vowed never to return.

She'd lived here with Lilith's grandmother, Nan, and the orphaned girls of the Grigori coven after her mother had died. Back then, her telepathy had been wide-open because she hadn't learned to control it yet. She'd also been a precocious child and always in trouble. Which meant those around her were usually mad at her, and she got the full brunt of their unfiltered thoughts.

Trina always ruins everything. Does she have to live here?

She knew exactly what everyone thought of her. And she'd spent her life trying to overcome those thoughts.

Her military record had been spotless . . . up until her invisibility problem. Her social life stellar . . . again, until people stopped seeing her. She'd even summoned her soul mate, Trevor—wealthy with All-American-boy good looks and charm—the kind of guy every girl wants to bring home to Mom and Dad . . . well, he'd looked good on the surface, anyway. Okay, so overcoming the coven's expectations hadn't gone well, but she'd get there.

At least she had Lilith.

When she'd driven home to Haven House from her apartment just outside the Bremerton Naval Yard, she'd been nervous as hell. She hadn't seen her BFF in two years, but there hadn't been cause for worry. Lilith had seen her as soon as she'd come up the drive, had bounded out of the house to greet her, and they'd clicked as if no time had passed.

They were together again and everything had been normal—*she'd* been normal. They'd sat down and had a few drinks. Laughed. Teased. They'd chatted out loud and then in their minds. Lilith had told her about her mate James, a vampire Guardian, and though she'd avoided telling Lilith about her life, she had told her she'd come back because she'd had a vision. She'd come back because Lilith would need her. She hadn't gotten into specifics—how in her vision a Darkness surrounded and killed her—she hadn't wanted to worry her.

"Come on, Trina. The pizza will be here soon."

She left her room and bounded down the stairs.

Turned out Lilith *had* been having problems—Julius Crowley, a vampire with a mesmerist talent had been stalking her. He'd even sent other daemons to try to kidnap her—though she'd fought them off with James' help. She was certain the darkness from her vision symbolized Crowley and his thugs.

Trina stumbled to a halt at the curved entrance to the kitchen; Lilith wasn't alone. Her mate, James, stood with her, his thick arms folded over his chest. At first glance, there wasn't any softness to him—his shaved scalp gleamed, his eyes held the glow of all nocturnal predators, and his chiseled features framed a scowl. He always scowled when he looked at her.

Not that she blamed him. He had every right to. Yesterday afternoon, she'd walked in to find Lilith unconscious on the floor and James standing over her covered in blood. She'd damned near lost her mind. She *did* lose control of her Magic. If Lilith hadn't woken when she had, she'd no longer have a mate. So, James could scowl all he wanted—she was just happy he could see her. She winked at him.

One dark brow lifted.

At least Lilith was smiling. Tall and thin, she'd always towered over Trina, but standing next to James, she looked petite. Willowy. She brushed her dark hair over her shoulder with a natural grace few possessed. The thing was, they weren't sure what Lilith was. When James had bitten her, Lilith hadn't transformed into a vampire, not all the way. She didn't have a shadow, her eyes glowed in the dark, and she was immortal. But she still had a heartbeat and a reflection, so she wasn't really a vampire. They had no idea what she was, nor why she and Lilith hadn't been able to communicate telepathically since then.

"Are you okay? You took off last night and I haven't seen you since."

"Yeah." Trina waved away Lilith's concern. "Just tired."

Where Lilith was tall, sweet, and small-breasted, with a creamy complexion, Trina was short, loud, on the clumsy side, and had the dark complexion of her Mayan ancestors. They were opposites, and yet they'd always meshed as friends in a perfect sort of way.

"Glad to hear it." James' chin notched up. "What in the hell happened?"

That was James. Always to the point. Direct. Honest to his own detriment. And she so was not taking the blame for last night. "You mean the part where your friend tried to mesmerize my friend so he could kill us all?"

Crowley had come to Haven House right after the botched transformation. He was young. Handsome. Creepy as fuck. He hadn't even noticed her when he'd stood on their doorstep, trying to mesmerize Lilith into inviting him into their home.

James scowl darkened. "He's not my goddamn friend. If he was, I wouldn't have showed her how to banish him from the property. I want to know what happened after that."

She shrugged. "I thought Lilith had a good plan."

Lilith bumped James' shoulder. "It was a good plan. We had no way of knowing Crowley had gotten to the coven."

The plan was simple: She'd go to her induction ceremony and once she was an official member of the coven, Trina would bop in and together with the coven, they'd overthrow their high-priestess, Rowena.

Except the coven had summoned James with the intent of destroying him.

"Ah." Trina nodded. "You mean the part where I saved your ass."

When she'd arrived at the ritual circle in Rowena's back yard, she'd found the entire coven had been mesmerized, Lilith had been bound, James trapped in a summoning circle, and Rowena and Crowley were arguing about what would happen next.

Trina had gotten to play the hero. She'd freed Lilith and James and woken the coven from Crowley's hypnosis. She'd been a bad-ass and it had felt so damn good. Everything had gone right . . . until it went wrong.

Lilith shrugged. "She saved both our asses."

"Jesus, Lil. Don't encourage her."

Trina grinned. She'd been a pain in his ass since she'd arrived. Mostly because she wanted his measure, but partly because it was so much fun. They needed a little fun after last night.

In the end, Rowena had died and Crowley escaped with the humans.

It wasn't ideal. They would have all preferred it if he were dead but Lilith, James, and the coven had all survived. That's what mattered most.

"Why don't you let me and Trina visit?" Lilith put her hand on James' arm. That's all it took. The grouchy male from seconds before turned into a big ol' teddy bear right before her eyes. When he gazed at Lilith, his features softened and his lips curved up at one corner.

Love. It was nauseating.

He leaned down and kissed Lilith. A quick melding of lips. Possessive. Demanding. So fucking sweet it hurt to watch. "Ugh. Standing right here, guys." Not that she wanted James or begrudged Lil. She just wanted someone . . . and at the same time, knew she'd lost that opportunity.

As James strode past, he smacked Trina's ass. "Behave yourself, Sunshine."

Her hands fisted and she turned toward his retreating back before she even realized what she was about to do.

"Satrina Lopez!"

She started. Shook out hands, releasing the build-up of Magic. When she turned back to Lilith, she plastered a smile on her face. "Just kidding."

Lilith's eyes narrowed.

"We're trying to get along." She did like James. He treated Lilith well— she'd never seen her friend so happy. "I just like to mess with him."

"I hope so." Lilith waved her closer. "I have news." Lilith winked.

"Which is?"

She shook her head. "I have to wait. The pizza will be here soon and we're expecting company, and—"

"Company?" She couldn't handle the coven right now. Lilith knew they didn't like her. "I wondered why you went to the trouble of ordering pizza when you and James can't eat it. Maybe I'll just head out—"

"No!" Lilith covered her mouth, trying to hide a smile. "Oh, gods, Trina. You're going to kill me." Her eyes crinkled and a laugh escaped. "I'm going to be dead by morning, I just know it."

Dear goddess, not another of Lilith's *plans*. "If you keep this up you will be. What's going on? Who's coming?"

"I don't know exactly." Lilith shrugged. "We'll find out soon enough. As for what's going on, I need to explain some things about what we found out about the Original."

"Crowley called you that. When he came here, he asked you if you were the Original." James had taken Lilith to see the Historian to find out what he meant, but they hadn't had time to tell her what they'd discovered. "What is it?"

"I'd rather wait until our guest arrives so I don't have to repeat myself—it's too risky."

She glanced around. They were alone. "It's not someone from the coven, is it?"

"No." Lilith sighed. "Look, I know they weren't very nice to us when we were all little, but they have changed. They were just scared kids back then."

Trina folded her arms over her chest. "So were we." That didn't excuse the thoughts they'd had. "So what, we're just waiting here?"

Lilith nodded. She seemed way too proud of herself. Scary, that. She leaned forward and lowered her voice. "What did happen last night . . . with the wave?"

Where to start.

Rowena had started several fires with her Magic during the fight. While James and Crowley fought, the flames had started to surround them. "James almost went head first into a burning bush." Her lips twitched—kind of apropos considering he'd been a priest when human. "He told me to put out the fire." Except her Magic went wonky and instead of conjuring a little water—she'd conjured a tidal wave which had sent everyone ass over teakettle. Crowley had gotten away in the deluge.

Lilith pressed her lips together—twenty bucks said she had the same thought about the burning bush. "Well, you did accomplish that."

Yes. Yes, she had. "Look, I'm sorry. I just wanted to help."

"You did." Lilith wrapped her in a hug. "I am so happy you're here."

"Me, too." She'd stayed away too long. Everything would be fine now that she was home. Her Magic was still acting up, but it would get better soon.

Lilith jerked away with a gasp. Her face twisted into a grimace as she stared down at her right arm. Her hand was blackened. Charred.

The Darkness she'd seen in her vision. Trina shook her head. She'd thought it was symbolic. She'd thought it represented Crowley... not that the blackness would literally creep over Lilith's skin.

"Trina?" Lilith staggered back, leaning against the old harvest-gold refrigerator. She looked down. Touched the blackness creeping up the pale skin of her right arm with her shaking left hand. That hand came away blackened, too. "Shit. What is it?"

Trina's heart beat so fast in her chest she couldn't catch her breath. "Come sit down." She put her hands on Lilith's shoulders, to guide her toward a chair and the blackness streaked up from around the collar of her shirt. She let go of Lilith and backed away.

It was her. Every time she touched Lilith . . .

In her vision, when the Darkness closed in around Lilith, she'd saved her. That's why she'd come home, to *save* Lilith.

Except maybe she wasn't meant to save her . . . What if she *was* the Darkness?

The Darkness inched up Lilith's arm and spread over her shoulders and neck, leaving the muscles sunken, the skin hard and brittle.

She reached out to help her friend, but snatched her hand back at the last second. She didn't dare touch her again. Instead, she backed away, bumped into one of the kitchen chairs, and jumped as it scraped across the hardwoods. "I don't know what's wrong." *I don't know how to fix this.*

This wasn't like what happened to Trevor. She hadn't even been angry. She hadn't had any violent thoughts. Tears pricked her eyes. Her mouth wobbled. "I don't know what to do, Lil. What do I do?" With each question her voice edged up in volume.

Lilith dropped down to one knee. She held her whole body stiff, rigid, as if she feared moving. "This isn't you. Can't be."

Bullshit. "What if it is?"

"Kat." Lilith grimaced, gasped. "Kat can help."

Of course. Kat was the coven's healer. She could fix any ailment.

"James!" Trina shouted for Lilith's mate as she ran out of the kitchen and through the foyer. She took the stairs two at a time. "James!" She shoved open the door to the guestroom, snatching her purse and keys off the still-packed suitcase sitting by the door. She paused long enough to push open the door to the room Lilith shared with James. He wasn't there. *Damn.* She started back down the stairs. "Where's James?"

"Here." He walked into the foyer from the living room, his gaze tracking her progress down the stairs. "What's with all the yelling?"

"Lil's sick."

His brows drew together as he ran his hand over his head. "Where is she?"

"The kitchen. She needs Kat. I'm gonna take—"

"I'll take her." He headed into the kitchen but stopped cold. "What the hell?" He glanced back at Trina, then at Lilith. "Were you overreaching, Lil?"

Witches who tried to perform spells beyond their skill could burn themselves in the process, but this, the Darkness creeping over Lilith's skin, wasn't that.

"We weren't using Magic," Trina said. At least, she didn't think she had, but her Magic had been so weird lately she really wasn't sure.

James scooped Lilith off the floor and started for the door. "I've got you, sweetheart."

"I gave her a hug." Lilith curled into her mate, tucking her head under his chin which muffled the rest of her words as he carried her through the foyer.

Trina started to follow, but James stopped at the door, blocking her exit. "You'd better stay here, Sunshine."

She wanted to argue. She should be there for Lilith, that's what friends did, right? They were there for each other. But this was her fault. It must be. Lilith had been fine until she'd touched her. "Okay."

Unable to help, she stood on the porch, chest tight and gut roiling, while he got Lilith settled in the passenger seat of her blue Camry. Within minutes, they were gone.

The sound of the car faded, leaving behind the skittering of fall leaves and the wind through the trees. For a long while, she stared out at the night-shrouded lawn. She went back into the house, not bothering to close the front door. Should she grab her things and head out herself? She'd been sure that coming here had been what she was meant to do. So sure that she could save Lilith. For once, she thought she'd be the hero and earn the coven's respect.

Instead, she'd hurt her best friend. Just like she'd hurt her mom. And

Trevor.

She stood in the foyer, staring at the closed door of the ritual room. The secret room sat directly under the split staircase that was the heart of Haven House—the rest of the house had been built around that room. It's where they'd all practiced Magic as coven kids. It's where she'd first realized she wasn't like the other witches. She had more power. Had to be more careful.

For a moment she could see them—the rest of the coven as little girls—all lined up like eleven perfectly aligned pegs, their faces contorted with disapproval. Worse, she could hear their thoughts, like when she was young. *You always mess everything up. Why can't you just keep your mouth shut? You shouldn't use Magic if you can't use it well. You always ruin everything.*

The coven had never liked her or Lilith very much when they were kids. They had accepted Lilith now that they were adults—made her their high-priestess—though she didn't expect the same treatment.

She'd spent her whole life trying to prove them wrong and for a long time, she had. She'd had a good life. She'd been successful.

They wouldn't see that, though. They'd see that she made it possible for Crowley to get away. They'd see Lilith and the Darkness creeping over her skin.

Goddess, please, fix whatever it is I did to her. Keep her safe.

A car pulled up outside, the headlights flashing through the open door, making her shadow stretch up the wall. The headlights flicked off.

Trina turned to stand in the doorway.

A delivery kid hopped out of the car with a steaming pizza box in hand. The teen ran up the porch steps, coming to a halt before the open door. He leaned in, looking both directions. "Hello?"

Goddess, no.

Shaking, she stood right in front of him. Far too close to tears. If she didn't speak, he'd never see her. Never even know she was there.

He stood so close, she smelled the coffee on his breath. "Hello? Anyone home?"

She cleared her throat. "Hi."

The kid jumped back a full three feet. "Holy shit." He laughed. "Sorry. Didn't see you, Miss." He shook his head. This time his laugh was hesitant.

She swallowed the lump in her throat.

"Man, guess I was daydreaming or something."

"Or something." She reached into her purse for her wallet.

"It's all paid, tip and everything." Again, he angled his head, looking past her, as if she'd already disappeared.

"Thanks." She took the box and closed the door.

Haven House hadn't made her visible.

Lilith had.

CHAPTER 3

Carnation, Washington

DUNCAN HAD BEEN ON THE private charter for ten hours. In that time, the whole damned world had gone pear-shaped. He'd intended to chat with the Watchers while he drove to his job, but ever since he'd turned on the radio, the local news had had him distracted.

He turned the radio up as he cruised down an arterial toward his destination. "Local phone services have been overwhelmed with more than fifteen-hundred missing persons reports in the last twelve hours. New information suggests the phenomenon is global, with several countries requesting aid from the United Nations. We may have initial global estimates by morning." He muted the radio and tried, for the umpteenth time, to ring Harry.

Again, he got a message from the operator that all lines were busy. *Shite.*

From what he'd learned so far, the humans had grounded air traffic and were asking people not to drive or operate machinery. Two planes had crashed and there had been countless auto collisions—the collateral death toll from the disappearances was rising.

Duncan pulled over at the end of the road between street lamps where trees and bushes would conceal his car. The area didn't appear inhabited, evergreens and ground cover surrounded both sides of the asphalt. He'd passed the last house almost a mile back. Ahead, the road turned to unpaved dirt. From the amount of overgrown foliage to either side, the lane wasn't used to seeing much traffic. Supposedly, his targets lived at the end of that lane. He shut off the engine, tucking the key into the pocket of his Mackintosh. While he understood Leo's expectations, he needed confirmation on what the Watchers wanted.

"All right, then. What are we doing tonight, kill and kidnap, or search and rescue?"

Despite the vehicle being off, the radio clicked on, playing Alanis Morissette's *Guardian.*

He rolled his eyes. "Right." Search and rescue it was. He picked up his iPod, left the car, and headed down a dirt road overgrown with vegetation. The brisk night air settled right under his skin. This job and the things happening in the world—they had him spooked.

Someone had been using the lane, but they hadn't been doing so for long. Deep grooves lined the muddy ground. Broken branches hung from the bushes to either side. While he walked he put in one ear bud. "You know, I have no idea how to go about this. Can you at least give me a description of who's in the house?"

His iPod came to life, playing "Mr. Cellophane" from *Chicago.* He pulled a face. What the hell? He didn't have any bloody show tunes on his device. "You lot are getting a bit tricky, in'nit?" As he continued on, he tried to glean some information from the lyrics. The song was about a man no one paid attention to which didn't give him any clue as to what the women might look like . . . unless they happened to be mannish or see-through. "Lot of help you are."

A sign came into view. A white-washed plank nailed into a moss-covered two-by-four. Someone had written *Haven House—All Lost Souls Welcome* in black paint that had faded from years of neglect. He stepped past the sign and the music cut off mid-note. He still had a full battery. "Guess that's all you've got to say, huh?"

The house came into view. An old monstrosity of Victorian revival. The two-story estate reminded him of something out of a Vincent Price movie. He stared at it, half expecting a spectral image to peer out of one of the darkened windows, except as he got closer, he noticed all the windows had been boarded up on the inside. Pasquino must have done that to keep his bolt-hole sunlight free. Damn, he wouldn't be able to sneak a peek to see who the hell he was dealing with.

Getting in wouldn't be easy. The green haze of a door shield protected the entrances, indicating at least one of those in residence was human. "Are all three of them in there?"

His iPod remained silent.

"Anything? Come on, you expect me to knock on the bloody door?"

Nothing. Weird. Usually they'd at least play something, just enough to tell him to sod off. This total silence . . . he didn't like it.

The place had seen better days. The yard hadn't been cared for and the house needed repair, but a little red Jaguar sat in the front drive and light trickled through a few of the boards blocking the windows on the first floor of the house. Someone was here.

He swallowed. He had no idea who might be in that house. Hell, he didn't even have clear instructions on what the Watchers wanted. He wasn't to harm the occupants, that had been clear enough, but then what? Did he give them a warning and walk away? Hide them? Bring them home like he had with Harry?

Whatever he did, he needed to get back to Harry quick. The lad had a habit of finding trouble when left on his own too long and *that* was when the world *wasn't* going to hell in a handbasket.

"What about Crowley? Do I need to worry about him?" At this point he didn't expect an answer and he didn't get one. He hated that Crowley had a part in this. The bastard was a damn good mesmerist. All he needed was a second of eye contact and he crawled right into a mind. Made his victims do things. Forget things. Remember stuff that never happened.

He strode across the yard to the convertible. The inside was tidy. A romance novel sat on the passenger's seat and a can of coke had been left in the cup holder.

"Right, then. Unless you lot have a better idea, I'm knocking." He stalled a few more seconds, hoping for some kind of information, but got nothing. Maybe he'd take a look around the back of the house before he knocked. Hopefully, those windows weren't boarded up and he could at least discover if friends or foes resided inside.

Something was wrong with this whole scenario.

CHAPTER 4

ALMOST THIRTY MINUTES HAD PASSED and she'd heard nothing. What if Kat couldn't heal Lilith? What if—?

"No." Lilith would be fine. She was the only person in the world who cared about her, the goddess wouldn't be so cruel as to take her away.

Trina flopped back on the loveseat in Haven House's living room and stared at the statue of Gaia, which sat cross-legged, her arms wrapped around her pregnant belly which held the Earth, sitting on the mantle. Perched atop lace trim doilies, surrounded by an assortment of candles and little bowls filled with offerings, Gaia was the main focal point in the room and while the statue always wore a faint smile, she was certain the real Earth Mother was frowning tonight—whether in concern or disapproval, she couldn't discern.

She turned her attention to the television. The anchor adjusted the mic pinned to her bright red jacket. "Two-hundred forty more people have been reported missing from the greater Seattle area since our last update, though authorities estimate that number is low as both land line phone services as well as cell phone services are still overwhelmed. Cell service companies are advising their customers to use text or email. If you have any information pertaining to the disappearances, please text the number below, email, or visit us on Facebook."

What was happening out there was terrifying. It reminded her of that bible story. They'd made television shows about it, too. What was it?

She looked up at Gaia again as if she might have the answer, but Gaia had nothing to say. "The Darkness is because of me, isn't it?" She didn't want that to be true, but she knew it was. She drew in a shaky breath. Somehow, she needed to discover what was wrong with her and how . . . or why, she'd infected Lilith.

"Should I call? I don't want to interrupt if Kat's still trying to heal her."

James' cat, George, hung across the back of the armchair. He lifted his head long enough to hiss. She must be disturbing his sleep.

She stuck her tongue out at the orange-striped feline, picked up her phone and texted Lilith: *Are you feeling better? Did you find out what happened? Have you seen the news? I'm freaking out. I don't know if I should stay or leave.*

On the television, the camera shifted to a male anchor. "In other news, Dr. Edwin Moss has reported that he's found a cure for the infected soldiers currently quarantined in the Revelations Industries Lab. We'll do our best to keep families updated on the progress of this story."

Trina's phone buzzed. *Please stay. I need you to be right where you are. I'm fine. Didn't even need Kat. My skin went back to normal on its own.*

Yeah, as soon as James drove away from the house, probably. Hey, wait a minute! She typed: *Bitch!*

Lilith must have already been typing her excuse for not calling right away and letting her stew for the last thirty minutes. *Got side-tracked with the news. Just wanted to see if I could get some answers before I called. I'm sorry!*

Trina snorted. She better be after leaving her here worrying.

Her phone buzzed again. *The coven's been studying the disappearances. They're certain it's the Rapture.*

The Rapture. That's what she'd been thinking of—where people were brought straight to Heaven, bodies and all.

Her phone buzzed. *Brenda had a vision, she says the End Times are starting because the humans have Crowley, but she can't get a look directly at Crowley or where he's at.*

Brenda's visions were never wrong. Why would Armageddon start just because humans had Crowley? True, daemon kind had done their best to remain out of human consciousness for the last . . . well, forever. But Armageddon? Seemed an overkill response.

She closed her eyes. What the hell was Crowley up to? What did he hope to gain from all this? As a mesmerist . . . he probably had those humans eating out of the palm of his hand, but why? Why now?

At least things couldn't get worse. But maybe she could make things right by getting Crowley away from the humans.

She pressed her hands against her eyes. "Come on, Lopez, think. Next steps. Where do you go from here?"

Sitting around doing nothing while the end of the world approached was not her style, but what could she do? She fingered the moonstone choker locked around her throat. Rowena, the late high priestess of the Grigori coven, had charmed it years ago to dampen the wearer's Magic. Well, specifically, to dampen *her* Magic. She'd been forced to wear it when she was younger because Rowena hadn't trusted her or her Magic. For a while it had completely inhibited her abilities, but she'd broken it, and after that it had only slowed her Magic to a somewhat manageable level.

She'd carried the damn thing around for years, with the hope that someday she could slip it around Rowena's neck. But after what happened with Lilith tonight, she'd put it on willingly, hoping it would prevent any more accidents until she could figure out why her Magic had become hair-trigger responsive and twice as powerful. Why, when she conjured only enough water to put out a few small fires, she'd gotten a tidal wave, instead. Whatever had affected her Magic must be what caused the blackness to creep over Lilith's skin when they touched. She couldn't take any more chances, not with Lilith or anyone else.

At the same time, she was desperate to make up for her mistake, find Julius Crowley, destroy him, and end Armageddon. The conflicting urges had her in a state of near panic. She didn't know where to start or what to tackle first. She didn't know if the humans who took Crowley were his allies or enemies, where they'd taken him, or why.

Her phone rang. She thumbed over the green button and put it to her ear. Before she could even say hello, Lilith started talking. "I know what you're doing. This isn't your fault."

"How'd you get through?" They just said all the lines were busy.

"Magic, dork."

She jumped off the couch to pace. "Yeah, well, best friends aren't supposed to lie." Everything wasn't okay. She strode through the living room, into the foyer and all the way to the kitchen before turning back. "I can't trust my Magic anymore. I've had trouble for almost two years now, but it's worse since coming back. The wave. The blackness. I don't know what's wrong with me."

"Don't say that. This *isn't* you."

The certainty in Lilith's voice made her pause. "What do you mean?"

"It's *my* fault."

She laughed. "That's ridiculous. You're the high priestess of the Grigori coven, the Original, you—"

"Yes. *That's* the problem." Lilith sighed. "It's not safe for me to talk. Look, go to Le Fey's place, okay?"

Trina's brows drew together. They'd nicknamed Rowena "Morgan Le

Fey" after hearing their mothers refer to her as such when they were kids. Neither she nor Lilith had ever spoken that name aloud; they'd only called her that when they were chatting telepathically.

"Go look up the subject we're talking about."

What? "The Original?"

"Yes."

Trina paused mid-step, replaying the conversation over in her head. Lilith was being very careful with her words. To anyone listening, she could be talking about anything. "Is someone listening?"

"*Yes.*"

What the hell? Was someone in the room with Lilith? Did they think her phone was bugged? It couldn't be the Watchers because they'd hear her side of the conversation, too. "Can they hear me?"

"No."

"Is it the coven?"

"No."

"James?"

"*No!*" Lilith sputtered. "You're so far off you're not even in the correct galaxy." She huffed. "Go do what I said."

Trina wet her lips. "I'm a little scared." It was a stupid thing to admit. She was used to being on her own. As long as she didn't draw attention to herself, no one could see her, much less harm her. Still, she was scared. She'd always relied on her Magic for so much and right now she couldn't trust it.

"I've, uh . . . *sent* for someone to, um, *help* you."

We're expecting company. Wonderful. She'd forgotten about that. "Who?"

"Just trust him, okay?"

Him? "No. Not until you tell me who he is."

"I don't *exactly* know. . . ."

"Lil–ith."

"Now, I don't want you to panic but I, uh . . . ." She sighed. "Well, remember the first time we watched *Indiana Jones*?"

Trina snorted. "How could I possibly forget? I was so enamored of Indy and Marion, I got all amped up about all of us girls in the coven finding our mates." Nan had been adamant that neither witches nor daemons had mates.

"Well. . . ." She cleared her throat. "You're welcome."

Trina stopped pacing. Lilith didn't *send* someone, she'd *summoned* Trina's mate. "Goddess, no. Tell me you didn't."

"I did."

"Lilith, this can't end well." She pressed her hand to her stomach. Lilith's spell, whatever it was, couldn't have worked. "I summoned my mate years ago. The man the Watchers sent. . . ." *He's dead now. My mate is dead.*

Her mate hadn't shown up as quickly as James had for Lilith. James had appeared on their doorstep after a few hours, almost twenty years ago. Two whole weeks after she'd performed the ceremony, Trevor had shown up. He'd walked right up to her, ignoring all the other women in the club. Goddess, he'd been handsome, so fucking charming. . . .

"You're not thinking clearly. Oh, honey. Look, I've got some bad news, maybe you should sit down," Lilith suggested.

Fuck that. "Just tell me."

"Brenda can't see you in her visions. Not ever. We're not sure why, but it stands to reason that if a seer can't see you . . . well, I don't think *they* heard your petition. I don't think they ever heard any of your petitions. Whoever showed up . . . *they* didn't send him."

She was talking about the Watchers. Trina sat. The Watchers couldn't see her? "Is that why you're being so vague? You don't want them to know what we're doing?"

"Yes."

She shook her head. The Watchers saw and heard everything. Everywhere. "If the Watchers don't know I exist . . . how the hell did you summon my mate?"

Someone knocked. Who the hell was at her door at three AM? "Someone's here."

Lilith scoffed. "You know who's there. Do you want me to stay on the line?"

Her mate. Her mate was on the other side of that door.

No. That was impossible. "I, uh, I don't want to do this." Her belly did a little flip. "I mean, how do you know? If the Watchers can't see me, how would they know who my mate is? You're not making sense."

"You're going to have to trust me. I can't tell you how I did it, not yet. But I don't want you to be alone. Remember what you told me when I called you all freaked out about James?"

Trina rolled her eyes. "'Enjoy him for a little while, keep his protection, and let him go.'"

"Somehow, I remember your advice being much brasher than that." The wry tone to Lilith's words made Trina smile. "You told me to do everything you would do. So now I'm giving that back, do everything you used to do."

Tears pricked the back of her eyes. Once upon a time, she'd been fearless and damn it, she wanted to be that person again. "I can't."

"Oh, honey. I did this because I want you happy. I know you've been hiding these last couple years and it has to stop."

The compassion in Lilith's voice nearly undid her. She'd almost called Lilith so many times over the last two years, but in the end, she could never find the words.

The wall rattled as someone knocked again.

Lilith sighed. "You'd better go."

"I can't do this."

"Why not?"

Because I killed him. I lost control and killed the man I thought was my mate. What if I kill this one, too? The words stuck in her throat, refusing to be spoken. "I gotta go."

"Okay. Good luck."

Trina hung up and slipped the phone into her back pocket, pausing to check that her sidearm was holstered at the small of her back. Good luck? There was nothing good about this. Her eyes burned with unshed tears, her hands shook, and she'd been rattled to her core. If that was her mate out there, he was in danger, both from Crowley as well as herself.

Then again, a brief interaction with whoever stood out there wouldn't send her over the edge. She touched the choker around her neck. It should keep her Magic to a manageable trickle. Besides, he wouldn't even be able to see her unless she spoke or touched him. She wiped her eyes, straightened her back, lifted her chin, and took a deep breath; it was okay, the guy on her doorstep was not her mate. He couldn't be; she'd killed her mate.

She opened the door wide.

Her first thought: If Hell needed bouncers, they'd look like this guy. She'd always had a particular type, and this man wasn't it; he was too big, too *everything*.

Trina forced her gaze up. He must be in his mid-to-late-thirties. He had the anatomy of a fighter, all hard planes and tight, corded muscles. The color of his eyes was obscured; they simply reflected the lights from the house. His hair had been shorn tight to his scalp, revealing a high forehead, chiseled features, and a scruff-covered square jaw. His nose had been broken, the bump adding to the almost overwhelming character of his features. He wasn't a handsome man, not in any sense of the word. He was too hard, too rugged. But he had an interesting face to go with an intriguing body.

The slightest frown must make him look downright mean, but now, wearing an amused expression, he appeared roguish. She had the distinct impression that he'd played the field a time or two . . . hundred.

"Is that appreciation in your eyes?" He winked.

He could see her? How long had she spent looking him over thinking he'd never be the wiser? No, damn it. He couldn't be her mate. He wasn't her type. She withdrew her Glock from its holster. Pointed it at him. "Who are you? Why are you here?"

His gaze rolled from the crown of her head to the black nail polish on her toes. He didn't even blink at the gun. "You human? You're giving off vibes I ain't never come across before." He tipped his head to the side.

She stared, taking a moment to shift through the jumbled mess that had come out of his mouth. He had a thick English accent, dropping half the sounds of the words, making him sound less James Bond and more Ray Winstone. She gasped. "Of course I'm human. What else would I be?"

He popped his bottom lip out, appearing to give the matter some thought. "Don't know, could be like me." He pulled the collar of his coat down to reveal a scar under his right ear—a jagged oval of webbed tissue. "But your heart's thrumming right quick." He cleared his throat. "And you ain't got the smell of a lycan. So you tell me, love. What are you?"

Slowly, she lowered her gun. The damned thing wouldn't do any good against a vampire anyway. Still, she was safe. The door shield would keep him out. "You're on my property. You do the talking."

"You're gonna put away your gun, just like that?"

She scoffed. "As if shooting you would do anything more than piss you off. I know you can't come any closer."

"Do you, now?" His lips twitched up at the corners. "Seems you know an awful lot. How 'bout this?" He pulled a chain out of his shirt to reveal a silver Guardian pendant. A devil's eye—an upside down y in a triangle—centered on an infinity symbol—a sideways figure eight. *Infinite danger.* "You know this?"

Lilith's mate wore the same symbol. All the Guardians did. He was testing her. The Vampiric Council forbade Guardians from telling humans anything more about daemon kind than they already knew. "You work for the Watchers."

"Yeah. They sent me."

Trina's mind raced. This guy, who, if he *was* a Guardian worked for both the Watchers and the Council, was throwing his allegiance out there as if it should put her at ease. But Crowley worked for the Council and the Watchers had never done her any favors. Hell, the Watchers didn't even know she existed according to Lilith, so they couldn't have sent him. "You know, I thought of how I can prove to you I'm human."

He folded his arms over his chest. "Oh?"

"Something I saw my BFF do to some unwanted company recently." Lilith had banished Julius Crowley from the house by speaking two words and some force had hurled him off the property and he hadn't been able to return.

She smiled sweetly while she fisted her hands, drawing energy from the Earth. It danced under her skin, lighting up all her nerves and making her heart race. "Go. Away."

He slid back a foot, his arms pin-wheeling as he caught his balance. He frowned. "What the hell was that?"

Why hadn't it worked? Was it her Magic? She narrowed her gaze. No. According to James, any human could banish a vampire from their property by speaking those two words, damn it! "Go away."

He wobbled a little, but nothing more.

"Go. Leave. Go away. I command you to depart." She waved her arms, shooing him. "Get off my property!"

He grinned. "Forget to take your meds, love?"

She slammed the door. Leaned back against it.

"Are you going to open up so we can chat?" His deep voice came through the closed door.

She remained silent.

"I can hear your heart beating. I know you're still there."

Why wouldn't he leave?

"All right, then. Nice chat. Good meeting you. Tea tomorrow? I'll come by around, oh, dusk. Sound good?" Silence stretched until her nerves were ready to shatter. He grumbled something unintelligible. The porch groaned under his weight as he left.

He'd be back. She either needed to relocate or find a way to get him to leave for good. She drew in a deep breath. Maybe if she took off the necklace, when he came tomorrow she could use her chaos Magic to confuse him—she had the ability to manipulate matter at the atomic level, even the energy currents within a mind. She'd send him back to wherever he came from. It'd be simple.

She sighed. The karmic kickback would be severe. She'd be sending him to certain death if he returned to the Council without completing his assignment . . . whatever that might be.

Besides, she couldn't rely on her Magic, not as haywire as it'd been. If she took the necklace off, she might end up killing him instead of banishing him.

First things first. She needed to get Rowena's Grimoire. Once she solved her little problem with her Magic, she'd get rid of the big dude, find Crowley and destroy him.

Her legs started to tremble—she wasn't just leaning against the door, but using her whole body as a barricade. She let out a shaky laugh. This was silly. He'd never get past the door shield.

But she hadn't been able to banish him and that could only mean one thing.

Dear goddess, he was her mate.

CHAPTER 5

The Astral Plane

THE THICK IRONS CLASPED AROUND Julius Crowley's wrists kept him suspended from the ceiling. His ankles, too, were bound, anchoring him to the floor. At one point, this room had been beautiful, with painted walls and sanded hardwoods. Art had hung from sliver hooks and decorated the shelves, like a small, fine-art gallery tucked into one neat little room.

Nothing but rubble remained. Water puddled on the floor. A couple of the lights still worked, which left the room in semi-darkness. Every statue had been smashed, every painting blurred with turpentine, everything was a shadow of what it had once been. Even him.

One item remained intact—a wind chime.

It was a silly, happy thing. Stupid, really. A conglomeration of gossamer strings tied to colorful glass butterflies that clinked with the slightest breeze. He couldn't remember why it was here, but it gave him something to focus on. Something bright and whole amid all the darkness and destruction.

He'd been focusing on that wind chime for a long fucking time.

Years.

Decades.

Centuries.

This—everything around him—wasn't real. It was a trick of a broken mind. A refuge from the horror of everyday life. When he couldn't take anymore reality, he turned inward and came here. But lately, even *here* had become an exercise in misery.

Except for the butterflies.

Mr. Crowley, we're going to clean you up and prepare you for a few tests.

Something tugged at him, prodding him. Not here in this room in his mind, but out *there* in the real world. Someone was doing something to his body. He shied away from the clinical rubber-clad hands, from the frigid slab at his back, the sudden chill on his skin.

Here, in this room in his mind, his skin broke out in gooseflesh as his clothing vanished.

Maybe he should go back. See what they were doing to him. See who *they* were.

He shook his head. Much more reality and he *would* break. Better to stay here in this boring, dreary room where nothing was real. Not that here was safe, but it was *safer*.

Above him, in the main part of the house, the floorboards creaked. Dust trickled down.

His whole body tensed. He wasn't alone. He hadn't been alone—even within the confines of his mind—in centuries. Something else roamed in here . . . in him . . . something terrible.

His gaze followed the footsteps across the ceiling. They came down the stairs behind him. They were far too soft to belong to the thing that lived here with him. Was Azazel fucking about? Trying to surprise him from sleep? It would be just like the bastard to force him back to reality. Azazel wanted him broken.

The door at the base of the stairs opened, sending the chimes spinning and tinkling in the resulting breeze. Rainbow lights spiraled across the walls. The scent of cinnamon permeated the air. That couldn't be Azazel. Not with a scent like that.

The intruder paused. Light footsteps hurried around to his front.

He'd seen her before—Kat was her name. She'd visited him a few weeks ago, but he hadn't expected to ever see her again. She reminded him of Katherine the Great, his mate, and the high-priestess of the old coven. Except Katherine had been tall, thin, and harsh as hell.

That was the thing about life-mates. It wasn't all Disney-style singing and googly eyes. Eventually, yes, a life-mate would bring happiness, passion, and love. But a life-mate's true purpose was to challenge their mate to be better than they were. As such, life-mates, especially when introduced before they were ready, could be brutal. When he'd met Katherine, he'd been ready—he'd fallen ass over tit in love. That's why he'd never seen her betrayal coming. Still, she'd fulfilled her duty as a life-mate. She'd taught him a lesson, one about trust and loyalty and how neither should be awarded until won in both word and deed. It was a lesson he'd never forget.

The top of this woman's head only reached mid-chest on him. Her frame was anything but thin—voluptuous would be a more apt word. Gorgeous, another. With wide hips and heavy breasts, she was softness personified. Her red hair stood out in a riot of curls around her head. Katherine would've hated her on sight.

He tried shrinking in on himself, he didn't want her seeing him like this. Didn't want her seeing all the scars. But there was nothing he could do. Her gaze stroked over him. A blush highlighted her cheeks as she bit her lip.

He felt it in his groin.

Her bright green gaze met his and didn't waver again. "I discovered your name. It's easier to find you on the astral now, Julius Crowley."

He closed his eyes. Yes, she would know his name now. They'd met her in the real world since her last visit. He, or rather the bastard residing in here with him, had ordered her death at one point, which is why he never expected to see her again.

She folded her arms under her breasts. "I think I know your other secret, too."

He snorted. She couldn't possibly.

A shiver stole over her. She glanced around as if searching for eavesdroppers. Leaned forward to whisper, "Who's in here with you?"

The air seemed to congeal in his chest. She was messing with things best left alone. "Don't." The single word came out more of a croak than a demand.

"See, my friend Claire, she's fantastic with dream Magic. I told her about this." She waved her arm around, indicating everything around them. "The house—how dilapidated and ruined everything is. You, chained-up in the basement surrounded by broken art. You know what she said?"

"Please stop." *Leave me alone. This is all I have.*

"She said in dreams, houses represent a person's body. In this case, yours."

Broken. Dilapidated. Ruined. "I don't need to hear this." She was going to ruin this. Make him think about what was happening out there to his body. To the world.

"And the basement is that person's last reserves. She fears that if you've anchored yourself all the way down here at the bottom, that you must be at the end of your rope. That you're close to giving up."

"I don't *want* to hear this." He'd been content, lying to himself for centuries—that he had some control. That he wasn't broken. That he never would be.

"And the other night . . .?"

He closed his eyes, trying to shut her out.

"Remember? When you ordered that thug to slit my throat. Right after the order left your mouth, you shouted for him to stop."

Jesus, she had the same tone as if she were telling him about the dress she'd worn that night. *He'd ordered her fucking throat slit.* "You're too sweet to die at the hands of an asshole like that."

"You sounded different when you ordered him to stop. Your voice. Your expression wasn't so . . . jaded." She came closer. Put her small hand on the rise of his pec. Her touch, so foreign, too light, almost burned. His breath hissed out.

Those bright green eyes of hers stared up. So trusting. She had no idea what an absolute bastard he was. "So tell me, Julius," she wet her lips, "are you crazy or are you possessed?"

Both. I've been possessed so long, I've gone mad.

"To be honest, possessed would be the easier of the two to fix, but either way, I'll find a way to help you." She grinned. "I'm a—"

"Why are you doing this?" Why wouldn't she leave him alone, for Christ's sake?

Her smile faded. "You're my mate."

A startled laugh burst out of him, bitter and strained. "My mate wouldn't deign to arch her dainty brow if doing so would save my fucked-up life. Try again."

Her brow arched. She lifted up on her tiptoes—"You shouldn't cuss."—and planted her soft lips right against his. All at once, it was far too much stimulation, and not enough. Part of him wanted to lean in. Part wanted to jerk away. Maybe she was his mate. Maybe she was ready now and would help instead of hurt him. Jesus, this was more warmth than he'd experienced in ages. More sweetness than he'd tasted in . . . . God help him, he couldn't remember. Unwanted tears pricked his eyes. It was so, so good. And it wasn't real.

This was a fucking dream.

Footsteps, heavy this time, tromped across the floorboards overhead.

He pulled back with a groan. "You have to go."

She shook her head. "This is your dream. You have control here."

Footfalls descended the stairs.

"Leave me." He had no control. Not anywhere. "Get out."

Her gaze traveled between him and the door at his back. She took a step away, twisting her pinky-finger with the fingers of her other hand. "I think you can make him leave."

She shouldn't have faith in him. He didn't. "You're wrong."

Behind him, the door swung open with enough force to send the wind chime into a cacophony of sound. Rainbow lights jerked, streaking across the walls as if in a panic.

He shouted, "Go!"

She jumped. Faded from the Astral as she woke back in the real world. But he remained.

The heavy footsteps neared from behind. The air grew heavy with the stench of decay. "Who were you talking to?"

"Myself." He winced. He'd answered too fast.

Behind him, Azazel drew in a long, deep breath. "Someone else was here."

"In my head?" He scoffed. "Anybody else moves in here, we'll be tripping over each other."

"I smell them." Azazel snorted, sending a burst of hot air over his shoulder. "Someone was here."

"If so, wouldn't that be a figment of my imagination?"

"Am I?" Azazel moved, pottery fragments crunching beneath his feet until Azazel stood before him, filling his vision.

Here, in his mind, Azazel never took the same shape and never appeared in his true form. Today was no exception. The fallen angel must have been feeling nostalgic, for he'd chosen the image of an ancient Greek legend—the Minotaur. The horned beast wasn't anything like how Homer described, though he could imagine *this* Minotaur as one of the infernal guardians Dante depicted in *Inferno*. This Minotaur was diseased; the flesh beneath its fur rotting, beginning to peel. Milky-white cataracts glazed over his eyes. Yeah, he looked like something straight out of one of Dante's hells.

He schooled his features, refusing to flinch. Showing weakness in front of Azazel wasn't wise. Instead, after giving him a long, insolent stare, he turned his gaze to the butterflies.

"I'll ask you one last time."

His putrid façade came so close, sour breath bathed over Julius, making him gag.

"Who was here?"

With nothing but force of will, he laughed in Azazel's face. Fear made his tone shrill. Made him sound insane.

Without another word, Azazel whipped away. In two strides he stood before the wind chime.

Julius' laughter came to an abrupt halt as his breath caught. He strained against his chains. He shouldn't react but that was the last decent thing here. The only thing keeping him somewhat in his right mind.

One of Azazel's thick arms shot out, striking down the butterflies. The glass shrieked in protest, shattering against the wall. The colorful lights disappeared.

He couldn't look away from the carnage. His vision blurred. The first tear left an itchy trail in its wake. What now? What did he have left? There was no point returning here again.

The door slammed behind Azazel, pushing a gust of wind toward Julius, delivering the lingering scent of cinnamon. He inhaled deeply.

He had the scent of cinnamon.

The memory of a redheaded angel.

The memory of her touch. Her kiss.

He had a reason to fight again.

CHAPTER 6

Carnation, WA

DUNCAN SAT IN HIS RENTED Escalade, gripped the steering wheel as if to anchor himself there, and stared out the windshield.

He *knew* that woman . . . or at least, he had *known* her. All the old feelings came back with a vehemence that bordered on cruelty. Back when he was human, they'd—

No. He slammed his hands against the steering wheel so hard the whole vehicle swayed. Wasn't her. Couldn't be.

The radio clicked on, playing Stevie Nick's *Talk to Me.*

He turned down the volume. "Bastards, the lot of you. Leaving me hanging like that. No warning. No nothing. *Now* you wanna chat?"

The radio clicked off.

"That had to rank as one of the strangest conversations in all me three hundred years. The target appears human." Brilliantly human with those dark eyes, petite frame, and an abundance of feminine assets. "She knows an unusual amount about daemon kind. I mean, she determined from the scar on me neck that her gun was useless." She understood the natural rules of vampirism—the door shield. She didn't ask him to expound on what a Watcher was. "Not surprising, maybe, if she knows Pasquino."

Interesting, too, that she'd tried to banish him but only managed to push him about. He'd seen humans banish daemons before, they had a natural right to protect their homes. But either she'd been conflicted over whether she wanted to banish him, or the powers that be were conflicted on if she had the right to do so. Maybe even conflicted on her status as human?

He was. He suspected she might be more than human. As soon as she'd opened her door, energy had crackled in the air around them, lifting the hair on his arms. Even more interesting, she appeared to be getting up as opposed to going to bed. Her hair and makeup looked fresh. The scent of coffee had filled the house. "What is she?"

The radio clicked on and a DJ said, "Tell us her name."

Duncan blinked. Three hundred years he'd worked for the Watchers. Never, not once, had they asked him a question. "Think maybe we got our wires crossed. Don't think I heard that right."

Again. "Tell us her name."

The numbers flashed over the screen of the radio as the channel changed. A newscaster's voice filled the car. "Don't ask. Don't tell."

What the fuck?

The dial spun. "Tell us her name." And spun. "Her name . . . name . . . name . . . name."

The hair at Duncan's nape lifted. What in the hell was going on? The Watchers were insane, everyone knew that, but they'd never acted quite this bizarre before.

A little girl's voice, maybe from a commercial said, "Stay out of this."

The dial spun. "Yakity Yak (Don't Talk Back)" blasted as the volume raised. Again, "Her name. Her name. Her name. Her name."

Were they arguing? Legend said there were two hundred Watchers, it stood to reason they wouldn't always see eye-to-eye. His phone buzzed in his pocket. The message: *Don't listen to electronic messages. Communicate by humans only.*

He hadn't even finished reading it before it buzzed again: *Don't listen to them. Listen to me. Say her name. Say her name. Say her name. Say her name.*

The second message went on and on.

They *were* arguing. And he was stuck in the middle of it. Which ones were the ones that had assigned him this job? Why did they only want to communicate through humans? Couldn't all Watchers take over a human body the same as they could take over the electronics they usually communicated with?

"I wish you fuckers would've picked someone else."

Did he? If they hadn't picked him, he wouldn't have gotten to see *her* again. Wouldn't even know she was here. The more he considered it, the more he was sure that was her. Satrina. He should know, he'd made love to her on a regular basis. She'd been his refuge.

Christ, things had been bad in those days. Charlie, his son, had been a bit of a thing. Gertie, she'd always been so angry. There had never been any peace in his house, so he'd often found himself in his mistress's bed.

He stared through the windshield at the path that led to Haven House. That *was* her. She looked different now, sure, but there were similarities.

Or maybe he only saw what he wanted to see. She was a fit woman and surprising enough, out of all the emotions he'd seen cross her face, disdain hadn't been one of them. Hell, not even Satrina had looked at him like that. She'd put up with him, but . . .

He wiped his hand over his stubble, noticed his hand shook and put it back on the steering wheel. "Forget it." He spoke the words aloud, letting them settle into his skin. "It doesn't matter anymore." Focus on your rules. Don't let your emotions show. Do your fucking job.

Either way, whether she was his Satrina or not, he couldn't leave her alone. Whatever might be going on with that woman, he had no desire to see her dead, or worse, in Leo or Crowley's clutches. "So, I'm thinking I'm on my own. I won't be chatting you up anytime soon."

Marilyn Manson's *Deep Six* came on.

The message was clear. He was on at least one Watcher's shite list—a place he had no desire to be.

He was in the process of fucking over the head of the Vampiric Council, for the benefit of a woman who might, or might not be the reincarnated soul of a past lover. He'd left Harry, who he was responsible for, alone in London. Humans were disappearing. The Watchers were fighting among themselves and now at least one of them wanted him ashed.

"Well, there's nowhere left to go but up, right?"

The radio went dead.

Headlights broke through the foliage leading to Haven House. A little red sports car came into view. He ducked.

Duncan smirked. He'd scared her out of her burrow. Nice.

As soon as she passed, he popped his head up, turned in his seat to watch until she'd made it around the bend in the road. Once her taillights disappeared, he put his car in gear and followed. He stayed well back, tailing her toward Main while he tried to ring Harry again. This time, the phone rang. And rang. And went to voicemail. *Christ*, what if he'd become one of the missing?

"Listen, pup, I know you're still brassed off 'bout being left behind, but could you give me a bell? Or at least answer your bloody phone? It'd be nice to know if Leo's got you, or, you know, if you've gone missing." He cut the call. "Fuck's sake."

Despite being after three AM, humans rushed around Main as they looted the shops for emergency supplies. Somewhere farther up the street a gunshot rang out. Humans screamed, scattering. Three men, their arms full of stuff, dashed out into the road. His target had to slam on her breaks and swerve to avoid them.

All hell was breaking loose in the small town of Carnation. He couldn't imagine what it might be like in the big cities. Damn. He shouldn't have left Harry in London.

They drove to the end of Main where a cemetery sat at the edge of town, then down an unlit arterial. There wasn't much around but farmland. As he turned, his headlights swung over tall grass and black-and-white spotted cows.

The woman stopped at the end of the road, right before a sharp turn. He parked in front of a farm on his left. Cut the lights.

His phone beeped and he checked the message. Harry: *Toss off.*

Duncan sighed. At least the little shite was still alive.

He set his phone aside and scanned the area. There wasn't much cover—a few trees along the road. He got out of the car. Shut the door.

Down the street the woman got out of her car and glanced back.

He ducked behind the Escalade.

Closing his eyes, he called up his Vampiric Talent. They all had one—a gift passed down from the fallen angel they'd descended from. He sorted through the familiars he'd gathered over the years, settling on an English Mastiff. The dog he'd bonded with had been a sweet, calm male who'd been as protective as hell. He'd suit this job nicely.

He allowed the familiar to take over, the other creature's form settling in over his. It was a tight fit, he preferred to shift to larger animals, but a smart woman wouldn't allow anything bigger than this mastiff close to her. Hell, this was a long shot.

He padded down the road in the mastiff's form, in time to see her enter a cottage-style home tucked back in the corner. She hadn't turned on any lights and no door shield protected the house. No one lived there.

He'd sneaked up closer, almost to the front door, when the smell hit. He paused. Sniffed the air. Death. The scent grew stronger round the side of the house. He padded through the back yard where tall blocks of stone stood in a circle—a modern rendition of Stonehenge.

What was this place?

The scent pulled him forward, past the circle, and into the woods. He jumped up on a fallen log near the river to survey the area. Bodies littered the forest. Bodies and ash. Daemons had fought humans here recently.

What in the hell was going on? Was this linked to the human disappearances? To his job?

The sound of heartbeats neared. He'd expected the woman and maybe someone from the house, but two men approached from the other direction.

"What a mess. Did they say what happened?"

"Do they ever?"

Duncan hunkered down to watch. Both wore some kind of uniform. A patch with the initials: RI, rode the right front breast of their shirts. Both had guns. Assault rifles from the look of it. The one on the left looked nervous as hell, kept messing with the safety on his weapon, jumping at every little noise.

"Relax, will ya?" The blond on the right kept his body relaxed, his weapon ready, his gaze watchful. He was the more experienced of the two—the dangerous one.

"What if whoever did this comes back before the clean-up crew arrives?"

Blondie turned to stare at the Noob. He shook his head. "We detain them."

Duncan didn't wait to hear more. He slunk through the underbrush back to the house to alert his target. He wouldn't be able to warn her in his familiar's form. He'd have to play this straight and hope to hell she didn't scream or run when she saw him. He shifted back into his true form, rolling his shoulders and cracking his neck as he strode up to the door.

Knock, or go in? It'd be easier on the woman if he knocked . . . but she could slip out the back right into those two thugs. Duncan entered the house, ducking a bit so he didn't bust his head on the frame. He closed the door. The small entryway—a five-by-five area of tile—led into a living room lit by a night-light. Books, papers, jars, and piles of stones littered every surface. To his right, an arch led to a dining room crowded with table and chairs. The house had a weight to it—a heaviness in the air that urged him to leave.

He stayed in place, speaking to the house at large. "Just here to warn you, there are two armed men outside, planning to detain anyone they come across."

While quiet before, the whole place went silent in an unnatural way.

"Look, I'm not here to hurt you. The Watchers sent me to protect you. I'm a friend."

The woman stuck her head out from behind a wall deeper in the home.

Straight black hair framed a narrow face punctuated with big, dark eyes. Her lips parted.

At least she wasn't a screamer.

He held his hands out to his sides showing her he wasn't armed. "Name's Duncan, love. I wanna help."

TRINA STRAIGHTENED AND CAME OUT from behind the wall, clutching the *Black Book of Daemonology* against her chest. She didn't need this right now. She'd just been reading about the Original. Just started to process through what it meant for Lilith to be the Original.

Her gaze narrowed. The door shield should've prevented his entrance. "How the hell did you get in here? You are a vampire, right?"

"Isn't your place." He glanced around. "Isn't anyone's, else there'd be a seal on the door." He tipped his head toward the right. "Is one of those bodies out there the owner?"

Indeed, Rowena had died last night. "I'm here. I'm human."

"Ah, but this isn't your home." He rubbed his palm over his stubbly chin. "You don't have any more right to be here than I do."

Her heart shuddered. *Shit.* Why hadn't she thought of that? Lilith had given her half-ownership of Haven House, but here, she was an interloper.

"Calm down." He eased a step closer. "That heart of yours sounds ready to take flight."

She backed away. "Stop. I don't want to hurt you, but I will."

He motioned toward the dining room. "How 'bout we have a seat? Chat things over?"

That might be good. Rowena's dining room was a tight fit for her with that mammoth table. If she could get him seated in there, thinking she meant to cooperate, she'd have half a chance to get a head start when she bolted. "Okay, you first."

Duncan entered the dining room. The seat at the head of the table was piled high with boxes. He sidled between the back of that chair and a sewing mannequin, almost toppling it as he squeezed past. He pulled out the chair across from her, easing into it, as if afraid it might break under his weight.

She took the chair closest to the entry, setting the book down on the table.

"Now, I'm not here to make you nervous, love."

She almost laughed. She couldn't picture anyone being comfortable around him, big as he was. "I'm not fond of daemons."

"Ah. So then it's not me looks or accent that's got your hackles up?"

"You do remind me of the villains in most of the historical romances I've read." He sounded like one, too.

He winked. "And you, love, you'd play the part of a duchess well. What with your straight-backed posture and your chin tilted just so."

Her cheeks heated. She didn't dress like a duchess with her combat boots, ripped jeans, and Disturbed concert tee. Had he meant that as a compliment or an insult? Goddess, this man was her mate? She'd never have chosen him. The Watchers couldn't have gotten their match right. "Duncan, can I be honest with you?"

"Rare thing, honesty. Though I do prefer it, meself. Go on."

"The Watchers aren't high on my trust scale."

"Are they on anyone's? Daft bastards, the lot of them. Never know what to expect when they're involved, know what I mean?"

She blinked. Strange, but when in motion, his features softened. "I, uh, yes. Yes, I do. And I've already shared with you my thoughts on daemons."

"Now, there"—he wagged his finger—"I think you're wrong. Daemons are an honest sort, they don't shy away from the dark truths of life the way humans do."

Her lips had parted while he spoke and she snapped her mouth closed. He was almost . . . *almost* . . . pleasant-looking when animated. "What I'm trying to say is, I don't think we suit."

"Suit?" His features scrunched up. "Why would we need to suit? Look, Duchess, I'm here in the capacity of a bodyguard. Don't need to 'suit' anything to guard your person. Just need to be able to fight. Now, then. Where are your friends?"

Stubborn man. Maybe she could at least squeeze some information from him. "You expect me to give you the location of my friends, who the Council has issued a kill order on, knowing that you work for the Council?"

"Know about that, do you?" He kissed his teeth.

She did now. "You admit it?"

He grinned. "Council tried to hire me to off one of you women, with a side order to dust James Pasquino if he got in the way."

She stared.

"What? You wanted honesty. Thought we were putting all our cards on the table."

She started to get up.

"Now, I said they *tried* to hire me."

"You're here." She paused. "You must have taken the job."

"Well, yeah, I—"

That was all she needed to hear. She grabbed the book and lurched out of the chair, smacking her thigh hard against the table, enough to make her eyes water.

He jumped up, too. "Wait—"

Shit. He was coming *over* the table, not around. She whirled. Made it a couple of steps before he caught hold of her wrist.

No Magic. Don't use Magic.

He pulled her back. "Now, we're having a nice little chin wag—"

She round-kicked his knee out from under him. He went down hard. She turned to run.

Don't use Magic. No Magic.

He grabbed her foot. She fell flat on her stomach, grunting with the impact as her cheek smacked the floor. The book flew out of her hands, skidding across the polished wood. *No Magic.* Kicking out with her free foot, her boot connected with his cheek.

He cursed.

She flinched. *Don't use Magic.* Scrambled up. Ran to the door, pausing to flip the lock.

He spun her around.

Don't use Magic. No Magic. Can't use Magic. Her heart thundered so hard her whole body twitched with the reverberations.

He still wore her shoe print. His lips had thinned into a harsh slash. Without a word he picked her up, holding her against the door, nose-to-nose. She fisted her hand and tried to throw a punch, but hindered by the proximity of the door, it was more awkward than effective.

He changed positions, using his linebacker's body to hold her in place, restraining her hands on either side of her head. Even his damn thigh blocked her from kneeing him in the groin.

"You goddamned, disease-riddled, spawn of a fu—"

"None of that, now, Duchess." The muscle in his jaw flexed. One eyelid twitched.

Shit. What had she started? "Let me go."

"What happened?" His gaze narrowed. "I told you I'm here to help. Why'd you run?"

Because he scared the hell out of her. Because it was easier to believe he was with the Council or the Watchers or Crowley than that he was hers. "Why'd you chase me?"

"Like I'd let a prize like you get away." He winked. "You gonna answer my question?"

The darkness wasn't creeping over his skin like it had with Lilith. He had her pinned to the door, his whole body pressed against hers and nothing bad was happening. She wasn't infecting him.

She opened her senses to him the tiniest bit, not enough to get into his head, she never used her telepathy anymore, but just enough to look at the colors of his aura. There was none of the bright reds and oranges, or harsh fluctuations of someone in a rage. His colors were blues, greens, yellows, and pinks—despite his stern expression he was amused. She closed her eyes, trying to calm herself. If she took those colors at face value, this man probably didn't have a mean bone in his body. And her touch didn't do anything bad to him.

"I don't like being alone with you."

"I'm your new bodyguard." He tipped his head to the side. "Guess you're gonna have to get used to me."

She forced herself to relax. "I overreacted. Got scared. That's all." She squirmed. "Let me down."

A slow grin curved his lips. "Think I like you where you are, love. Feel like I know you better already."

Now that he'd drawn her attention to their intimate position, her body started to respond to all those thick muscles pressed up against her. She wet her lips. "Don't call me that."

"What?" He stared her mouth. "Love?"

He wasn't handsome. He wasn't. Yet her nipples tightened, and her belly tingled. "It's too personal."

He leaned in, his warm breath fanned her lips. "Oh, but we're going to get personal, you and me."

"No." The denial came out in a breathless whisper. "We're not."

"Very, very personal. Love."

"I told y—" Her words got lost against his lips. He wasn't punishing or brutish or unskilled, which is what she'd expected. He seduced, nipping, nudging. Gentling her to a calmer place before slanting his mouth over hers and letting her taste his hunger.

Goddess help her, it had been far too long.

She forgot about how big he was, how mean he looked, how she didn't want anything to do with men, much less her mate. All that hard male snug up against her had languid heat spreading through her veins. She moaned. Wanted more. She nipped his lip. Cuddled closer.

When he pulled away, his hazel eyes had turned a shade darker than before. "That's better, now, in'nit?" He squeezed her ass.

Goddess help her, she'd wrapped her legs around his waist. "Let me down."

He raised his arms, grinning. "You're holding on to me, not the other way 'round."

Her cheeks heated. She tightened her grip around his neck long enough to lower her feet to the floor. "Stay away from me, Duncan."

"Ain't a chance in hell you're chasing me off now."

CHAPTER 7

Carnation, WA

DUNCAN STEPPED AWAY FROM THE infuriating woman the Watchers expected him to protect. She didn't appear inclined to make his job easy, but he'd be lying if he said he wasn't enjoying her. "Now that we've been intimate and all, think you'd be willing to tell me your name?"

Her mouth opened and closed as though choosing and discarding several potential responses. Finally, she sighed. "Trina."

"Trina." He nodded. "Mm, like that." Damn. Her name was a little too reminiscent of his past. Was Leo fucking with him? Had he set this whole thing up? But to what end?

"Good for you." She pushed past him to get farther into the house.

"Now, Duchess, here I am trying to be amenable." He shook his head. "You're not even making an effort."

She spun around. Pointed. "I gave you my name. Use it."

"Is Trina short from something else?"

"Satrina. Satrina Isabella Cortez Lopez." She huffed. "Happy?"

Happy? Not Hardly. Gobsmacked? Utterly. She had that same gorgeous, dusky skin tone. But where his Satrina had lived life with an ambivalent indifference to whatever happened to transpire around her, this Satrina seemed wary of damned near everything—at least where he was concerned. He swallowed. "Think I'll use Duchess. Fits better."

Her chin went up another notch.

"How 'bout this; I'll quit being antagonistic if you make me job easier and leave before those two blokes outside think to scrutinize the house."

"You're assuming I believe there's anyone out there."

He stepped closer. "Two lads armed with assault rifles. They got RI embroidered on their uniforms—"

Her skin paled.

Now they were getting somewhere. "Who are they, then?"

She glanced around as her heart thundered, looking like she was about to panic. She inhaled a deep breath and swiped her hand down the front of the hooded skeleton on her t-shirt. "You have to get away from me. It's not safe and you're going to get in my way. I don't need your protection. I don't need anyone."

Funny. She sounded like Harry, all earnest toughness and false bravado. Hell, he didn't know her well, she might be sincere . . . but his instincts said she lied. From what he'd seen thus far, she needed someone more than anyone he'd ever met outside of Harry. Why the hell was she traipsing about unprotected?

"Why'd your friends abandon you?" *Why does the Council want you?*

Some emotion crossed her face, tightening the muscles around her eyes and mouth. She looked away. "It's not safe for them to be around me and they're smart enough to realize that."

They were smart. He wasn't. Nice. "So far I haven't suffered any ill effects." He tipped his head to the side. "Aside from an intimate look at the bottom of your shoe, that is. Far as I can see, you do need help. I've had the drop on you twice now."

"How do you figure?"

"When I came in here, I could've gotten you before you realized you weren't alone." He bobbed his head toward the door. "And now, when I had you pinned to the wall."

When she came closer, he couldn't mistake the pleading in her eyes for anything but outright concern. "Please go away."

He folded his arms over his chest. She was worried about him? Not since he'd been a lad could he remember being the recipient of such a thing. He wasn't sure how to react. Especially since if he were to do what she asked, he'd be worse off, which contradicted her sentiment. "If I leave, not only am I ash, but the lad I protect will be, too. I'll take me chances with you, Duchess. Ain't got no other choice. Now, mind telling me why we're here?"

She turned with a growl, flinging her arms up.

He flinched. Caught himself and straightened. Christ, what was wrong with him? She was a bit of a thing and if she was a reincarnated soul from his past, she was Satrina, not Gertie.

At least Trina hadn't noticed. She'd covered her eyes with her hand.

"This is nuts." She dropped her arm to her side, paced away a few steps, stopping at an overstuffed bookshelf. "So what are your orders?" She took out her phone and used the flashlight to illuminate the bindings of the books. Great, they were risking getting caught here because she needed new reading material.

He walked closer to her. "From the Watchers?"

"Yeah." She picked up the thick book she'd had earlier off the floor and shoved it at him. "Make yourself useful."

Least she'd stopped arguing. "They've made it clear none of you are to be harmed. That's it so far . . . just that I'm to protect you. So, again, it'd be helpful to know where the other two are."

"You don't need to worry about them." She added another book to the one he held. "They're in the safest place on Earth."

They were safe. So, why wasn't she? "Why aren't you with them?"

"Because I'm the fuck-up."

The words shot out of her with such vehemence, he almost took a step back.

"Shit. This is the one I need." She yanked another book out from beneath a bunch of others. The whole shelf teetered. He caught the shelves before it lurched forward, but was too late to prevent the books from tumbling off the shelves. She jumped back, avoiding getting buried in the heavy tomes, but there was nothing to be done about the racket.

They both froze, their gazes locked on the sliding glass door at the back of the house.

For a few seconds, her racing heart was the only sound . . . then there were two more. "Hide." He started to take his hand from the bookshelf, but the bloody thing teetered again.

Trina dove behind the couch as a beam of light swung through the sliding glass door. There was no way in hell they hadn't seen her—the back of the couch *faced* the sliding glass door.

Shite.

The light settled on him, dazzling his eyes.

Duncan smiled. Waved. *Fuck me.*

They tried the door. It slid open.

Jesus, who the hell had lived here that they hadn't locked any of their bloody doors?

"What're you doing here?" The blond guy spoke, his voice shaking. He was scared. They both were, considering how fast their hearts raced.

Duncan hefted the books in one hand. "Nothing nefarious, lads. Just looking to elevate me education."

The two crept closer. One kept his light trained on him, the other swung his in a wide arc, searching the room. They came closer, walking right past where Trina lay behind the couch, stopping in front of him. How the hell had they not seen her? Did they not think her a threat because she was a woman?

This would be easier if Guardians were allowed to kill humans, but that was a rule he didn't dare break. He just needed to take them down long enough to get Trina out of here.

Blondie spoke into a mike on his shoulder. "HQ? I got one. Silver eyes, like you said."

What the hell? Did everyone in Washington know about vampires?

Blondie must've been wearing an earpiece—he was quiet for a moment. Nodded to his buddy. "We're holding him."

The other guy pulled cuffs from the back of his belt. "Put the books down."

"Gladly." Duncan threw them at Blondie. Pulled the bookshelf down on the Noob at the same time.

They shouted. Cursed.

Duncan dove for their guns. He got hold of one, throwing it in Trina's direction. He grabbed the barrel of the other. The bastard fired. The shot went wide, but fire lanced over his palm as the barrel heated. He released Blondie's weapon.

The Noob struggled to his feet and Duncan cold-cocked him. The lad dropped like a ragdoll.

"Don't move." Blondie stood, his weapon pointed at Duncan's face.

Slowly, he straightened. Damn, he was already ugly enough, didn't need a bullet adding injury to insult.

Trina popped up from behind the couch with the other assault rifle. She leveled it at Blondie's back.

Duncan dove to the side as she pulled the trigger. The room lit up. Fire streaked through his midsection. He hit the ground. Throbbing pain radiated out from his stomach and back.

For fuck's sake, that hurt.

He gripped his side. Blondie was dead—the bullet must've tore right through him considering all the blood. He lifted his hand long enough to stare at the blackened hole in his abdomen. Had he been human, he'd be taking his last breath right now, bleeding all over the carpet. But as Trina had put it, all this did was piss him off.

"Fuck, Duchess. Thought you weren't going to shoot me."

*S*HE ALWAYS SCREWS EVERYTHING UP.
Not this time. She could fix this. She *would* fix this. Blood stained Duncan's shirt, his coat, and droplets splattered on his face. Trina's stomach knotted and heaved. "Oh, Gaia. Oh, goddess. No, no, no."

She stumbled out from behind the couch, tripped over the dead man's feet and almost toppled onto Duncan. She caught herself and knelt at his side. When she reached for him, he jerked away.

She ruins everything she touches.

Her stomach bottomed out. That was the second time he'd done that. He had to be six-six or six-seven and built like a brick shithouse. The way he'd taken on those two mercs from RI—no fear, no hesitation. She hated that she'd made him afraid of her. "I'm not gonna hurt you." *Like he's going to believe that after you shot him.* "Anymore."

One dark brow crept high on his forehead.

She wiped some of the blood from his face with the side of her hand, cleaning her palm off on the carpet. "I'm sorry. So, so sorry." She couldn't do anything right lately. "I didn't think the bullet would go through."

He motioned to the dead guy. "That skinny little shite? Your Glock might've given you a clean shot but those assault rifles are meant to go through cement block like butter."

"I know." She covered her eyes.

"You knew?"

Ah, goddess. She was making herself sound even worse. "Well, in the Navy . . . I mean, theoretically I knew, but I forgot. I never saw any action. I've been out awhile. I should've used my Glock, but the rifle was right there, and I only planned to scare him at first but when I saw his gun in your face . . . ." She yanked up his shirt, tucking it up under his arms out of her way. "It's not too bad." There was little blood under his shirt, just enough to hint that he'd fed recently, all the gore covering him belonged to the other guy. A tiny round black hole marked the wound. "Turn over." He rolled to his side. When the bullet exited, it had left a ragged, gaping hole the size of a grapefruit. "Damn." He had a thin layer of flesh and muscle and below that, where a human would have blood, organs, and bone, only blackness.

"Feels as big as my fist."

"Yeah." It was one thing to acknowledge that he was a vampire. Another altogether to be faced with the reality of his curse. He was empty inside, filled with nothing but the dark Magic keeping him undead. All of the external functions that made him look human on the outside—the rise and fall of his chest, sweat, tears, spit, they were all nothing more than permanent glamours.

They needed to cover that wound. "Rowena must have had a first aid kit. Hold on."

She ran into the kitchen. He couldn't bleed to death, but the Darkness that filled him would leak out, diminishing his energy and life force. That wound, if not cared for, would destroy him. She rummaged through the kitchen, pulling open drawers. Nothing.

Goddess, please help me. Don't let him die. Upstairs in the main bathroom, she found a first aid kit under the sink. She pulled out a package of bandages and returned to Duncan. "Lift your shirt."

Grumbling under his breath, he sat up, tugging his shirt to his chin.

"Does it hurt?" She knelt beside him, packed a wad of sterilized padding over the larger wound in his back, taped it into place, and wrapped a bandage around his middle.

"Of course it hurts." He grunted as she pulled the bandage tighter. "Might look different than you on the inside, might not die as easily, but everything *feels* the same as when I was human. When I'm impatient, I get a rush of adrenaline, though there isn't any in me. And when I'm embarrassed, I blush, though there's not really any blood to rush to me head. And when I'm nervous, me stomach knots just the same as yours, even though there's nothin' there. I 'spose it's all in me mind . . . maybe euphoric recall or phantom pains of what I think I should feel, but it's real enough to me."

How strange must that be? She had to stretch to fit her arms around him and every time she had to reach to pass the bandage roll to her other hand, her cheek brushed the rise of his muscular peck, his hardened nipple. She'd known he was a large man, expected him to be muscular, but damn . . . . "You're going to need to rest."

"Can't do that here. That blond bloke reported us."

"Yeah." She reached around him again, inhaling his outdoorsy scent. Even if the mercs hadn't reported them, Rowena's house wouldn't be a safe haven; none of her windows were boarded. Only thin white curtains covered the windows.

"Just got into town." His voice was low, husky. "Dawn's coming. I ain't got nowhere to stay."

She closed her eyes. In other words, she either needed to take him home or finish him off. Once she invited him into the house . . . goddess, she'd never get rid of him. Maybe she didn't want to. How would she have handled tonight if he hadn't been there? Probably the same . . . though minus shooting an ally. She had to admit that she appreciated not being alone. She was so damn tired of being alone. Maybe Lilith was right. He didn't seem to be adversely affected by her—his skin hadn't charred or turned black. And maybe having him around . . . maybe she could get her confidence back.

Goddess, was she actually considering this after what had just happened? "I'm starting to think the Watchers don't like you much."

"Why's that?"

"They sent you to me. I meant what I said before, I'm a fuck up. I've known you what? A couple hours and I've already accidentally shot you." She tucked in the end of the bandage. When she sat up, her head collided with his chin.

"Bloody hell, love." He touched his jaw. "You sure you haven't decided to dust me?"

"Sorry." She rubbed the sore spot on the back of her head. She needed to calm down. She'd always been clumsiest when nervous or upset.

He slouched back against the wall and jerked his thumb toward the unconscious man next to him. "We need to make scarce before our friend wakes up."

The books. "Give me a minute." She picked through the tomes littering the floor until she found the two she needed and then knelt next to Duncan. "Come on, big guy." She slid her arm around his back under his Mackintosh and helped him to his feet.

He staggered a bit with his first step. "Christ."

"Are you sure you can make it?"

"Don't worry, I got a bit of time before I crash."

They needed to get back home fast. There was no way she could lift his weight if his body shut down to recover, and she couldn't risk using Magic. Gods, she hoped these books contained the information she needed so she could use her Magic again. She juggled them a bit in her arm, trying to get a better grip.

Together, they made their way outside into the cool early-morning air. Duncan drew in a deep breath. "That house, I don't know what it was, but I didn't like it in there."

"People leave a mark on their environment. Sometimes it's pleasant—a scent or a feeling of warmth, other times it's a stain." She guided him down the two steps that led to the drive.

"And who lived here?"

"Her name was Rowena." She swallowed. "She was my legal guardian." *The high priestess of our coven.*

At the front drive, he came to an abrupt halt, forcing her to stop.

Four cars sat in the street. One tucked up tight blocking in her Jag. Several mercs in RI uniforms stood in various positions around the area, petrified mid-motion.

What the hell did they want? They'd showed up a few nights back when Rowena had tried to exchange Lilith for Crowley's help in mesmerizing the coven to do her bidding.

One man was bent over, looking into her car with a flashlight. Three others had stopped mid-stride toward the house. Another sat in one of the vehicles, his hand on the door, his leg hanging out, as if he'd frozen when exiting the car.

"Come on." He tugged her into motion.

"What if they . . ?"

"Look at their eyes."

Only the whites showed. They were in trance, or possessed or—

"The Watchers have them."

She tore her gaze from the tableau to give Duncan her attention as they walked. "How do you know?"

"Guardians didn't always get kill orders via text. Back in the day, a stranger would approach, their eyes would roll up, and they'd freeze like that." He waved a hand toward her car. "You need anything in there?"

"I left my purse at Haven House. The registration has my name on it, but the address is in Bremerton."

The men began speaking in a monotone, though none moved and their eyes still faced inward. "When the Original comes, she'll come to thee as three . . . ."

She stopped. Lilith was the Original, the reincarnated soul of the first woman. But what was this about coming as three?

"Keep walking, love. They wake as soon as they deliver their message."

"All as human first, then as daemons are set free . . . ."

They hurried past, Duncan leaning heavier on her as they went.

The men continued. "The Beacon burning bright. The Shadow hidden from sight. The blighted, damned Knight."

Why did that sound so familiar?

He pointed to an SUV parked in a drive farther up the road. "That's mine." He pressed the keys into her hand. "You better drive."

She helped him into the passenger's seat and closed the door, glancing back the way they'd come. The men were still frozen. Still talking.

The Beacon. The Shadow. The Knight. She'd heard this poem before. Somewhere. Maybe when she was a child?

Behind her, the car door opened. "Duchess?"

"Coming." She hurried around the car and climbed in. He had the seat pushed all the way back, so she had to adjust it until she could reach the pedals and lower the steering wheel before she backed out of the drive.

The Beacon had to be Lilith. She'd always been so optimistic. Had a way of bringing light to any situation, no matter how dark things got.

Trina slowed the car as she entered downtown Carnation. The town looked like something out of the Twilight Zone. Idling cars dotted the two-lane road. While still early, 6:57 AM, the radio said, people were on the sidewalks, frozen in acts of civil unrest. Men and women petrified mid-run, their facial expressions mixtures of fear and somber determination, their arms filled with stolen goods. One woman had frozen as she swung a bat at a window, she'd been captured in time just before the wood collided with glass.

Duncan rolled down his window when she pulled up at the light. A chorus of monotone voices recited the same message. "...are set free. The Beacon burning bright. The shadow hidden from sight. The blighted—"

"Bloody hell." He shook his head. "They have the whole damn town in trance. Like they weren't quite sure how to get the message delivered."

Like they knew the person they wanted to communicate with was in town, but unsure where. Like they couldn't see him or her. A shiver lifted gooseflesh on her arms. She cranked up the heat. *The Shadow hidden from sight.*

He glanced at her. "Don't suppose you know who the Original is?"

When the light changed, she returned her gaze to the road but she didn't move. Should she tell him? The Watchers weren't treating Lilith being the Original like a secret. Julius Crowley knew. She had to assume the Vampiric Council did, too. If she planned to allow Duncan to stick around, as her ally, he needed as much information as their enemies. The question came back to whether or not she intended to keep Duncan for the time being.

"Sun's rising, love." He shifted in his seat, grimacing.

The horizon *had* turned a lighter shade of violet streaked with pink. She hit the gas as the streetlight changed to red.

Duncan had made it clear he intended to fulfill his duty to the Watchers. To the Watchers, not to her. While that news had been disheartening—he didn't seem to have any idea they might be destined mates—it also made her decision easier. He wouldn't expect anything from her. Which was perfect, because she didn't have anything but disappointment and pain to give. But if she was careful, if she didn't use Magic, maybe she could keep him for a little while.

"Should I take from your silence that you know, but you don't trust me enough to say?"

"The Original was the first woman." That wasn't so hard. No one else could hear her if Lilith was right. *Oh, honey. Why would you think they're any different from anyone else?*

"What, in a biblical sense? Like Eve?"

She nodded. "I was reading about it when you showed up. Before the goddess made Eve from Adam's rib, she made Adam and Lilith from the mud and gave them dominion over the Earth. Lilith wouldn't submit to Adam. She wanted to be treated as his equal. When he refused, she left Eden and Adam got a new wife."

"That's it?"

"Well, no. When she left, she took a lover—"

"I thought Adam was the only man."

She turned off Main. "Her lover was an angel." *Samael.* "She was already a witch and he turned her into a vampire, making her the first daemon. They couldn't have kids, though. Lilith could only create lesser daemons—some kind of minion or something. When she went back to Eden to see how Adam fared, she discovered Eve had children and got jealous. Vowed to kill any unprotected infants and make them her own."

He let out a low whistle. "That must've pissed them off."

"The goddess punished her, but I'm not sure how; I didn't get that far. That's why I grabbed the *Black Book of Daemonology*. I'm hoping the rest of the story is in there."

"And this other book?" He stroked his hand over Rowena's Grimoire.

"Lilith suggested I look up information on the Original in there . . . for a different reason." No need to scare him by telling him about her Magic.

"So this Original is returning and we have to stop her?"

"I hope not. She's my best friend." The full weight of his attention settled on her. "I think she's going to be our savior from the End Times, I'm just not sure how."

"She's returned to help the beings she once tormented?" He scoffed.

She slowed as she drove onto the dirt road leading to Haven House, wincing as the overgrown vegetation surrounding the lane scraped down the sides of the SUV. "Everyone deserves a chance at redemption."

At least she hoped they did. She needed redemption. She needed to prove the coven wrong. She needed find a way to regain control of her Magic, destroy Crowley, and stop Armageddon so she could prove to everyone, including herself, that she didn't always fuck everything up.

London, England
Vampiric Council Chambers

FIFTEEN SENTRIES STOOD BEFORE LEOPOLD. Huge males, bigger than Sinclair, even. The shortest couldn't be much shy of seven foot and was wide across as the old knotted willow that used to stand on his family's property. They were solid muscle, all of them, so much so that their necks were almost as wide as their heads.

Now that they were here, he wasn't sure how to proceed. With the Watchers privy to his every action, his every word, how did one go about tricking them? He couldn't. The best he could hope to do, was to get his chess pieces into place without the Watchers figuring out his true intentions until it was too late.

He pulled a slip of paper out of his pocket. "Two of you will go to this address. Protect the gates. Kill anyone or anything that tries to get inside."

One Sentry came forward. He took the paper, motioned to another Sentry and the two of them left. The gate they would protect was his own. The Watchers knew that—there was no way to hide it—but no one here on Earth knew where he lived.

He withdrew another paper, with another address. "I'll require three Sentries for this job. Timing is essential. Augustina Saar must be destroyed."

A few of the Sentries broke rank long enough to share speaking glances. Not many daemons would want to fight Augustina, but the Sentries would see it as a challenge and they loved nothing better.

Three stepped forward at the same time.

He handed the slip of paper to the closest. "I don't care how she dies, but I want it done quickly. Kill anyone she's with. When you're finished, wait for further instructions."

With a little luck they'd reach Augustina before either of Sinclair's targets did. By now, it might be a moot point, they may have already met her. They may already know what they were and understand how much power they possessed. Which was why . . . . "I need one Sentry to stand at our portal and let me know if there's any change."

They hesitated this time. Guarding an inactive portal wasn't a glorious assignment. The Original had shut the portals to Machon three hundred years ago and she was the only one who could re-open them. If Augustina had any sense of strategy, she'd send the women there to gather allies among daemon kind. It was the best they could hope to do since they were still missing the third part of the Original. The Knight was well out of their reach, he'd made damned sure of that.

Not even the Watcher inside Crowley had figured out what he'd done.

"I have intelligence that suggests the portal may open, and none on the other side are fond of the Council."

Not after he'd tried to eradicate all who opposed him. Not after he'd had the coven destroyed. Julius—the thing inside him, was supposed to have finished the job long before now. Leopold had done his part, he'd provided the bastard with Julius' body. He'd kept the secret, never speaking out loud about how he'd helped the Watcher escape Machon. But the Watcher had gotten pissed when Julius Crowley had trapped him inside his body and the portal to Machon had closed. The Watcher stopped everything, refusing to dust the remaining Guardian until he was free from Crowley.

Now the coven was back and as strong as ever. He couldn't take them on, not as powerful as they were . . . but the Watcher could destroy them all.

All he had to do was get to the Original before the Watcher. That was his last remaining bargaining chip: To hold the key to the Watcher's freedom.

The hint of the possibility of some action was incentive enough. One stepped forward, bowed and left.

"The rest of you remain on guard. No leave until further notice."

CHAPTER 8

Carnation, WA

DUNCAN STUDIED TRINA AS SHE parked in front of Haven House. "What aren't you telling me? This friend of yours, she's a vampire? A witch?"

"Both—James bit her; now she's immortal but she still has a heartbeat and a reflection."

He shook his head. "Impossible. If she were transformed, she'd lose her Magic when her Vampiric talent took over. Besides, all the witches are dead."

She leaned her head back against the head rest. "We're Grigori."

Grigori? Weren't they those balding monks who made calendars? No, wait, they were Gregorian.

His confusion must've showed because she added, "As in the Grigori Coven." She got out of the car and slammed the door closed.

Bloody great. Rumor had it the Council had ordered the entire coven destroyed centuries ago during the Clearances. If they'd returned, why did Leo only want one of them dead? It was common knowledge that they'd eventually reincarnate, so did he not know the others had returned?

He must not. Had he, he'd have started a war in the effort to get rid of them. The coven could oust the current Council and return daemon kind to the way they had been before Leo took over.

This wasn't what he'd signed up for. Christ, he thought he'd come here, put three people into hiding and head home. He stared out the windshield.

There wouldn't be any going home. When Leo found out . . . *Christ*.

He couldn't leave Trina on her own, not if he wanted to live with himself. Which left him at loose ends with Harry—he couldn't keep the lad safe while on the run.

Fuck's sake, this was a mess. He shoved his door open, which required far more effort than usual. Despite Trina's care, his energy was diminishing fast. The front door of Haven House looked to be a million miles away. He needed blood. Hopefully, Pasquino had a stash inside.

She came around to take the books and help him out of the car. While he wished he didn't need assistance, he'd have fallen flat without her help. They climbed the porch steps together. She left him leaning against the side of the house as she went inside. She could've left him there. The door shield would keep him out. He'd have no chance in hell of finding cover before sunrise.

Instead, she faced him. "I need your name."

"Duncan Sinclair."

She shook her head. "If we're going to do this, we're doing it right. Give me your full name."

The woman was madder than a box of frogs. Someone who knew what they were doing could do a lot of damage with his full name. A witch could work all types of Magic on him. "Is this necessary?"

"You're asking me to open my home to you."

"After you shot me!" The windows on either side of the door reflected the first rays of sunlight cresting over the trees. He didn't have time to muck about.

"I'll be vulnerable to you once I invite you in. If you want my trust, you have to give me yours."

"When we become Guardian, they expect us to kill anyone who knows our full names."

Her eyes widened, she started to take a step back. Then she straightened, thrusting her chin up. "You can try."

He couldn't help but grin. "You're too cheeky for your own good." He dragged his hand over his stubble. "Duncan Samael Sinclair."

For a long while, she stared.

"You leaving me out here?"

She started out of her daydream. "Duncan Samael Sinclair, you are welcome here." She swallowed hard. "My home is your home."

Now *he* was standing there staring like a bloody cabbage. She could've stopped at her invitation, giving him access until he left, but no, she'd given him total access to her, permitting him future access to any house she entered with no conditions. "Why'd you do that?"

"I've decided to keep you a while longer." She shrugged.

He shouldn't take it as a compliment, nor as a sign she might be warming to him, still warmth flooded him down to his toes. "Yeah?"

"Not that it'll matter if you continue to stand out there."

Right. Dawn. He pulled himself away from the house and went inside, glancing around at the odd conglomeration of cozy modern furniture nestled within the antique architecture. Deep rosewood wainscoting paneled the walls. A split staircase, leading to an upstairs landing, dominated the entry. Centered beneath, between the two curved staircases was a door protected with another door seal. "Anyone in there?"

"No. It's a ritual room."

A place of Magic—not meant for his kind. To the left of the entry, an archway led to a kitchen. There was an exit there and another door that maybe led to a basement or pantry.

Trina motioned him to the right, to the living room.

Paintings of ancient myths lay over acanthus wallpaper. An assortment of candles and little bowls covered the mantle over the fireplace. To the right of the fireplace, what *almost* looked like a cat lay over the high-back of an armchair.

He paused. To anyone else, it probably did look like a plain-Jane orange-striped tabby. To him it was slightly misshaped as if something bigger lived inside the cat. He motioned to the beast. "What the hell is that?"

"James' cat, George."

The feline-thing hissed.

No. Something about the creature was off. Way off. "That ain't a cat." He stumbled toward the loveseat—the biggest piece of furniture in the room and half fell, half sat. He'd heal fast enough, but if he didn't start conserving his energy, he'd lose consciousness while his body repaired. That worried him. He didn't like the idea of Trina being unprotected. He glanced at George. Not with that thing in the house. "You sure you trust it?"

She stroked her hand down George's fur. Instead of purring, he growled, though he didn't lift his head. "He's not the nicest cat I've ever met, but he was possessed . . . and exorcized recently. I feel a little sorry for the grouchy boy."

He shot the beast another side-long glance. That might explain the taint of daemon surrounding it, but he didn't quite buy it. As a shifter, if there was one thing he knew, it was animals. And that wasn't like any animal he'd ever seen.

She sat at the edge of an armchair, facing him with her big books on her lap. "Can I get you anything?"

He raised an eyebrow. "You offering a snack?" He shouldn't tease, he couldn't help himself.

She narrowed her eyes. "Don't even think about it."

Huh. Never, in all the time he'd spent with Satrina, had he ever managed to get a rise out of her. This Trina he liked better. She showed her emotions. "Well, if there's no blood to be had—"

"James has a cold storage safe upstairs."

"You know about that?" He'd been planning to wait for her to go to sleep before searching the premises for Pasquino's cooler. Every Guardian had one. "Why don't you see if there's anything in there. Should be set to our universal code." He rattled off the combination.

While she went upstairs, he called Harry. The lad picked up on the second ring.

"What?"

Well, praise Jesus. "You all right?"

"You know what? You have to stop treating me like a kid. This is beyond ridiculous. For fuck's sake, Duncan, you went to the Council. You were *there*. If you'd told me you were going—"

"You're not ready, pup." Harry had been trying to talk him into taking on the Council for years. He understood. The lad wanted revenge for whatever had been done to him, but he couldn't allow it to happen before Harry had a chance at winning the fight.

"You know what? Fuck you and the horse you rode in on. I didn't ask for this. None of it. Now I'm stuck in this goddamned mausoleum of days gone by—"

Damn, the lad was in a rare mood. "All right, then. Just wanted to make sure you were still alive."

"—while you're out there doing whatever the fuck you're doing."

"Do you think this is enough?" Trina walked in, her gaze measuring the two bags of blood she held in her hands. She glanced up, saw him on the phone and winced. *Sorry.*

"You're with a woman?" Harry scoffed. "Oh, that's fucking rich—" His voice grew louder with every word.

"Gotta go. Keep the monitors on. Stay safe." He cut the call on one of the lad's more colorful curses.

Trina lifted a brow.

"My charge. He ain't too happy with me leaving him behind."

"He shouldn't talk to you like that." She handed him one bag and set the other on the ottoman.

"You heard?" He popped the cap off the bag.

She sat in the armchair. "He was yelling."

He shrugged. "Sometimes things ain't as simple as they seem. He's been through ten lifetimes worth of pain, and he's a bit of a thing."

"With a mouth like that?"

How to explain Harry? "The Council did things to him. Don't know what, but they had him for a long time. By the time I got to him, he was more animal than anything. He didn't want to live, but I saved him anyway. Have had him for almost a decade now. He still has panic attacks. Nightmares. Feel like, if cussing gives him a sense of control . . . far be it from me to take that away." He motioned to the books she'd left next to the armchair. "Why don't we take a look-see at those and try to figure out what's going on?"

TRINA STARED DOWN AT THE book. "This is Rowena's Grimoire. She cursed the Original. She killed the women of the last coven— our mothers. She wasn't a good person." She shook her head. "Part of me is afraid to open the damn thing."

"Give it. I'll do it."

"No." The denial came quick, vehement, surprising her. "I need to see for myself."

"Understood." He patted the loveseat. "Why don't you come over here?"

Her mouth went dry. She shouldn't. She shouldn't try to lean on him or take support from him. She couldn't rely on him. Not ever. Still, she joined him on the loveseat. With a trembling hand, she opened the book.

The first few pages were written in the rounded scrawl of a teenaged cheerleader. The spells, rudimentary and morally suspect.

He squinted down at the book. "Is that a cheating spell?"

"Mm." She paused, looking over the words before flipping the page. "And a love potion. Interesting."

"Why?" He took a long swig of blood.

"Our creed says, 'If it harms none, do what you will.' These spells, they're all harmful."

"Not outright. It isn't as though she's killing people."

She pinned him with her gaze. "She did. Eventually. Once you start playing in the Darkness, it's easy to get lost."

"We're daemons." He winked. "It's our job to toe the line and do what others don't have the stomach for."

She looked away. The book outlined Rowena's slow escalation from minor infringements on human lives to the outright murder of her coven sisters.

As she flipped through pages, the handwriting changed, along with the difficulty of the spells.

"What's that?" Duncan put his hand on the page to keep her from turning it. "The Thirteen Steps to Hell?"

For a moment, she wasn't sure. She scanned the page, caught the words "Maltby Cemetery" amid Rowena's scrawl. She laughed. "It's an old urban legend. If you walk down these steps in this cemetery, they say you disappear." She rolled her eyes. "If you survive long enough to reach the bottom, you see yourself burning in the flames of hell and go mad."

He frowned. "Isn't there a kernel of truth to every legend?"

"The owner poured cement over them years ago. They don't even exist anymore." She turned the pages. Rowena had dedicated several pages to the steps before she came to a page that had "The Original" scrawled across the top. "Here."

Duncan leaned closer.

She read it out loud. "When the Original is no longer cursed, she'll come to thee as three. All as humans first, then as daemons are set free: the Beacon burning bright, the Shadow hidden from sight, the blighted, damned Knight." She chewed her lip. "I thought the Original was one person, not three."

Duncan pulled the other book out from under Rowena's Grimoire, set it on top and opened it. He flipped through to The Original, and they both leaned forward to read.

She'd read most of the story at Rowena's house before Duncan had interrupted her. Lilith and Adam were created as equals. Lilith refused to lie beneath Adam and she left Eden. When she saw Eve pregnant, she'd grown jealous and vowed to kill any unprotected infants. The goddess confronted Lilith and they'd fought. She scanned to the battle between Lilith and the goddess, where she'd left off earlier.

"Damn." He pointed to the same section she'd been reading. "Her soul was split in two."

"That accounts for two people, not three."

"Says those who shared in her blood or Magic were also cursed to reincarnate in human form until they learned some lesson." He set the book aside. "That angel she took for a lover turned her into a vampire, right? So they shared blood. Maybe he's the Knight."

Maybe. She glanced at him sideways. Wouldn't that be him? *Samael.*

Rowena had three words circled, Beacon, Shadow, and Knight. A line was drawn from each, pointing to a name scrawled in the margin. Lilith's name was linked to the Beacon, but the next name made the breath stall in her lungs. The line linking the Shadow pointed to her name.

The room spun for a moment. Not that she was surprised, it did explain a lot. Why she disappeared when Lilith—the light—wasn't around. Why Rowena had always been afraid of her. Why her Magic had changed when James transformed Lilith into a vampire. She just didn't *want* to believe it. Besides, it left too many unanswered questions. If she were part of the Original, why did she infect Lilith when they touched? Why did the Council only want one of them alive? Why did Crowley? Why could the Watchers hear Lilith, but not her?

"You didn't know?"

"Rowena could've been wrong."

"What do *you* think?"

What did she think? Being the Shadow-half of the Original wasn't exactly flattering. In psychology, the Shadow represented the part of each person they'd rather hide—the part that could turn mean when backed into a corner, that could kill. She chewed on her lip. The Shadow of the Original. Was that like a shadow-self?

Goddess, help me. Her mind raced, piecing through the last couple years when everything had gone wrong.

What if she'd triggered this when she'd killed Trevor? He'd been an ass, but he hadn't deserved to die. She hadn't meant to kill him.

Everything had been fine until that event. That's when she'd started going invisible. She'd been terrified that she'd get caught. She'd been . . . . Dear goddess, what if she'd done it to herself—caused her own invisibility because she'd been so scared?

When Trevor died, she'd only had a couple weeks left of her enlistment. She completed her enlistment, but had always expected the MPs to come calling. Those last two weeks had been hell.

When she'd gotten out of the Navy, she'd holed up in a little studio apartment just off base. She'd quit calling Lilith. Refused to answer Lilith's texts or tell her where she was because she'd been so scared the police would come knocking and she didn't want to get Lilith involved.

What if she'd triggered the Shadow-self of the Original within herself? What if she'd made herself invisible to avoid punishment for her crime? What if she was escalating like Rowena had without even realizing it? She'd almost killed James the same way she'd killed Trevor. Her actions had allowed Crowley to get away. She'd shot Duncan who was only here to help. She hadn't planned to do any of those things . . . they'd just happened. Maybe because she tended to be impulsive. Maybe because of bad luck. What if the Shadow aspect of the Original was making her do things—things that would allow the bad guys to win?

No. She was a good person, damn it.

"Hey." Duncan reached over and tipped her chin his way. "What do you think of all this?"

"I think I don't know what to think." She returned her attention to the book. "Looks like she couldn't make up her mind about the Knight." Several names that had been written in had been scribbled out: Brenda, Sherry, Meredith. Below them, one name was circled: James.

He leaned in even more, his arm pressing up against hers and pointed. "What does that say?"

The tightly curved letters were almost illegible. "Knight Templar?"

"So James is the Knight?"

Again, maybe. Why would Lilith's mate be the Knight but not hers? Or were they both, like her and Lilith were both part of the Original? Neither made sense as she read the poem again. She shrugged. "Rowena was a little, uh, bat-shit crazy there at the end. I mean, why assume any of us were part of the Original?"

He grinned. "Says right there at the bottom, love." He pointed to the bottom of the page. *Souls gravitate to those they've known before.*

"You believe that?"

He rested back against the cushions. "Ain't been around as long as others, but long enough to re-meet those I've known before. Not all, but some." His gaze bored into hers as if trying to instill some extra meaning to his words. He didn't seem so scary now. Didn't seem big in a threatening way. There was something about him that was peaceful. Something that reached right inside her, slowing her heart to a steady rhythm.

Focus. She returned her attention to the book. Lilith thought Rowena might have had information on the Original that would help her figure out why her skin had turned black when they touched, but there were no answers here. Even if she was the Shadow to Lilith's Beacon, shouldn't they be able to be together if they shared part of the same soul?

She flipped the page and wished she hadn't. "Rowena wrote everything down. The spells. The dates. Which of our moms she used each spell on." All of them were there, except hers. Her mother had died in a car crash—not because of Rowena, but because of her.

"Thorough for a head case. What was she doing there at the end?"

She flipped to the last few pages. One name in particular caught her eye. "Julius Crowley."

Duncan lowered the PVC bag. "She knew him? You know him?"

"They were working together. I don't think it was for long and it didn't work out the way either of them expected, but . . . ." She read some of the entry. "He wanted access to Lilith in exchange for making the coven obey Rowena."

"The coven didn't like her?"

"From what Lilith told me, the coven was rebelling against Rowena's plans to start a war with the Council." She read a little more. "She planned to betray him from the start. Rowena did a dream spell on someone named Dr. Edwin Moss. Told him about Crowley's healing capabilities. At least she told him to keep Crowley's eyes covered." She sat back. "Why do that? Why the hell does that name sound familiar?" She pulled out her phone and searched the name. Immediately, the news stories about RI and their race to save the soldiers came up. "Oh, dear goddess, I can't believe I didn't make the connection." She typed in 'Where is revelations industries located?'

"What?"

"He's the director of RI."

"Those men that tried to detain us . . . they work for this Moss bloke?"

"Yeah." Smyrna Island. RI was located on a little island out in Oceania. She pulled up the map and pictures. She'd been to the island once while in the Navy—they'd done practice maneuvers there. There wasn't much she could do with the information now. She needed to gain control of her Magic before they went after Crowley or she'd risk making things worse. "Moss is the director of a bioweapons company. The last director sold one of RI's new bio-weapons to our enemies, who infected a whole squadron of our troops. They're dying from exposure—the bio-weapon was stolen before they'd made an antibody. Moss was on the news all last week, begging the science community to help him find a cure."

"And Rowena gave him Crowley." He sagged back against the couch. "A vampire with a mesmerist talent and bioweapons. Nothing good can come from that."

CHAPTER 9

Smyrna Island, Pacific Oceania
U.S. Department of Defense
Revelations Industries, Inc.

JULIUS CROWLEY WOKE WITH A start. He'd been having a pleasant dream . . . well, not pleasant exactly, he'd been chained up in a house. In an old basement, which wasn't nice at all. But there was this gorgeous, voluptuous redhead. She'd kissed him. Told him she belonged to him and that everything would be okay. It was bullshit, of course, but it had been pleasant.

Christ, it was stifling under the hood. He couldn't see, the sounds around him were muffled. The air he dragged in tasted stale and thin. The rest of him was cold as bejesus. Something pinned his limbs to the icy slab at his back, pinching his skin tight under some kind of restraints.

This wasn't the first time he'd been forced into a hood and he doubted it'd be the last. But, damn, he hated it. He'd been forced to wear one too many times over the centuries, thanks to his Vampiric talent.

What the hell had happened? Everything was blank. Everything was— He *wanted* everything to be blank. Memories tried to return, but he pushed them away. He didn't want to think. Didn't want to remember. He just wanted away from wherever he was.

Where the hell are we?

He got no answer. He wanted to go back to sleep but his body shivered from cold and stress. There'd be no more sleep for a long while.

This happened more often lately—this abrupt return to consciousness when he least wanted it. For decades, he'd been able to recede into his own mind, disconnecting himself from what Azazel did with his body, refusing to acknowledge the pain. The guilt. Now that Azazel was so active, finding that quiet place away had become almost impossible.

Possession—yeah, it was a bitch.

The first time Azazel had seized his body, Julius had wanted nothing more than for the fallen angel to get the fuck out. After he did leave, once Julius had witnessed firsthand the power of a Watcher unconstrained by a host body, he'd realized he needed to restrict the Watcher from accessing all his power. Julius had done the one thing in his power to protect humanity—he'd held on to the bastard the next time Azazel possessed him. Trapped him inside his body, limiting his power.

That little brainstorm had proved to be the stupidest, most reckless, painful, and arrogant thing he'd ever done, because now they were stuck. He'd been paying the price for his rash move for over three centuries.

Chalk another line on the wall there, boss.

The hair on his bare arms prickled as someone came near, he strained to hear over his breathing. Each heavy breath echoed under the hood, muffling and distorting sounds from without. Which side were they on? What were they doing? The low whine of some type of spinning mechanism filled the room. His muscles tensed.

Azazel's voice filled his mind. *Host, you must see this.*

For a moment, he could see. Not with his eyes, but inside his head. They were in a sterile room—white and stainless steel—and he was spread out naked on a gurney, strapped down and hooded. A fat little man loomed over him, holding a long, thin tool with a spinning blade on the end.

"Oh, God."

Laughter bloomed inside his head. The vision disappeared, leaving him surrounded by the darkness of the hood.

You sick bastard, one of these days—the fat man started to speak, and he silenced his mind to listen.

"When we first brought you in, we catalogued a number of open wounds and bruises on your body, but—"

"Who are you?"

He ignored the question. "—within twenty-four hours, they had all healed. Nothing short of miraculous."

Julius tried again. "Where am I?"

The whine of the saw stopped. "My name is Moss, Mr. Crowley. We spoke yesterday, do you remember?"

He hadn't spoken to Moss. He didn't even remember how he came to be here, wherever here was. Unless . . . shit. Azazel. *What kind of sick deal did you make? Why are you doing this?*

Azazel remained quiet.

"Interesting. I'll have to make a note of your memory loss. That could be a problem. To recap: We have several sick men here who need to recover. As you can imagine, we find your healing capabilities quite interesting—you're immune to the bioweapon—but I'll need more precise measurements. For one thing, I have no way of knowing how old those injuries were. My notes must be thorough if I'm going to gain approval to proceed."

This wasn't happening. What the hell had Azazel gotten him into? What could he hope to gain from this? Was it another of his twisted punishments?

"I'm going to cut the tip of your finger off so I can measure how long it takes to grow back."

"What?" He struggled, but with his limbs restrained all he managed to do was smack his head on the table. *Get us out of here. I know you can. Why would you allow—*

The saw started again.

Goddamn it! Make him stop, you fucking—

The pain came.

All his muscles seized under the sudden attack of acute agony. It was too much effort to even drag in a stale breath of air around the blinding fire.

His thoughts shattered.

CHAPTER 10

Carnation, WA

TRINA STARED AT HER TAROT reading. Everything pointed to major turmoil. To the fate of the world resting on her shoulders.

The goddess must be as crazy as the Watchers.

The Shadow. Fucking great. The more she thought about it, the angrier she got. She jammed the top edge of each of the Tarot cards from her reading into the frame of her mirror with far more force than necessary. There were more capable witches in the coven. Did it mean she was evil? The violent, horrible part of the Original? Was she meant to spend the rest of her life fighting against such impulses? Did it mean that no matter how hard she tried, she'd always taint what she touched?

She ruins everything.

She rested her elbows on the dresser next to a small pot of dirt which once housed a sick fern. Now it held a little, once-white rabbit in a yellow sundress impaled on a Popsicle stick. She ran her fingertip down the rabbit's head. Sun-bleached and dusty, the condition of the toy solidified the fact that she did, indeed, ruin everything. Even a stupid yarn bunny wasn't safe.

Someone rapped on her door. She jerked around to stare.

The door opened. Duncan popped his head around the corner. "Heard you up, love. Can't protect you from the other room." He stepped in, closed the door and leaned on it, folding his arms across his chest.

As if she needed protection. She took him in from beneath her lashes.

Unlike James, who always dressed for comfort, Duncan appeared to put more thought into his clothing. No worn jeans or tees for him. Even now, half put together and wounded, he looked fresh off the page of some Calvin Klein ad; a fresh, trendy designer shirt hung open over low-riding chinos. *The goddess had taken her time creating that body*. He was all sharp lines, hard planes, and tightly packed muscle. Handsome or not, his potent male energy commanded her attention.

She blinked. When the hell had she started being *attracted* to him? She should've never invited him into her home. "Get out."

He gifted her with a lopsided grin that threatened to turn her to mush. "Are you deaf?"

"If I was, I wouldn't have heard you trying to walk through the floorboards, would I, Duchess?"

She ground her teeth together.

"Just wanna talk." He held his hands up in a placating gesture. "I hurt like hell and now that I've fed I can't seem to sleep." He pointed to the chair sitting at an angle in the corner near the door. "Can I sit? You stay on that side of the room, I'll sit over here, and we'll both behave."

He gimped over to the chair and sat. This wasn't a good idea. She had no desire to get close to him. Knew better than to risk his safety by having him anywhere near her right now. But she couldn't continue to sit around here feeling sorry for herself. Hell, if they talked a while, maybe she'd discover Duncan was just as much of an ass as Trevor had been. Then she wouldn't feel so bad when it was time to part ways.

In the end, she sat on the bed and pulled the remaining pillow into her lap, holding the feather-stuffed sack in front of her like a shield.

He glanced around, his gaze pausing on her suitcases, on the items on the dresser, the cards hanging from her mirror.

Quiet seconds ticked by. She began to fidget. She didn't want to discuss her problems and she sucked at small talk. "What did you want to talk about?"

The full weight of his attention fixed on her. "Anything. I'm knackered. Something dull enough to put me to sleep."

"Let's talk about you."

"You do know how to wound a male." He chuckled, which forced her own reluctant grin. Duncan Sinclair was a dangerous man—he wasn't easy to dislike.

"Ask me anything." He crossed an ankle over his knee, wincing. His head rested on the cushioned back, his elbows on the arm pads. He appeared relaxed enough to fall asleep at any second.

"Where are you from?"

His lips quirked. "What, the accent didn't give me away?"

"Obviously England, but where?"

"Bow Bell, love. I'm true-blue Cockney."

She arched her brow.

"Back in the day we had the gentry, the poor, and the Cockney; working class riff-raff born near St. Mary-le-Bow's church in London. If you heard the bells from where you were born, you were considered a Cockney. Nowadays it just means you have a charming accent."

"That is one of the strangest things I've ever heard." His chest rumbled with quiet laughter and she smiled again. "When was 'back in the day'?"

"Oh, what . . .? Would've been around fifteen-sixteen to fifteen forty-eight."

He'd been thirty-two when transformed. "What's it like?"

"The sixteenth century?"

"No, well . . . yeah, that too, I guess, but living for so long."

"Poor choice of words, that." He stared at the ceiling. "Right, so, as a human I wanted to put food on the table, keep a roof over our heads. Now, I can't remember specifically what I look like." He grinned. "Which may be a good thing. I don't recall how food tastes, not even when I catch the scent, nor what sunlight felt like. That's the hardest part."

She'd never thought too much about what it would be like to not have a reflection or eat regular food. She couldn't imagine forgetting the flavor of chocolate. "Not remembering?"

"Nah, more . . . knowing I didn't *experience* things enough. I never bothered to pay attention to the mundane stuff I did and saw a thousand times over. Now there're no specifics to recall."

"Oh."

His eyes met her gaze.

"I didn't expect a serious answer."

"Mm." His lips curved. "I've been around awhile. You can't go long without noticing some of the darker aspects of life." He bobbed his head to the side. "And death. I have a serious and thankless job. What I'm trying to say is I prefer to keep things on the light, yeah? Makes the nights pass smoother, keeps the wrong people from paying me mind, but don't mistake it with me being light in the head."

"And fifteen forty-eight?"

"Right," he muttered on an exhale. "Pretty much the same as now." At her scoff, he added, "Minus all the modern conveniences and cleanliness." He cleared his throat. "This is nice. Had a feeling you'd be a bit of all right once you retracted your claws." When she didn't comment, he continued, "I think you and me are more alike than you want to admit."

She failed to stifle her laugh and it came out as a snort.

His brow shot up.

She coughed, tried to bluster through. "Sorry, but I can't find any similarity. I grew up in the States, graduated, and served in the Navy. You . . . ." She let her words trail off.

"What? I'm an uneducated villain from the wrong side of town?"

"I didn't—"

"You're handing me your CV, in'nit?" His accent became almost too thick to understand. "Listing off your accomplishments to weigh against mine. But what? You don't have anything on me yet? Nothing to compare, good or bad?"

"I was going to say I can't find any similarities and I got embarrassed and the thought came out wrong. *But we are nothing alike.*"

"How?"

Her mind went blank. She didn't even understand why they were arguing.

"I'll hand-feed you a couple. We're opposite sex and were brought up in different countries. So, come on. How else?"

"Listen to—"

His cheeks flushed. "You shouldn't make snap judgments based on a person's speech."

"I was going to say, 'Listen to how arrogant you sound.'"

His cheeks reddened more.

"Why are you mad?"

"I ain't. Said what I had to say." His accent smoothed out with his temper. He leaned forward as if he were going to rise to leave.

"What were your parents like?" She wasn't ready for their talk to end.

He paused. Settled back in the chair. "My father was a butcher, had a shop in Cheapside."

"Did you follow in his footsteps?" She couldn't quite see him doing that kind of work.

"Nah. I—" He rubbed the back of his neck.

She waited for him to say more.

He shrugged. "I was a pugilist and a filch."

"What's that?"

"A boxer. During dry spells, a thief." His gaze met hers. "A villain."

She grinned. It suited him. "Sounds hazardous."

"I tend to have an unusual amount of luck."

"Not enough." She grinned. "Did you break your nose in a fight?"

He grew still, his expression guarded. "Of a sort." His gaze zeroed in on her suitcases. "So, you've been away. Where?"

"The Navy. I did ten years." She hated lying, but ten . . . eight, who would ever know?

"You liked the service?"

No. Yes. She shrugged. "I had a freedom I didn't have here."

"In the military?" His tone dripped skepticism.

How could she explain? "Have you ever felt . . .?" She held her hands up. "I don't know . . . like parts of you were missing?"

"Empty inside?"

She nodded.

He leaned forward. "Yes."

Why was she telling him this? Lilith was her best friend. She'd always told her everything—at least everything she was willing to say out loud. But his gaze held steady—intent and understanding—and the words spilled out. "I don't remember ever *not* feeling like that and when I"—*was forced into the military*—"joined the military, I didn't have Rowena or the coven hovering over me and I could do things that made the emptiness go away for a little while. Does that make sense?"

"Drink. Women . . . ." He bobbed his head. "Well, women for me." He winked. "Lots of mates who weren't true friends because I never talked to them about anything important." He sat back. "Parties and rows. Filching and conning." His gaze met hers. "I get that. Went through a similar phase."

"Except whenever I was still again . . . whenever I was alone . . . ."

"The emptiness was worse than ever."

She stared at the brutish man sitting in her recliner. "*Yes.*"

His bottom lip popped out. He nodded. "Took me a long, long time to figure out I was distracting myself, not fixing the problem."

"Yes." Her eyes widened. He did understand. Maybe they *were* more alike that she realized. "I even asked the Watchers to send me my mate. I thought that would fix the problem."

"Didn't it?" He tipped his head.

She needed to stop before she said too much. "It didn't work out."

His gaze dropped to where she rubbed her hand over her tattoo. *During this life, I belong to no man.*

"If you say so." His gaze turned intent on hers, in the pregnant silence. Then, his expression softened. He settled back into the chair again. He cocked his head toward the mirror attached to her dresser. "What d'ya got there?"

"Tarot cards. Whenever I do a reading for myself, I pin them up." She'd hoped to find solace in the cards. Unfortunately, her spread had nothing comforting to say.

"What do they mean, then?"

She settled on giving him the barest of details. "Uh, well, the Ten of Swords indicates change." Actually, she had a feeling it indicated transformation . . . as into a vampire and she just wasn't okay with that.

"Fitting. The next?"

"Judgment is about past mistakes." And not letting them rule your future actions. "The Hierophant"—his eyes narrowed on the card as she spoke—"suggests I'll need to make a trade"—a sacrifice—"for what I want."

He tipped his head to the side. "And the last set?"

Instinct told her he knew she lied. Knew she was feeding him half-truths. Still, she continued, focusing on the cards: The World crossed by Death. "They refer to the Rapture." To a major transformation needed to even get close to her goal of stopping Armageddon. Typically, the cards were read in order, first this, then that, so if the Ten of Swords predicted her transformation into a vampire . . . what the hell kind of transformation was involved in the last set of cards?

He regarded her for a long moment, lips pursed, nodding slowly. She needed every ounce of composure she had not to squirm.

"You know," he kept his words conversational, but his tone held a note of challenge, "the Tarot originated in Europe—fourteenth century or so. *Tarocchi*, they called it. These here are remakes of the Rider–Waite deck."

Well, shit.

His lips quirked. "See, historically speaking, the poor tend to be a superstitious lot. They're most apt to put credence into such things as divination and witches. Yeah?"

Her stomach did a little summersault. "I suppose they were popular in Cheapside."

"Very." He flashed a brilliant smile. *Checkmate,* that smile said. *I caught you* telling me half-truths.

Maybe he knew she wasn't giving him the whole truth, but she doubted he could read them. "What's your take?"

"Well, let's see now." He pulled himself out of his chair, wincing, his hand pressed tight to his side, and crossed the room to the cards. "I'd have to say the Ten of Swords speaks of major changes. It's warning you, as a person who likes to command her environment, you can't retain control. Your whole world will be altered. The card is telling you not to fight fate. Resistance causes pain."

She swallowed hard. He had talent. His reading was correct.

"Judgment wants you to stop judging yourself. New things are coming. Don't let past mistakes scare you off unfamiliar experiences. I'd say this card indicated a special someone in your future." He leaned on the wall. "Intense feelings." He winked. "And great sex."

"Duncan." She instilled a warning in his name.

"Yeah, yeah." He straightened with a chuckle. "The Hierophant might be what you said, maybe, if someone else drew the card." He grew serious. "For you, this indicates big compromises to fulfill your goal. Dangerous things. Hard choices. This last set, The World crossed by Death, everything considered, the literal translation is fitting—it being the Rapture an' all." He ran his finger over the little sun-bleached rabbit the same way she had earlier. "Even so, we could be a bit more philosophical. The World indicates you'll near your goal, but not achieve success as you're thinking of it now. Death suggests the goal will require a major transformation on your part. Since Death crosses your desire, that change will be something you'd rather not do: A sacrifice."

He turned back to her and she snapped her mouth closed. "You've studied Tarot?"

Shaking his head, his bottom lip popped out in a thoughtful expression. "Knew someone who did. Watched her read sometimes."

He'd done more than watch. "It takes study of the occult to understand the symbolism. Most people don't learn that from just watching."

"Most people don't take the time to learn anything other than what they're told to know."

"You're cynical."

"A cynic can't imagine the possibility of better things. My problem is, I can." His heavy-lidded gaze shifted away. He returned to his seat, stretched out his legs and crossed them at his ankles. His little performance must have zapped the remainder of his energy.

"They're beautiful, don't you think? Same as Monet or Van Gogh, just in a different way. Always thought they belonged in a gallery."

She glanced at the Tarot cards. They'd never been more than a tool of her trade, but now that he'd mentioned it, they were beautiful. "You like art?"

"Mm. Took a holiday once." He let his head rest on his chair, turning his hooded eyes to her. "What? Guardians get pay and benefits same as anyone." His eyelids slid closed. "But, yeah, I had a hard time getting up in the evenings. All seemed pointless. I couldn't rationalize my job anymore—going out each night, destroying this daemon or that one. What gave me the right? And the humans who lived because of me interference, did they deserve a second chance? Did I save humans who would do good with their life or, being how I'm a daemon, did I precipitate evil?"

Good question. One she'd often thought about, too. Her Magic was a dark thing. Deadly. Uncontrollable. So what was her purpose in life as the Shadow-self of the Original? To precipitate evil? Was there anything good that could come from her gifts? She pulled herself out of her thoughts. "What year did you take your holiday?"

"Recent. The nineteen hundreds. 'Forty-five. August." He stretched, folding his arms over his chest, settling in the chair. "Decided I needed something beautiful in me life. Something to remind me what I fought for every night. I ended up at the Louvre, in Paris. Back then, they had the place locked up tight. Half the art had been crated, but what still hung out . . . . Amazing."

She strained to hear. As he relaxed his accent became heavier, something she hadn't thought possible.

"First night, I ended up in a statuary room. The lights were off, not a living soul 'round. All that gleaming white marble and limestone. Like walking through a strange tomb where the bodies were frozen instead of buried. Reminded me of the stories of Medusa, you know, in Greek mythology. Felt a bit like her. Unwillingly turned into a monster, unwanted by society, destroying everything I encountered. Had a kinship with her."

Her throat grew tight as she listened to her most secret thoughts being voiced. She'd never considered someone else might feel the same.

"After that, I started spending some of me pay. Buying up art, books, music, anything to try to remind me of the beauty humans were capable of. I always searched for that elusive . . . beautiful . . . *something*."

Her breath caught, she leaned forward. His voice had grown husky, his accented words trailing off until she strained to hear. She should let him sleep, but she wanted to know. She needed the same thing in her life. Wanted it desperately. For a long time, she sat there, picking at the loose threads on her bedspread. Afraid to ask, but wanting to know if he found it, needing know what it was. He appeared at peace with himself and the world—so he must have, right? "What was it? Your something beautiful?"

"Mm." His weight shifted and he started to snore softly.

She sighed, settling back on the mattress.

What had happened in 'forty-five that had challenged his faith in mankind? A personal event? Maybe something that made him flinch every time she motioned with her hands?

She'd wanted to dislike him. To find a way to keep her distance because she did pose a threat to him. But during their conversation, she'd forgotten to keep him at a distance. He'd sucked her into their discussion and she'd begun to like him.

Her gaze followed the hard lines of his body. Goddess preserve her, he was a reformed bad boy with a body made for sin. Almost as if he were made for her. Once upon a time she'd have jumped at an opportunity with such a man. But life had taught her caution.

Curling up under the covers, she pulled out her phone and searched August, 1945. The first results said it all: The end of World War II. Hiroshima. Nagasaki. The conclusion of one abomination and the beginning of another—definitely a year to challenge a man's faith in humanity.

And Duncan Samael Sinclair had gone off in search of something beautiful.

CHAPTER II

A MAD LITTLE DRUMMER WOKE DUNCAN a few hours later. The erratic beat, punctuated by staccato, wordless lyrics pulled him from his dreams. He forced away the haze of sleep, recognizing the rhythm as a heart in the throes of terror, accented by soft, spasmodic whimpers. This wasn't the sweet rhythmic lullaby he'd drifted off to.

He pressed his hand to his wound, easing out of the armchair to investigate. Restless in her sleep, Trina had knocked her pillow to the floor and had the sheets tangled around her legs. Why did he find her so damn fascinating? Because he'd known her before? Because she was better than before? She looked so much like Satrina, but she was different. More emotional. More . . . just more.

When he sat at the edge of the bed, the mattress sagged under his weight and she rolled, curling around him. Logically, because the bed dipped toward him, but in his mind he rather fancied she did so to get closer. He stroked his hand down her arm, her skin dark under his pale, callused fingers. She moaned, throwing her arm over his thighs.

"Mm, I'm not such a bad sort when you don't have to look at me, eh?"

She let out a soft whimper in response. Moisture glistened on her dark lashes. He had to restrain himself from shaking her awake and demanding to know what she dreamt of. His response was illogical. Inappropriate. It was damn near all-consuming.

Rule Three: Never love.

Hell, he needed to be careful with this one. She reminded him of Harry—the way she hid any weakness by turning prickly. He saw something in her, some pain she'd buried and nurtured into a shield to keep others away. Yeah, he needed to be careful, but he'd always been a sucker for a challenge.

If she belonged to him, he'd curl up behind her and hold her through the nightmares. She didn't, though. She'd pitch a fit if she woke to find him in her bed. Instead, he slipped one arm under her shoulders and the other under her knees and stood, groaning at the pull on his wounds. He carried her to the armchair, settling her in his lap. This evening, when she woke, she could slag him off to her heart's content. He'd tell her . . . what? His actions were compulsive? Compassionate? No. they were possessive—and he doubted she'd like to hear that.

Rule One: Never let true emotion show.

She could stuff her displeasure. He wasn't any happier about this whole mess than her. He wanted her. Had every intention of having her. But she wasn't the type of woman to be left behind and relationships were not his strong suit.

The last one . . . ah, Gertie. He'd tried to love her. She had been his wife, supposed to have been his helpmate. Instead, she'd become the bane of his existence—the longer he had her in his grasp the more she changed into something unlovable. He'd found solace with Satrina, though she'd been a cold woman, always keeping him at arm's length.

Then they'd all died. All within a few days. Satrina disappeared, never to be heard from again, and his wife and son . . . . His gut twisted into an unyielding knot.

Yeah, Gertie had been his own personal hell and Satrina hadn't been much better. To set himself up for such a thing again would be daft.

Trina sighed, drawing his attention back to the present. Her head listed to the side, the pointed diamond-shaped stones in her choker digging into her neck. It was a menacing-looking bauble and broken, to boot. One of the milky-white stones was cracked. Most of the stone was missing from another. Odd that she'd changed into a pair of baggy shorts and a tank top for bed, but hadn't removed her jewelry.

He lifted her, crossed his ankle over his knee and settled her bum into the pocket his leg made. He nudged her head into the crook of his elbow so the choker wouldn't dig into her.

She was different from the women he usually seduced. Even the abstract designs inked around her upper arm had a gothic bent to them. Small in stature; her head didn't even reach his shoulders. With her narrow waist and slender, toned limbs, she was petite everywhere except for the full breasts attempting to spill out of her tank top.

Despite all that, she had an upper-crust aura about her—maybe because of her impeccable posture or the inscrutable expression she wore to try to hide her thoughts or perhaps because of the fragile pride she wrapped herself in. Whatever the reason, it made him want to push her buttons until that pristine mask shattered so he could get to the woman underneath. And he had every intention of getting to her. Soon as she started trusting him.

His lips quirked. Damn but she'd been shocked as hell when he caught her lying about those Tarot cards. Embarrassed, too. She wouldn't try to trick him again.

His gaze settled on her mouth, the saucy bow shape, the full lower lip. Christ, the things he'd like to do to that mouth. She'd shoot him again if she had any inkling.

Yeah, she'd be his. At least, for a little while. She'd already started to get curious about him. She watched him whenever she thought he wasn't paying her mind.

Ugly as he was, he had never understood his appeal, but for whatever reason, he had the devil's luck with women. Well, at least with getting them into the sack. He discovered real fast not to expect more—a hard-learned lesson that he'd never forget.

TRINA WOKE TO A GENTLE rocking, almost like that of a ship. The comforting motion tipped her from side to side, following the ebb and flow. She turned her head into her warm pillow. Inhaled earthy things—trees and rain . . . she shouldn't smell any of those things in the ocean.

Wait . . . she wasn't in the Navy anymore.

Soft rhythmic inhalations and exhalations kept time with the rocking motion.

Duncan.

She came awake with a start, launching herself out of his lap. She whirled around, fisting her hands at her sides, ready to berate him with a barrage of scathing put downs. Magic thrummed through her veins alongside a potent rush of adrenaline.

No Magic. Don't use Magic. She paused. Forced her hands to unclench.

At her hesitation, he grinned like a Cheshire cat. "All you had to do was ask, Duchess. No need sneaking into me arms while I'm asleep."

"Why you arrogant, little b—"

"Careful now. Ain't nothing little about me."

Her gaze dropped to his lap where an impressive erection pushed against his fly.

"Penny for your thoughts?" His lips spread in a knowing smile.

She forced her gaze up. "You damn well know you're the one who accosted me in my sleep you . . . you perverted deviant. You want me—"

In less than a heartbeat he had her backed to the wall. An icy tendril of apprehension crept up her spine. Her Magic spiked, demanding release. She tamped the urge down again.

With him looming over her, she didn't even reach his shoulders in height and she couldn't help but notice the flex of muscle in his chest, how thick his biceps were or how broad his shoulders. Goddess preserve her, this man could do a person some damage.

No Magic.

She didn't want to hurt him. Not unless he did something to deserve her wrath, so she waited, ready to defend herself.

He didn't touch her, instead he braced his arms on the wall to either side of her, leaving her room to escape. Gave her time to do so, in fact, but she stayed, entranced by the fire in his hazel eyes.

"Yeah, I want you." He leaned in. Let his body press against hers long enough for her to feel his erection hard and hot through their clothing. "You feel me?"

"Yeah, I get it, you want to fuck me." She used her most derisive tone, hating the shakiness of her voice.

"Oh, no." He shook his head once. "No, not with you. You're not the kind of woman created for a mindless fuck. No, a woman like you . . . . Should I tell you what it'd be like? Would you like that, love?"

"Don't call me that." Too late, she realized the breathlessness of her voice denied any truth to her words. She'd always wanted to be some-one's love. But it wasn't meant to be. Not for her. She lifted her chin. "I don't like it."

"You do." He tipped his head to the side, studying her. "See, when the time is right, I'm gonna strip these clothes off you like they were fancy paper on a pressy. Not with the clumsiness of an excited five-year-old on Christmas morn, but with the reverence of a man who's never got-ten a pressy before and maybe never will again." His voice sounded like silk pulled across velvet, smooth and soft, but still rough from slumber, catching here and there before sliding along again in its fluid, effortless baritone.

"I'll peel them away, prolonging the anticipation, savoring the experience, making a memory of each second. When we're both starkers, *love*, I'll do the same to you. I'll kiss those pouting lips of yours, coaxing you to open for me so I can taste you again." He bit his bottom lip, bowing his head as if to kiss her, but stopped shy. "You remember me kiss, yeah? Remember me loving your mouth? How I taste?" He leaned close enough for her to feel his words on her lips, to taste each breath he exhaled, but didn't come close enough for anything more. "I'll touch every inch of your skin with me hands, lick every bit of flesh, undoing any reservations you have."

He awakened senses she'd thought long dead, making her burn, but denying her the relief of his touch. Her head spun, scattering her thoughts as she became intoxicated on desire.

"And your breasts. Ah, you've got magnificent breasts. I can almost feel their weight in me palm, imagine your nipples hardening in me mouth, straining for more."

As affected by the erotic pictures he painted as she, his breath had turned ragged. His gaze never left hers, holding her captive in a way his hands never could.

"You'll be begging, writhing against me, pleading with me to fill you with me cock. And I'll be hard for you—bursting with the need to be inside you. But not yet. First, I'll want to taste you. . . . " His thigh nudged hers apart, slid against the apex of her legs. "Here."

Unable to look away, her cheeks burned. He must feel the heat, the dampness through their clothes.

"Don't blush, love. Don't be embarrassed. You're wet for me. I like that. Makes me ache all the more for you. So much I can't stand much more. You like it, too—that I'm so damn hot for you. You like the idea of me mouth on your pussy, me tongue sliding over your clit. That'll be the first time I make you come. But I have a secret, love."

He leaned in until his chest brushed her breasts, making them ache, until the scruff on his jaw scratched her cheek, until his heavy breath caressed her ear, causing her to shiver. "It won't be anywhere near the last."

Duncan pushed back to arm's length.

Her hands twitched, wanting to pull him in until he pressed her to the wall. Until he fulfilled each act he'd described.

His gaze stroked over her as if trying to memorize the moment in its finest detail. She waited for him to lean in and kiss her. She waited for him to touch her. For more erotic words.

She waited in vain.

"But not now." He lowered his arms to his sides. "Get dressed, Duchess. I'll be waiting downstairs." He inclined his head to her and left the room.

A shuddering breath shook loose. Damn, he was dangerous. He'd hardly touched her but he'd left her in such a state of arousal she had little doubt the slightest stimulus would send her careening over the edge. Never had she been so aroused, much less by something as simple as words.

Maybe he really was hers. A soul created for her and her alone.

No. The Watchers couldn't see her. They didn't know her well enough to fulfill the spell the coven had cast requesting her mate.

This had nothing to do with him, or them being mated or true love. She hadn't been with a man in two years. Too much abstinence had turned her to mush. That's all this was.

She nodded. Lust could be sated and forgotten. If Duncan wouldn't let her push him away, she'd sleep with him and be done with him. Their curiosity would be satisfied and they could both move on.

CHAPTER 12

Smyrna Island, Pacific Oceania
U.S. Department of Defense
Revelations Industries, Inc.

JULIUS CROWLEY ALLOWED HIS MIND to quiet, his control slipping away as the Watcher took over.

Images flashed through his mind at such speeds he had no hope of garnering any information. *The red-headed woman from his dream leaning over Lilith—one side of Lilith's face sunken and black, James Pasquino pacing at the foot of Lilith's bed. Leopold, hunkered down in his hidey-hole with his wife. A young boy he didn't recognize sitting in a library, staring at a wall of monitors, sipping blood from a bag. Sentries standing guard at the gate of an abandoned townhome. Different Sentries disembarking from a Cessna on a private airstrip surrounded by evergreens.*

None of it made sense. Though he recognized most of them, the scenes themselves had no context. The single grain of truth: Azazel was keeping tabs on everyone involved in this mess.

Azazel narrowed the scope of his vision. *A u-shaped tropical island. A sizeable-looking military facility. Glass and stainless-steel hallways.*

Forcing himself to relax, Julius made his consciousness as small and unnoticeable as possible. He hid in his shared body, watching and listening. A vision of his surroundings filled his mind.

A fat little man entered the lab. Chubby. Glasses. He used his forefinger to push them up the rise of his nose. Computers, measuring equipment, beakers, and centrifuges filled the room. Windows ran along one wall, tilted to look down onto a lower floor of the building.

A memory flashed through his mind of this same guy standing over him with a bone-saw. Moss.

Moss hummed as he approached. Like before, he wore green scrubs with a white lab coat.

His stomach roiled. Did that mean he intended to play surgeon again?

"You did well in that last test, Mr. Crowley."

"You will call me Great One." The words had tripped out of his mouth with no effort from him. He clamped his mouth shut.

Moss' brows lifted as walked around the edge of the gurney to straighten some instruments laid out on a sterile tray. "I'm going to repeat the experiment."

Moss' voice echoed in his head as he heard the words both with his ears and in the vision.

"Again? Why? You got your precise measurement. How 'bout you fuck off instead."

Moss flashed a tight smile. "I'd like to see how much you can regenerate. What will happen if I make the next cut at the first knuckle, for instance?"

He opened his mouth to argue but his throat seized. He struggled against the pressure filling his throat, filling all of him. Resistance always made this more painful.

Azazel spoke through him. "Why stop at the first knuckle? Take the whole finger."

Moss slid his glasses up his nose. "I had considered doing that." A door hissed open as it slid to the side. Moss turned as a brunette in dark-blue scrubs entered. She had a small computer tablet in her hand. "I think we're ready to begin with Mr. Crowley, LeAnne. I'd like you to record everything."

"Great One. I grow tired of reminding you. However, my host will be happy to assist you in any experiment you deem necessary. It's most important you progress quickly. You must save the soldiers."

As if Azazel cared what happened to the soldiers. No, Azazel wanted something else, he just couldn't figure out what. Did he expect the good doctor to allow them to bite the soldiers? What would that do? Create a few more vampires?

"Is that so?" Moss harrumphed. "Well, I have been having trouble retaining any of the samples I've taken. As soon as I remove the tissue, it dissolves into a sooty substance."

Julius almost rolled his eyes. That was the thing about vampires—they were long dead. Once you removed tissue from the dark Magic keeping them alive, it faded to the ages. Whatever Azazel had hoped Moss could do, was doomed.

LeAnne's eyebrows drew together. "Is that normal?"

Azazel chuckled. "For my kind, yes. Add blood to the vial before you take the sample. It will preserve whatever tissue you decide to take."

Moss turned toward the woman, giving her instructions as he put gloves on.

Azazel's voice filled his mind. "You see, host? You lack faith. Everything is under control."

The whole thing seemed anti-climactic, truth be told. He talked to Azazel in his head. "Ooh, the big bad Watcher is teaching the human how to make vampires. Big fucking deal."

Azazel corrected him. "Not vampires. Nephilim."

Julius froze. Nephilim? He'd seen Azazel create them once. The creatures had decimated an entire town within minutes. They'd destroyed the old coven. His mate. It's why he sacrificed himself to trap the Watcher inside his body in the first place. "You have to be outside my body to make those."

"Or the good doctor needs to remove a bit of me, when he removes a lot of you. I may be invisible and stuck inside your weak form, but I am solid. I am real." As if to prove his point, Azazel stretched until Julius was sure his skin would split from the pressure.

Christ. The Nephilim were relentless. Hungry. Thoughtless. Once created, their disease spread like wildfire. And Azazel had told Moss how to do it.

Hello, Nephilim. Bye-bye civilization.

Moss picked up the bone saw. "I've decided to take you up on your generous offer, Mr. Crowley—"

The restraint holding down his right arm released. For a split-second, Julius thought Azazel had had enough of his games. Thought he might be getting them the hell out of there. Azazel forced Julius' arm to jerk out, his fingers closing around Moss' throat.

The woman screamed.

Moss sputtered, clawing at his hand, gouging his skin.

Azazel forced his hand tighter. "If you must address me, call me Great One."

"G-g-great One."

They released Moss. He stumbled back, panting. Azazel forced Julius to lay his arm back in the restraint and it clasped around his wrist again. "You may proceed."

CHAPTER 13

Carnation, WA

TRINA TOOK HER TIME SHOWERING and dressing, drawing out the chore as long as possible. When she couldn't find any other reason to stall, she called Lilith.

James answered. "Yeah?"

"Where's Lilith?"

He was silent so long, she repeated her question. Finally, he said, "The darkness came back right after you talked to her."

"What?" Her gut churned.

"Started in her hand and around her ear . . . everywhere the phone touched. It's not going away this time. Kat hasn't been able to help her. Lil keeps saying it's not your fault. Keeps asking if you got the Grimoire."

"I . . . ." This couldn't be happening. How could she infect Lilith over the phone? "I did, but I didn't find any answers. Not about why this keeps happening."

"Look, I planned to visit the Historian, but . . . ."

He didn't want to leave Lilith. She closed her eyes. "I'll go. Text me the address."

"Okay. I gotta go. She's restless." The phone went silent as he hung up.

She glanced at the clock. They couldn't leave for another half hour. Not if she intended to take Duncan with her. Tears pricked the backs of her eyes, but she refused to cry. That would be like admitting they couldn't heal Lilith. She refused to give her friend up yet. The Historian would have answers. They'd figure this out.

Her stomach grumbled and though she didn't feel like eating, she should. She needed to keep strong for the night ahead. She headed downstairs.

Not ready to talk to Duncan—not about what happened upstairs, at least—she tiptoed straight to the kitchen. She glanced over her shoulder into the living room where the television was set to CNN, the volume too low for her to make out the newscaster's report. She turned into the kitchen and damn near jumped out of her socks.

"Evening, Duchess." He sat at the kitchen table, the *Black Book of Daemonology* open in front of him.

"You scared the shit out of me." She pressed her hand over her thundering heart.

He shrugged. "Should've been looking where you're going instead of sneaking around like a thief."

Ignoring his barb, she went to the fridge. Lilith didn't have much. A couple yogurts, a box of pinwheels, cream cheese, soda. May as well add a stop at the grocery store to her mental to-do list—if the looters left anything. Hell, she could slip "looting food" right between "avoiding Duncan" and "saving the world."

After she selected a yogurt she went in search of utensils. Found them in the second drawer she opened, grabbed a spoon, and leaned against the counter. *Come on, look at him. At least pretend everything is normal.* She forced her gaze up. He wasn't a handsome man, but wasn't ugly, either. He did have a fantastic body . . . but he wasn't the type of guy she usually got hot and bothered for.

"You're making eyes at me again." He winked. "Gonna give me a big head."

She snorted, using her spoon to indicate his high forehead and close-clipped hair. "So, is that a Guardian requirement or something?" James kept his head shaved bald. Duncan didn't have much keeping him from the same state.

"What, being 'andsome?" He tipped back in his chair.

She rolled her eyes. "No, the whole lack of hair thing."

"Now, why hide something this gorgeous with long locks of hair?" He shot her a feral grin, flashing straight white teeth.

Goddess help her, she loved that he had no problem poking fun at himself.

"You always this cheeky first thing in the evening, Duchess?"

Then he had to go and irritate her. "Why won't you use my damn name?"

He patted his knee. "Maybe if you come ask real nice-like."

She planted her hand on her hip. "Showing off your misogynistic tendencies, today? What's tomorrow, caveman speak?"

The low rumble of his laughter rolled over her. "Does that usually work? Do big words and a bit of contempt scare the lads off?"

She froze with her spoon in her mouth. It *had* always worked, damn him. That and her wardrobe choices tended to keep men away....when they could see her. At least the kind of men who'd have been a challenge for her—the kind of men a woman fought for and kept. She set aside the yogurt and spoon, her appetite gone. "What do you want, Duncan?"

"How about some information for starters. We'll get to the rest later."

If he insisted on digging himself in any further there might not be a later. She didn't want to be responsible for anyone else's death.

"Come on, I ain't gonna be much help if I don't know what I'm bloody well doing, now can I? We'll both end up dead if we're working at odds."

Her mouth went dry. He was right. She either needed to tell him everything or get rid of him now. She started searching for a glass. Took four tries before she found the right cabinet. Why had Lilith put them by the refrigerator instead of next to the sink like a normal person?

"How is it, you don't know where anything is in your own home?"

She filled her glass at the tap. "I've only been back a couple days. When Lilith took possession of the house, she put me down as co-owner." She took a long drink, staring out at the twilight beyond the kitchen window. What should she do? If she were honest, she had no desire to go on this mission alone.

"When did you get out of the Navy?"

"Two years—" She closed her eyes. If she wanted to keep her secrets she damned well better start paying attention to the conversation. She hadn't even told Lilith that.

"Ah. Makes more sense. You don't have the bearing of someone who'd recently been in service. Why'd you stay away so long?"

Gods, there were a ton of reasons. Because no one knew she'd been discharged two years ago. Because she hadn't wanted to come back to the coven in a shambles. Because it was so much easier to hide in her apartment in Bremerton than to accept what she'd done and move on. "My mother, for one thing."

"I thought she'd passed."

"She did." She turned to him. "It's silly, but while away, I pretended that she was still alive. Here in Carnation. Waiting for me to come home."

A small smile curved his lips. "That's not silly."

"She passed when I was seven. I had plenty of time to come to terms with the fact she'd died, but still, when I left . . . ."

"All beings have one thing in common, the need to feel cared for."

Did that mean he wanted the same? He'd been around a long time and must have learned to circumvent some of the more impractical aspects of living. Love. Caring. Intimacy. Goddess knew, she'd spent the last two years trying to avoid them.

FOR A MOMENT THERE, SHE'D allowed herself to be open with him, vulnerable. Now, though, her whole expression closed off. It was time to change the subject. He tipped his chair back on its rear legs. "What's the plan for tonight?"

Trina began to pace across the kitchen. Must be a habit with her, pacing when anxious.

"I talked to James. Lilith isn't doing well. He'd planned to go visit the Historian to ask about Crowley."

"Which one?"

"Augustina Saar."

His eyebrow rose. "Interesting. Last I heard, Leo ordered Pasquino to ash her." Guess he wasn't the only one who shirked the Council's more questionable orders.

"Well, he didn't. I guess she's like an oracle."

He nodded.

"But James is afraid to leave Lilith. Now that it's dark, we should go—"

She started past again and Duncan grabbed her hand, keeping her in place. "That's fine. Before we go, I'd like to see your Magic in action."

Like a hedgehog caught in the porch lights, her whole body stilled.

"Don't want to risk getting in a fight and being surprised by whatever it is you do."

Her eyes closed. She turned her face away.

"What are you scared of?"

That got her temper up. She skewered him with her glare. "My Magic isn't acting right."

"Show me."

"It won't be much." She touched the choker at her throat. "This is a dampener that keeps my abilities at a minimum so I can control them."

He almost smiled. She feared disappointing him? "Understood. I won't expect much, but I want to know if you can protect yourself in a fight."

"Don't move." She fisted her hands at her sides.

The whole house splintered inward.

He damned near jumped out of his own skin. He did grab hold of Trina to shield her, not that they had much room to move in.

The whole bloody thing imploded, freezing millimeters from where they were. Pipes, beams, siding and drywall all slivered into sharp, jagged spikes that aimed straight at them.

"I have chaos Magic." Her words were muffled against his chest. "I can manipulate things on an atomic level. Even get into a mind or an aura."

"You can get into a mind . . . like read it?" He didn't like the idea of that. He had plenty of secrets no one would understand.

"I don't do that anymore. It's not pleasant getting all that unfiltered information. Except with Lil—up until James transformed her, I used to leave a door opened for her so we could communicate without being heard. Now, I can't hear her anymore."

"Jesus." He swallowed. That wasn't any sort of normal Magic he'd ever heard of. Satrina had been a whiz at precognition and Tarot. He'd expected something similar. Two minutes ago, he'd thought things were bad, having to protect her from both the Council and Crowley. Now . . . who the hell *wasn't* going to want a piece of this woman and the power she possessed?

Not to mention he was a tad bit afraid of her now. "Thought that dampener thingy made your Magic less powerful."

The house returned to rights. She squirmed out of his lap. "Without the dampener, my Magic is *too* strong. My problem isn't protecting myself. It's trying not to kill everyone else when I use it."

Hell, yeah; she scared the shite out of him.

CHAPTER 14

Smyrna Island, Pacific Oceania
U.S. Department of Defense
Revelations Industries, Inc.

JULIUS CROWLEY WAVERED IN AND out of consciousness. He longed for the deep oblivion of sleep to dull the constraining hood and the pain of Moss' experiments, but Azazel began to stir, capturing his attention.

Visions flashed through his mind. He didn't dare try to focus on the spectacle of everything that was happening now, at this moment, everywhere in the world. He waited as Azazel brought his attention down to one event.

The island came into focus first, the wind-whipped palms, the white sand beaches, then the facility. The name and logo etched into front doors—four running horses; one each of red, green, white, and black beneath which read: REVELATIONS INDUSTRIES, INC.

Julius' gut rolled. Another little detail of Azazel's joke.

Ha, ha, very funny. Dickhead.

The vision narrowed further to a room inside the building. Dr. Moss sat in a tiny office, tapping away on a computer. Papers and energy drinks littered his desk. Sweat dripped down his temples. He mopped at his brow, pushing his glasses up his pug nose.

LeAnne scowled. "You're going to have to take a break soon, sir. I brought some data you might want to read through."

Moss raised his bleary eyes. "Data?"

"Yes." She smoothed her free hand down her plain brown dress. "I did some research on the Great Ones."

Moss' gaze shot heavenward. "I don't have time for nonsense. I've had a break-through."

"You don't know what he is. . . ."

He turned back to his notes. "The most logical answer is that he's an extra-terrestrial."

"Even if he is, that doesn't mean that these old poems weren't written about his kind. People from thousands of years ago explained strange phenomena any way they could. At least read this." She shoved some papers at him. "I don't think you understand what you're dealing with."

Julius wanted to grin. Unlike Moss, LeAnne had some serious doubts.

Moss stood. "I don't have time for this. You'll never believe the extraordinary things I've found in the last couple of hours. Mr. Crowley is unlike anything I've ever studied."

"The Great Ones are bad news. He's a fallen angel."

Moss kept talking, his voice trembling with the intensity of his excitement as he struggled to impart every detail of his experiments. ". . . The subject is also showing some regeneration capabilities. We removed the tip of his pinky. Within hours tissue grew back perfectly. We weren't as successful when we amputated an entire digit. The finger did regenerate, but—"

"Sir." She shook the papers. "Even if Crowley is pretending to be a Great One, or trying to emulate them—"

"I encountered some abnormalities. Regeneration is a rather reptilian feature. Goes along with their need for external sources of heat, I suppose. The sample I took—"

The papers she'd been shaking dropped to her side. "You got a viable sample?"

That sample was more dangerous than any bio-weapon RI might cook up on their own.

"I tried a form of cryogenics first, of course, which didn't work at all. But when I did what he told me to do, it worked perfectly. His sample altered my blood. Attacked it. I've never seen anything so aggressive. I had to feed the sample in order to keep the specimen intact."

"Aggressive?" She shivered. "You need to stop. What if he's telling the truth? These legends I found say the Great Ones can't lie."

"You're being ridiculous. I plan to start treating soldiers this evening. I'll remove a pint of their blood, add Crowley's DNA, and reintroduce the blood back to the patient. I should have a full report for you to transcribe by morning."

She backed away. "Don't you need to do more testing?"

"What? No. I need approval from the IRB board. Their representatives are on the way now. I don't foresee any problems, though. I'll begin treatments as soon

as they leave." He paused, studying LeAnne. "Maybe you should take the next couple of days off."

Azazel chuckled. "Soon, host." Azazel used Julius' voice. "Soon you'll get a front row seat to what the world should have become."

Should have become? He couldn't imagine what Azazel might think the world *should* have been like. "Everything has happened as it should."

"No." The denial echoed in the sterile lab, even with the hood buffering the sound of the shout. "We were first. The Grigori were the first of all creatures, of the angels, even. Our children should have inherited the Earth. Mankind was meant to be nothing more than feed."

"You're wrong." Julius took control of his voice. "That plan failed. God washed your sins away with the Great Deluge. It'll fail again."

"You've always been pathetically optimistic in your beliefs, host. But God, the angels, they promised to never interfere again. They'll not break their promise. They can't stop me. I'll enjoy watching your hope fade to despair."

CHAPTER 15

DUNCAN PULLED UP TO A little cottage-style home in the middle of the woods. The green haze of a door-shield protected the house, signaling at least one human resided inside. Shutters covered the front windows, preventing him from being able to tell if any lights were on inside, but the front porch lamp glowed in welcome. "You sure this is the right house?"

She stared out the window. "This is the address James gave me."

He turned off the engine and got out of the car. His wound had almost healed, but still sent a twinge of pain through his skin. He scanned the darkened forest at the edges of the property. They were in the lower Cascades, less than an hour from the Haven House. There were no sounds of traffic or planes, just the low chirp of frogs and the rattle of leaves in the wind.

"You stick tight to me." He took hold of her hand, leading the way to the front door. He knocked. After a few moments, he knocked again.

A clatter came from behind the door, followed by a masculine curse.

Duncan glanced at Trina, who shrugged.

The door swung open to reveal a bare-chested blond-haired man in blue jeans and a robe that hung open in the front. Ignoring Trina, he eyed Duncan with a heavy-lidded gaze before taking a long swig of his beer. "I have to admit, I didn't"—he hiccupped—"expect an a-ssas-sin-in to be quite so polite as to knock." By the sound of things, he'd had more than one drink.

"We're not assassins." Trina held her hand out. "My name is—"

He did a double take. "Where'd you come from?" His gaze narrowed. "You're not here to send us to the great beyond?"

Duncan shook his head. "Just want to talk, mate."

"Well, then." He hiccupped. Swayed. "Fuck off."

The door slammed shut. The lock clicked into place.

Duncan closed his eyes. "Please tell me that sotted cabbage ain't the Historian."

"No. We're looking for a female."

"Right. Augustina—I'd forgotten." He motioned to the door. "It's a protected house, Duchess. I can't enter without an invitation . . . unless you happen to be inside already."

With a huff and a roll of her eyes, she held up her fisted hand in front of the door. As she spread her fingers, the door dissolved into trillions of tiny white dots. When she moved forward they scattered like tiny ping-pong balls. The door shield dissolved as she entered the house. He followed, holding his breath so he didn't inhale anything, brushing the tiny bits away from his face and shirt. Once they were both inside, she swept her hand back toward the door. All the tiny specks of white flew back into their places as the door solidified again.

"You're brilliant." *Terrifying, but brilliant.*

The blond-haired human came around the corner at the end of the hall. "How'd you get in here?"

Duncan put himself between Trina and the human. "Have an appointment with the Historian."

"Ya don't." The blond waved them away. "She'll be pissed as hell. She don't hold her liquor well as I do." His whole body jerked with another hiccup.

Augustina was drinking liquor? He'd always assumed she was a vampire, but apparently not. "Do this often, do you?" He'd never had much patience for drunks.

He shook his head. "Never. Figured if we were going to die tonight, we may as well try something new." He shuffled off down the hall, waving for them to follow. Halfway, he paused and turned toward Duncan. "Suggested trying all the positions in the Kama Sutra, but she felt it'd be undignified to get caught with our pants down." He waggled his brows.

What the bloody hell was going on in this house? "Oh? You expecting Guardians?"

"Nah." He waved the question away. "Sentries."

That's the last thing they needed. Sentries were Black Tamanouses, not vampires. Nothing as simple as a door shield would stop them. He pulled Trina close. "It's not safe. Let's go."

"What are Sentries?"

"The Vampiric Council's personal guard. If they're coming, you don't need to be here."

The guy slumped against the wall. "You two coming or going?"

He held up his hand, signaling they needed a moment.

"We need to see the Historian." She brushed passed him, pushing his hand down.

Duncan let out a string of curses.

The drunk opened a door at the end of the hall that led to a dark room. "Go on. I still need to get her another drink."

Trina slipped into the room while Duncan got hung up trying to sidle around the drunken fool in the small hallway. He didn't like this. While the Guardian tended to have a set code of ethics, the Sentries were warped by their constant involvement with the Council. He didn't want the unscrupulous bastards anywhere near Trina.

When he got into the room, he came up short. He wasn't sure what he'd been expecting. Maybe a little old lady with thick glasses surrounded by huge volumes of books. But the woman appeared no older than thirty. Thin, shapely, she lay sprawled across an armchair, her head resting on one arm with her long auburn hair trailing over the side, her jean-clad legs dangling over the other. "Did you get my drink, darling?"

The massive room had a small sitting area in the entry—four armchairs positioned around a low table—but farther in, the ceiling rose two stories high. That part of the room had been left barren. Why? What kind of daemon was she?

"Robert?" The woman turned her head. Her eyes widened. She struggled into a sitting position before getting to her feet. "It's not often someone can sneak up on me. You're not who I was expecting. Where's Robert?"

Why was she ignoring Trina? What was it with people? "Getting you another drink."

"Ah, very good." She nodded. Blinked. "Who are you?"

Trina stepped forward. "James Pasquino sent us to—"

The woman's attention jerked to Trina. Her eyes widened. "Oh, my." The woman walked a tight circle around Trina. "Amazing. James told me about you, of course, but I wasn't certain I believed him." She touched Trina's cheek. "I didn't see you."

A shiver made Trina's body jerk.

Duncan pulled her back against him. "You blind?"

He'd directed his question to the Historian, but Trina answered. "For a couple years now, people don't see me unless I draw their attention. Except if Lilith's around."

"I see you."

She met his gaze. "Yes. You do."

That might explain why those mercs didn't see her but he still called bullshite. He expected her to believe she'd been in the military and been invisible? How the hell had that worked? As soon as they got out of here, he had some questions and she damn well better stop lying.

The Historian waved them away. "You shouldn't have come. It isn't safe. The Sentries will arrive any time now."

Trina shook her head. "Why are you sitting here waiting for them? Come with us, we'll protect you."

"All Historians have the sight." Augustina scoffed. "It's both a blessing and a curse. Not only can I see what will happen if I stay, I can also see what will happen if I run. If I fight. If I go into hiding again."

Robert entered the room and handed Augustina a martini. His free hand slipped around her waist.

The Historian leaned into him, brushing his cheek with hers. He'd always envied couples who had such affinity for each other.

Her attention returned to them. "Trust me, it is for the best of all involved if we meet our end now."

Duncan gave Trina a squeeze. "Ask your questions. I need to get you out of here before they arrive."

TRINA SWALLOWED. THE KNOTS IN her gut wound tighter. The Historian had an aura of stern gentleness, much like that of a mother interacting with her child, but still, she feared what the Historian might say. Not that she doubted she would tell the truth. She'd helped James and Lilith. She'd help her and Duncan if only because of her debt to James.

The Historian sighed. "We may as well be comfortable." She waved them toward the chairs as she sat. Robert half sat, half leaned on the arm of her chair. "You may call me Augustina, by the way."

Trina sat in the chair adjacent to Augustina's. Duncan took position behind her. No doubt because he had a good view of the entire room and the door. The fact that he was worried about the Sentries had her spooked, too. She introduced herself and Duncan, and, sensing his impatience, got down to business. "A couple of days ago, we discovered that whenever I touch Lilith, her skin turns black. Now, even talking to her on the phone infects her. I think it's because of the changes in my Magic, but I don't know how to fix that, either."

Augustina nodded. "Tell me about the changes."

Where to start? Did she start with her accident with Trevor? No. That had been a case of her not paying attention. What had been happening lately was different. "It's more powerful the last few days, despite wearing this dampener." She touched her choker. "This minimizes my Magic to a level I can control, but I don't trust myself."

Augustina took a sip of her martini. "Ah, you see, dear, *that* is part the problem." Augustina stood and began walking around them. "You're one of the most powerful beings on two worlds. The shadow-self of the Original. The dark part of her soul, so explain to me why you have come here in this form."

Her gut twisted as she remembered the Ten of Swords. "What other form would I come in? This is the only one I have."

"The Original is both vampire and witch. You are only witch. You have access to both James and Duncan; they can transform you, yet you are still human. Why?"

Was she crazy? "A witch who becomes a vampire loses her Magic."

Augustina stopped in front of her. "A witch, yes. Not the Original. Has Lilith lost her Magic?"

No. If anything Lilith's Magic had gotten stronger after James bit her . . . *shit*. "This started when James tried to transform Lil." Lilith's Magic had gotten stronger and hers had, too. "Except before we could communicate telepathically and afterward we couldn't."

"You'll likely be able to do so once you've accepted who you are. So, I'll ask again. Why have you not submitted to transformation?"

Her throat swelled. "I don't know if I believe that I'm part of the Original."

"Liar."

She shifted in her seat as her face heated.

Augustina pointed to Trina's left arm. "Take your arm out of the sleeve."

Trina sat up and wriggled free of her jacket, jumping a little when Augustina grabbed her arm and pulled up the sleeve of her shirt to bare her shoulder.

A small smile curved her lips. "Sneaky. Tried to hide it with a tattoo, huh?

Not just any tattoo. It was a spell that read: *During this life, I belong to no man*. At the time, she'd been devastated by what she'd done to Trevor. She didn't want to risk hurting anyone else. Now ... now she had a mate and she had no idea what that spell might do to him.

"What?" Duncan leaned over to look, too.

"I have a birthmark. A reversed crescent moon."

"Exactly the opposite of Lilith's." Her gaze focused on Trina. "Try again, and tell me the truth this time. Why have you not submitted?"

All her old fears came bubbling up to the surface. Everything she'd spent her life fighting against. "I mess things up. Everything. Ever since I was a kid. No matter how good my intentions, I make things worse. I hurt people. I don't intend to ... sometimes it's a careless thought, an angry word. Sometimes it's nothing I consciously did. While I was away from here ... from the coven and Haven House, things were better for a while. I had a good life ... and then .... Just look at Lil. I came back to help her, but because of me, Crowley got away, Armageddon started, Lilith is sick and seems to be getting sicker."

"Mm." Augustina nodded. "Soon she'll become the Shadow which you emulate."

Her stomach sank. "What do you mean?"

"She'll disappear."

Her chest grew tight. She was killing her best friend just by existing. This couldn't be happening.

Duncan came around the side of her chair. "She's part of the Original, in'nit? Shouldn't you be showing a little respect?"

"Bah. She's nothing."

Trina flinched. "I don't want to be evil. I don't want to always cause hurt and pain and death."

Augustina slammed back the remainder of her drink. She ignored her, speaking to Duncan, instead. "Until she accepts herself, she can't be more than nothing." She pointed the glass toward her. "Bad things come to those who deny their true selves, girly. Pain comes to those who resist."

A tear slipped from her eye and she dashed it away. "I am my true self."

"You lie." She leaned over Trina, bracing her hands on the arms of the chair. The scent of strong spirits laced her breath. "You lie. You've been lying. What's worse is all the lies you tell, you've told yourself. You've lied to yourself for so long, you believe them."

Duncan eased the Historian back. "Easy, now."

The Historian's full attention shifted to Duncan. "You won't be saying that for long, Guardian; her lies will affect you, too."

Trina straightened. "You mean I'll affect him like I do Lilith?"

"Maybe." She shrugged. "Maybe in other ways."

Duncan tapped his fingers against the back of her seat. "You've seen this, for certain?"

"No." She ran her hands through her hair, turning her attention to Trina. "I can't see you in my visions. Common sense dictates that when one part of a being functions abnormally, all parts are affected. A broken bone in the smallest toe will cause a limp, damaging the knee, the hip, the spine . . . the temperament of the body. You and Lilith are parts of a whole, dear. Her mate is part of her." She slid a meaningful glance up to Duncan before spearing her with a speaking look. *Duncan was her mate—a part of her—so he'd be affected, too.*

Her stomach knotted. "And if I become a vampire, she'll be better?" *He'll stay safe?*

"Should." She shrugged. "You need to embrace who you are. You are the queen of daemon kind. That might not always look pretty, you may have to do difficult things to hold your place, but your throne, your people await you on Machon. Your people will see you. They will know you. But until you accept yourself, you, Lilith"—she set a pointed glance on Duncan—"and all those around you, will suffer."

"You make it sound so easy. Too easy." But she didn't know. She hadn't seen her or her future any more than the Watchers had.

"Easy?" Augustina laughed. "Nothing about this is going to be easy. You and Lilith together are daemon kind's judge, jury, and executioner. Together, you are our law. And soon, all of daemon kind, including the Watchers, will look to you for guidance. It's not going to be easy. Sometimes it'll be violent. Bloody. Terrifying. But we need you."

Could she do that? Could Lilith? It all sounded so surreal.

Augustina nodded to Duncan. "That's why the Watchers sent you him. Why they sent James to Lilith. You both need someone who will watch your backs. Someone loyal."

"What about Crowley?" Duncan asked. "And the Council? Why do they want her?"

Augustina took her seat again and Robert took her hand in his. She pulled his hand to her lips and kissed it. "It's cloudy. All I know is what I've seen from visions of Leopold, but I don't see everything the way the Watchers do—he's a snake. He made some kind of deal with Crowley years ago. That I know. Crowley hasn't completed his end of the bargain, but Leopold completed his. That I know. Crowley has disappeared without a word and Leopold is scared. That I know. Leopold is surrounding himself with Sentries and has sent some here for me. While he hasn't said so out loud, I wouldn't be surprised if he sends them to you next. Whatever his ultimate plan, he's aware of the Watchers and doesn't want them to know—but they're not stupid. If I can figure out what he's up to, so can they." She met Trina's gaze. "As for Crowley, he's as invisible to me as you are."

Trina looked at Duncan. "Who's Leopold?"

"He's the bloody wanker who leads the Council. Shady, that one." Duncan folded his arms over his chest. "Isn't that odd? That you can't see Crowley?"

"Not really. I can't see Watchers. Or Trina. There are others I've met throughout my lifetime that I couldn't see in visions. Aside from those anomalies, there's Magic—a shielding that can be placed over a person or dwelling, that hides those inside from seers and Watchers temporarily."

His gaze returned to Augustina. "What bargain did he make?"

She shrugged. "Leopold has never spoken of it."

Trina shifted in her seat. "Are you sure what's happening with Lilith has to do with me and not Crowley? Humans captured him—"

"What?" Augustina leaned so far forward she almost tipped out of her chair. "Humans have possession of Crowley?" She swayed as she glanced back at Robert. "I guess now we know what started Armageddon." Her gaze returned to Trina. "You need to submit to transformation as soon as possible."

Trina nodded, though she wasn't sure if she could go through with a transformation.

"This is a big decision for her," Duncan said. "We have time, don't we? I mean, ain't there a bunch of events that happen before Armageddon? War, famine, destruction of crops, and all that?"

They all turned, staring.

Robert snorted. "Where have you been? War has been ongoing for centuries. Famine, failed crops, animals dying off in great numbers, plagues."

"Have you not heard the progressively worsening news in the last three centuries?" Augustina asked.

"All that's been going on for ages. I—"

"Yes, as predicted. Now everything comes to a head. We have the Cause in one hand. The Effect in the other." She lifted her right hand, palm up. "One is the true symbol of evil—the true cause of Armageddon." She raised her left hand, palm up. "And in the other a scapegoat—an easy victory. It's your job to figure out who's who and destroy the one that needs destroying. That is what will stop the End Times. Go to Machon. Talk to the Watchers. Gather your allies."

Machon? What good would that do? "The Watchers can't see me."

"In visions, no. But if you stand before them, they can. Even better, you and Lilith can see and speak to them without an aid. You're the only two who can. Together, you and Lilith are the only beings alive who can match the power of a Watcher. That's why you're both so special, because you're as strong as they are. You're the only one who can fight Crowley."

What did the Watchers have to do with Crowley? "I don't understand. What—"

Augustina's head jerked to the side. "They're here." She stood. "The Sentries."

Duncan pulled Trina up. "What's the quickest way out?"

"The door in the back of the room. Robert will show you." She squeezed Trina's arm. "I'll hold them off long enough for you to get away. Believe in yourself, allow Duncan to transform you. Things will begin to go your way."

Trina lurched forward, wrapping Augustina in an awkward hug. "Thank you."

"Go."

Duncan pulled her away toward the back of the room, but Trina didn't take her eyes off Augustina. As she walked to the middle of the room, Augustina's skin split open. The flesh didn't tear, there was no blood, but her skin came apart at hidden seams along her limbs, torso, and head. A knotty black substance spilled out, expanding and lifting the remaining strips of her flesh until they were smooth, cream-colored battle scars. Its oblong, amoeba-like body resembled a corrupted, twisted brain with several clawed limbs bursting out at odd angles. Three eyes of different sizes and colors appeared in the front of the pulsing mass.

Duncan's hand settled on her hip. "She's a baldander. She'll hold them off. Hell, she can kill them, if she wants."

Three brawny men burst into the room dressed all in black.

"And those are Sentries." He tugged on her arm.

Even as the Sentries strode into the room, they began changing. Their skulls split like the lobes of a Venus-fly trap, revealing rows of jagged teeth. Each fold held an eye, half a nose, and half a mouth creating a gruesome illusion of terrible wounds when parted and a normal human when the halves melded together.

Duncan tugged at her again, but she couldn't tear her gaze away from their transformation. He picked her up, hauling her over his shoulder. She flipped her hair out of her eyes.

Their arms elongated, snapped and cracked as the joints moved. The legs did the same until the males stood at least six feet tall on four, thin, multi-jointed legs, their cavernous, toothy maws yawning.

Robert shouted, "Run!"

Trina's attention snapped to Robert, who held open a door that had been hidden a moment before. Duncan sprinted toward the opening.

She hit his back. "We shouldn't leave her."

Robert waved them on, urging them to get out. "Go!"

He paused as they came abreast of Robert. "Come with us."

"You know how it is." He smiled. "We can't leave our mates." He gave Duncan a shove and slammed the door shut. The whole building rumbled as one of the beings inside let loose a mighty roar.

Duncan set her down, but held on to her hand as he ran. "We'll have to leave the car. Another Sentry might be waiting out front."

She fell into step beside him, glancing back once. Poor Augustina. Poor Robert. If that was the couple's best option, she couldn't imagine how horrible their end might have been had they chosen a different path.

CHAPTER 16

Smyrna Island, Pacific Oceania
U.S. Department of Defense
Revelations Industries, Inc.

MOSS NEARED THE GURNEY. *"RUBY, General Pitch." He made a small flourish with his hands. "This is Mr. Julius Crowley."*

The woman's attention fixed on where his body was strapped to a gurney. She gasped and her hand covered her mouth.

Julius' attention sharpened. Would this woman help him? Did her reaction mean she might be sympathetic to his cause, or did the amount of scars lacing his skin disgust her? From wrists to ankles to neck, scars webbed every surface usually covered by clothing. Most from knife wounds. Azazel loved that fucking knife.

His gut twisted. He hated being on display. He should be grateful Moss had at least been considerate enough to throw a sheet over his hips but couldn't muster any enthusiasm for such an emotion. Not here. Not now.

"Is someone there?" Julius' voice sounded weak and raspy from beneath the hood—Azazel loved playing games. "I don't want to be here. I've been kidnapped. My rights . . . I want a lawyer."

Moss rolled his eyes. Julius could relate.

Ruby gasped, again. "Dr. Moss, I believe you assured me you weren't impinging on this man's human rights."

"I think you'll find I've done no such thing." Moss reached across the gurney to pick up a scalpel.

Julius' stomach roiled. He braced himself.

"Observe." He pressed the sharp blade to Julius' abdomen.

Unable to keep himself from reacting, Julius clenched his teeth as the blade bit deep into his flesh. He gasped.

"Dr. Moss!" Ruby grabbed Moss' arm, which pushed the scalpel deeper.

"Stand down, Moss." The General's voice echoed against the barren walls.

Julius tried to control his reaction. Much more and Azazel would notice he was conscious and watching. The vision would disappear and he'd be locked in unknowing blindness beneath the hood while those bastards did things to him.

"Watch." Moss dragged the blade across Julius' flesh, making a two-inch incision.

He couldn't restrain his shout.

"I won't stand here a—"

"Wait." General Pitch leaned closer. "He's not bleeding."

Moss pushed the edges of the wound aside.

Sweet baby Jesus, that hurt like a mother fucker.

They both leaned forward.

The General pulled the surgical light closer. "He's empty. My God."

"Good guess." Azazel used Julius' voice. "But you can call me Great One."

Julius struggled to maintain focus through the searing burn in his gut. He didn't want to risk missing anything, not when things were critical. He panted through the pain, clinging to the vision like a life line.

Ruby wet her lips. "Is he an extraterrestrial?"

"Well, I am other-worldly." Azazel chuckled.

Moss scowled. "We haven't been able to get any straight answers from him." He shrugged. "Our best guess is he may be."

The General motioned to Julius. "You think he's the answer?"

Moss nodded. "Crowley is immune to everything we've thrown at him. His DNA is the answer."

"This is unprecedented." Ruby paced away. Turned back to the men. "I can't begin to imagine what the FDA's recommendation would be. The approval process might take years; he's not even human."

Moss took her hand in his. "After the public scandals of events like Operation Orange, the military doesn't need any more bad press, Ruby. The public knows we lost our bio-weapon to the enemy. That it's been used against us. And they're watching. So far, the American people have been distracted by everything else going on in the news, but that won't last."

Moss strode to one of the windows looking down into the surrounding pods. He motioned her over. The perspective of Azazel's vision shifted, allowing him to see below where seventeen men were housed in hospital beds, covered in IVs and *breathing tubes. A priest performed last rites for one. A minister sat with another. "They continue to deteriorate. We lost another last week."*

Ruby nodded. "I understand your concern, but—"

"With the IRB's approval, I can start clinical trials. We can save them if we don't have to wait for the FDA."

No wonder these people interested Azazel, they had the power to allow or deny the continuation of Moss' experiments. They could stop Armageddon.

Or they could start it.

"Think about the ramifications of going through the full approval process," Moss continued. "The religious lobby alone would lock the decision up for decades."

Her lips pressed together. "He's not human. I doubt they'd lift a finger in protest."

Azazel spoke and Julius' voice drifted through the lab. "Not one but many, the horseman white. All their followers walk the path of light. The promise of heaven is halo bright. But the faithful are blinded—evil, can't sight."

Ruby's attention riveted on Julius' hood during the recital. "Is he even sane?"

"Quite." Dr. Moss didn't look so sure. "I'm afraid he takes perverse pleasure in his jokes and creepiness."

"I suppose it doesn't matter." She rubbed her palms up her arms. "As long as he's the key we're looking for."

Julius almost moaned. No angel of mercy this one; she'd herald in the end of the world without ever realizing it.

Ruby's gaze shot to the hood as Azazel continued. "The horseman of red; she rides alone. Compassion and peace she can't condone. Her sword of fire all men bemoan. As kingdoms fall and kings dethroned."

What was Azazel doing? Was he so confident in his success he didn't fear frightening them off?

Moss raised his voice. "Mr. Crowley, that's enough."

"When can you start treatment, Moss?" Pitch returned to the gurney, his attention fixed on Julius' wound, a wound healing even now. "I've got sick men on the field I need for fighting."

"A horseman of black in his robes of night, brandishes his scythe bringing hunger and strife."

Moss turned toward his backers with an apologetic smile. "He's reciting an old Apocryphal poem. He talks non-stop most of the time."

"Mankind will rally, and all will fight. Only death will reward you during this plight."

The General appeared to take Azazel's antics in stride, though a small scowl marred his features. Ruby, on the other hand, didn't look well. Good. If Azazel kept pressing his luck she'd never give her approval.

"I said, enough." Dr. Moss' demand echoed in the lab.

Of course Azazel didn't listen, but this time when he spoke from beneath the hood, the voice no longer sounded like it belonged to Julius. This voice was inhuman. Guttural. It sent a shiver up his spine. "A pestilence follows the horseman pale."

Dr. Moss took a step back.

They all took a step back.

"No weapon he carries, no chainmail."

Dr. Moss moved to lift the hood, then snatched his hand back.

"The apocalypse he hails. Arrogance his cross. This nobody lab rat by the name of Moss."

Moss raised a trembling hand to mop at his brow. He swallowed hard, glancing at the others. He chuckled as if he were in on the joke, but his laugh sounded strained, forced. "I believe you forgot your line, Mr. Crowley. I've heard this poem before. The last two lines should be 'A plague he bestows in unimaginable scale. We cry for mercy, but he will prevail.'"

When Azazel spoke again, Julius' voice returned to normal. Amused. "Oh, it'll all be the same in the end."

Chapter 17

You know how it is, we can't leave our mates.

Duncan paced himself, ignoring the stitch in his side from his healing wound and staying behind Trina as they ran through the forest alongside the road. She panted, clutching her side, but didn't slow down. They were well away from Augustina's little cabin.

What the hell might be going through her mind right now? Couldn't be anything good. With her distain for daemon kind she must be doing her head in trying to think of a way to get out of transformation and still save her friend.

"We're good, Duchess." He sucked in a breath.

She didn't slow her pace. He didn't like how fast her heart beat, nor how hard she gasped for air. He sped up, put his hand on her shoulder, forcing her to slow. Still, she resisted. "Stop." He picked her up off her feet, stopped, and set her down.

"They're dying!" Tears streaked down her face. Her breath came so hard and fast he started to worry she might hyperventilate. She jerked her hand out of his and started walking again.

"But you're not." He followed her, ready to grab her should she try to run again. "I'm not any happier than you to leave them back there, but you heard them. They knew what they were doing. I'll be damned if I watch you sacrifice yourself trying to save those who don't want to be saved."

"We should've . . ." She flung her hand out.

He spun her around pulled her into his arms. "Come here."

"What're you—"

"I'm not letting go until you settle down. Your heart's beating too fast. Your breathing's too shallow. You need to walk. You understand? Calm yourself."

She nodded and he released her, keeping hold of her hand as they walked. "I don't know what to do."

"Shush." He gave her hand a little squeeze, as if with a little pressure he could still her trembling. "Give it a minute. Don't think. Don't talk."

"I can't."

"You can."

"No, I mean I can't . . . do this. When James transformed Lilith she turned into an immortal human. And I'm the opposite of her, so what if you transform me and I turn into a mortal vampire? I can't . . . let you bite me."

He didn't have a ready response for that worry, so he shot her a side-long glance. "I'm not hungry, but thanks."

"Wha—?" She let out a little chuckle. "That was lame."

"Yeah, it was." Damn, he liked this woman, but good God was her life a train wreck. Robert's comment continued to echo in his head. *You know how it is, we can't leave our mates.* The worst part? The more he considered the idea of having Trina as a mate, the more he liked the idea.

Still, he had some questions for her. Needed to find a way to get her to trust him and quit lying to him.

"When you said people can't see you until you draw attention to your-self, what did you mean? Is it a spell or something?"

"No. It's just . . . like that. They don't see me. When those two RI guys caught us at Rowena's they didn't see me. They should've, the back of the couch faced the sliding glass door. I saw them . . . but they didn't notice me."

"That's probably a good thing."

"If I hadn't spoken to Augustina, she wouldn't have, either."

He paused, forced her to look at him. Things weren't quite adding up and it bothered him. If he was going to risk his skin for her, she needed to start 'fessin' up. "How did you serve in the Navy if they couldn't see you?"

"I wasn't always like this." They started walking again. "Not as a kid; back then I was notorious."

That he could relate to.

"It wasn't until after I left. The first four years were fine. I didn't notice anything unusual. I enjoyed being enlisted, being accepted. Part of something bigger than myself. When it came time, I re-upped for another four years."

"What changed?"

"Lilith came to visit quite often. She made purchases for the coven's online store and traveled a lot. It just worked out that we ended up in nearby ports quite often."

"Didn't think you could tell people where you were docking."

"We can't. But . . . you know . . . Magic." She shrugged. "She'd come when I had a bit of leave and we'd hang out. Then . . . we both got busy and didn't have time to visit."

He guided her deeper inside the tree line. "The longer you were apart—"

"—the more I disappeared." She kicked a stone, making it skip through the dirt. "My friends wouldn't say 'hi' in the passageways unless I did first. My captain started marking me absent for meetings. I got sent to Captain's Mast for dereliction of duty—while on watch, three people came on board but none of them saw me." She shrugged. "I was reading. I shouldn't have been. I didn't notice them. It went from bad to worse fast. I was at the end of my second enlistment, so I just didn't re-up."

"You lasted eight years. Where were you the other two?"

She shrugged. "I stayed in Bremerton. Started a web design business. I told the coven—Lilith, everyone—I was still enlisted. I mean what do you say, 'Hey, I know we haven't seen each other in a while, but I've actually disappeared?' No one knows . . . well, except you, now."

He liked that, knowing one of her secrets. He stared at her as they walked. Something still wasn't adding up. There was more to the story. Like why the hell hadn't she come back? Most people ran to a safe place when the world went upside down. Something else had kept her away. He just hoped to hell her past didn't start interfering with her immediate future. They had enough to deal with.

Smyrna Island
Revelations Industries Laboratory

"THEY'RE OUT OF CONTROL!"

In the stifling pitch of the hood, Julius' mouth spread into an evil smirk—Azazel seemed pleased.

It was done.

In the distance, somewhere outside of the room they were in, people screamed. The scent of blood tinged the air, making his mouth water.

Azazel spoke to Moss through Julius. "Out of control?"

"You should've warned us." Moss' voice cracked.

"Why, because the accommodations have been so luxurious? Because of your kid-glove treatment?"

Julius agreed. This place was a fucking nightmare.

"My staff is dying." Moss' voice trailed off. "Oh, my God. My God." He sounded hoarse, raw. A man didn't sound like that unless he'd been jolted past the limits of understanding and reason. "Tell me what to do. Anything. How do I stop them?"

"Tell me where we are." Why ask something Azazel already knew?

"The observation pod."

"You can see them from here—the Nephilim?"

Bastard. This whole conversation was for *his* benefit—so he could imagine what the other two were seeing while stifled under his hood and chained down to the gurney, helpless.

"Y-yes. Yes. They're on the other side of the glass, below us in the infirmary."

Azazel smiled. "It's simple. Use your mesmerist abilities to subdue them."

"My abilities . . .?" Moss stammered. "You think this is funny?"

"Oh, right. I guess that would be my job."

"Hurry, Mr. Cro—"

"Don't call me that." His voice echoed in the room.

"G-Great One. Please, hurry, Great One."

"Take off the hood."

Julius perked up. Finally, Azazel would get them out of this house of horrors. But then what? The Nephilim had been created. The few seconds Julius could gain control wouldn't be enough to stop them. He'd have to bide his time and pray the Original had a plan.

Moss shook his head. "No. You can do things with your eyes."

"I guess we're at an impasse." Azazel sighed.

"You have to help them."

"You *have* to take off the hood. Why don't you turn me toward the window? If you stand behind me . . . ." *Said the fox to the mole.*

"Oh, yes, that would work."

For such an intelligent man, Moss could be a complete moron. The gurney jerked when he kicked off the break and rolled Julius over to the window. The bed tipped until he hung in a semi up-right position. Moss lifted the hood. Fresh, cool air flooded over his face for the first time in days. The strap securing his eyes shut came off next.

Julius squinted against the emergency strobe. He felt Azazel's impatience as strong as his own. Though for different reasons, they both needed to see what was happening below. Bit by bit Julius' eyes adjusted to the harsh illumination. When his vision cleared, his gut churned.

Seventeen Nephilim were feeding in the room below. They were abominations—humanoid in form, but larger, stronger. Their abnormal muscle-mass made them appear twisted and misshapen and their jagged teeth and yellow eyes as evil as they were.

"What's taking so long?" Moss shifted his weight.

His lips spread into another grin. Azazel's pride welled up, filling him near to bursting. Azazel took full control, flicking Julius' gaze to the reflective surface of the window. As a vampire, he had no reflection but Azazel did.

Fixated on the destruction beyond the window's surface, Moss was slow to notice the reflection of the burnt, twisted skeleton. Slowly, by degrees, his attention shifted.

Moss stopped babbling. He froze, as if that would make him less of a target. His breathing grew shallower, faster. His gaze turned from the scene beyond the window, to its surface.

Moss met his eyes. Azazel took over Moss' mind with Julius' talent.

While he pitied Moss, he refused to stop Azazel. Moss was the pale horseman, the proof of his part in Armageddon visible through the window. He had to die before he caused more trouble.

"You will suffer, Moss. Like an enclosed fly desperate for fresh air." Azazel laughed. "Release me." Sadistic bastard. He could've freed them himself, but always he had to display his control over others.

The doc complied with naught but a soft whimper of protest as he triggered the mechanism. The manacles opened.

His muscles, anemic from his incarceration, didn't want to work and he dropped to the floor. He'd pay for slowing Azazel down. The Watcher forced him to stand, to stretch, rotating his wrists and ankles, each in turn while he observed the scene below, paying no heed to the agony of pins and needles that Julius experienced.

Seventeen Nephilim. Already, they had killed twice that many RI staff. They bathed in the blood as they fed. Some of the bodies were starting to transform.

"So smart, aren't you?" They turned to Moss. "You're nothing. An insignificant pest. A fly. Do what the flies do. Find your freedom from this room if you can."

They walked over to a desk, picked up the phone and dialed Leopold, while watching Moss.

Moss turned to the observation window. Launched himself at the glass much the way a trapped fly slammed itself against glass panes when trying to escape a house. The window rattled.

Leopold came onto the line. "Hello?"

"It's me."

"Juli . . . " He cut himself off with a curse. "Great One? Where the hell have you been?"

Across the room, Moss backed up several feet.

"I've been a bit tied up." Julius would've rolled his eyes if he could. "I'm ready now. The Nephilim are here."

"It's about damned time. So now you'll bring me the Original and destroy the Guardian."

"No." Azazel waited while Leopold cursed a blue streak.

Moss ran at the window, arms hanging at his sides. His nose broke with a sickening crack. Blood splattered across the window.

The scent of fresh blood rode in on his next inhalation. *Christ, he was thirsty.*

Azazel chuckled. The sick bastard loved playing with his damned food.

Moss started back to the middle of the room. Reflexive tears streamed down his cheeks, thinning the blood from his ruined face.

"It seems while I've been . . . otherwise engaged, you've been busy."

"I didn't know where you went." Leopold's voice shook. "You could've been killed for all I knew. I had to proceed."

When Moss reached the center of the room he turned around, prepared to rush the window in his soundless, mindless escape.

"So you sent Duncan Sinclair, of all people? I wonder why."

"He's a mindless twit. He'll do what he's told. The Watchers vouched for him."

"Ah, but which Watchers? Those who may be on my side, or those who oppose me?"

Leopold remained silent.

Moss impacted the glass again. The plexiglass shook. He flopped against the glass a few times before turning around again.

"I think I'll pay you a visit."

"Wha—? I'm here in the Council Chambers as always."

Christ, what an idiot. Just because Azazel had never before called him on his shit, didn't mean he wasn't aware of Leopold's tricks. "Even my host is disgusted with you." Leopold was a projector. He projected his targets deepest desires—even his own. The epitome of a narcissist, the sick fuck desired nothing as much as himself. "I'll see you soon."

"At the Council Chambers."

"Fine. But it had better be *you* at the Council Chambers."

Julius' hand lifted, halting Moss as they hung up the phone. "Come here, human, my host needs to feed, else he'll be useless."

Moss offered the tender artery in his neck with no protest. Julius tried to turn away. He had no desire to aide Azazel, but the Watcher had full control of his body and, God help him, he was thirsty.

The sick bastard took pleasure in tearing Moss apart. In making the feeding so much more painful than needed. When finished, he turned them to the viewing windows as if nothing happened.

CHAPTER 18

Carnation, WA

WHEN THEY GOT HOME, TRINA plopped down on the couch, flipping on the television. He understood her need for distraction, but she had some decisions to make. He leaned against the wall. "Look, I know this is a lot to—"

She waved her hand impatiently. Turned the volume up.

He came around to see the telly. Still set to CNN, the graphic in the background showed the same logo as those two lads at Rowena's house had on their shirts.

"RI director, Dr. Edwin Moss, is injecting the infected with a new experimental treatment. We should know in the next few hours if it has worked. In other news, air traffic is still grounded while authorities try to pinpoint the cause of the mass-disappearances . . . ."

"Fuck." Trina stood. Sat back down.

New experimental treatment?

"Rowena sent Crowley there. Fuck. Edwin Moss is the guy she did the dream spell on. We're out of time. *Fuck. Fuck. Fuck.*"

Yeah. This was bad, but there wasn't a damned thing they could do. The sun would rise soon. He tried to instill a little levity in the situation. "You're inner sailor is showing, Duchess."

"We have to stop them. If they have Crowley . . . . What do you want to bet that experimental treatment has something to do with him?"

That wasn't a bet he cared to take, but they couldn't take off half-cocked with dawn approaching. "No." He folded his arms over his chest. "It'll be dawn soon. You're not going alone."

Her chin jerked up. "I know where it is. I looked it up. The facility is out in Oceania on an island called Smyrna."

"How the hell are we going to get there?"

She glanced at the clock. "With the time zone lag, we've probably got about three hours of darkness. I can't promise it'll be a fun ride, but I know a spell that will get us there."

Spell-travel? "Well, never thought I'd be able to mark 'traveling by spell' off my bucket list."

She wet her lips. "It'll be a risk, I don't want to lie to you. With my Magic acting up, I can't guarantee we'll get there safely."

What the hell did she expect him to do with that information? Run, screaming, in the other direction? They had to get Crowley away from the humans. "I trust you."

She held out her hand.

He entwined their fingers.

"I'm not sure what we'll be walking into. Last time I was at Smyrna, there was nothing there. It used to be a nature preserve."

"Get us there. I'll take care of the rest."

Trina closed her eyes. Her lips moved as she silently spoke a spell.

Strange sensations assailed Duncan's skin like thousands of raindrops pelting him as his body separated into billions of tiny molecules. The infinitesimal atoms split apart, making him appear similar to the figures in Georges Seurat's *Sunday Afternoon on the Island of La Grande Jatte*. Trina had the same rough, dotted texture.

"Bloody hell." Even his voice had taken on a fragmented quality as though coming through a poor connection on an old phone line.

Like a click of a slide, one moment they were there, standing in the house, in the next he stood ankle-deep in water. All around, screaming, snarling, shouts, and gunfire drowned out the waves lapping at his boots.

Aside from a couple of too-bright floodlights aimed their way, it was dark. With his eyes still dazzled by the bright lights at Haven House, he could hear the danger, but not see it.

Trina's grip tightened on his hand. They both froze, the red-tinged waves lapping at their feet. As his eyes started to adjust, he glanced around. Behind them, the two sides of the u-shaped island curved around, almost enclosing the small bay. The island was narrow enough to see a Navy ship docked on the other side of the island, the lights of the ship highlighting the bland, slate gray of the towering vessel. To their right, about a hundred yards out, stairs rose to a red-brick building. Floodlights sitting on the roof lit the area, highlighting where the beach rose about ten feet to a mesa, which was why he couldn't see the threat—they were up there, over the rise. Palm trees stood in clusters around the sandy beach. Bodies littered the ground. Some wore Navy uniforms, some lab coats. A few of the dead wore civvies, name tags still hanging around their necks.

"Look." Trina pointed to their left where one of the bodies—a woman in a red dress suit—started to thrash.

Trina started toward her.

He gripped her arm, stopping her. "Wait."

The woman's skin rippled and stretched as she twisted in the sand. Her nails elongated, and her muscles bulked, ripping her clothes at the seams.

Jesus, she was transforming. He just wasn't sure what the hell she was transforming into. What had they been doing here? He strode over to the woman, pulling his Guardian blade. The etchings down the center of the knife revealed a slat of wood caught between the two halves of the blade—the perfect daemon-killer. He didn't hesitate. He brought his knife down, sinking it into her chest as he went to one knee next to her.

As soon as the wood in the blade hit her flesh, the woman's body crumpled, dissolving into ash, leaving nothing but her jewelry and name tag: Ruby Braith, IRB. He glanced back at Trina. "Kill anyone who's been bit."

She took a step back. "Maybe there's a cure . . . maybe—"

Some beach wood lay nearby in the sand. "They're transforming but I don't know into what. Must be some kind of vampire-hybrid because they react the same to wood." He pulled off a smaller branch—thick, smooth, maybe a foot long, with one pointy, jagged end, and tossed it to her. "Use this. Your gun won't work."

He pulled his second blade out of his leg sheath and climbed the rise to see if there was anyone left to save. "Stay back."

⊘

THEY SHOULDN'T HAVE COME.

She'd thought they'd arrive, break into the facility, and kill Crowley. She hadn't expected *this*. Wasn't ready for this. Gripping the branch Duncan gave her tighter, she followed him up the steep incline. At the top, she stopped.

Duncan didn't.

He walked right into the fray. Humans in lab coats and military uniforms were fighting for their lives, trying to fend off the creatures. She didn't know what they were—not vampires. They were mis-formed, bulging with muscle mass. They had little resemblance to the humans they must have been.

A scream lodged in her throat as Duncan walked head-on into the first of the creatures, spinning when he was at arm's length and sinking his blade into the creature's throat. He was ruthless, brutal, destroying one after another.

There were too many. He'd be overwhelmed in minutes if the humans didn't shoot him first. The guns didn't have much effect on the creatures, slowed them down a bit, but nothing more.

She started to rip off her choker but hesitated. In the distance a lone figure stood still, watching. Nothing more than a silhouette against the lights from the ship. The captain? Someone from RI? He stood with calm authority. He might be able to direct her to Crowley. She ran toward him, skirting around the melee, staying low to avoid getting hit by stray bullets. Her gaze kept wanting to return to the fight to see how Duncan fared. She caught one last glimpse of him before more creatures swarmed the area, blocking her view.

Her attention returned to the lone figure. "Hey!" She waved her arms as she climbed the small hill. "Hey!"

He turned toward her, but didn't speak.

"I'm looking for someone named Julius Crowley. They brought him here a couple of"—she sucked in a deep breath, trying to regulate her breathing as she climbed the last few steps to the top—"days ago."

"You've found him." He walked into the light.

Trina looked up into his face—a young, handsome trustworthy face covered in blood. His sand-colored blond hair was longish with a bit of curl; blood stiffened it in places, too. She met his brown doe-eyes … *shit!* Shifted her gaze away. Damn it, she knew better!

"Too late, little witch. I've already got you."

No. She didn't feel any different. It must take him longer than that to get into her mind.

Trust us, little witch. I can help you. I can make you powerful.

No. She turned. "Stop it." Began walking. Thank the goddess she hadn't taken her necklace off. He'd gotten in her head. He could make her do things.

"Stop."

Her whole body froze, refusing to take another step. He hadn't even raised his voice. She'd barely heard him over the noise of the creatures and the gunfire below.

Stay with us, little witch. We'll keep you safe. "They're beautiful, don't you think?" He stood next to her. "Look at them."

She made no effort to obey.

"Look!"

Her whole body jerked, forcing her to stare into the fight below. She couldn't even blink her eyes. Duncan had positioned himself with his back toward the remaining humans, deep furrows slashed across his cheek and nose where one of the creatures had clawed him. *Goddess, please keep him safe.*

"They're not fettered by conscience nor morality. They will always focus on their purpose in life: to feed and repopulate." He stepped into her line of vision, waving one arm wide. "Meet my children, the Nephilim." He smiled. Stepped closer. "Now, I have one little spell for you to cast . . . and you can be on your way." *Relax, little witch. Speak the words we want to hear. Cast the spell.*

She tried to shake her head, to shout a denial, but her body wouldn't respond. What was he after? Did he think she'd transport his hideous children to the mainland?

"I want you to perform an exorcism." *Exorcize us. Everything will be better once we're free.*

Shock rolled through her. He was possessed? She didn't even have time to process that before the words rose in her mind, the bible verse needed, the ritual—everything she'd need to say and do to perform the spell.

"One little spell." *Exorcize us. Free us and we'll leave you be.*

She almost believed him. Almost. After all, he had the full force of her chaos Magic at his disposal. All he wanted was freedom. Her mouth started to open.

No. She drew on her Magic, clamping her jaw shut.

"You do know how to perform an exorcism, don't you? Lilith did. I've seen her perform one." *Exorcize us. Psalm 91. Speak the words.* "But not you. No, I never see you."

She could've been their secret weapon. She could've snuck up on him. Instead, she'd bungled this whole mission. Announced herself. Looked him in the eyes. *Shit.*

Speak the words. Do it. Free us.

Her jaw ached. Throbbed with the need to speak. Even her tongue strained against the inside of her mouth, desperate to follow his will.

"Quit fighting me, little witch. You are no match for my power. Not on your own." *Speak the words. We'll let you go if you say the words.*

A tear ran down her cheek as she struggled. Her throat hummed as the words tried to spill out of her. Through the pain, the absolute betrayal of her body, she started to formulate a plan because when she couldn't resist any longer, she had a feeling the words would shoot out of her like cannon fire. What if she could twist the words and say a different spell?

"Careful." He came closer. "Make sure you speak the right words, little witch. We wouldn't want any problems." *Whosoever dwells in the shelter of the . . . Speak the words, witch. Free us.*

Pain spiked through her skull. Her head began to throb as if her brain were swelling, pushing against her eyes and sinuses. Tears flowed down her face, leaving itchy trails.

She drew on her Magic again, allowing it to pulse through her.

"Quit resisting." *Speak the words. You're safe. We won't hurt you today. Not yet. Not too much.*

"Whosoever dwells in—" She snapped her mouth shut. *No!*

"Good, little witch."

She forced her attention back to fighting his suggestions. Pulled more energy from the Earth, letting it pulse through her. She couldn't speak the spell. She couldn't set him free.

A fresh spike of pain slashed through her head and strangled sound broke from her lips. Warm, wet liquid trickled from her nose. She couldn't resist forever. Black dots checkered across her vision. Her fingers ached. Burned.

He curled his fingers around her throat. Started to squeeze. Her heart thudded hard in her chest. Her lungs began to burn. Everything around her shifted as the first wave of dizziness set in and her mind began to wander. "Whosoever dwells in the shelter of the Most High—"

Crowley jerked his hand back with a shout.

She sucked in a hard breath, holding it when the urge to speak the spell came back two-fold.

Crowley held his hand up between them. It was black. The skin brittle, the small muscles beneath the skin sunken like dried prunes. Slowly, the blackness edged up his wrist, wasting everything as it went. He took a step back, eyes wide.

The same thing had happened to Lilith. The same . . . Why the hell did she infect him but not Duncan?

He looked down at himself. "You." His mouth twisted and he laughed. "All this time. . . ." He shook his head. "Leopold will pay for this, the shit."

He backed up, twirling his good arm overhead. A black circle opened above him, a place where no stars showed, and where the edges were a lighter gray.

With his blackened hand, he pointed. "You and I, little witch, we'll meet again. Soon."

A rush of wind blew up into the void, growing stronger, bending the palm trees and raising the sand in little whirlwinds. Stronger, it sucked him right up into the circle.

His talent released her. She'd been straining so hard against his will, when the resistance disappeared, she collapsed to the ground, choking. Her throat was raw and when she wiped her hand under her nose, it came away covered in blood. Her hands . . . the veins beneath the skin had turned black. She'd overreached with her Magic, trying to hold his suggestions at bay.

The noise from the creatures grew louder as they, too, were dragged along and sucked up into the portal before it closed with a pop.

The wind died.

Her ears rang in the silence.

"Trina!" Duncan paced the clearing, shouting her name.

"Here." But her voice came out little more than a croak. She clutched at her throat, dragged herself to her feet and stumbled down the hill.

There were survivors. Not many, but a few. They held their guns, pointing them in Duncan's direction as if they weren't sure if he were friend or foe.

"Duchess." His clothes were shredded and the gouges across his cheek and nose looked like macabre war-paint.

"Your face." He had more scratches on his arms. His chest.

"We'll sort it out when we get home." He took hold of her chin, tipping her face into the light. "Crowley?"

"I forgot he was a mesmerist. I forgot and . . . ." She started trembling so much, her voice shook. "I fucked up." *Again.*

"Okay." He pulled her into his arms. He was warm from exertion and solid and she didn't deserve such consideration after what happened. Goddess help her she'd walked right up to Crowley and announced her presence. The Nephilim were loose. Crowley was free.

Bad things come to those who deny their true selves, girly. Pain comes to those who resist.

"We'll get another chance."

No. *She* wouldn't. She couldn't keep screwing up. She'd have to let

Duncan transform her. Lilith would heal and Lilith could fight Crowley. She couldn't risk another mistake.

She couldn't risk Duncan again. "You almost died."

"I'm not nowhere near ash." He squeezed her. "A few scratches is all."

She snorted. "Because of me. I insisted we come."

"You sped up our arrival, that's all." He pushed her to arm's length. "You sure you're all right?"

No. But she didn't speak, just stood there, shivering.

"Anything starting to hurt now that the excitement is done?" He pulled a handkerchief out of his pocket, spit on it. Scrubbed it under her nose.

"What are you—?" She snatched the cloth out of his hand.

"Just a bit of blood, love. There." He grinned, winked. "Now you look a bit more human."

"I don't believe you did that." But she dabbed the thing under her nose again, making sure he hadn't missed any.

"Those hands of yours okay?"

They burned. Ached. But it wouldn't last for long. "They'll be fine." The damn handkerchief smelled like him, like rain in the desert. "It smells like you."

He grinned. "Like that, do you?"

A snarl came from their left and his smile disappeared. He took two steps to the side, pulled his blade and let the stray Nephilim drive itself onto his knife. The creature dissolved into a spray of ash. "Must not have been fully transformed when Crowley made his getaway. Guess we should take a quick look about and make sure there ain't any others that got left behind."

She nodded.

"Stick close, Duchess. Some of these bodies may still transform."

They headed back toward the building, pausing so Duncan could stab those lying in the sand to make sure they were dead and not in the dormant phase of transformation. Two humans followed them, watching their every move. "We've got company."

"Good." He went up the steps to the building and pulled open the door. "Maybe they'll bloody well learn something."

Nothing moved within the interior of RI. Anything that had been alive in here either had died or transformed long enough ago to have left the building. There were only a handful of rooms and they made quick work of clearing them. Once they were done, they turned to leave.

The two humans who followed raised their weapons. "Who are you?"

She fisted her hands. "Want me to take care of them?"

His hand settled on her shoulder and he squeezed. "Me name's Duncan." He folded his arms over his chest, tipping his head toward the guns. "This is an odd way to show appreciation, considering we helped you."

"Did you?" The nametag on his uniform identified him as S. Mason. "Where'd they go?"

"Don't know, mate. I suppose if you turn on the news, you'll be finding out soon enough."

Mason pointed his gun. "You let him get away."

Duncan held up his hands. "Now, just because he got away, doesn't mean we *let* him get away. You saw what happened. Most of them got sucked out of here."

Trina put her hand on his arm. "We should go." Before these two lost it. She tightened her grip on Duncan. *Quickly, safely . . . .*

"Look, if you need help, say my name out loud. We'll find you."

The Watchers would hear them say his name. They'd let Duncan know.

She closed her eyes and focused on home. *Quickly, safely take us there, in my mind I show you where.*

Mason shouted for them to stop.

Then they were home.

CHAPTER 19

A**S SOON AS THEY APPEARED** in Haven House's kitchen, Trina started gathering supplies. Duncan watched her for a time, he was worried about her, about those hands, but maybe she needed to keep busy. To keep her mind from rehashing what happened.

"Do those scratches hurt? Burn?"

"They itch so bad I'm wanting to get in there with a Brillo Pad."

Her lips twitched. She selected another jar out of the drawer, shut it, and pointed toward the table. "Come on."

Though she tried to act normal, her hands shook. Her eyes were wide, dilated. She showed all the physical signs of shock. Their little mission hadn't gone well. He'd expected Crowley to be in a cell somewhere, not out and about. And those creatures . . . he'd never seen anything like them. "I'd rather go in there." He motioned to the living room.

"Okay."

Once there, he sat on the floor in front of the ottoman and patted the cushion. "It'll be easier for you to work if you're not having to reach up, in'it?"

She sat, put some sort of astringent on a clean white cloth and started cleaning the wounds on his nose.

He winced at the sting. "Feel free to scrub it out good. I won't hold it against you."

The corner of her mouth curved. Trembled. Fell. "They're free." A shudder ran through her, one so strong it made her whole body jerk. "Crowley and those monsters." Her gaze focused on her task as she cleaned his wounds.

He put his hands on her knees. "Talk to me, Duchess. Whatever you tell me won't make me think no less of you."

She pressed her lips together.

"Crowley is hated among Guardians. We've all had a run-in with the bastard at some point. He's gotten to me before."

Her gaze flicked to his. She went to work scrubbing out another cut. "What did he want you to do?"

"Ignore a kill order. This daemon . . . he was a real bastard. Damn near as bad a Crowley."

"Did you?" She dabbed some sort of cream in the freshly scrubbed wound and the burning stopped.

"They were both gone before I realized what had happened."

She started scrubbing at his neck. "And later?"

"What about it?" He grimaced.

"Did he make you do anything else?"

He tipped his head to the side, trying to see her eyes better. "Are you worried he's still in your mind?"

Another shiver rolled through her. She nodded.

"No." He pulled her onto his lap, wrapping his arms around her. "He can't do that. Once the link is broken, it's done. I'm sorry, love. I should've warned you before we left. He's a sneaky bastard, that one."

"I knew better. I saw him mesmerize Lilith. I wasn't expecting him to be loose and then it was too late."

What all could Crowley have used her for? With her Chaos Magic . . . he couldn't begin to imagine what he might have had her do. "What did he want?"

She sat back on his thighs. "He wanted me to perform an exorcism."

Exorcism? He'd thought she'd cast that portal thingy that let them get away. "Did you . . . what am I saying, of course you did. He had you mesmer—"

"I resisted. I don't know how exactly, I kept flooding Magic through myself and I resisted."

He'd never heard of anyone resisting Crowley. He was an arse, but damned good at using his talent. He'd had centuries to perfect it. On the other hand, Trina had some scary-ass Magic. "Did he say why? What's possessing him?"

"No." She bit her lip.

"Duchess?" He brushed the silky strands of her hair back, tethering them behind her ear and for the first time he noticed the blackened fingerprints around her throat. Crowley's luck had run out. The fucker was ash, he just didn't know it yet. "You're holding something back. I can't help you through this if I don't know everything."

"His skin turned black. When he touched me." Her hand went to her throat, her fingers clawing as if she could still feel his hand on her skin.

Gently, he pulled her hand down.

"He laughed about it." She speared her fingers through her hair. "When the darkness infected Lilith it was painful for her." She met his gaze. "Crowley laughed as if it didn't matter."

"Okay." He put both his hands along her jawline, cupping her face and making her look at him. "I ain't getting burned." *You know how it is with your mate.*

"Just you." Her eyes welled with tears. "Everyone else I touch, I infect. What if that changes? What if I start infecting you, too?" Her hand flung out to the side. "And now the Nephilim are free—"

"Nephilim?" He sat back. That wasn't good.

"That's what he called those monsters. He introduced them as his children, the Nephilim. I think I should call—"

"I think you should go take a shower. Put some comfortable clothes on. Eat. Rest. Then, if you want to chat some more, we can." He needed to think. *Nephilim?*

She flung herself against his chest, tucking her head beneath his chin.

This time, a shiver ran through him. Awkwardly, he gave her a pat. "You're gonna be fine, Duchess. You'll see."

"I'm more worried about you." For a moment, she sat back on his thighs and looked him over, her gaze tracing each of the scratches. Then she stood and turned to leave.

He patted her bum. "I'm gonna be fine, too."

She froze. Turned and stared with a look that hovered between incredulous and outraged.

Shite. He held up his hands. "Look, I didn't think that one through. You can smack my arse if it makes you feel better."

Her eyes narrowed but she left without another word.

Christ. They were in some serious shite. Nephilim were the product of angels and humans. They hadn't walked the Earth since before the Great Deluge. Said so right in the fucking bible. At least now he understood why Armageddon had started. Had Crowley called them his "children" . . . or was it the being possessing Crowley? A Watcher, maybe? That would explain why the Watchers were fighting. That might explain why they only wanted to talk via human—maybe the Watcher possessing Crowley couldn't put humans in a trance while possessing another body. It did explain why Trina and Lilith were coming into their powers now. And why Augustina couldn't see Crowley.

Shite. Augustina.

He wasn't the only one Trina had touched without ill effects.

She'd hugged Augustina.

So had Augustina been immune like him? Or did Trina not infect any-one but Lilith and Crowley?

CHAPTER 20

AMAZING WHAT A SHOWER AND a fresh change of clothes could do for a male. Duncan felt halfway human. Well, maybe he wouldn't go quite that far, but he did feel a fair shake better than he had. He'd fed and the wounds from the Nephilim had almost healed. The gunshot wound healed, leaving a scar. But all the bruises had turned deep purples and blues.

He left the bathroom, finishing buttoning his shirt as he went down to the kitchen.

Trina sat at the table looking for all the world like she'd shot her favorite dog.

"What's up?"

"I talked to James. Lilith is getting worse."

"Ah." He leaned his hip against the counter. This must be killing her trying to decide between the rest of her life and Lilith's. "I hope he didn't try to pressure you into anything."

"I didn't tell him what Augustina said."

He nodded. Probably for the best.

"Our moms were close."

"Oh?" She must mean her and Lilith's mums.

She crossed her arms on the table and rested her chin on them. "I remember mine telling people that Lilith and I were best friends since we were in the cradle. Her mom used to introduce me as her niece even though we weren't related."

"That doesn't mean you have to do this. You need to make the choice that's best for you."

"Lilith wouldn't have hesitated. I'll always hate myself a little for the fact that I have." She sat up and dragged her hands through her hair. "Lilith could've beat Crowley. She and James would have already if not for me."

He didn't have a ready reply for that, though he didn't think it was true. While he hadn't seen James or Lilith fight, he didn't think anyone would've fared much better than they had under the circumstances.

She stood. "I need to do this. I knew I did when I drew the Ten of Swords—the card of transformations." She walked up to him and thrust out her arm, offering him her wrist.

Now what? If he did as she asked, would she end up hating him? What if he refused and her friend disappeared? Bloody hell, neither option would leave him smelling like roses.

"Wait." She snatched her arm back and paced again, shaking her arms out at her sides. "I need a minute."

He admired that even scared, she still intended to go through with the transformation. "You're giving me a headache, love." He unfolded himself from his lounge and strode toward the living room, scooping her up as he passed.

"Put me down." She thumped him on his chest to emphasize her demand.

"How 'bout you shut it." He gave her a little shake to settle her down as he stalked over to the big arm chair and sat.

She tried to get up.

He pulled her down on his lap, held her hands in one of his and arranged her the way he wanted her, shoving her head down on his shoulder. "Quit fighting me, I'm bloody well comforting you and you're gonna let me."

She went limp, allowing him to pull her tight into his embrace. Awkwardly, he alternated between rubbing and patting her back while he tried to think of something appropriate to say. Some comforting sentiment.

"If you keep doing that I'm going to burp."

"Shite. Sorry."

Her shoulders shook. For a paralyzing moment he thought he'd made her cry. A giggle escaped.

The awkwardness evaporated. "Are you sure you want to do this?"

"Yeah."

Biting her didn't fall within the boundaries of his plan to earn her trust, damn it.

"Tell me what to expect." She whispered her worry against his neck. "Will I be myself? Will I have control?"

Control? Not bloody likely. Neophytes were inconsolable in their first bloodlust, but he'd take care of her. The thing was, as the Original she wasn't supposed to turn into a vampire exactly. He didn't know what to expect. "I won't let you do anything you'll regret."

She placed a soft, chaste kiss on the scruff on his chin before offering her wrist again. "Hurry."

He rearranged their positions to better be able to restrain her, tucking both her legs under one of his. He took her wrist in one hand, her forearm tight to his chest, his triceps resting across her chest and brought it to his mouth. "I'm sorry about this, yeah?" He tightened his hold and bit down into her tender flesh.

Sweet, metallic blood filled his mouth. Like a drug, it overwhelmed his sense of reason, clouding his mind. She screamed, writhing and straining to get away, but the scene had a disconnected quality, like he saw and heard everything through the haze of intoxication.

A vision filled his mind.

A little girl, dark-haired with big brown eyes. She stood outside a house, looking into a window. Next to her a tall redhead, Rowena, pulled her hooded cape tighter around her. Her green eyes almost glowed. "Stop ignoring me, Trina."

She listened, but the girls inside interested her more. None of their mouths moved—they all sat quietly, somberly, playing with dolls under the supervision of an older woman—still, she heard them. She always messes everything up. Why can't we have one normal day? Too bad she didn't die in the crash with her mom.

Rowena knelt down next to her. "I'm your high priestess. Even your mommy had to obey me. If you want to come back inside, you need to put this on."

Trina tried to fight, but his muscles locked, holding her in place. Blood gushed into his mouth in waves with the rhythm of her heart. Her nails dug into his neck.

Rowena's mind was silent. "I can't hear your thoughts anymore." She stared at Rowena. "Why can't I hear your thoughts?"

"Never mind that." She held out the choker. "Put this on. Be a good little witch."

Her gaze shifted to the window, to the girls inside. Don't know why she has to live here anyway. She's weird. She's always getting all the attention.

"I'm never going to be like the others, am I?"

"No. You're a dark creature. You can't come inside unless you wear this."

She lifted her hair, giving her back to Rowena. The choker tightened around her neck.

The voices went silent.

Nature went silent.

Everything did, as if she were seeing the world through a clear plastic box. She couldn't feel Rowena's aura. Couldn't feel the energy of the Earth. Nor her Magic.

She screamed. She screamed and she ran in circles and she dropped to the damp grass, clawing at her neck.

Rowena stood over her. "It's for your own good. For the good of us all."

Duncan needed to let go. This vision, the violent thoughts playing through his mind, they needed to stop, but his instincts urged him for a little more, another taste.

Deep scratches marred her skin around the choker. "I can't hear anything! I can't feel anything!"

"Yes, you can. Your Magic is gone, not your senses. Though no one would know it to look at you." She pulled Trina up by the elbow and swatted her backside. "Stop your nonsense."

"I can't feel anything."

Her struggles grew weaker, her voice hoarse and whisper-soft as she neared the end. "Wish you dead."

Pain, beginning as a dull ache flared through his head. His chest grew tight. With every draw from her wrist the crushing agony intensified. His stomach roiled and a violent tremor shook his frame. He was killing his mate.

He had to let go.

At last, his body deigned to listen. He pulled her arm away. He covered her wound with his hand to block the smell; trying to keep her from bleeding out before the transformation.

"Sod it." He'd known it might be difficult to pull away, but nothing like that.

He pulled her limp body closer.

"Come on, Trina, yell at me." He rocked her, burying his face in her silky mane. "Slag me off with your quick wit."

She remained quiet, but inside his mind, the vision continued.

Inside the house, the girls stared. Frowning. Narrow-eyed. All of them, except one. One little girl with pale skin and long brown hair had tears running down her face. "I can't hear you."

Trina sniffed. "I know. I can't hear anyone. I can't feel anything."

Rowena shook her. "You can. You answered her." She pointed at the other little girl. "No more trouble from you, either, Lilith, or you'll be wearing a collar, too."

Trina whirled on her high-priestess. "Wish you dead."

Rowena let Trina go. Took a step back. A little trail of blood leaked from her nose.

She wiped at it. Her eyes grew wide. "You shouldn't be able to do that."

One of the stones in the collar cracked. Trina didn't break eye contact.

"You'll all end up in foster care." Rowena lifted her hand to point at them. "You'll be separated if you hurt me. You'll never see Lilith again."

"Trina!" Lilith ran to her side, putting her arm around her shoulders.

Trina dropped her gaze and wet her lips. "Sorry."

The two little girls walked away. Trina glanced back long enough to see the result. Long enough to catch Rowena and the other girls' fear.

The vision disappeared.

Jesus. Just now, she'd said the same thing. *Wish you dead.* The pain in his head . . . had she not been so far gone, what would've happened to him? Or had her spell failed because he was her mate?

He couldn't decide what horrified him more, Rowena's treatment of the girls, the fact that such a young Trina had almost killed Rowena in cold-blood, the fact that she'd just tried to kill him, or the fact that she lay limp in his arms. He stood, cradling her to his chest while he paced. It couldn't be healthy, her having had that as her last human memory. Then again, he couldn't remember what his last thoughts had been of. Nor did he recall the process being this peaceful, this quiet.

"You know, Duchess, I was getting used to the idea of giving you hell for all eternity. I mean, I could live without that whole mind-meld thing you just dropped on me, but you know, I'd rather you didn't die." Her heart wound down like a clockwork toy. Stopped. *Shite.* "I don't think it's supposed to be like this."

What had he done?

He closed his eyes, slamming his head into the wall behind him once, twice. Harder. "Just like you to throw a spanner in the works, Sinclair." He brushed away the hair falling across her shoulder, combing the strands with his fingers and lifted Trina's arm for a closer look at the bite mark. Using the edge of his shirt he wiped the remaining blood away, revealing an uneven oval scar. She'd healed.

She wasn't dead.

Relief washed through him as her heart started beating again. Her chest rose. She opened her eyes.

"Trina." He hugged her, laughing. "I thought I'd botched the whole thing."

She didn't say anything but turned toward his neck. Her mouth pressed to his skin. Her lips brushed his throat as they parted.

"Oh, no." He pulled her away. "No biting other vampires, love. It'll make short work of us both."

She remained focused on the prize: his neck.

"Are you listening? You bite me, we're both ash."

Her muscles tensed. She attacked. He struggled, trying not to hurt her. She lunged, much stronger now, and his muscles shook with the effort to hold her back without hurting her.

"How about we get you a snack." He rearranged his grip and picked her up, avoiding her mouth. This was a common mistake neophytes made. They hadn't mastered different scents yet. Vampires didn't have blood and biting him would destroy them both.

He carried her upstairs, trying in vain to keep her legs away from the banister. She kicked, trying to throw them off balance and making him stumble.

Once in James' room, he changed his hold again, using his weight to pin her against the wall while he punched in the universal code for James' cooler safe. He pulled out a unit of blood, popped the cap off with his teeth and held the bag to her mouth.

Her attention shifted as soon as she caught the scent and she took long gulps of blood.

Her phone started ringing. Christ, what a night. He fished it out of her back pocket. "It's Lilith."

She stared back at him while she sucked down her dinner, uncomprehending.

He got another bag of blood ready while he answered the phone. "Hello."

A masculine voice said, "You're not Trina."

"And you're not Lilith."

"Where is she?"

"Feeding." He handed Trina the next bag, taking her empty. "Lilith?"

James sighed. "The same. It happened out of the blue. One minute I thought she was dying . . . the next, the blackness receded and she attacked me."

"So they are linked." The wildness receded from Trina's eyes. "The Historian suspected as much. She had a theory if Trina was transformed that Lilith would heal since they each have half of the Original's soul." Trina would have a fit that he'd revealed that little tidbit, but they should bloody-well know what she sacrificed and why.

"Have her call us in the morning."

"Will do." He hung up and handed her a fourth unit of blood. It was like feeding a baby elephant.

Halfway through, wariness crept into her eyes. He did remember that. Waking up mid-suck with the understanding that he was guzzling a substance he would've found disgusting twenty minutes ago. "Don't think too hard. You need it. What you're going through is normal. You know . . . for vampire daemons."

Her eyes widened. "Lil."

"I talked to James. She's fine. She's feeding, too." He should've asked if Lilith still had a heartbeat. Trina did. She wasn't truly a vampire. Nor was she still human the way she'd guzzled down that blood.

When he offered her a fifth bag, she held up her hand. "I don't think I've ever experienced that kind of thirst." She grimaced. "How often will that happen?"

"Couple times a month at first. Eventually, you can go longer between feedings."

She nodded and pulled away from the wall. Ran her hands down her shirt as if to straighten it and stilled, her head cocking to the side. Her eyes closing.

He should tell her what happened—about the vision. He just wasn't sure how.

She rubbed her wrist, traced the fresh oval scar with a finger. Her eyes met his, the lust-filled look she gave him stripping the air from his lungs.

Oh, yeah. He remembered that, too. The way his body had become ultra-sensitive right after the change. Mentally, he shook himself. He needed to tell her about the vision. "Look, when I bit you—"

She shivered and her usual guarded mask returned. "You don't need to explain. I knew the risks."

Hell, she'd been through enough tonight. Maybe he'd leave that little revelation for some other day. "You need anything else?"

*A*NYTHING?

Everything was different. Not in a bad way, but in a heightened sense. She felt more aware. More alive. Duncan's scent filled every inhale, earthy, fresh and very male. Her senses all locked in on high gear, focused on him. With each breath, her nipples scraped against her bra, her shirt against her skin. Her whole body was . . . needful. "You know last night, when we first woke up?"

His brows drew together. "What of it?"

She shifted her weight and, oh, goddess, why had she worn lace panties? "Did you mean it? What you said?"

"Ah." His brow smoothed and the corner of his mouth curved. "Every word."

She shouldn't do this, it wasn't safe for him. But every nerve in her body was sensitive right now. Goddess help her, she could even feel the touch of his aura on hers.

Then again, he was her mate, maybe he was immune to her Magic. Maybe she *couldn't* hurt him. Either way, right now, she needed him. "Show me."

The words had hardly gotten out before he had her in his arms. His mouth slanted over hers and he lifted her off her feet while he walked down the hall.

He swung her around, closed the bedroom door, and pressed her against it in one swift move. His large hands framed her face, angling her for a deeper kiss as his body pressed against hers.

His leg nudged between hers, teasing, stirring a sweet emptiness. This wasn't a directionless desire. She wanted Duncan. Needed *him.*

Only him.

Little thrills shocked through her as his hands stroked down her back to her bottom where he palmed her cheeks, pulling her higher onto his thigh.

She gasped.

Urgent, her fingers stumbled along the buttons on his shirt, eager to feel his skin. She managed to slide a couple from their moors before he grabbed his collar, tugging the material over his head. The second or two he took stretched for an eternity until his mouth settled again on hers.

Trina pulled at the leather straps of the knife sheath, dragging them over shoulders, down his muscular arms before letting the whole thing fall to the floor, barely registering its heavy clunk on the hardwoods.

He gathered her hair, twisting the locks around in his fist, forcing her head back. She shuddered as he licked and nipped her lips before deepening the kiss; his tongue skimming along her teeth before mating once again with hers.

Lifting her higher in his arms, he swung around, took two steps and landed on top of her, on the bed.

His weight pressed her down, jarring her to another time, another place. Trapped, she froze as icy spasms of fear cooled her ardor. *Heavy weight pressed down on her, crushing her. She couldn't breathe . . .*

Be good, my dark angel.

Her eyes snapped open and her mother stared down. Blood leaked from her eyes. From her nose.

No! She sucked in air. Reached up, looking for the anchor of the headboard. Needed to pull herself out from under the stifling weight. Her hand grasped nothing but air at the foot of the bed. She tried pushing herself out from under him but her legs tangled with his and the pillows.

"Duchess?" The voice sounded far away.

Magic curled around her, the words on the tip of her tongue, *wish you dead.*

"Wish you . . . *No!*" She wouldn't. She shoved against his weight, using Magic. Tendrils of energy launched him back, throwing him against the headboard. He grunted.

Once free, she flung herself from the bed. Sanity returned with brutal force. Mid-flight, she stopped as the enormity of what she'd done sank in. She'd almost killed him.

"Duchess?"

Damn, she screwed this up. A few seconds of uncontrolled panic and he must be furious. She couldn't blame him, she'd be angry to have someone throw themselves at her one moment and freak out the next.

She headed for the door.

"Bloody 'ell," his voice came out in a ragged breath. "I didn't know. I thought you wanted me, too."

Goddess help her, she did want him. Ached for him. With one glance over her shoulder she lost her inner battle. *Shit.* She couldn't allow him to think he'd done anything wrong.

It wasn't him. Or a hang-up about sex. It was the weight. It was being trapped. And it had screwed up every relationship she'd ever tried to have. She couldn't take back what she'd done, but she should explain. He deserved that much.

CHAPTER 21

"TALK TO ME, LOVE."

Trina leaned back against the door, her expression inscrutable. She appeared calmer now, but she hadn't released him. Her binding spell didn't hurt, but she'd pinned him—his bum planted on the mattress, his back pressed to the cool wood, his arms spread wide and locked in place against the headboard.

What the hell happened? He'd never taken an unwilling woman and never would. When the denial had erupted from her he'd backed off. He'd been stunned, though, by the terror on her face.

"Talk to me. Yeah? I can't get away until you let me and I'm quite comfortable, you know, if you're worried."

The left corner of her lips twitched up a fraction. "That . . . ." She made a little waving motion with her hand. "That wasn't your fault."

The knots twisting his gut eased. Thank God for small favors. Now he needed to figure out what the hell *had* happened. "Come on, chat with me." He nodded toward the edge of the bed.

She sat on the mattress, crossing her legs. With her back ramrod straight and features schooled, she looked like she might shatter into a million pieces any second. "I'm sorry." Color rose high on her cheeks. Her gaze strayed to the door.

"You want to tell me what happened?"

"I—" Her voice cracked on the one syllable. Her lips twisted and pressed together.

His gaze followed hers to where she picked at a loose thread on the duvet.

She needed a few minutes of the mundane to collect herself. "I've always liked purple."

Her gaze shot to his.

He nodded to the duvet. "It's a good color, rich, kind of exotic. Back in the day, yeah, only royalty had purple fabric. The dye was too expensive even for the gentry. Even that, uh, Beau Brummell chap, never had any purple to sport."

"Bo?"

"Fancy fop from back in the day. Never mind him, ain't important."

She continued to stare as if he were daft. Good, her mind had focused on something else. He prattled on, "I had this fight once, part of the prize was the tiniest bit of purple dye. We were all mad for it."

"What did you use it for?" Her voice sounded steadier.

He grinned. She'd assumed he won. "Everyone had their opinion, but most agreed I should sell the stuff. Well, I didn't even have enough for a whole shirt, yeah." He shrugged. "So, I used the dye on me boy's nappie."

Trina burst out in laughter.

"Ah, I wish you'd been there. No one else found it amusing, let me tell you."

"You made that up." She turned toward him, sitting Indian-style. Her knee brushed his thigh.

"If only." He grimaced. "Would have saved my nose."

"Oh, stop."

Their laughter faded and he perused her room, looking for inspiration for another anecdote, if needed.

"It doesn't—" She tipped her head back to stare at the ceiling. "What happened doesn't have anything to do with sex. Or with you, or any man."

The violent energy that had been thrumming through him settled. She hadn't been raped. "That's . . . good." Simple words, maybe, but heartfelt.

"I get . . . sort of . . . claustrophobic. When I'm weighed down. I don't like to be on the bottom."

He concealed his reaction to her soft confession, surprised she admitted even that much. "Okay."

"Okay?"

"I've always been partial to bottom myself." He spoke in the same tone he might have used to say he preferred sleeping on the left.

"You're not angry?" She studied him as if she'd never seen anything like him. "You're not going to tell me I'm being foolish?"

"No."

"Why?"

"I've found that what may seem the silliest of preferences are often bred from self-preservation and conditioning. For me—" He hesitated, never having told anyone this secret and finding the admission more difficult than he'd expected. He rushed the words out. "I can't sleep with my feet uncovered." Bloody hell, what a manly confession. Damn near akin to "I can't sleep without my blankey."

Her brow furrowed. "Why?"

He leaned his head back. "We had vermin in the choky. The rats, they'd get hungry."

Understanding lit in her eyes. Something changed in her demeanor, calmed. A small smile curved her lips. "Why do you prefer the bottom?"

"Ah. That's all owing to the view."

She grinned as they lapsed into silence. Her gaze drifted to the Tarot cards pinned to the wall. "Do you still want me?"

He had to strain to hear. "I've never wanted a woman more."

Those midnight eyes of hers fixed on his. Women had always been easy for him to figure out, at least in the small capacity he allowed himself to know them. This one, though, was an enigma, one he would be happy to spend his existence puzzling out.

She rose to her knees and crawled onto his lap.

Unsure of what to say, he held his tongue. Instead, he concentrated on keeping his body under control. Tried not to notice how she stared at his lips.

"Can I?" Her thumb touched the corner of his mouth. "I want to see . . . ."

He gave the barest of nods.

She leaned in, brushing her lips to his in a sweet tease of a kiss. Once. Twice. She lingered, her tongue tickling a path across his bottom lip.

He couldn't contain the groan stirring in his chest.

She jerked back, staring.

He fought the urge to cajole. *Come on, Duchess, kiss me blind.*

Grinning, she rewarded him with another kiss, deeper. Hotter. Straddling his legs, her hands curved around his neck. Her body pressed into his and she kissed the breath right out of him.

He surrendered any ideas of remaining un-aroused. Something about her stirred him. Maybe her slightly sweet taste, the scent of lemongrass lacing her hair, her satiny skin, or the way her body fit his. He craved her like a man lost at sea craves fresh water.

Her mouth was wild, her pelvis rubbed against his and he moaned low in his throat. Wanting her to do it again, he tried moving his hands to direct her to his desire before he remembered she'd bound him. "Again."

"This?" She rotated her hips against him in a wicked lap dance that caused fresh bolts of need to sizzle through his body. Their labored breathing timed her movements. Just when he thought he couldn't stand any more she pulled away.

Her hands slipped around his throat, palms flat against his skin, fingers touching at the back of his neck, thumbs stretched toward his Adams apple.

She applied the slightest of pressure as she stretched her hand farther around his neck. If she wanted to see if her thumbs would touch, she'd never make it. Her hands were too small. His neck too thick.

Her lips parted, she shifted in his lap. "Anyone ever tell you that you're a very"—her gaze met his—"large man?"

"Maybe once or twice." Christ, if she kept wriggling like that, she'd see exactly how large. She did it again. This time her eyes closed. The minx was doing it on purpose. "Keep that up, Duchess, I'll give you something just the right size to wrap your hands around."

Her eyes opened. "I want you." Her statement added that last inch of steel to his cock. "But I can't be worrying that you'll do something that might . . . make me hurt you."

Ah. She intended to leave him like this. *If* he gave her the go ahead. As if there were a question in all that. He'd rather touch her. He wanted that thick, black hair twisted around his fingers. Wanted to learn the weight of her breasts. Stroke every last inch of her skin. Lick and nip at every ticklish spot on her body. Find a way into every nook and cranny she had.

He'd need to convince her she wanted all that, too. He leaned forward, much as he could, and couldn't quite reach her. "Come here."

Her eyes stayed open and she swayed closer, but not quite close enough to make it easy for him. He grinned. "Tease." He strained that last centimeter. Bit down gently on her bottom lip and sat back against the wall, taking her with him.

Those dark eyes widened.

That's right. You don't have as much control as you thought you did.

He stroked his tongue over her lip before releasing her. "It's hard to kiss you when you're all the way over there."

A smile flashed over her lips. A blush stained her cheeks. "I'm nervous. It's been a while."

"Think I've got you beat there." Her hands drove him to distraction, stoking over his chest and shoulders, her gaze followed their every path.

"Oh? How long?"

"Since I took Harry in. Almost five years."

Her hands paused their exploration. Her gaze lifted.

"Don't worry, Duchess, I still remember what to do."

This time, she laughed. Her hands slipped over his shoulders and she pressed herself close. All those feminine curves snug against him. "Guess it couldn't have changed all that much."

When he shook his head, they bumped noses. She laughed again. Low. Sultry. The sound made his cock twitch. "Last I heard, people still get naked first."

"I heard they kiss." She shifted in his lap. The heat of her sank right into him. "Maybe rub up against each other a little."

His breath shuddered out. "Yeah." He nudged her a bit with his chin to get her into position, teasing the corner of her mouth with little kisses. "Like this, yeah?"

"Mm. Yes." She shook her head.

Christ, she was sweet.

"Maybe like this?" He parted his lips, letting her breath waft over them. Letting her taste his scent. Her lips parted, too. She leaned in and he leaned back. She whimpered. *Enough teasing.* He took possession of her mouth. Swept in and tasted her; sweet, salt and the tiniest tang of blood.

She clung, her nails digging into his shoulder, her heat pressing down on him, making shivers flit over his flesh. Her breasts rubbed against his chest through her clothes. She shivered.

He lifted his knees, forcing her up, and sucked on one nipple though the thin bra and tee she wore. Her arms closed around his head, pressing him closer. "Goddess, yes."

Her nipple hardened, but all he tasted was the cotton of her shirt. He wanted her skin, damn it. "Take the damn thing off." He needed her naked. Wanted all that silky skin riding over his.

Her gaze met his, desire clashing with challenge. She must be used to riding heard over her men in the past. "Off." She'd learn to like his way.

She pulled her shirt over her head, tossed it aside.

He devoured every nuance of her bared flesh with his gaze. The color of warm tawny beige, her skin had a fresh, soft look that promised to feel of satin. She had an incredible figure, petite yet curvy, her flat belly had a small dip of a navel. She ran her fingers over one of the lacy cups of her bra. "This, too?"

He followed the motion of her hand, along the edge of the cup to where the damn thing clasped in front. When would they start making the damn things with Velcro? He could've managed Velcro even with his arms bound. "You remember what I said the other evening?"

Her eyes darkened, she bit her lip.

Yeah, she remembered. "Bet right now every last inch of your body is hypersensitive." He stroked his tongue over the rise of her breast. "Bet you can feel the air sliding into your body, and over your skin with your every move." He bit down on the edge of her bra, dragged it down until her breast spilled out. "Beautiful." He traced the outline of her areole with his tongue.

Her breath hitched.

"Bet you can feel every fiber of those clothes you're in. Now, I can play nice. Fulfill every last one of my promises. Or—" He dragged his stubbly cheek down the curve of her breast.

The bra disappeared. She didn't take time to remove it, instead spell-casting it off.

Don't you dare smile, you'll get her all riled up. He drew her nipple into his mouth, sucking lightly, then harder until—

"Oh."

There, that's what she liked. He kept it up until she writhed in his lap, every shift and wriggle sending tingles of need straight to his cock.

"Dunc."

Switched to the other breast and repeated until she moaned. Teethed lightly on the bud. "You want more?" He nipped the underside of her breast, stroked his tongue over the spot.

"Yeah."

"Take the rest off, Duchess. Let me look at you."

She sat back on his thighs, her gaze following the path of her fingers as they roamed over his skin. No one had ever admired him like that before. Never. He couldn't drag his gaze away from the way she looked at him.

This wasn't an adventure to her. She wasn't using him to forget or hurt someone else, like Gertie. Unlike Satrina, she wasn't posing for him, or holding back. He felt wanted. Needed by her unbridled efforts to arouse and please.

She leaned in, her mouth trailing behind her hands, exploring the contours of his torso with bold inflaming strokes and heady kisses. Lower, down the ridges of his stomach, her breasts brushed over his erection, his thighs, as her tongue delved into his navel. She undid the front of his trousers. Her knuckles ghosted over his cock. *Jesus.*

He needed to look away long enough to regain control, but he couldn't. Not when she sat up, hooking her fingers around the waist band of both his pants and boxers and hauled them down the length of his legs. Certainly not when she stood to shimmy out of her jeans. Definitely not when she kissed her way back up his legs, nipping at every sensitive spot she found along the way. If he had looked away, he'd have missed her satisfied smiles when his muscles tensed under her lips. And he sure as hell wouldn't have been prepared for her next move.

She enveloped him in the heat of her mouth. No teasing first. No shy touches. Just straight down his length and he damn near came. He groaned. His lids slid shut. His head fell back as she dipped lower, taking in more of him, stroking his cock with her velvet tongue. When he opened his eyes, it was to find her staring up at him while she worked him. Watching. Taking in his every reaction. Not judging. Not looking at him with disgust. She acted as if she cared, and damn it, he could love her for that alone. She was his mate. His. He set his teeth against the exquisite pleasure. He needed to be inside her. Now. "Gotta stop. You're gonna make me come."

"Isn't that the point?"

"Come here."

She got to her knees, held on to his shoulders as she spread her legs to sit over him. When she settled in his lap, her pussy nestled right up against the length of his cock. All that wet heat so damn close. "Let me up."

Her eyes clouded. "I told you—"

"I gave you my name, damn it. You gave me access to any house you're ever in. You want this—" He flexed his hips which made his length slide against her.

She gasped.

Chills washed over him. "—you give me your trust."

She worried her bottom lip between her teeth.

He flexed his hips again and, Jesus, that felt good. "Give me your trust, Duchess. I'll keep us both safe."

Whatever had been holding him to the wall, released him. Slowly, he lowered his arms, giving her a chance to get used to the idea. He brushed her hair back over her shoulders, gathered it at the base of her neck. Twisted it around his fist. "You trust me?"

A shadow of doubt flitted over her face, but she nodded. It was enough. For now.

He pulled back on her hair gently, forcing her mouth up to his. "I'm not going to pin you down. You're going to trust me to keep my own ass on the mattress."

A little more confidence entered her expression. Again she nodded. She squirmed against him. "Dunc."

He trailed his tongue over her bottom lip. "You want this?" He bit down, drawing her lip out before releasing her. Slanted his mouth over hers while cupping her bum in his free hand. Pressed her harder onto his length.

Christ, much more of that and he'd be done. He spread his legs, sliding her back so he could get his hand between them. Under her. She was so damn wet his finger slid right into her. Her breasts rubbed against his chest as she shifted and pressed down, looking for more.

He added a finger. Just that little bit and he filled her from wall to wall. Damn, this was going to be a tight fit. He pressed his forehead to hers.

Her hands wrapped around his cock. Stroked. Squeezed the head. "Fuck." Everything in him wanted in her now. The need to take thrummed through him, sending shivers over his skin, making his breath hitch.

Without pulling his fingers away from her, he pushed her back on the bed. Kneeled over her.

Her eyes widened and he paused. "No weight." He slid his fingers out of her, pushed them back in. "Want to taste you, love."

SHE COULDN'T QUITE TELL WHICH was more overpowering, her desire, the sweet tension flooding through her, or anxiety that he might forget their agreement. He'd promised to keep his ass on the bed but his bum faced the ceiling. Still, he didn't try to put any weight on her. He sat back on his heels, leaned down, and—

An inarticulate sound strangled out of her throat as sensation burst over her like lightning—intense, white-hot. Her fingers clenched in the bed sheets as his slick, persistent tongue stroked over her. Her breasts throbbed. Her belly bottomed out. Shivers darted over her skin. When he closed his lips around her clit and sucked . . . her breath caught as pleasure burst over her, made her twitch and convulse. His fingers rode in and out of her, drawing out her orgasm, slowing in time with the pulses of her body. Even though she'd come with enough force to make her want to sleep for a week, when he slid his fingers out, she whimpered. Reached out to bring him back.

He pulled her back into his lap, to the ambiguous safety of his embrace. His cock brushed against her pussy and need started building again. His mouth slanted over hers.

"Taste that?"

She did. She tasted herself on him, caught her scent on his skin and while it shouldn't turn her on, it did. He smelled of her. Tasted of her. His mouth tracked down to her neck and she let her head fall back. Shivered when his teeth scraped over her throat. Shuddered when he sucked at a spot below her collar bone.

She held on to him, her arms spread wide to accommodate his shoulders, her legs spread wide to accommodate the rest of him. He was so damn big it was an effort to wrap herself around him.

That turned her on, too.

Goddess, she wanted him. It had been so damn long since she'd been with anyone. To be with her mate, even if only this once, meant everything.

"More." She rubbed her cheek against his. Nipped his ear lobe before drawing it into her mouth. She wanted her scent all over him.

The blunt head of his cock pressed against her entrance. Thick. Solid. She lifted herself a tad, just enough and as he breached her, she bit down on his shoulder.

"Mm, that's it."

"Damn it, Dunc." He was huge everywhere. She sank her nails into his shoulder, the back of his neck. Breathed through the stretch.

"I've got you."

That he did. He had her wrapped around him. He had her halfway impaled on him. Had her twisted around his damn finger. "More." It came out far more as a plea than the demand she'd intended.

His hips turned strong as iron as he flexed, giving her something to push down on. Inch by inch. His calloused hands curled around the outside of her thighs. Her hands cupped his head. Her forehead rested against his. Mouth open. Eyes closed. Inch by blissful-fucking-inch until he was seated deep inside her. Her muscles trembled around him.

She opened her eyes to find him staring back.

You're mine. He wasn't a handsome man. But right now, with him filling her, surrounding her, his gorgeous hazel eyes filling her vision . . . she'd never seen a more beautiful man.

"You're beautiful." His breath came in shuddering pants between parted lips despite the fact they weren't moving. "Ah, Duchess, you have no idea what you do to me."

Warmth swelled in her chest. He was giving her a line, one used on any number of women before her she was sure, but for tonight she'd let herself believe it.

For tonight, he belonged to her. *You're mine.*

He kissed her, urgent, possessive as they rocked against each other, finding their rhythm. He cupped her breasts, rolling the nipples between his fingers. She arched back in response, her hips moving in a circular motion, grinding down, seeking pleasure for them both.

As the tide of their passion crested, his rough hands caged her ribs, urged her up so she could experience the length of him sliding out, gliding back to fill her. He lifted her again.

Deep, coiling tension settled in her core, her muscles growing taut, straining. She whimpered. Each slick glide made the tension wind tighter. She raised up and lowered again until they were flesh to flesh. The scent of their arousal rode in on each breath. His muscles flexed under her hands with each thrust. His gaze never left hers as he pumped into her. His hands slid up her back, gripping her shoulders from behind, adding more force to every thrust, deepening each stroke until release raged through her.

She screamed his name. Her inner muscles clenched, gripping him in her silken heat.

Duncan tensed. Shuddering beneath her, as orgasm claimed him, too.

While they waited for their breathing to quiet she allowed him to hold her. It was nice nestling up to someone solid and strong. Her mate. But it couldn't last. Not even with him. Especially not with him. She didn't trust herself. Nor her Magic.

After her near miss earlier . . . .

This couldn't happen again. She'd lost control tonight when she'd slammed him against the wall. What if she'd spoken the words instead? What if she'd torn him apart on an atomic level? There were so many things that could've gone wrong . . . .

"Shh." He kissed her hair and she realized she was trembling. He pulled the duvet out from under them, scooted down to lie amid the pillows, and covered them both.

She had to let him go but he was the first good thing to happen to her in a long time. She tightened her grasp as she rested on top of him, her legs intertwined with his, her head tucked under his chin. One of his hands stroked her back. Had anyone ever treated her so sweet? She shouldn't allow it, this tenderness. All this would make walking away later more difficult, but she craved the contact, even if he just held her a few moments more.

Their breathing returned to normal in slow increments. He'd want to go now, right? Hell, he didn't even realize they were mated. He'd expect this to be a one night stand. He'd get up and dress in semi-awkward silence and slip out while she'd pretend to sleep. That's how these things ended. It would be a good thing, help them maintain distance. And if she pretended to sleep, she couldn't ask him to stay.

To make his departure easier, she slid to his side, but couldn't resist resting her head on his shoulder. Tracing the Guardian symbol he wore around his neck, she tried to ease the tightness in her throat.

She had to let him go.

He sat up. He was leaving. He was going and . . . he was taking a long damn time.

She opened her eyes in time to see him kick up the end of the duvet so it folded under his feet. He took the time to re-arrange her legs, cocooning her feet in the blanket, too. When he lay back, he gathered her into his embrace, holding her close and let out a lusty sigh. Nothing impatient, more an 'ain't this cozy' kind of sigh.

She no longer trembled.

Now, she shook like a fall leaf in a strong November wind. Moisture stung her eyes. Her chest ached. Worse than all the turmoil roiling around inside was she couldn't fathom why she was so upset.

CHAPTER 22

DUNCAN STOOD ON THE DOCK *of a ship. With each wave the whole vessel tipped from side to side. Big, slow rocks that threw his equilibrium off as it hit each precipice. Water crashed against the vessel, splashing up over the edges. All the lights on the ship were out. The moon peeked out from thick, fast-flying puffy clouds.*

He opened his eyes. Jesus, that was weird. He hadn't even been asleep really, more drifting, yet he could almost taste the salty air.

Trina moaned in her sleep.

When he closed his eyes, the scene returned. *The moon broke through long enough for him to make out two people farther along the deck. He strode closer, eyeing the edge of the ship. They shouldn't be this close to the edge. Not much of anything stood between them and the sea. He headed toward them, glancing around. A rocket launcher sat in the center of the deck. A fucking rocket launcher.*

Christ, this wasn't his dream. It was hers.

The guy threw up his hands. "What do you want me to say?"

"I don't know." Her hand fisted, settling on her hip. "Because last time you said it would never happen again and guess what?"

"Look, Trina. Honey. I'm sorry."

Duncan winced. He sounded far more patronizing than sorry.

"Why can't you keep it in your pants?"

"I don't know. Why can't you act halfway normal in bed? Why do you always have to be on top? In control? It's stupid."

"I wish I never met you. I wish none of this ever happened. You don't deserve to breathe the same air as the rest of us." This time, she walked away.

Dumbass followed. "Oh? What? You wish I was dead?"

She spun around long enough to say. "Yeah. I wish you were dead." She was headed straight for Duncan, tears in her eyes.

Christ, would she see him? When she woke, would she know he'd been here in her dream? Not that he knew how to stop this, but he was seeing things he had no right to see.

The guy made a weird noise, half cough, half gurgle.

She turned back just before she would've plowed into Duncan.

Her ex's whole body went rigid, his arms pulled up against his chest, his eyes rolled back.

"Trevor?"

The moon made another appearance, streaming light down between a break in the clouds, bringing Trevor's features into focus. Blood streamed from his eyes. His nose. He took a step back. Another.

"Trevor?" She ran toward him. "Duncan?"

The guy's face changed until Duncan was staring at himself. Blackness crept over his skin—his arms and neck—laying waste to the muscle beneath. Leaving his skin charred, brittle. It crawled over his chin and cheek, his bleeding eyes widening. He took that last step back as the ship rolled.

Duncan's eyes shot open. His hand went to his eyes, searching for blood, for ... *Fuck. You can't bleed like that, dumb shite, only humans can.* He inhaled a slow, deep breath, brushed Trina's hair from his face, and tried to relax.

She moaned, throwing her arm over his chest, snuggling closer.

Daft woman. Here she was trying to get closer, seeking protection from what was going on in her mind while in her dreams, she'd destroyed him.

It seemed more of a fear than a wish. A valid one considering what she could do with her Magic. He should be terrified of her.

What the hell was he doing? The thing about having chosen the wrong woman once, was trusting that he wasn't making the same mistake again. It was always difficult to admit to screwing up. Harder still to admit to being bested by someone smaller. Never would he admit out loud any of what happened with Gertie. Made him look weak. Pathetic. He'd worked through his shit. Went through all the fucking stages of grieving, anger, and whatever. He was over it. Didn't ever think of the past no more.

Except now that he had a dark-skinned beauty pushing every single one of his goddamned buttons ... maybe he'd been lying to himself. He was over Gertie, yeah. Satrina, too. He'd forgiven them both. What ate at him, was if he could trust again. Having Trina's dreams floating through the ether, straight into his head, wasn't helping matters. Her subconscious was torturing them both.

Earlier, when she'd thrown him up against the wall, all he'd been thinking about was what had her so damned scared. Thing was, that no matter how big he was, no matter how well he fought, she could end him without lifting a finger.

The power she had was rather humbling. Had a way of knocking the Alpha in him right on his arse.

What would he do if she ended up like Gertie? Angry. Resentful. Mean as a badger with a sore paw? With Gertie he had always walked away. With Trina—he'd never stand a chance. *He should be terrified of her.*

So why wasn't he? Was he being foolhardy? Reckless? He'd only known her a few days. With all the shite going on around them . . . she wasn't falling apart. Or lashing out. She was working overtime, taking precautions against using her Magic. So she slipped up once and threw him against the wall. As devastated as she was, he didn't think she'd do so again.

Shite. Was he making excuses for her? He took his time, mulling it over. No. That had been a defensive maneuver, not an attack. And what happened during the transformation—he couldn't hold that against her. All vampires turned psycho until that first feeding.

Then again, holding back like she did wore on a body. Eventually, she'd need to rest and her Magic might do as it would while left unchecked. Kind of like how that telepathy of hers reached him whenever she was unconscious. She was wearing herself out.

Maybe that's why he wasn't too worried. She was twisting herself into knots trying to keep everyone else safe.

Lying here thinking about it, the problems she had with her Magic didn't make sense. How could someone so focused on not hurting people, be overwhelmed with Magic that did just that?

She moaned in her sleep.

He closed his eyes. Her dream was still going, as if running on a continuous loop. Time to wake her up. He let out a nice, loud cough in the silence.

TRINA WOKE WITH A START, her arms and legs flailing against a nightmare.

"I've got ya." Duncan's sleep-roughened voice pushed away the last dregs of her nightmare. He curled up behind her, holding her to his chest, steady and warm. He cooed nonsensical words to her while she collected herself. "Ya want to chat?"

"No."

"You worried about tonight? About going to Machon to find the Watchers?"

For a little while, she'd forgotten about that. Augustina told them they should go there, but they hadn't made any specific plans. "No. I'm not going. Lilith will do a better job than I ever could."

Behind her, he propped himself on an elbow. "Why would you say that?"

She glanced back. His eyes glowed silver, picking up the filaments of light from the clock. "Think about it. Why would anyone choose the Darkness over the Light? The Shadow over the Beacon?"

"Ah. It's all about perspective, love."

She curled tighter on her side. There weren't many ways to look at the situation. She was a danger to everyone, including Duncan. With her at the helm of this mission, failure was guaranteed. "I'm the Shadow-self of the Original. Evil. Everything I've tried to do lately has turned to shit, and this mission won't be any different."

He was quiet for a long time. So long, in fact, she had the urge to give him a good hard glare over her shoulder. Shouldn't he at least offer some sort of platitude to make her feel better? They were lying next to each other naked, after all.

"Couple years back, I was standing on a platform in Oxford Circus—"

Goddess, help her. Did the man have a story for every fucking situation?

"—that's a tube station in London—waiting for the last train. It's always crowded on the weekends. People coming home from the pubs or a day in London proper. Seen this one woman, hustling two little ones along toward the edge of the platform. Didn't think much of it, thought she wanted to make sure she got them on ahead of the crush, you know. 'Cept when the Express came barreling past the station, she jumped. With the kids." He shook his head. "She had perfect timing. Didn't even hit the ground. All three of them must've died on impact fast as that train went through."

Why the hell was he telling her this? She rolled onto her back. "That's horrible."

"Was. Bad thing she did, killing those kids." He shrugged. "That's not the point of me story, though. See, all those people, milling about, waiting for the last train . . . . We all saw the same thing, but everyone reacted a bit different. Some went to help—always heroes in those situations."

She arched her brow at his wry tone.

"I'm not taking a piss, just saying is all. There was no way those three survived, so those who went running over—they were either hopelessly optimistic, or morbidly curious. Yeah?"

She tipped her head, conceding his point.

"Others cried or hugged. Some whispered to their companions, shaking their heads. Some prayed. Couple people got sick. Others stared into space, in shock. This one woman, late-twenties, well-dressed, fit—she started screaming. The kind of scream that sets your hair to standing, know what I mean?"

She nodded, though she'd learned that 'know what I mean,' was a rhetorical question.

"Down there in the tunnels with the cement floors and tiled walls, she sounded like an air-raid siren. She'd wail and then pause to catch her breath. The echo faded just as she'd start in again.

"At first, people were sympathetic. They asked her companion if she was all right, if they could do anything, if she knew the victims. But she didn't. And when she wouldn't stop screaming, they got annoyed. People started telling her to shut up. Started asking her companion to shut her up. The companion got red-faced, even tried slapping the woman to get her to stop. Those whispering about the victims, started whispering about the attention-seeking woman."

"Some people handle trauma better than others." She rolled back on her side, away from him. If this was a fucking lecture on how she needed to adjust her behavior he could go take a leap off a tall bridge.

He scoffed. "Bullshit. We all handle trauma the same. Some of us meet the Darkness as babes and some as adults. We all have that screaming moment. We just forget. Maybe because we're ashamed. Maybe because we were too young to remember. Personally, I think she had the right of it."

Damn him, now she was curious where he was going with this. "Why?"

"We'd all witnessed horror that night. All of us. We'd seen a woman kill herself and murder her two young children. It was an atrocity. That woman was the only one there who wasn't a jaded asshole. Bet she lived her whole life up until that point without meeting the Darkness. One of those 'blessed people,' who's never lost someone close or seen evil. All the rest of them, they damn well knew it, too. They knew and they hated her for it. That's why they turned on her."

"That's the point to the story?"

"The point is, love. It's not you, it's them."

She rolled over onto her back. "What?"

"That lady saw death. She understood that two children were killed. That something terrible had happened to make that mother do what she did. She understood that she was going to die, too. Maybe not right then, but eventually. She understood what we all were going to have to face someday and it horrified her. Split her wide open. She's the only one there that got it.

"This is a terrible responsibility that's been handed to you. You understand what failing means. You understand that success might not be much better. And you fear both. You fear whether you're up for the task. You've seen the Darkness, been the Darkness, and have a healthy respect for it. That's why I'm happy you have this burden." He stroked his thumb down her cheek. "You won't underestimate it."

"I might not succeed."

He spread his hand on the curve of her hip and squeezed. "We're dealing with forces greater than ourselves now, love. If you don't succeed, no one was meant to. If you do, it's because it was meant to be."

She sucked in a deep breath as if a great weight had been lifted off her and she could breathe again. He was right. She couldn't change the goddess' will. No one could. If this was the End Times, she couldn't stop it even if she did everything with perfect precision. Which meant that if this wasn't the End Times, even if she fumbled her way through and did everything wrong, in the end, she'd succeed.

She reached up and cupped his face with one palm. He wasn't a handsome man, but he was a dear man. One who was attractive because of who he was, not what he looked like.

At dusk, she'd go and do what the goddess wanted. Find Machon. Find the Watchers and find a way to beat Crowley. At dusk, she'd tell Duncan that this could never happen again. She'd keep him safe from her.

But for now, she needed him. Needed him to know how grateful she was to him. Needed to bond with him again. Her mate.

In silent demand, she lifted her face to his.

His mouth covered hers in a gentle assault chasing away her worries and leaving her burning. He rolled to his back, taking her with him.

There was no foreplay, no urgency. Just a slow, languid joining. A healing endeavor and she'd never experienced anything like it. Every movement was purposeful and deliberate as their bodies strained and melded. They held each other in an unyielding embrace as if they couldn't get close enough and when they reached their climax, its intensity left them both boneless and sated.

She drifted back into the darkness with her mate still buried deep within her.

CHAPTER 23

TRINA WALKED INTO THE BEDROOM fresh from the shower, with a towel wrapped around her and tucked under her arm. Duncan hadn't moved yet. He still lay in bed, sprawled out on his back with his head resting on one forearm. The sheets lay low over his hips. Every inch of his tightly packed abs and broad chest bared for her perusal. She'd kissed every inch of that chest earlier. Had even left a hickey on the rise of his left peck.

Her cheeks heated. *Everything* heated.

Damn it, she didn't want to let him go. She'd much rather climb back into bed with him, feel that thick cock of his—

Her phone started ringing, jerking her out of her fantasy.

Duncan drew in a deep breath, but didn't open his eyes. "You took off your pants at the foot of the bed, love." A slow grin stretched his lips. "Shimmying and shaken', those beautiful breasts a jigglin'."

A full body blush warmed her skin as she walked around the end of the bed, found her clothes and dug her phone out of her jeans. Lilith smiled up at her.

She answered as she left the room. "Lil?"

"James."

Her heart wedged right up in her throat. She closed the bedroom door behind her and began pacing the hallway.

"Where's Lilith? Duncan said she was better."

"She's right here, glaring daggers at me. I—"

Lilith yelled from the background, "He's being an overprotective asshat."

Trina smiled. Nothing could have reassured her more that Lilith was okay. "Ah, she's starting to see things my way, James."

He snorted. "Shut up, Sunshine. I know you like me. Everything okay over there?"

She rolled her eyes. Now that Lilith was safe, he'd go back to trying to protect everyone else. "Yeah. Look, I should probably, um, update you on everything I've found out. I tried to go after Crowley last night, but it didn't go so well." She got as far as telling him about the Nephilim before he interrupted.

"Ah. Why am I not surprised you had something to do with those creatures."

She growled. His teasing was not doing anything good for her new-found intentions to go to Machon. "You know?"

"Everybody knows. It's all over the news."

"Hold on." She ran down the stairs and turned on the television. Sure enough, there was an aerial view of a city from a news chopper—people were running in every direction. There was blood. Fallen bodies disappearing right before her eyes as they transformed. "The Nephilim don't show up on camera."

"No, that's what tipped us off that we were dealing with some kind of daemon. The coven is trying to track them as we speak, but they're jumping all over the place. By the time they follow them to one city, they're gone. My team just arrived. We're going to try to contain the problem with the coven's help. See if we can't hold them down somewhere until sunrise."

Fat chance. "You'll need a different plan. The reason they're gone by the time you get there is because Crowley's transporting them." She ran her hand through her hair. "Augustina suggested we go to Machon and ask the Watchers how to beat Crowley and I think that's a good idea."

"Ah, so you know what he is?"

"Crowley?"

"Yeah, it took me awhile, too, and I used to be a priest. I'll give you a minute."

Why would having been a priest help him figure it out? They were back to riddles again. Back to them not being able to give her infor-mation. Why? It had to be because of the being inside Crowley or the Nephilim. The Nephilim.

"Goddess, help us." It was a Watcher. Nephilim were mentioned in the bible. So were the Watchers. The goddess had caused the Great Deluge—wiping out almost everything in the effort to rid the world of Nephilim. "That's why you didn't tell me outright, you didn't want the other Watch-ers to overhear. Are you wanting to keep the Watcher in Crowley from knowing you know?"

"He already knows."

"You're afraid the others will side with the Watcher possessing Crowley?"

"The thought has crossed my mind. Let us know what you find out. I guess the best we can do is keep the human carnage to a minimum. Be careful, you hear?"

"I will. Hopefully, we'll have some news soon. I'll call later." She hung up. Somehow, they were going to have to get the Watcher out of Crowley and . . . and what? Kill it? Banish it?

She headed back upstairs, running Duncan's advice through her head again. *If you don't succeed, no one was meant to. And if you do, it's because it was meant to be.* It kept her from panicking too much at the idea of eventually fighting a Watcher. *One disaster at a time.* First she needed to talk to Duncan.

The bed creaked and she paused, staring at her bedroom door. *Goddess give me strength.* She entered her room to find him sitting at the edge of the bed, the comforter draped over his lap. Sleepy and bed-rumpled, he winked. "You get to chat with Lilith?"

"Sort of." She rubbed her arm. "Duncan, I . . . ."

"We in a hurry?"

She shook her head.

He patted the mattress beside him.

Now that she stood here, facing him, her confidence wavered. She'd much rather crawl back into bed than have this discussion. Maybe just once more. She bit her lip, swaying closer.

The memory of her nightmare returned. Blood seeping from his eyes and nose as he convulsed. The blackness creeping over his skin. "No." She shook her head to clear it and said it again with more conviction. "No. You and I need to talk."

His lips pursed and he made that sound she hated—like he was sucking air. He grabbed his pants. "Go on, then."

"Last night was—"

"Incredible."

"Yeah. It was." She cleared her throat. He wasn't making this easy. "We've both have a lot going on and—"

"I'm protecting you." He shrugged. "Not much else going on."

"Right." She tucked the towel tighter around her. Why hadn't she waited until she'd gotten dressed? "We can't sleep with each other again."

"Why?"

Her mouth opened, closed, and opened again.

"Don't worry, I ain't gonna keep after you. I've had someone who didn't want me and I want no part of that again." He stood and pulled his pants on, chatting away as if none of this affected him. "And I've had someone who put up with me. Can live without that in me life, I can tell you. But I'm curious."

Now that she knew him, she couldn't imagine ever treating him like that. Who the hell were these women? "You deserve better." She motioned to him. "You're a good—"

He held up his hand. "Now don't go lying. I know what I am and what I ain't. I'm not handsome, so don't go there."

"I was going to say good. You're a good man." She wet her lips. That sounded lame.

He squinted and wrinkled his nose. "That the best you can do?"

"You have a great body."

"Oh?" He waggled his brows. "Hear I'm good in bed, too."

She smiled, ruefully. "Yeah, you are."

"Now, don't go changing your mind on me, love. You had your chance." He held his arms wide. "So why are you willing to give up all of this?"

He wasn't going to let her off the hook. She swallowed. She couldn't tell him about her past, nor the nightmare she'd had. She'd never told anyone, not even Lilith.

"Ah." He bobbed his head. "Think I'm not strong enough? You worried you're going to hurt me?"

How the hell did he do that? He read her so easily. Most people stared right through her, but he *saw* her. *Understood her.* "Of course not." She swallowed past the lump in her throat. He was *everything* she'd ever wanted. And she had to let him go. "We haven't . . . known each other for long, and—"

"We're mated, time doesn't matter."

He *knew*. He knew they were mated. And still he stood there as if this discussion didn't matter, while she was sure she must be bleeding internally.

"What matters is honesty. And I don't think you're being honest with either of us." He sighed and shook his head. "Look, I need a shower. I'll meet you downstairs." He snapped up the rest of his clothes and boots and left, closing the door without a sound.

She'd have rather he slammed it. She sure as hell wanted to slam something. That hadn't gone well at all. There hadn't been any yelling. No angry words. No violence. What had she expected? That he would argue? That he would try to change her mind?

Yet she was devastated. Her stomach knotted and her chest hurt and she wanted to cry but couldn't. She went to her dresser, opened the drawer and pulled out his handkerchief. She'd kept the damned thing. Couldn't even bring herself to wash it, because it wouldn't smell like him anymore. She brought it to her nose and inhaled.

Now, don't go changing your mind on me, love. You had your chance.

No, she couldn't change her mind. As hard as this had been, as much as she hurt right now . . . what would it be like a week from now, a month from now? She couldn't risk his safety. She had to stay strong.

Trina glanced up into the mirror and…It had finally happened. She'd completely disappeared.

I'D RATHER BE DEAD THAN *tied to a nobody like you.*
Duncan closed the bathroom door and leaned against it, rubbing the heel of his hand against his chest. Rule One: Never let true emotions show.

You're ugly. Poor. Rough. I hate you.

He tried to ignore the voice in his head. Funny how after all these years he couldn't remember Gertie's face, but he sure as hell remembered her words.

Your son is going to grow up to be ugly. Rough. Poor. And I hate him, too.

He stripped down and climbed into the shower. Yanked the navy-blue curtain closed.

With a few jerks of his hand he turned the water on, tensing under the icy spray.

One indiscretion shouldn't cost a woman everything. I never should have laid with you. Let you put those animal paws on me. It will never happen again.

"Shut up." He closed his eyes and tried to push the memories away. Trina was nothing like Gertie. She was scared, not mean-hearted. They were different, damn it.

We can't sleep with each other again.

Okay, maybe there were some similarities. Enough to trigger all the baggage he thought he'd stowed in the deepest part of his consciousness.

But they were different, too.

Gertie may have been his wife, but Trina was his mate. And mated dae-mons were a beautiful sight to see. He needed to give Trina time. A little space. She'd figure things out. She'd accept him. "Don't force things. Let it happen."

He meant what he said, he wouldn't chase after her. She'd need to fig-ure all this out on her own. She'd need to learn to trust him. To realize she *needed* him, damn it. Because otherwise . . . .

He refused to be someone's placeholder, or someone's regret. Not ever again.

Nor could he walk away. Not if he wanted to continue to live in a way that would honor his son's memory. So where did that leave him?

The water heated. He pressed his palms to the wall and hung his head so the water trailed like a curtain over his face.

If she *was* protecting him, there was hope. She must care for him a bit. Still, it meant that she had some of the same ideas about him that Gertie had had.

You're weak. You're going to ruin us. You can't even keep food on the table.

At least he didn't have to worry about the last one. He had a big, beau-tiful home in the heart of London. A town home he'd decked out and made as safe as possible.

So how did he prove to her he could take care of himself? Show her that she wouldn't hurt him? She wouldn't. She spent too much time worrying about it.

It was that Magic of hers.

The witch. He straightened and opened his eyes. Something about the way Rowena had thought made his skin crawl, but she'd been smart, too. And she hadn't liked Trina at all. Maybe he'd go check out her place . . . see if he couldn't find a clue as to what was wrong with Trina's Magic.

CHAPTER 24

TRINA PACKED A BACKPACK WITH enough to get her through a few days. She had no idea how long they'd be in Machon, but hoped it wouldn't be more than a day or two. She dropped her bag next to Duncan's by the stairs and went to the living room. When they petitioned the Watchers, she'd need an offering, a token of respect. While not the greatest gift, she took the polished stones from Gaia's offering bowl and stuck them in her pocket. At least she would have something.

Now she just needed to wait for Duncan. She went into the kitchen, poured herself a glass of milk and had it halfway to her lips before she remembered she couldn't drink it. She'd always liked the scent of milk, but today . . . while fresh, the scent wasn't appetizing. Still, the glass was cold in her hand, soothing, familiar, so she took it with her to the living room. Sat and rested her arm on the cushion with the glass hanging from her fingers like she'd have done if she were still human.

Except she couldn't drink it.

That wasn't the only change she'd experienced this evening. Any doubts she had about Duncan being her mate had been put to rest as soon as he'd left. He hadn't gone far, no farther than the edge of town by the feel of it. But that was the problem, she *felt* him. As if a thread linked them and pulled taut with each mile he drove.

Now what? They were truly mated. They would always sense each other's presence even when apart. *Especially* when apart.

She set the glass down. The tenseness started to lessen—he was coming back. What did she do when he got here? Would he want to talk about what happened? That would be bad. If he put up the slightest resistance to her plan, she'd crumble. As difficult as it had been to tell him no the first time . . . she didn't know if she was strong enough to have that conversation again.

She stood and started pacing. If she stayed with him, eventually they'd fight. She'd lose her temper and that would put him at risk. But how could she walk away when she felt his presence growing thinner with each mile that separated them?

A knock on the door drew her out of her thoughts. Her hand went to the small of her back as she double-checked that she had her sidearm. She approached the door, put her ear to the wood and listened. Julius Crowley couldn't even step onto the property since Lilith had banished him. The Nephilim wouldn't bother knocking. Nor would Lilith or James.

It had to be one of the women from the coven.

She opened the door and stepped back.

A boy stood on the stoop. Maybe twelve or fourteen, she'd never been good at guessing children's ages. And this one—she had no idea if he was small for his age, or if he looked older than he was. He still had that awkward appearance of adolescence, with a mop of sand-colored blond hair, too-big teeth and bright blue eyes, his body still thin and wiry, though his shoulders were wider than his waist . . . so maybe small for his age.

He used his foot to push the door farther open. He didn't make any move to enter, nor did he call out. He looked around from where he stood, keeping one hand behind him, the other on the strap of his backpack. His gaze stopped at the base of the stairs where she and Duncan had left their bags.

A thief? *Shit.* Part of her wanted to reach over and close the door—he had the wrong house. On the other hand, knowing Nephilim could show up at any time . . . she couldn't leave him roaming around alone. "Can I help you?"

Usually, she scared the crap out of people when she did that, but this kid was more grounded than the majority of the population. His only show of surprise was a slight widening of those gorgeous eyes. He glanced at his watch, as if unbothered by her sudden appearance. "I'm looking for my, uh . . . dad. Duncan. You seen him?"

Dad? The kid didn't look anything like Duncan, but he had mentioned a charge named Harry. Still, while the speech pattern was similar to Duncan's he sounded more American than British. "What's your name?"

"Harrison. Calls me Harry, though. Or pup, depending on his mood." The kid adjusted the backpack slung over his scrawny shoulder. "He gonna be back soon?"

"Yeah." She shook her head. "How'd you know he's not here?"

"Got my ways." A wide smile spread across his face. "You the one the Watchers sent him here to protect?" He waggled his brows. "Starting to see why he's been taking his time, you're kinda cute. What's your name?"

Great, he must be taking lessons from Duncan. "Trina Lopez."

"Nice to meet you, Lopez." He shot her a toothy grin and walked past her.

"I'm Harrison Cayce." No, he didn't walk, he swaggered inside, all five feet four inches, ninety-some-odd pounds of him, flipping his hair from his eyes. He didn't move like a kid. "Is Duncan expecting you?"

"No." He smiled. "He's gonna be pissed as hell at the both of us, that's for sure."

Her hand went to the small of her back. He hadn't moved his hand from the small of his. "Oh? Why's that?"

"Me, because I didn't stay put. I left his house and traveled here by myself." He tipped his head to the side. "You, because you opened the door."

Harry's posture remained relaxed, but she watched for any tensing of his muscles, any sign that he might attack. "What happens when he gets angry?"

He let out a long, low whistle. "Life sucks when the old man is unhappy."

She swallowed. Great. Duncan wasn't exactly pleased with her. Though so far he only seemed to have two settings, unaffected and scorching passion. "How so?"

His brow crept up so high on his forehead, it disappeared beneath his bangs. "Seriously? You haven't pissed him off yet?"

"Tell me already."

His lips quirked and he walked past her into the living room. Sure enough, he had a knife tucked into his belt loop at his back. He sat in the armchair, crossing an ankle over his knee. "He's got this sick and twisted . . . ."

"What?"

"Need to tell stories." His eyes flashed, and the quirk of his lips spread into a wide smile.

"Ha. Ha."

"I'm serious. He tells these overblown, long-winded stories. You know, the kind with some sort of moral at the end . . . except the son of a bitch doesn't spell it out for you, he makes you think about it."

She folded her arms over her chest and repressed a smile. Yeah. This kid knew her mate.

"Usually, they're about him. Something he did or saw or heard . . . and he's good at it, you know? So you get sucked in. You find yourself going back and *thinking* about shit." He shook his head. "It's annoying as fuck."

It was disturbing to see such a young kid cuss the way he did. "Somehow, I have the feeling the two of you are quite similar."

His eyes widened, narrowed. "You taking a piss?"

"What does that even mean?"

"A Mickey? Poking fun?"

"No, I—"

"What the hell are you doing here?"

Duncan stood in the entryway, his big hands fisted at his sides. His hard gaze shifted between Harry and her. "And you? You let a vampire you don't know waltz into your house?"

Yeah, he was pissed. As thick as his accent usually was, it was even more pronounced now.

Harry grinned. "Told you."

Wait. Her gaze widened on Harry. "You're a vampire?"

He grinned.

"Bullshit. You walked in without an invitat—"

"Is there a human living here?" Harry's brows lifted. "'Cause I don't see any."

Trina sobered. Shit. She was a vampire now. Both she and Lilith were, so the house wasn't protected. And it hadn't even occurred to her that he might be a vampire. She didn't think they were allowed to transform children. "How old are you?"

"Twenty-one. Sixteen when I was transformed."

Sixteen? She'd been thinking closer to fourteen. Her expression must've reflected her disbelief because he shrugged. "I was a late bloomer."

He was stuck in that adolescent body. Vampires didn't age. His hair would grow along with his mind and emotions, but Harry's body never would. Aging internally while being stranded in the physical body of a youth must be its own special brand of hell. Harry grew restless in his chair. Goddess preserve, who did this to him?

Duncan strode farther into the room. "You bloody little fool, do you know what a risk it was coming here?"

Could Duncan have transformed the boy?

He glanced at Trina, did a double-take, and frowned. "Don't insult me. I'm not the one who did that." He motioned to Harry. "I'm a shifter. He's a splitter. We'd have the same talent if I'd done it."

Shifter? Did that make her a shifter, too? What the hell was a shifter?

Harry stood. He jerked his chin up. "All right?"

"It's all Pete Tong, pup. You shouldn't have come."

Who the hell was Pete Tong? Another vampire?

Duncan scowled. "We got Barney Rubble enough without me dustbin lid going off on the frog and toad with no dicky bird, yeah? Anyone could've seen ya balling around, ya fucking berk."

It was some kind of code. They were keeping secrets from her, damn it.

Harry didn't back down. Despite being shorter than her and thinner by far, he took a step closer to Duncan, puffing his chest out. "Ya should've thought about that, afore ya left me on me Jack Jones. Your dead loss came sneaking up the table and chairs like a fucking tea leaf, mate. Him 'an his china plates, they went all kinds of Guy Fawkes on the place."

Duncan jerked back as though he'd been punched.

Guy Fawkes—didn't he try to blow up Parliament? The look of absolute shock on Duncan's face had her reaching for him.

"Everything?"

"I, uh . . . ." Harry patted his coat, dug into the pocket and pulled out a small wooden box. "Nabbed this on the way out."

He grabbed the boy and pulled him into a bear hug. "You're barking, you little fool."

Harry squirmed out of the embrace and thrust the box at Duncan. "Take it. You're lucky I happened to be watching the security tellys and saw what they were doing."

"Jesus, pup. I'm sorry as hell I wasn't there. You all right?"

Instead of answering, Harry tipped his head toward her. "So while I dodged ash, you're over here wetting your Hampton in treacle."

Duncan's expression darkened. "Belt up. It's not like that."

She poked Harry in the shoulder. "I don't know what you said, but I don't think I like it."

He ignored her and stared at Duncan. "What's it like, then?"

"Apologize to the lady first."

She stared at Duncan. Why would he stick up for her after what happened this morning?

Harry's chin went up a notch, his lips puckering for a moment before he kissed his teeth. "Ma'am, I'm sorry if I offended. I'm furious with big D here, but I had no right to allow that animosity to extend to you." He sounded like an American kid again.

"Yeah, well, whatever language you two were talking in, don't do it again. If you want privacy . . . leave."

Harry rolled his eyes. "One last thing, then English the whole way." He turned to Duncan. "You're headed for buckets and pails. And that's if you're lucky." Harry snorted. "You're gonna get yourself dusted breaking your damned rules."

"What's he talking about?" Her gaze bounced between the two of them. They didn't take their eyes off each other. "Tell me."

Duncan gave a minute shake of his head.

Harry opened his mouth.

"Don't." He pointed at Harry. "Don't go rabbiting on about things that don't concern her."

Now she had to know. "Tell me."

"The Council issued a kill order on D." Harry jerked his chin toward Duncan.

The room spun. "What?" She'd been so focused on protecting him from herself, she'd forgotten about the Council.

Duncan ushered her to a seat and pushed her into it. "Look what you did, pup."

She bounced right back up. "Why didn't you say something?" She'd completely forgotten about why he'd initially come. Hadn't even thought of what repercussions he'd face for failing to do his duty.

"He had three nights." Harry sat in the armchair and this time George joined him, curling up on the boy's lap like they'd known each other for years.

Duncan snorted. "Been two."

"Jesus, D, learn to fucking count."

"Been here two nights."

"And traveling for most of one. Two plus one equals—"

"Fuck off, 'arry. No one counts travel time."

"Harry. With a fucking H, D. Buy a consonant once in a while, won't you? And the Council does count travel time, you bloody—"

Trina held up her arms for silence. "Enough." She took a deep breath and met Duncan's gaze. "I'm so sorry. If you need to go home to straighten anything out—"

Harry snorted. "He doesn't have one anymore."

She stared. "What?"

"That's what I told him. Leo burned his house to the ground. I'd have been dust, too, if the old man here wasn't so freaking paranoid."

CHAPTER 25

DUNCAN SAT. HE'D BEEN TOLD once that everything came up roses once a daemon found their life mate. What a load of rubbish. If anything, everything was in a tight downward spiral.

He'd found out fuck-all at Rowena's place. He'd hoped she'd left something behind that would prove that damn necklace Trina wore warped her Magic. Thought he'd just waltz over there and solve their problems and Trina would fall back into his arms.

There wasn't going to be an easy fix.

He squeezed the box Harry brought him in his hands, hoping to stop them from trembling. He'd lived in that townhome most his life, now. Collected a massive library of books and art. Everything him and the lad owned was gone.

At least they each had a rucksack with a few changes of clothes. But hell, now what did he have to offer Trina? Not much.

He turned the box over and ran his thumb over the words carved into the bottom—*Never walk away.*

"So what are we doing?" Harry cuddled George to his chest and for the first time, the beast purred. "Saw the bags by the stairs. We headed out?"

His gaze didn't lift from the box. He lifted the lid and touched the scrap of purple fabric inside. How had Harry known how important this was? He didn't remember taking it out around the lad. "Gotta talk to the Watchers."

"So talk."

Trina cleared her throat. "The problem is, I interfere with their vision. If we want to talk to them, we have to go see them."

Harry laughed. "Ri-ight. Then have D go somewhere else and chat with them."

"We can't risk all the Watchers hearing us. They're not all on our side." Trina turned to Duncan. "I think I figured out where to go."

Duncan lifted his brow.

"Remember in Rowena's Grimoire? All those pages she had about the Thirteen Steps to Hell?"

"You said it was a legend."

"But you said yourself there's a kernel of truth in every tall tale. She was a sick woman, but she was smart. She wouldn't have spent so much time researching the steps if she didn't think them important."

Harry glanced back and forth between them. "You're serious about this?"

He sat back against the cushions and filled Harry in on what they were up against.

"So you're going to open the gates to Machon? Let every daemon on that side have access to all the humans on this side? It's going to be a fucking massacre."

The lad had reason to worry. He still had a human family. His parents were alive and well and would be affected with whatever decision they made. Everyone would. "They'll be okay." He'd made sure of it. The Cayce family knew if they were ever in trouble to speak his name out loud. Harry didn't know that, though. The lad had never been open to talking about his parents nor had he ever been willing to so much as write them a letter.

"You can't guarantee that. You don't know for sure."

"What I know is that if we don't figure this out, what happens to the humans on this side of the portal is the end game." Duncan threw his hands up. "So choose. Either daemons have access to humans, or all humans die."

Harry shifted his gaze to Trina. "See what I mean? At least it wasn't a big long-ass story, but he put the question to me, knowing damn well there isn't any choice to be made."

"Fuck me." He stood and walked out of the room. He didn't have patience for this. Didn't need another opinion clouding the options when he and Trina were already at odds. How the hell was he supposed to get the woman to give him a chance when Harry would be making his life difficult at every turn?

"Hey, D."

"What!"

The lad held up a glass of milk.

Trina stared at it with wide eyes.

Walking closer, the smell hit him before he could make out the chunks floating on the surface. "It's off."

"I just poured that. Hasn't been out more than half an hour."

He'd never heard of such a thing. How could milk go off like that? The house wasn't warm, in fact there was a bit of a chill . . . His gaze shifted to the door. To the windows. "Grab your bags and run."

The two of them stared, unmoving.

"That." He pointed to the milk. "Can't be good. Something's coming for us and this house isn't protected anymore."

That lit a fire under their arses.

Duncan grabbed his rucksack and slung it over his shoulder. He headed for the door.

"Wait!" Trina's shout stopped him cold. "Spell travel."

The faint sound of growling came through the door. The Nephilim. They were here. He backed away from the door. "Yeah, okay." He turned and grabbed hold of her hand.

Harry slipped past and ran back to the living room.

"Get your arse back here, pup!"

The Nephilim were getting louder. Closer. Outside, the porch groaned. Something snarled.

Harry returned with his scrawny arms full of sleepy feline.

Christ, that was the last thing they needed. "Leave the beast here."

Claws scraped against the door.

"No. We aren't leaving anyone behind who might get hurt and that includes the cat."

Trina grabbed hold of both of them. "It's fine." She closed her eyes and started the spell.

Somewhere in the house a window shattered.

They started to fade. Their bodies separating into the tiny particles.

The door flung open. Duncan turned to fight. Trina's grip tightened. The door and the creatures breaching the house disappeared in a blink.

They were outside. The night was cool and damp. Clouds obscured the light from the moon. A row of tombstones studded the overgrown grass to their right and next to them was a large square of cement.

"Sorry about that." Trina winced. "I've never tried to spell travel with a group before. It'll be quicker next time."

Duncan squeezed her hand. "You did fine."

She gave him a small smile and glanced around. "This is it. Maltby

Cemetery." Trina pulled her hand away from his and Harry's and walked closer to the cement pad.

He nodded. "How far are we from Haven House?"

"Maybe twenty miles. We're in Monroe."

The cemetery was quiet but for some light traffic on a nearby road. "Let's be quick. Don't know how long until they find us again."

"Crowley must have sent them to the house." Trina shook her head. "But he couldn't have known we were there, he can't see me."

"Don't know." But he'd be damned if they took any more risks like that. "We stay on the move from here out."

"Your phone, D." Harry shifted George in his arms. "Shut off your phone. That's how I found you. I did a reverse GPS location search. It's Council-issued."

"Shit. And Crowley's tight with the Council." He dug out his phone, powered it off and stuffed it into his pocket. "If they're working together, we'll have to keep watch for Sentries, too."

Trina stepped to the side, put a hand on his arm to angle him away from Harry and whispered. "You don't have to stay with me. I understand if—"

She was gutting him. Bit by bit without mercy. "Look, yeah. I made a promise to"—*me son*—"someone once that I would never walk away from a problem. I intend to do the job the Watchers assigned me. I'll keep you safe and I'll get you back home."

She didn't even look at him.

"All right. It's your show. Let's get to it."

KEEP IT TOGETHER. KEEP MOVING forward. She fisted her hands, closed her eyes and visualized the cement, the billions of tiny particles splitting apart, floating, and changing into the tiny particles that made up the air around them. She couldn't make a particle disappear completely, but at the atomic level, the same stuff made up everything. Neurons. Protons.

Harry whistled.

She opened her eyes and looked straight down thirteen steps that led nowhere. Darkness cloaked the bottom, the moonlight too faint to reach the depth.

"That's it?" Duncan started for the steps.

"Don't." She stopped him. "Let me." The vague shape of something shifted in the shadows.

He blocked her path. "You're staying with me."

For a second she thought he didn't intend to let her put an end to them. And for the first time, she had to acknowledge that that's what she'd wanted all along. For him to demand her attention. For him—for someone—to fight for her. To want *her*. Not because it was easy, but because they cared.

"Just because you don't want me, doesn't me I'm not going to do my job. I'm here to protect you, not stand by while you do the dangerous stuff."

She rubbed her hand over her chest, as if she could sooth the hallow ache that had settled deep under her ribs. He might be hiding it well—focusing on business instead of the personal mess she'd created this afternoon, but she'd hurt him. All she wanted to do was hold him close and soothe the rejection she'd dished out. But she had to let him go. She had to keep him safe. Better he be hurt than ash.

"Stay behind me." She didn't wait for a response, but walked around him and settled her gaze at the bottom of the steps. She didn't trust whatever was down there. She slid her foot onto the first step, the one level with the muddy earth. The sole of her shoe scraped across the uneven surface, sending a shiver up her spine.

Duncan stepped up behind her, so close his hip brushed against her bum. His breath touched the cradle of her neck as he leaned down and took hold of her hand. He lifted it, resting the heel of his hand on her shoulder, entwining his fingers with hers. "Rowena had notes about people disappearing on these steps. Where you go, I go."

With effort, she resisted the urge to lean back into him. "You with us, Harry?"

"Yep."

She lowered her foot. The Earth held its breath on the second step. The wind stopped. The faint sound of traffic, the rattling leaves—everything went silent.

The legends made sense now. Something was different about this place, unsettling.

On the third step, everything tilted and blurred. For a few seconds she thought she was falling. Her free hand flew out to her side of its own accord as instinct took over and her body tried to fight the sense of vertigo.

Duncan didn't let her go, his fingers tightened around hers. Steadying.

Grounding. She breathed through dizziness. Anchored her energy to the Earth and the world righted itself.

She went down another step. The scent of rotten eggs stuffed into a decomposing corpse rolled over her. Sulfur. Decay. She could taste the oily scent. Her stomach roiled. Churned.

"Shite." Duncan jostled her as he caught his balance.

"You okay, D?"

"Yeah."

She took her hand from the wall and covered her mouth and nose with her shirt.

Down. Her skin crawled. Her hair stood on end. Doubt crowded her determination. They shouldn't be here. This place wasn't meant for the living. Not even the living dead. She took a deep breath through her mouth, through her shirt, and wiped her eyes. They'd started to water.

Another step. Six so far. They weren't even halfway. Her mind filled with dark things. Images. Flashes of faces. Her mother staring as blood leaked from her eyes and nose. She blinked. Swept her hand out in front of her as if she could swat the image away like a fly.

"You sure we're in the right place?"

She turned all the way around. "I don't—" Her hair lifted, like when someone tried to sneak up and brushed her aura. She whipped around. She'd expected something awful to be there, below her on the stairs, but . . . nothing. She scanned the darkness at the bottom and again, the shadows moved. "I don't know."

He let go of her hand and his arm snaked around her shoulder. "No. It's this place. It's making us doubt. We came here for a reason and we're going to the bottom."

His arm was heavy around her shoulders. She'd never allowed anyone to do that to her, but not only did she allow him, she held onto his wrist, anchoring him there. "You okay, Harry?"

"I'm thinking I want this over and done, Lopez. Get us to the bottom already."

Down.

The world spun around her on the seventh step. Though not the stone and earth walls. Not the stairs. Nor the blackness pooling at the bottom.

The car spun, streetlights and headlights flashed in her vision. Her mother screamed. Tires squealed. Glass shattered.

Trina recoiled from the memory.

"I've got you." Duncan's words whispered in her ear.

What the hell?

Duncan sat next to her, the world outside the car tilting as the car rolled over and over until it hit something with enough force that she lost consciousness.

She must have psychically dragged him into her vision. He was right there with her in the darkness with her mom. She'd never let anyone into her mind. Never even talked about this and now he *knew.*

"Work through it." His voice filled her ears, drowning out the high-pitched whine of sirens. "Go down again. Get past it." But with every word, his voice faded, coming from farther away. "Get it over with."

Sliding her foot forward, she found the edge, but she couldn't force her foot down.

"Wake up, Satrina." Her mother. No one else used her full name. *"Satrina, wake up for Mommy."*

She opened her eyes, but the darkness was so complete she couldn't see anything. Something heavy pinned her down, crushing her into her seat and pressing the seatbelt buckle against her back. She smelled gas. Burnt rubber. "Can't breathe, Mommy. Help me."

"I know, baby."

Panic started to well up. Why couldn't she see? "Where are we?"

"We're still in the car. You remember the accident?"

Trina closed her eyes, but the vision remained. She understood now why people lost their minds on the thirteen steps. "It's not real. It's not real." Her hand went to her hip, where it felt like a real seatbelt dug into her.

The buckle pressing into her hurt. "Are you okay? Am I okay? Something heavy is on me. Get it off." The something heavy took a deep breath as a sob wracked through her mom.

"I can't. I can't move. But the firemen are here and they're going to cut us out of the car. I need you to listen, baby."

"I can't breathe, Mommy."

Goddess help her she didn't know if she could do this. She'd thought she'd lost these memories long ago. She'd never been able to remember what happened. Not like this.

"Yes. You can. You are breathing. I know you're uncomfortable, but you have to listen."

In the darkness, Duncan said, "I'm right here. I've got you."

She damn well knew she had a tight grip on Duncan. Knew he stood at her back, but she couldn't feel him anymore. Nor the steps beneath her shoes. She tried to force her foot down another step and failed. She couldn't move. The weight had her pinned down.

Mommy cried. She couldn't see her or what was wrong. She stilled. "You're hurt."

"Baby, I love you so much. You're my dark little angel."

"Mommy . . .?"

"And you're going to do great things. You have purpose, Satrina. Just like your namesake. 'When the Original is no longer cursed, she'll come to thee as three. All as humans first, then as daemons are set free: the Beacon burning bright, the Shadow hidden from sight, the blighted, damned Knight.' Remember, Satrina."

Mommy never wanted to talk about her name. About the ancient one she'd named her for. "I'm scared."

"Me, too, baby. Listen to me. When the firemen open up the car, Mommy is going to go away."

"No."

"I have to. But I'm going to keep you safe. They're going to leave us here for a while, Satrina."

"How can you go away if we're gonna be stuck here?"

"My body will still be here. The weight . . . they think the weight will keep you safe, baby. But there's too much pressure . . . when they open the car . . . ." Her voice cracked. She sniffed. "The coven is your family now. Do good by them."

"Duchess!" Duncan's sharp tone made her look to her side. It was too dark to see him.

"Ma'am?" A deep male voice, muffled but full of authority. "We're ready."

"Love you, baby."

"Mommy, no! I'm sorry. Don't go away!"

Mommy's voice wobbled. "Go ahead."

Metal screeched and screamed. Pain spiked through her skull and made her sinus' feel too big in her head. The weight, which had been crushing her before, became even heavier.

"I'm picking you up, Duchess. Don't freak out on me. I'm gonna walk us down the rest of the steps."

Light flooded over them, so much brighter than any of the lights she'd remembered from before. Great big square lights lit everything up bright as day. She couldn't see much. No more than a sliver between the seat cushion and the weight stifling her. She caught a glimpse of yellow and gray firefighter pants. He knelt down and his face came into view. "You and me, we're going to wait here a while."

"Where's my mommy?"

"She's keeping you safe, baby girl."

Behind him, she caught a glimpse of another man—one who shouldn't have been there—pacing. Duncan raked his hands over his head in a desperate gesture. With each step, his body shrank, thinned to adolescence until he didn't look much older than Harry.

A voice she didn't recognize called out to him. "Duncan?"

She strained to see around the firefighter. To see who called Duncan.

"Mum?" He walked out of sight.

The firefighter touched her. He smiled. "What's your name?"

"Satrina." She shifted one of her arms, got it loose and started prodding the heaviness crushing her. Part of it was the driver's seat. Part of it was soft and warm and smelled like Mommy.

That couldn't be right. The weight squishing into her couldn't be her.

"Well, Satrina, we're going to move the weight off you a little at a time. We've got to give your body time to adjust." He motioned to someone and a moment later he had a clean white cloth and a bottle of liquid. "I'm going to clean you up a little bit. And my buddies here, they're going to pull the weight up just a little. I need you to be patient for me and I need you to keep looking toward me." The weight lessened to how it had been before they'd pried the car open. Hair brushed over her cheek. Mommy's hair.

She kept her eyes focused on the fireman but she felt Mommy's gaze on her. She just knew she stared at her. She wanted to look because Mommy always had a smile and something to tease her about, but she didn't want to look because she might have the sad face on. Or the mad face. Or maybe she wouldn't be there at all.

She'd been mad at Mommy. Said things to her she shouldn't have said and when Mommy turned to give her a swat . . .

Harry walked right in the middle of the scene, a fat, orange tabby-cat spilling over in his arms. "Hey!" He grabbed Duncan and stalked toward Trina. "Twenty minutes we've been standing on these damn steps. What the hell is going on?" Duncan didn't resist, but he kept looking back, his attention staying with something she couldn't see.

"Hey!" Harry shook him. "It's this place. It's got you stuck." He pointed to her. "Help me get her out of there."

Duncan's eyes widened as they met hers. He looked down at himself. Started to look back and shook his head. "You're not supposed to be here."

"Fuck's sake." Harry set the cat down, put both hands to Duncan's back and shoved.

Duncan disappeared.

"You, too, Lopez." Harry motioned to her. "Let's go. This isn't good for you."

He was right. She didn't want to be here. She didn't want to relive this. Though it was nice to have had her mother back for a moment. Her hand twisted in Mommy's blouse. The vision might restart. She might have enough control the next time to ask all the questions she'd longed to ask her over the years. She might not get lost next time through. "Maybe a little longer."

"No."

Harry put his foot on the remnants of the car, grabbed her arm and pulled her out from under her mother's body. *She glanced back as she stood and saw Mommy. The red where the whites of her eyes should've been. The bloody tears. The sadness and fear in her final expression. Her mother blinked and turned her head. "There's no turning back now, my dark angel. No half-measures."*

Harry gave her a hard shove.

Duncan grabbed hold of her before she stumbled down any more steps.

She ran her fingers under her eyes and wiped away the tears. Goddess help her she could still feel the weight of her mother's body. A shiver wracked through her. "I know this is shitty of me to ask, but I can still feel—"

He pulled her into his arms and rubbed his hands over her back. "I know. Me, too."

Goddess help her, she'd never felt safer than when surrounded by this big man. "Who called you? I couldn't see where you went." She wasn't even sure if it had been a man or a woman.

"That's for the best." He pulled her away a bit and met her gaze. Whatever he'd seen in the vision had shaken him. "Ready?"

No. She'd much rather stay in his arms a while longer. "Yeah." She turned to find Harry and George staring at them both.

"This is the thanks I get for dragging the two of you out of there?"

In a monotone, she said, "Yeah, Harry. Thanks."

Duncan's, "Good going, pup," wasn't much more enthusiastic.

He rolled his eyes. "Look, there's like six more steps to go. What say we jump the remainder? I'm not keen on watching the two of you disappear on me again."

Trina nodded at the same time Duncan said, "All right."

They stood three astride on the step. The darkness swirled and pulsed at the bottom.

"One."

Both Harry and Duncan entwined their fingers with hers.

"Two."
George stared down into the darkness and hissed.
"Three."

CHAPTER 26

THEY LANDED HARD. PAIN SHOT up her ankles and she stumbled forward, catching herself before she ran into a metal chair that was bolted down to the cement slab at the bottom. "Don't turn around. Rowena's notes said people have gone mad seeing themselves burn in hell's flames." Distant voices screamed behind them. The heat of fire warmed her back. Eventually, they'd have to turn around, but she wasn't ready yet.

Down here, the darkness was a physical entity, swirling and morphing. "Something's behind us."

She eyed Duncan from the corner of her eye. The longer she stood there, the more she felt it—something silent and menacing pacing behind them, lifting the hairs at her nape. "Don't turn around."

Before them, the darkness solidified into a hooded figure. When the figure looked up, her breath caught.

It was her. Sort of. The hooded woman had the same face, though a little thinner, the same hair, though hers was curly. The other woman was a tad older, an inch or two taller, and she wore old-fashioned clothes. A past-life version of her.

Duncan took a step closer, his brow creased. "Satrina?"

Trina's attention whipped to Duncan. *He'd known her before?*

She glanced between the hooded woman and Duncan. He tried to touch her cheek and his hand went right through her. Satrina didn't even acknowledge him with a glance.

Souls are drawn to those they've known before. Part of her wanted to turn around, leave, and pretend she didn't just see the wistful longing on her mate's face.

Satrina's focus stayed with Trina. "I knew you'd come."

Trina blurted out her most pressing question. "What's behind us?" Something was there. Pacing. Watching.

Satrina ignored the question. "The year is fifteen eighty-nine. Katherine, my high-priestess, asked me"—she nodded to Trina—"us, to create a spell that will close and protect the gates of Machon should anything happen to the coven. Something difficult that will keep those unworthy from reaching the gate."

"I almost didn't make it."

"We are leaving everything—our children, our lovers and our homes—to go after Katherine's mate tonight. She won't tell us why; she can't risk the wrong people overhearing, but she's warned us we may not come back. Something awful has happened."

Duncan glanced at her. "Ask her what she knew of Crowley."

"I don't think she can hear you, D." Harry tipped his head to the side. "She's like those animatronics at Disneyland, pre-programmed with a message but in ghost form."

"He's right." Trina nodded toward Satrina. "She's not answering my questions. She pauses when we talk, but once we're quiet, she continues on as if she weren't interrupted. Watch."

They all quieted and Satrina continued. "Recently, the Guardians presented Katherine's mate to the coven as a way to peacefully take back the Council from Leopold and his supporters. Katherine knows Mr. Crowley far better than I, but from what I've seen of him, I do think he can help daemon kind."

Okay, now they were getting somewhere. "They must've planned to have Crowley mesmerize Leopold into stepping down from the Council. Something went wrong—"

"No doubt Leopold figured out the plan," Duncan said. "And turned Crowley to his side."

"—and Katherine had Satrina close the gates of Machon before going after Crowley."

"That must have been the Clearances." Harry shifted George to his other arm, but the cat didn't take his dilated eyes off whatever was stalking behind them.

The old coven had been eradicated during the Clearances. Rowena had thought the vampires on the Council were responsible and had wanted to decimate the vampire population in retaliation.

Satrina continued. "Most daemons support our coven. They know when the Original comes, she'd be born a witch. They revere us. If we do not survive tonight, the gates will close to protect our allies."

"Jesus." Duncan met her gaze. "That must be the deal Augustina told us about. She said Leo and Crowley made a deal—Leo upheld his part, but Crowley hasn't yet. How much do you want to bet Leopold wanted Crowley to dust everyone who opposed him? That's why the Clearances happened. The coven found out and closed the gates to stop him. The daemons wouldn't have had a chance against Crowley—not the way he is now."

Possessed by a Watcher? No, not even daemon kind stood a chance against a Watcher. "The question is, how and when did the Watcher possess Crowley?"

Duncan shrugged.

"Maybe she'll tell us." They waited.

"Daemon kind will be safe until the Original comes—When the Original comes, she'll come to thee as three. The beacon burning bright, the shadow hidden from sight, the blighted damned knight. Any of the three may open the portals, but once open, they're open to all daemons."

That didn't sound too bad.

"A word of caution, though. The daemons on the other side may not be pleased to see you; it takes strong Magic to create a spell that will survive the witch."

But *that* did. "Shit."

Duncan glanced at her. "What's wrong? What does she mean?"

"All Magic requires a sacrifice. Small spells require an expenditure of energy and if a witch over-reaches, she damages herself."

"Like when the veins in your hands turned black?"

She nodded. "Big spells, like what she did, require a larger expenditure—a sacrifice." She didn't want to know what Satrina had done to seal the portals. Whatever the sacrifice, it must've been big.

After they remained silent a few seconds, Satrina continued. "The leaders of the tribes know what will happen if my spell activates. They understand the necessity of closing the portal to protect everyone in Machon. They agreed to the conditions of the spell to preserve their people. It's the people you may need to watch out for. Those whose loved ones were part of the sacrifice may harbor some resentment."

What was the sacrifice?

"When my spell activated, all the young in Machon died."

Her gaze tripped up to Duncan's. "That's one hell of a sacrifice."

He cursed. "She didn't leave us much to work with, did she?"

"Wait." Harry's face paled. "If a sacrifice was required to close the portal, won't one be needed to open it?"

Trina closed her eyes. "Maybe." It depended on how Satrina had cast the spell. "Let's hear what else she has to say."

"Upon the Original's return, Magic will return to Machon. The young will return to Machon. Many will love you for that alone. However, once you walk through the portal, you can't come back. As part of the agreement made with the tribes, you will belong to the daemons. To the Darkness."

So, no sacrifice, but a deal made with daemon kind. She pressed her hand to her belly. She had to stay forever? She couldn't leave, *ever*?

"Since you are only a part of one soul, only *one of you* must always be in Machon. When you're ready to proceed, stand before me and I will give you the key."

Ready to proceed? Either she or Lilith or the Knight—whoever that was—had to remain in Machon at all times. She couldn't make that decision for Lilith. If she walked through the portal, she had to do so expecting she'd never leave. "I don't even know what's on the other side. I can't make a decision like—" She snapped her fingers.

What the hell should she do? She couldn't go home—if Haven House had even survived the Nephilim. She didn't want to tell the coven she'd refused to do her part. She didn't want to risk facing Crowley again without knowing how to beat him. *Shit.* Maybe this was what the Hierophant signified—the card indicated a sacrifice was needed to get close to her goal—and if she walked through the portal, she'd sacrifice her freedom, her life here to get to the Watcher. "I promised myself I'd fix this." Armageddon. Crowley. The Nephilim. If she couldn't carry out her own promises, what the hell did she have left?

Duncan touched her shoulder to draw her attention. "We don't have to do this. Not tonight."

"I let Crowley get away. Twice." The night he tried to kidnap Lilith, and again on Smyrna Island. "We have to know how to beat him and that means talking to one of the Watchers." She reached into her pocket, holding tight to his handkerchief. "You don't have to come."

He shrugged. "Me house is ash. Yours is overrun with Nephilim. A holiday in hell sounds like just the thing."

"Harry?"

"You kidding? Duncan never takes me anywhere. I'm in."

"Okay." She smoothed her hands over her shirt. "Then we just need the key." She stepped closer to Satrina.

Satrina smiled. "I am your key." She grabbed Trina, ramming herself right into her.

All the air left her as their bodies collided. Merged. Became one. She leaned forward and wretched.

Duncan grabbed her and pulled her against his chest. "Stay calm. No getting sick."

For a moment her body twisted on the inside, too full, disordered.

"Slow breaths. You're okay."

She leaned into Duncan, drawing from his strength and after a moment or two, everything settled into place. Her breathing evened out. Her heart returned to a steady beat. She took stock of herself and for the first time ever, the consummate emptiness she'd lived with . . . was gone. She put her hand on Duncan's chest. "I'm okay." Okay . . . yeah. Maybe better than okay. *I can do this.*

He helped her to her feet. "You sure? Was that supposed to happen?"

She straightened her shirt and ran her hands down her pants, brushing off the dirt. "Yeah. I think so." *Hoped so.*

"Now what?"

"Rowena's notes on the legend said that when you reach the bottom and turn to the stairs you'll see the portal to hell. It said most who saw the portal, saw themselves in the flames. They lost their minds." Trina stayed where she was. So did they.

"Right." Duncan cleared his throat. "Let's think about this logically. Yeah?"

She wet her lips. Something back there was watching them. Waiting. "I'm open to logic."

On the other side of her, George growled. A loud, menacing sound ending with a low-pitched hiss.

"Aside from Satrina, everything we've experience thus far has been an illusion."

She nodded. "Of our own making."

"Right." He squeezed her hand. "So whatever we see isn't going to be real, but it'll be our fears or expectations, right?"

"Yeah."

"Logically, all we have to do is close our eyes, turn around and walk forward."

Trina's attention snapped to him. "Close our eyes? What if this part isn't an illusion? I can *feel* something back there."

"Me, too. But it hasn't *done* anything."

"He's right." Harry stroked his hand over George's fur, soothing him.

"Okay." Goddess, please let them be right about this. "Count of three. Eyes closed and we turn around."

"One." She closed her eyes. "Two." Took a deep breath. "Three." She turned around.

A wave of heat washed over her and she hesitated.

The weight of Duncan's arm settled on her shoulders, urging her forward. Together, they walked into the heat. Shouts and crying came from all around them.

Still, he forced her forward.

The heat increased until she was sure her flesh would start to bubble and melt. The agonizing screams made her stomach roil.

And then it disappeared. Cool air washed over her and everything went silent.

Gooseflesh rose on her skin and she shivered. "Are we through?"

Harry cleared his throat. "Ho-ly shit."

She had her face tipped down and when she opened her eyes, the first thing she saw was the ground. The grass. Black in the center and rimmed with white as if covered in frost, though it was soft beneath her shoes. She stared at it a long while, gathering her nerve before lifting her gaze to take in Machon.

When they'd discussed crossing through the portal into Machon she'd envisioned passing into a different dimension, a reflection of the world she recognized. But maybe the portal allowed them to step across space and time right onto the surface of another planet.

A short fence ran the perimeter of the meadow, some kind of rough, black stone fashioned into obelisks and positioned one next to the other with their pointy ends straight up. There must be a gate somewhere, but she didn't see one. And beyond, a forest surrounded the area.

The alien trees all sported a bright white, fleshy bark covering a deep, glowing-red core. The iridescent foliage varied from pale pinks to pale blues to deep, glowing reds. The flora reminded her of a bioluminescent species she'd seen pictures of, the kind of plants growing in the depths of the ocean where no light ever reached.

Even the sounds were alien. Unseen life warbled and hissed in the distance. Something took flight from high in the trees. She tried catching a glimpse, but the creature sped past in a blur.

"Goddess be blessed." Her gaze lifted to the heavy, molten moon hanging low in the sky—not distant like the moon she'd grown used to, rather so close she could make out all the curves of the orb and the chunks of dark matter surfing over the molten liquid beneath.

Though unwilling to look away from her new surroundings she did pull her pack off, found her hoodie and donned it.

She turned a slow, tight half circle and came face-to-face with Duncan.

"Welcome home." He stared at her in that way of his, making her stomach flutter and her breath catch. "Maybe now that you're here, everything will fall into place for you."

Wouldn't that be nice? To regain control of her life. Her Magic. She opened her mouth to say something, maybe to give an apology for ending things or to ask for one from him for walking away, but she didn't know where to start.

Then sanity returned. He'd be safer this way. She shoved her hands into her pockets and fisted his handkerchief in her hand.

"Shit." Harry stumbled back, his arms pin-wheeled, and he fell on his ass. "What the hell happened to George?"

George . . . wasn't a cat anymore. The small creature had shrunk to about the size of a large ferret with armor-like white scales covering the top of its body from its nose to its flat, reptilian tail. Short, midnight fur covered the rest of him. Its diamond-shaped head resembled a snake's— flat, with a wide toothy mouth. Small horns poked out of the top of its head above two overly large, inky eyes.

Harry crab-walked backward. The creature followed, tongue lolling as if it were a game.

"I told you that wasn't a fucking cat. What is it?" Duncan stormed past Harry and the little creature swiped the air, warning him back. Duncan managed to grip the creature in his large hands and tossed him away like a football.

George spun midair, hit the ground on all fours and, with a leap, he charged back, his inky eyes fixed on Harry. She tried to grab the thing as it ran past, but it dodged around her.

Duncan grabbed Harry, pulling him behind him, but the little creature tried to go around, under, over, anyway he could to get to Harry. Duncan had the lad behind him, in front, up in his arms, cursing the whole time. The persistent little imp wouldn't be deterred.

If the creature morphed, it must still be George. Must still have the same nature as the animal she'd known on Earth. Trina held up her arm. "Wait."

Duncan froze with Harry slung over one arm and his leg stuck out in the opposite direction.

The two reminded her of a novelty balance toy. She pressed her lips together. Laughing at them would get her nowhere. "Let them go and see what happens."

Duncan's brow lifted. "Are you daft?"

"Did you see the teeth?" Harry asked.

"George didn't hurt Harry."

Harry rolled his eyes. "She's right. Just startled me when I glanced down, expecting to see a cat in my arms and found that thing, instead."

She propped her hand on her hip. "Is he hurting you?"

"No." Duncan growled, but lowered his leg, allowing George to crawl up him and onto Harry. "Don't know how he does that. He's not using his claws to climb." He shook his head.

George paused halfway up Duncan's chest and hissed.

She followed its line of sight, saw a blur of a white streak through the fleshy branches overhead. "He doesn't like something up there."

Duncan scanned the trees. "I didn't get a good look at it."

"Me, either." George finished his climb and jumped to Harry. He nuzzled Harry's chin with his diamond-shaped head, letting out a gurgle of pleasure. Tentatively, Harry gave it a pat.

"See." She stroked her hand over George's scales. "Seems friendly enough now. He was never that happy as a cat."

Duncan snorted. "Nothing's happy when it's not being what it's meant to be."

She lifted her gaze to meet the challenge in his. "You have something to say?"

"I said it."

Harry jerked his chin toward her. "Can you zap us to the tower?"

"Not without knowing where it is." She'd never been here before. She needed to at least see the tower. "Besides, until I know how my Magic is going to react to this place, I think it's best if I don't use it unless absolutely necessary."

"You see this?" Duncan motioned to a boulder that had been polished and engraved on one side.

IN MEMORANDUM OF OUR SACRIFICED CHILDREN

JUNE 1588

MAY THIS PORTAL NEVER BE OPENED AGAIN.

Great. So the daemons here weren't exactly looking forward to the Original's return. The grove of trees surrounding the meadow stretched in every direction. A chill spider-walked up her spine and she pressed her hand to her belly. "We should find the tower." Preferably before they ran into any daemons.

They spread out, walking along the perimeter of the fencing. Up close, she realized the individual black obelisks were porous. They were made of some kind of volcanic rock. She found a lever sticking out between two. "I think I found it." She pulled the handle. Three of the obelisks lowered into the ground. A siren went off.

She swung around.

Duncan waved her on as he ran her way, Harry right behind him. "Go. Go!"

The banshee wail startled strange birds and insects as large as her hand from where they'd been hidden in the surrounding trees. The whole grove came alive as the creatures scrambled to escape the noise.

She took two steps out of the gate and stopped. Not everything had run. Dozens of creatures like George were scrambling down trees, surrounding them. They sat there with their wide, toothy mouths unhinged, tongues lolling like reptilian puppies.

"Jesus." Duncan slowed to a halt. He tugged on her arm. "Let's go." He pushed Harry ahead of him.

All the creatures followed.

Duncan stopped.

So did they.

He took a step to the left, dragging Harry and her with him.

The creatures followed.

"Great." He turned to go around the enclosure they'd been in, and came up short. "Damn." They stood on a cliff overlooking a valley. In the distance, a tower rose high above the horizon.

She nodded. "Okay. We know where we're going now." She couldn't be sure, but it looked like there was some kind of landing near the top.

"I'd prefer to walk." Duncan motioned to the tower. "We don't know what the hell we're going to be walking into if you zap us there."

"Good point." A Watcher lived in that tower and they had no idea what to expect.

More of the creatures had gathered. They were everywhere, surrounding them, edging closer. George hissed and curled himself tighter around

Harry's head.

"They don't seem aggressive, but he"—Duncan pointed to George—
"sure doesn't like them."

"Do you think they're dangerous?"

They scurried along, jumping over others to find empty patches of
ground to sit and watch them. All those inky eyes tracking their progress.
There was no clear path left.

Harry struggled to remove George from his head. "Get off!" He lowered his voice. "Look, they're friendly, you grouchy little shit." He reached
out to touch one.

Duncan jerked him back. "Don't."

"What's a matter?" Harry arched his brow. "Is the big bad vampire
scared of the itty-bitty—"

Duncan popped the kid on the back of the head. "Enou—"

The minions swarmed. Growling and snarling, teeth and claws bared.
All headed for Duncan.

She didn't even think, just put a hand on both Duncan and Harry and
spell-traveled.

A MOMENT BEFORE THE AIR HAD been cold on his skin and now
it was hot as . . . well, hell. The scent of sulfur laced the air. He
glanced at Trina. "Thanks."

George curled around Harry's neck and hissed, his inky eyes fixed on
Duncan. What the hell was wrong with it?

Trina flicked George on the nose. "None of that. Bad. No." George
stopped, but his gaze didn't waver. "This one seems to be protecting
Harry."

The kid grinned. "Maybe they all were. Better be careful, D."

"Whatever, pup." He walked to the end of the balcony and stood at the
low wall. Steam covered everything. "Can you do something about this?
I want to see what we're looking at."

She mumbled a spell under her breath and held her hands high over her
head. With a quick, outward, downward sweeping motion of her arms the
mist blew away, leaving them a clear view.

Far below them a moat of lava churned, and beyond that the blackened
ground sprawled for miles before the walls of a city rose in the distance and icy peaks of mountains stretched across the horizon. He walked

around the curved balcony and let out a low whistle. "Look." He pointed at strains of sunlight cresting the horizon.

"Sunrise?" Harry asked.

"Can't be." Trina leaned against the low wall enclosing the entryway. "Legend claims there's no sunlight in Machon."

A terminator line. "Not on this side. The planet must not rotate on an axis like Earth," Duncan said. "It's locked into an orbit like our moon." But beyond that line eternal day would burn anything that ventured too close. A lake of fire, just like it said in the Bible.

"Yeah, well, sounds like hell to me," Harry said.

He watched for a few more minutes, his eyes dazzled by the line of bright light stretching across the seeable horizon. He had no idea what the Watchers were like. If he thought she'd allow it, he'd have Trina wait here, but Augustina said she and Lilith were the only beings able to see or speak to the Watcher without an aid. Nothing for it; he had to bring her in.

"Kasdeja lives here."

He forced his attention away from the horizon. "How do you know?"

"There." She pointed to the top of the archway where KASDEJA had been etched into the stone. "He was one of the twenty leaders of the two hundred fallen angels. Taught mankind to fight with spells and weapons." She shrugged. "He's a fire Watcher. At least, when we do spells, we use fire to represent him."

"Great."

Harry cleared his throat. "Sure you don't want to shop around for another tower? Might be something safer, maybe a Watcher of fuzzy bunnies."

He rolled his eyes. "Let me check it out before we all go bobbing in there. I won't try to talk to him without you, just want to make sure it's safe. Yeah?"

She wet her lips. "Not a chance in hell."

Yeah, he hadn't expected that to work. She had no faith in him. "Fine." He strode through a large stone archway that opened into an immense chamber. No one was around, but he had the distinct sensation of being observed as they made their way deeper in.

The doorway appeared tiny from the center of the chamber, as if he'd eaten one of Lewis Carroll's cookies in Wonderland. What needed such a gargantuan space in which to reside?

He turned a full circle, searching for any clues as to what they were about to meet. Arches ran across one end of the curved room and off to one side, was a large mound of something. Upon closer inspection he found a fortune. Gold and silver, jade and diamonds, all tossed in a pile. "Bloody hell." He let out a low whistle that bounced off the walls. "This Watcher gig pays well."

"What's that?" Trina joined him.

Harry reached forward.

"No, don't." She stayed his hand. "This is Kasdeja's house. Those belong to him. My mom used to tell me stories about the old coven making a pilgrimage every year to petition the Watchers. They'd bring gifts and—"

Gifts? Duncan looked at Trina. "Did we bring a gift?"

She nodded. "Nothing this fancy, though."

He snorted. "Why do I have a bad feeling about this?"

George growled low in his throat. Harry bent, running his hand along the floor and held his hand up for inspection. "Know what you mean." He held up his hand for Duncan. Cupped inside, he held a gray, powdery substance. Ash. "The whole floor is covered with it."

"Bloody hell."

There were a lot of destroyed daemons on the floor.

TRINA WASN'T SURE WHAT SHE'D expected, but this—a massive empty room—wasn't it. Augustina had said she'd be able to see the Watchers. Talk with them. "Maybe the Watcher that's possessing Crowley lived here."

The whole building shook.

"That didn't sound good," Harry said.

The second time, they looked at each other.

Duncan's brows drew together. "Footsteps?"

The third time, they turned around.

A fiery-colored dragon lumbered through arches on the other side of the room.

"Fuck me running," Harry whispered.

Her gaze narrowed on the thing. Both Duncan and Harry saw it—that wasn't the Watcher, so what was it?

Harry elbowed Duncan. "Ask it your question."

His face scrunched up. "It's a dragon."

"Ask." Harry gave him a little shove. "It's what we came for."

He glanced at her and she shrugged. "I have no idea. Maybe it's a . . . guard or something."

"Uh, hey there, mate."

The autumn beast came closer, lowered his head until the snout hung mere inches from Duncan. Hot tendrils of smoke poured from its nostrils.

It wasn't a real dragon. Insects made up the scales—red ants, yellow wasps, tan scorpions—giving the creature a mottled hue of fiery colors, but they were moving, climbing over each other, making the scales change from red to brown to yellow to orange.

Her stomach flipped. "Dunc, come back here." She didn't like how close he stood to that thing. Scorpion stingers made up the jagged teeth protruding from its mouth. "It's an avatar."

He glanced over his shoulder. "What?"

"*That* is an avatar." Augustina had said she'd be able to see the actual Watcher, but she wasn't seeing anything different from Duncan and Harry. "Watchers are invisible." How the hell was she supposed to see this thing if it was invisible? "They were stripped of their flesh as part of their punishment so the Watchers couldn't conspire with each other. He's using the insects to create a way to interact with us."

Duncan glanced at her. "But you can see it? Augustina said you could."

"I don't know. He might be under all those bugs."

She stuck her hand into her pocket to get the stones. "Great Watcher, a gift for thee." Duncan's handkerchief came out with the stones and she turned to the side, away from everyone to stuff it back in. With the stones in her hands, she straightened and held her cupped hands out above her bowed head.

And what should I do with those? Spend the next millennia polishing them?

She lowered her hands. *Shit.* "I'd like to offer you a gift. What would you like?"

A gift or a bribe? The dragon came closer still, the mouth hanging open to showcase the stinging bugs. *I want electronics in every tower on Machon. That is a gift I will put to good use.*

She frowned. "He wants us to put electronics in the towers."

"That's how the Watchers communicate with the Guardians." Duncan gave her a meaningful glance. "The Watchers can control electronics—talk through them."

Kasdeja and the others would be able to talk among themselves. Conspire without anyone else seeing their messages. She may gain *his* favor by doing as he asked, but the goddess wouldn't be pleased. "No."

The dragon opened his giant maw.

"Run!" They all ran, spreading out.

She and Duncan dove underneath the dragon's chin as the first tendrils of fire burst from beast's mouth. She didn't see Harry and the place they'd been standing was an inferno of fire now. "Harry!"

Charred, blackened, and burning bugs dropped around her as she regained her feet. She slapped at her hair and clothes, brushing them away.

Duncan yanked her to the side, keeping her from being stomped by the dragon's clawed feet. She stumbled to her knees.

He helped her up, took her hand, jerking her into motion. "We gotta get out from under it."

"Where's Harry?" She didn't see him. "Harry!"

Duncan led her first one way, then another, trying to find their way out from underneath the dragon, but between the avatar's movements and sheer size of it they remained below it, no matter which way he went.

Her vision blurred and she swiped the tears from her eyes. Where was he? Her heart slammed against her ribs. "Harry?"

Duncan shouted for him, too.

"Way to go, Lopez. I think you pissed it off."

Harry sounded like he'd made it to the far side, near the door.

Duncan squeezed her hand. Shouted to Harry, "Get outta here."

Harry's denial echoed through the chamber. "Not without you."

They dodged to the side, narrowly avoiding a clawed foot. "I'm going to throttle the little shite."

When Harry came into view, he was standing still, as if he'd forgotten how to move. George wasn't with him. Had the Watcher gotten the little creature?

"Duncan." She pointed.

The dragon took notice at the same time. Lumbered toward him.

"Move your arse," Duncan yelled.

The dragon's head swung around, zeroing in on Harry.

The lad ducked, raising his arms over his head, before being consumed by flames. At the same time, the dragon's tail swished past them, catching Duncan square in the chest. She lost her grip on his hand as he was thrown across the room. He landed in a heap next to the Watcher's unwanted hoard of jewels.

She glanced back to where she'd last seen Harry . . . and gaped. No less than half a dozen Harrys—one quite crispy—dodged about the room.

Harry's a splitter, yeah. I'm a shifter. At least she now knew what a splitter was.

All the Harry's headed for the door, zinging across the chamber to avoid swiping paws, snapping jaws and bursts of flame.

All except one—the one with George flattened against the boy's chest, hissing at the dragon over his shoulder. He hauled ass across the chamber, straight for Duncan.

She'd had enough. Thinking to draw the beast's attention away from them, she called out, "Kasdeja!" Her voice reverberated through the chamber. "Choose a different gift. One I can offer without offending the goddess."

You. He continued to chase Harry's copies around the room. *I want to remember what it's like to have flesh while we talk.*

He wanted to possess her. Wasn't that how the other Watcher escaped?

Stones pinged across the floor as Duncan scrambled out of the Watcher's stash.

Kasdeja swung round.

If she left her body while he . . . borrowed it . . . it would limit the time Kasdeja could stay inside her. A body couldn't exist without its essence. And Duncan knew what questions to ask.

Fire blazed from Kasdeja's mouth as he zeroed in on Duncan.

"Okay!" She closed her eyes. She might regret this. "I agree but you can't harm us. You have to answer all our questions."

The fire subsided. The dragon turned back to her. *Deal.*

The dragon walked around her, looming closer.

THOUGH DUNCAN DIDN'T KNOW THE particulars, he didn't like this. Lines of strain appeared around Trina's mouth, her eyes, and tension made her shoulders stiff.

He got to his feet and ran. "Wait."

Trina's eyes rolled back into her head and she slumped to the floor.

"What happened?" Harry ran toward her, too.

By the time he reached her, her body started jerking back into motion. She gained her feet through a series of halting, toddler-like motions. Her spine straightened, then her neck. Her eyelids opened. The back of her eyes filled her sockets; an empty, unseeing whiteness.

Behind her the dragon dismantled, the ungoverned insects behaving again as they should.

"Your request," came a deep voice from her slack mouth. Her knees bent. Straightened. Her arms went out to the sides and her limp hands flapped.

Harry wet his lips. "Make him get out."

Yeah, this was wrong. What the hell was he doing with her? "Look, mate." His hand went to his blade, pulling it from the sheath. "How 'bout ya come back outta there."

Trina's slack mouth opened around Kasdeja's laughter.

Shivers raced across his skin. Damn it. What now? "You got your gift. What else do ya want?"

"Perhaps I want freedom."

Right. And how would they stop him now that he had Trina's body? "That's beyond my humble capabilities, mate. This is a prison, in'nit?"

"You don't know much, vampire. I can leave. I just need a host. No one would be wiser until I was long gone and this tower began to crumble." Trina's face came close, her sightless eyes staring into his. "I could use you." She swung drunkenly toward Harry, and George swatted her. "Or you. Or even this one." Her hands slid up her torso, over her breasts. "I like this one."

"Don't." He held up his blade. "Don't touch her."

"Or what?" Eerie laughter bubbled out of Trina's mouth again. "Will you destroy me with your blade? Sacrifice her to save her virtue?"

Shite. "Maybe."

"Ha! I feel nothing. No pain. No pleasure." Her hands stroked over her body again. "But here's the key: She does. I could crush her from the inside out and I wouldn't feel a thing. But she would."

"Stop." Harry pinned Duncan with a glare. "He's stalling. Get him to answer your questions."

Trina focused on Harry. "You've yet to ask and your chance to do so is dwindling."

Harry elbowed Duncan. "Ask."

Duncan's gaze shifted from Harry to Trina's vacant expression. "Dwindling how?"

"Your little witch didn't want to chance me taking her body, so she left. If she's away from her shell too long she may never find her way back before it dies."

"Hurry, D."

He wasn't sure what, or how to ask. The legends said the Watchers couldn't lie, but that didn't mean they couldn't withhold important facts or twist the details to suit themselves.

"Jesus, Duncan. Did you hear him? We have to hurry."

He held up his hand. "Belt up, I'm thinking." This Watcher had never seen Trina before. He had no idea *whose* body he possessed or what that body could do. *Shite.* He didn't want to feed information to the bastard without knowing if he was on their side or not.

"Before we start, yeah, I want you to tell me exactly what your punishment is." The Watchers weren't supposed to interact with each other, but now that one possessed Crowley—did Kasdeja know about him?

"Confinement from my brothers—I cannot see or hear them inside this tower or out."

Harry pulled George off his head, and relocated him to his shoulder. "Who are your brothers?"

"The angels."

Duncan asked, "Why were you punished?"

"Have you ever watched someone struggle to do something you find simple? Watch them stumbling along when you could pick them up and carry them a short distance? That is the main reason we came to Earth. Ancient humans never mastered their environment. They lived short, strife-ridden lives, unable to conquer the elements, the animals, even the flora. How many times did I watch them poison themselves as they experimented in search of food or medicine? How many men died on the hunt due to inferior weapons and tactics? Or froze? We could stand their suffering no longer. Not when we had the answers."

"You expect us to believe you wanted to help?" Harry asked.

"Sometimes even the worst disasters are inlaid with the best of intentions. Though we also had selfish reasons for what we did. We struck a deal with the humans: Their daughters for our knowledge. We were gods among the men and they jumped at the chance to know what we did. We taught the humans to make more efficient weapons and we taught them strategy. They created war. We taught them medicine. They used it to kill. We taught them Magic and they bastardized that as well. All the while worshiping us for our gifts. We saw our actions were evil and we turned on the men we once tried to help.

"We bit our wives, wanting to turn them to daemons to hurt their fathers and brothers. We'd seen it done when our brother Samael turned his mate Lilith into a daemon. But our mates didn't have the powerful Magic of the Original. They didn't turn into a vampire-witch daemon, they transformed into Nephilim. And the Nephilim turned on their families and friends. We could not destroy our own kin. So, we watched them multiply.

"By the fifth bite removed from ours, the Nephilim retained something of themselves from before the change. Less powerful, they retained their humanity. These creatures were unlike the Nephilim. They had more of the characteristics that the Original developed when her mate bit her. So we called them vampires. But it was too late. God created the great flood to destroy the Nephilim. And we were punished for seventy generations in the great lake of fire. And now those of us who are repentant live in the towers, helping keep the balance."

Duncan leaned down to brush a scorpion from his pant leg. The fucking things were everywhere. "Where are the un-repentant Watchers?"

"Some of our brothers still wallow in the flames, refusing to repent. Some have been destroyed. Watchers aren't much different from humans. Some accepted our failure. Others blamed men or God. They're the ones you must be prepared for—the wayward Watchers."

George sat up on his hind legs, swatting a large flying bug into his mouth. It crunched wetly as he chewed.

Harry gave him a pat. "How do we destroy a wayward Watcher?"

"Do you know his name?"

Duncan shook his head.

"Then you can't destroy him."

Fuck.

He shared a look with Harry, who kicked the ash at his feet. "This is a waste of time. He's not going to help us. I bet he wants Armageddon."

"I do not," Kasdeja said. "But if you do not ask the right question, I cannot give you the answers you seek. I do not read minds. . . ." He narrowed Trina's eyes into slits. "I have not seen you for a while, Duncan Samael Sinclair. Why is that?"

Samael. The Original's mate. That's why Trina had stared at him gape-mouthed when he'd told her his name. So she knew they were mated. She knew and she'd still tried to end things. *This can't happen again.*

Kasdeja repeated his question. "Where have you been, vampire?"

Kasdeja would figure things out right quick if he gave him too much time to think. "Okay, if we can't destroy a wayward Watcher, can we imprison him?"

"Maybe. If you lure him here. The easiest—" Trina's eyes widened. A too-wide smile stretched her lips. "Yes. It would be easiest if you had the cooperation of the Original." Kasdeja giggled and Trina's arms wrapped around herself. "Sneaky, sneaky witch."

Duncan took a step closer. Pointed his blade at her. "I will destroy her before I allow you to use her, so don't try it."

"Your hand is shaking, daemon."

"Don't test me."

Kasdeja leaned forward until the point of his blade pressed against the soft hallow of Trina's throat. "You're a lucky vampire. Lucky, lucky, lucky. I'm the one who sent you to her." He straightened. "Bring Lilith to Machon. The two women must unite and become the Original. Together, she can raise a tower and force the wayward Watcher within."

"How do they unite?" Duncan asked.

"They will know."

It must be instinctual. Something they'd know when they needed to unite.

"The Original has always been most powerful here, under the light of the full moon. But you must wait for the wayward Watcher's weakest moment, when the moon is new on Earth. That gives you two nights to prepare."

"Prepare for what?"

"War." Trina's sightless eyes stared straight into Duncan. "Do you think the wayward Watcher will come willingly? If he is wayward, he will use everything at his disposal to fight. Gather your allies."

"And the coven can summon Cr—?" Shite, that was close. "The coven can summon the being the Watcher possessed?"

The corner of Trina's mouth curved. "Got himself stuck, did he?" He giggled again. "And I must assume he possessed a daemon, since humans cannot be summoned."

Shite.

"They must know the daemon's full name. This isn't a spell the Grigori coven will have ever used. It's dark Magic. Try looking within the *Black Book of Daemonology.*"

"Do you know his name, D?" Harry asked. "His whole name?"

"I don't." He didn't know as though anyone would. Had no way of knowing how long the Watcher had possessed Crowley, though he assumed it was around the time of the Clearances. Somehow, it was all connected.

"You could ask me." Kasdeja made Trina spin on one foot. Stumbled. Righted herself.

"Yeah, you'd like that, wouldn't you?"

"I would." Kesdeja's playfulness vanished. "I find I do not like to be surprised. I did not like finding you in my tower and not realizing you were coming. I do not like not knowing what there is to know." Kasdeja lifted Trina's arms, stroked her fingers through her hair. "I do kind of like having a body again."

"Stop." He took a threatening step forward.

"You'll hurt her." Harry stalled him with a hand to his chest. He leaned close and whispered, "What's the likelihood anyone will know *his* middle name?"

"I don't know." Duncan threw his hands up. "This sucks." Crowley was far older than him. He had to assume Pasquino didn't know Crowley's full name, because he and Lilith had never tried summoning him. He'd have to take the risk and ask Kasdeja because he sure as hell wasn't coming back for more information later. "Crowley. Julius Crowley."

"Now that's a name I haven't heard for a long time. I'd forgotten he existed." Trina's eyes closed. "The Tanin'iver, Julius Elisha Crowley. He's a very old soul. Maybe the oldest of all the souls."

"Thank you." He nodded. They could summon Crowley now. "Can you get the coven here?"

"Yes. Right now, they fight the Nephilim. When they are done, I will send them to the Citadel to meet you."

"And the Guardians?"

"I am sorry. The Guardians are gone. Only you and James still live—at least as far as I can see."

Bloody hell. All of them? That was most everyone he knew.

"Your time comes to an end, vampire. If you have more questions, ask them quickly."

"No, we're do—"

Duncan held up his hand to stay Harry. "Can she hear us? Trina?"

Harry smacked his arm. "What are you doing? Get him out of her."

"Yes. Though most beings don't remember anything after they wake from possession."

"This mated thing . . . If she doesn't . . . " *Want me.* "If she decides she doesn't want to be mated, how do I release her from the bond?"

"Die."

Bullshite. "Come on. There has to be another way. We can't be the first mated pair in history that doesn't suit."

"You're not. There once was a witch who thought so little of her mate, she sacrificed him to the greater good."

"And what happened?"

"Everything affects everything else, daemon. Her ambitions were greater than her love, and now, here you are, looking for a way to stop what she started. Souls migrate to those they've known before. Everything is connected."

That he understood. "I knew her in a previous life, she didn't want much from me then, either." He shook his head. "So what, if I can't find a way to get her to . . . ." He glanced at Harry and lowered his voice. "You know?"

"Love you?"

Jesus, the bastard spoke loud enough for all of Machon to hear. His face heated.

"You will suffer. You will wish you were dead. I only know what I see and hear, daemon. But you, I'm not sure you are seeing what's right in front of you." The Watcher pulled something out of her pocket, and waved it with a flourish. His handkerchief. "Earlier, when she offered me her gift, this came out of her pocket and she hid it from you. It is yours, right?" Kasdeja ran the cloth under her nose. "Strange she carries your cloth and yet cares nothing for you."

He stared at the linen square. Warmth flooded him to his toes. "I don't even know what the problem is." He didn't want to mention she was having trouble with her Magic. Kasdeja didn't need to know about that.

"Nor do I. I cannot see her unless she's standing before me. Woo her."

"Fuck's sake. You think I haven't tried? One minute she's sprawled over me naked and screaming my name and the next she's telling me I have to stay away." He paced away a few steps. "I think she's worried she'll hurt me, which . . . ." *Completely emasculated him.* "So tell me, oh, great mighty one, how should I be wooing her?"

Trina's face tipped side to side as Kasdeja studied him. "You're angry with her. Hurt."

"Of course I'm—" He glanced at Harry, who watched everything with interest and lowered his voice. "'Course I am." Why shouldn't he be hurt? His mate, the one person made solely for him, rejected him. Didn't trust him to take care of himself. How wasn't that hurtful?

"Have you tried to change her mind?"

"Why, so she can shut me down again? I've been there and done that with one of her past lives. It ain't happening again."

"Mm." Kasdeja stared down Trina's nose at him. "Remember Charlie."

He took a step back, sucking in a hard breath. *His son?*

"Remember when he learned to walk? Wobbling his way around the house? You poured yourself some tea. Dark. No sugar. No milk. Steaming hot—the way you always liked."

Jesus.

"You turned around with cup in hand, stumbled over his blanket and when you put your arms out to stop your fall, you spilled the tea."

"It was an accident." He didn't know why he said that, it didn't matter if it was an accident, his chest still ached from the memory.

Trina took a wobbly step closer. "Remember how loud he cried when the hot liquid hit his bare leg? How he screamed when his skin blistered. He hated you."

"No. Charlie never hated a soul. Not even his mother."

"Didn't he? You hurt him. Surely he wanted nothing to do with you." Trina's head tipped to the side, farther than if she had done so herself. "Oh, wait, that's right. You burned him. He cried. Then he crawled into your lap and you both shed a few tears while you hugged."

Again, he glanced at Harry. "There's nothing worse than hurting your kid." He stared at Trina, wishing he could fight the bastard inside her. "What's your point?"

"You like stories, vampire. Figure it out."

His cheek twitched.

Harry leaned closer. "She hurt you because she told you to stay away and instead of trying to work things out, you're pouting. You're not like Charlie."

Duncan growled.

Kasdeja nodded Trina's head, like a rag doll with no stuffing in her neck. "You're not forgiving her. You're holding on to your hurt. You're too proud to try and change her mind."

What did they want from him? "I'm here!"

"Physically! I don't understand thoughts. I can't hear them. Or see them. I understand what I see. What you're telling me. You haven't fought, you're taking the easy way out and walking away."

"For her!" She didn't want him. Damn it. And he didn't want her to suffer. He didn't want to go through seeing her suffer. Of hating him. Hurting him. Of watching her turn into something ugly before disappearing altogether. He went through that with Gertie. With Satrina. He couldn't stand to go through it again. "I couldn't protect my last family and I can't fail again. I'd rather let her go than live through all that again."

"Then you've already failed."

Trina started to slump to the floor and this time he caught her. She lay limp in his arms. "This is twice now I've had you unconscious in my arms. There's not going to be a third, you hear me, you daft woman?"

He held her close, tipping her head back. He touched her cheek, whispering nonsensical words of encouragement for her to come back. He smoothed the hair back with a shaking hand, drew his finger down her cheek. He could love her. Hell, he did love her. That's why her rejection, her absolute lack of in faith in him, hurt so damn much.

"Come on." Harry wandered toward the edge of the room. "Sit down or she'll have a kink in her neck."

Duncan carried her to the edge of the room and sat with his back to the wall. Harry joined him. George leapt down and took a sniff of Trina's hair before curling up in the lad's lap.

He adjusted her until her head rested in the crook of his arm. He closed his eyes and leaned his head against the wall, unable to look at her lifeless body any longer. There were no visions this time and it bothered him. Reminded him she wasn't in there. Made him worry she wouldn't find her way back.

"Can I ask you something?" Harry asked.

"What?"

"What happened to him?"

He opened his eyes. "Who?"

"Charlie." He checked his watch.

Jesus, he didn't want to talk about this. "He's dead."

"Yeah, but—"

"I failed him and his mother. But mostly him." He leaned his head back on the wall. "I couldn't control . . . couldn't make things right." He looked down at Trina. "And now history's repeating itself."

"Doesn't have to."

No, it didn't. What would happen if he quit burying what he felt? What would happen if he told her he wouldn't allow her to blow him off? What if he tried a little longer? A little harder? Charlie had never given up. His little boy had woken with a smile on his face and love in his heart every day. No one could resist his charms. Not because he was needed. Not because he forced the issue. Just because he was who he was.

Harry nodded to Trina. "She reminds me of Em."

Duncan combed his fingers through Trina's hair. Harry had talked about Ember before; she had been his best friend before the Council had taken him. "Maybe you'll see her again one day."

"Trina treats me like I'm normal." He pressed his lips into a thin line. "No one else does but you."

They lapsed into silence. Behind Harry, the bugs were gathering. Building on themselves. Re-creating the dragon avatar.

"Kasdeja is right, you know." Harry jerked his chin toward Trina. "You shouldn't let her walk away."

How the hell did all this make the lad feel? He was stuck in that body, but full grown. At Harry's age, Duncan had been bouncing from bed to bed. He must want more. "Someday you'll—"

Harry cut him off. "Don't. I couldn't stand the company of a woman who found me attractive in this body. Not even Em. It's twisted."

"I was gonna say, someday maybe we'll find a way to change that. It's not like you don't have the time to wait."

Harry snorted. "Kind of farfetched, but I guess anything's possible."

Now if Trina would come back, they could call it a night.

TRINA OPENED HER EYES. DUNCAN leaned above her, his brows drawn down, and she had the urge to stroke her finger between them to ease away the worry lines.

"You two gonna kiss?" Harry teased.

She came to her senses with a start, scrambling out of Duncan's lap. She glanced around as she adjusted her clothing. A shiver shook her.

"This is gonna stop now, Duchess." He glowered as he got to his feet.

"What?" Why was he using her nickname again? What the hell had happened?

"This." He motioned to their surroundings. "I'm not having it anymore. What were you thinking? No more presenting dragons with gifts, no more fighting mesmerists behind me back, no more transformations or out-of-body experiences. And no more possession. No more." He paced away a few steps and strode back. He stuck a finger in her face as he lectured and she had the distinct urge to bite it. "If anyone is going to possess your body, it's damn well gonna be me. And I sure as hell don't want you floating around the ceiling when it's happening."

She glanced at Harry, who stared at Duncan with the same gape-mouthed expression she must be wearing. She'd never seen him get this worked up. He must have lost his mind or he wouldn't have made such an asinine statement. Not in front of Harry. She should smack him. Instead, the warm and fuzzies wrapped right around her heart.

And she couldn't have him. Couldn't risk his life. She turned on her heel and stalked off.

"Are you all right?" His voice softened. "Kasdeja didn't hurt you, did he?"

She stopped, studying her dusty boots while she regained some semblance of rational thought. "I don't remember."

The dragon waddled toward her and lowered its head.

"What's he look like?" Harry jerked his head toward the dragon.

Augustina had said she'd be able to see the Watcher's true form. "Kasdeja, I have yet to see a Watcher to know what I seek. Will you show yourself to me?"

His great head bobbed once.

Insects scurried away from both ends. The tail and muzzle began to dissolve. Her gaze trailed after the insects scurrying into cracks in the walls and the floor. As the last of the insects skittered away, he stood.

She craned her neck in effort to take him all in. Not even Duncan reached the height of his knees. Although humanoid in form, Kasdeja was nothing more than bones and all of them appeared twisted and elongated. Burnt. Even his skull was stretched, giving him an alien-esque look, with large, slanted sockets and spindly teeth. The skeletal remains of wings jutted out behind him—remnants of his divine heritage. He must've been beautiful at one time.

"Well?" Harry stared. "What does he look like?"

"Regret." A surge of compassion for Kasdeja overwhelmed her and she put her hand on the porous bone of his femur in a gesture of comfort.

Kasdeja's voice filled her mind, *The jewelry you wear around your neck . . . remove it. It's bastardizing your Magic.*

She shook her head. "It keeps it manageable. Helps me control it."

The Magic that made that was evil. It's tainted.

Rowena made it. After seeing the Magic she'd been performing in her Grimoire. Hope filled her. Maybe. Maybe it was the cause of her problems. Maybe things would get better if she just took it off. She unclasped the choker and tucked it into her backpack.

Now that you are in Machon, where you were always meant to be, your Magic will heal. As will you. Go southeast to the Citadel. You will find allies there.

She nodded. "Thank you."

CHAPTER 27

TRINA SPELL-TRAVELED THEM TO THE base of the tower and they headed southeast. She went ahead with Harry and George, leaving Duncan to follow. He'd done two complete about-faces in less than twenty-four hours and she wasn't sure what to think. She mocked, *"Don't be changing your mind now. . . ."*

"What?" Harry asked.

"Muttering to myself. That's all." She took a furtive glance over her shoulder to gauge the distance between them and Duncan. Several yards back, he scanned the area as he walked.

"What's got you foaming at the mouth?"

"Cavemen."

"Seriously? He's ancient, but he's not quite that old."

George swiped at her hair.

"Sometimes he does things that irritate the hell out of me." She nodded. This felt good, airing her grievances.

"Oh? Like what?"

"When he makes that weird sucky sound."

Harry kissed his teeth.

"Yes." She stopped walking. "Why do that?"

"Don't know." Harry tugged her along.

She glanced back to check on Duncan again and this time he caught her. He flashed her a grin and winked.

She tripped over her own feet. He was flirting with her again?

"Nice." Harry drew out the word as he steadied her. "Very stealthy."

"Oh, shut up."

"Why don't you go talk to him?" His blue eyes bored into hers. "Sort out whatever's eating you. The two of you've been acting like you're in the middle of a divorce—half-clingy, half-pushy."

"No. It's better this way. There's no point in encouraging him." The dirt crunched beneath her feet. Here, close to the tower and the lava fields, there were no plants. Nothing but cracked dirt as far as she could see.

"Except you want to."

She whipped her face around to look at him. "What?"

"Encourage him."

She snorted.

He grinned, throwing his thumb over his shoulder. "Oh, so what was your little maneuver about?"

"I'm making sure he didn't sneak up on us while we're talking."

He laughed. Even George made suspicious gurgling noises.

She suspected the little creature was far more intelligent than a house cat. They lapsed into silence. They were walking uphill at a slow grade and tree tops had come into view over the rise ahead.

"What do you want to know, Lopez?"

"Huh?"

"Seems like you're wanting to ask me something about him." He threw his head back to indicate Duncan.

"Oh, well, I wondered how you ended up together," she said. "I mean you don't seem to like him much. You're always cussing at him and giving him shit. Why stick around?"

"I think if I looked my age, what you're thinking of as arguing and disrespect might sound more like two guys ribbing each other."

"Ribbing? That's why you're always baiting him?"

"No. I have chronic short-man complex." He gave her a somber shake of the head. "I bait him to ease my inferiority issues." He leaned into her. "I'm sure you'd be able to cure me in one night."

She glanced at him askance. "I'm trying to be serious."

He leaned close. "Seriousness leads to depression."

"Harry."

"Lopez," he mimicked.

She strode ahead, irritated with his diversionary tactics.

"Wait up." He jogged to her side, holding on to George's thick tail. "D will have a melt-down if you're walking alone."

"Answer my question."

He sighed. "I take perverse pleasure in annoying him. It's a guy thing; you won't understand."

"Is that what he's doing when he calls you 'pup'?"

"Meh. We have kind of an odd relationship." He rolled his eyes. "My dad, he used to call me 'son.' By the time I hit my preteens I hated it. Thought 'son' made me sound like a kid, you know. I'd complain and he'd call me son anyway. I'm sure if I was home and human and twenty-six, he'd still call me son and I'd still grumble."

"So, 'pup' is an endearment?"

He shrugged.

Damn. "I didn't think you liked him."

"I didn't when he first took me in."

She stopped. That's not the story Duncan told her. "Took you?"

"Rescued me." George tried to sit on Harry's head, and he grabbed the small creature, putting him back on his shoulder. "Duncan isn't responsible for my current predicament, but he made sure I survived and for a time, that seemed worse."

"What happened?" An uncomfortable silence followed. "Damn. I shouldn't have asked, I—"

"I went to England for vacation with my parents. During one of the tours . . . well, next thing I woke up chained to a bed with an aching head."

A bed? Inside, Trina blanched. She didn't like the direction of this story.

George curled itself around his neck, cooing in sympathy.

"A vampire kidnapped me." His voice cracked and he stopped speaking. His eyes held a haunted, hunted quality before he shook it off.

Gods, he'd only been a kid.

"The Vampiric Council found out and had a fit. Not out of concern for me, mind you, the bastards were worried about themselves and what the Watchers might do since I was transformed before maturity. They punished my captor and called in D to destroy me."

"Which he didn't do."

"I hated him the first year." Absently, he scratched George under the chin, returning the creature's affection. "I tried to destroy him at every opportunity. I wasn't strong enough to hurt him and he wouldn't let me hurt myself. Every day he'd listen to me scream and yell, curse and throw things. He'd clean up the messes, talk me through the nightmares, and brought me blood."

"What changed your mind about him? About surviving?"

He shook his head in bewilderment. "The son of a bitch wore me down."

She smiled.

"I quit fighting. I mean, he never asked anything of me. He didn't yell or beat me. Hell, I tried to make him lose his temper to prove he was up to no good. Then I didn't know how to act or how to apologize. I caused him endless trouble and I wanted to make up for everything, but didn't know how."

Again, he gave her a flummoxed expression. "He knew. D comes strolling in one night and unlocked the door to the cell. Told me not to run off because any daemon I came across would destroy me. Said if I planned on staying I needed to earn my keep."

"Doing what?"

Harry grinned. "You sound as suspicious as I did. He wanted I.T. support."

"What?"

"Right? He looks so fit and healthy it's easy to forget he's a fucking antique." He laughed. "He wanted me to bring him into the tech age in exchange for instruction on fighting and splitting."

"Seriously?"

Harry glanced over his shoulder before leaning closer and whispering, "You should've seen the closet full of electronic corpses he had. Computers with all the peripherals, killer spy gear gadgets, surround sound, gaming consoles. We're talking tens of thousands of British pounds worth of stuff. A total kid's fantasy—" He put his hand to his mouth to stifle a laugh. "He wanted to use that stuff so damn bad. Had techie magazines and 'how to' books and he was completely fucking inept. The noob destroyed half the devices pulling them apart to try to, and I quote, 'Fix the soddin' rubbish.'"

She bit her lip to keep from laughing.

"I swear his office rivals the command center at NASA. He's got our entire goddamn neighborhood wired." His step faltered. "I mean, he did . . . man, I still can't believe it's all gone. That was his sanctuary." He kicked at a rock in their path.

Somehow, she'd find a way to replace it all. They wouldn't have lost everything if it weren't for her. "What's he like as a teacher?"

Harry shrugged. "He wouldn't accept less than my best. He's not even a splitter, but he researched my talent and worked with me until I mastered it. Taught me to box, use a knife, a gun. Taught me everything he knows. Still, he won't let me fight."

"Why?"

He faced her, holding his thin arms out while they walked. "I have no muscle, no weight to put behind my moves. He's been promising me for ages he'd find a way to get me close to the Council. Hell, he's dying for a chance at Leopold, but he won't. Not because he can't. Not because he wouldn't win. Because I'd be a liability."

She hated to admit it, but Duncan was right. Even with skill, Harry was too small to be much of a threat to anyone. "He'll rescind his promise to get you close to the Council?"

"No, he'll stall until he figures out a way for me to get revenge in as fair a fight as possible, which might take eons."

Pounding footsteps made her look back.

"What the hell are you two doing?" Duncan ran past, moving faster than she'd expect for such a big guy. Her gaze followed, watching the flex of his bum. *Stop it*! She looked up and froze.

Thirty or so daemons—human-looking for the most part—approached, weapons drawn. A militia.

CHAPTER 28

DUNCAN CAME TO A STOP. "That's far enough."

One of the daemons came forward out of the pack. A blond male and while sturdy and muscular, he had nothing on Duncan's size. "We've come for the female." His gaze shifted past Duncan and locked onto hers. He could see her. They all could. Augustina's words came back to her: *Your people will see you. They will know you.*

"She's mine."

A little thrill went through her and she tamped it down. He wasn't claiming her, just saying they couldn't have her.

"Listen to the foreigner, Levi."

Trina's gaze swung to her right. *Shit.* Another, even larger, militia stood there—close to a hundred daemons. And this crew *looked* like daemons. The leader—the one who had spoken—had deep blue skin with thick black tribal tattoos covering most of his chest and arms. Horns. Barbed tails.

"Holy hell," Harry whispered. He grabbed her arm and pulled her behind him.

"I can see over your head, twerp."

"Stay put."

Duncan backed up a few steps, angling himself to keep both groups in sight. "Telling you what I told him, mate. She's with me and she's staying with me." If he were closer, she'd spell-travel them out of here.

The blue giant stared her way. Bowed his head slightly which made the little silver hoops hanging from his left horn wink in the moonlight.

Levi shouted. He ran forward, drawing his sword. So did his men.

She grabbed Harry's shoulders. "Who the hell has swords nowadays?"

"Them."

Duncan bent his knees. Spread his arms, his little six-inch knife gripped in one hand as if that would help.

The blue giant drew a sword as well, his men following his cry as he ran toward the rest.

"This is bullshit." She stepped around Harry and swept her arm out in front of her, letting her Magic change the consistency of the dry, cracked ground.

Both militias stumbled as their feet stuck.

Their boots sank with their next steps. Shouts and curses punctuated their struggles.

Harry elbowed her. "Nice."

Slowly, they began to sink.

Duncan twisted around, pinning her with a glare. "You serious?" He wasn't sinking quite as fast as the others; he had the sense not to struggle.

She shrugged. "You were in the way."

He rolled his eyes, crossing his arms over his chest. He turned to the Levi, his tone dripping sarcasm. "You still want the female?"

Levi spit. "She'll be our prisoner. We're not allowing her to leave again, not now we've gotten our Magic back."

She eased closer to better hear them. "I'm not leaving. I'm here to stay."

The blue giant grinned. "Most welcome you are to do so, *Gasan*. I'm Dumuzid." He said it again, slower. "Doom-oo-zid. My friends call me Doom."

"You call her your queen already?" Levi waved his arm at Doom. "You're going to trust her again? You saw what she did!"

"With the permission of all our leaders." Doom pointed at Levi. "Does Meneus know what you're doing?"

Levi struggled harder to get his feet free. "He'll be hanging off the end of my sword along with the rest of you bastards."

Her attention wavered between the two groups. Despite his appearance, she liked Doom. He'd bowed his head to her—not a lot, but enough to get the point across. "Am I your friend, Doom?"

He smiled wide enough to flash his fangs. "I do hope so, *Gasan*." She couldn't place his accent, almost middle-eastern but not quite.

"Where were you from? Originally?"

"Sumeria." He'd sunken down to his waist and lifted his arms to keep them out of the muck. "And you?"

"Washington."

His brows drew together. "Never heard of it."

"Duchess, we're all sinking here while you're chatting up your new friend."

Her gaze shot to his, took in his bored expression. "What do you want me to do with them all?"

"No more half-measures."

No half-measures. Shit. If she let Levi and his group go, they'd cause havoc forever. Sounded like they'd been doing so since she'd last been here. So what did she do with them?

Harry came up behind her, whispered, "Before the good guys can't breathe anymore, Lopez."

Levi made the decision for her. He lifted his sword, cocked his arm back as if he intended to throw it like a spear, his gaze focused on Duncan.

She mouthed, *wish you dead*. Didn't think about it. Didn't consider the ramifications. She couldn't allow him to hurt Duncan.

Levi's whole body seized. The sword dropped from his hand and sank into the spongy ground. He clawed at his face. His throat. Blood leaked from his eyes and nose as he began to convulse.

Seconds later, he died.

Her stomach twisted. He was dead. She'd judged him after knowing him a few moments and she still had the others to deal with. Her gaze shifted to Duncan. He still appeared bored as hell.

She turned her attention to Levi's men. Her Magic hadn't affected them. She'd performed her spell, directed her Magic to her target, and it had stayed focused where she wanted it. Goddess be praised, Kasdeja had been right. Now that she'd taken off the necklace or maybe because she was in Machon or maybe because of both, her Magic was working properly again.

Maybe using her Magic to kill would never be necessary again. Maybe if she released Levi's men, let them spread the word that she'd returned and planned to stay, it would settle this particular grievance. "Do you want the same fate?"

A chorus of "No" went up. They dropped their weapons.

"I'm here to stay and anyone who doesn't support me is my enemy. Spread the word." She nodded to herself. That sounded good, right? Authoritative. Bad-ass. Now if she could stop shaking she'd be doing okay.

Duncan had sunk to his chin in muck. One dark brow raised.

Shit. Now she had to get them out of the ground. Using her Magic, she started at the bottom and made the particles denser so it'd push them back up to the top. Her heart leapt a bit in her chest when Duncan lifted up. She had control of her Magic again. Granted, she needed to be patient and test it again to make sure, but if she didn't have any more problems, all that remained between her and Duncan was the spell she'd tattooed on her arm. *I will never belong to any man.*

Could the coven reverse that spell? Maybe in time they could be together. "This is good. Everything's gonna be okay."

Harry leaned toward her. "Uh, Lopez, the more bored he looks, the more pissed he is. I've only seen that particular expression once."

She continued the spell, taking care to make sure everyone came up together as she hardened the ground under them. If that was the case, Duncan was pissed as fuck. "What'd you do?" She glanced at Harry. "When you saw that expression last."

"I shocked myself trying to make a Taser out of his electronics." He leaned closer. "And he got that look as soon as you started crying."

She turned and wiped away the evidence. She hadn't realized. . . . "I'm fine."

"Sure. But you don't have to convince me."

Duncan pulled himself free of the last few inches. Headed straight for her. "I shouldn't have said what I did. Next time you let me take care of it."

"I'm fine, damn it. The message needed to be sent. We'll be safer for it."

He raised his hand as if to touch her cheek, but dirt covered him. His hand fisted and he lowered it. "You did good."

She bit her lip. "Remember what you said about precipitating evil since we were daemons?" When he nodded, she added, "I think you were right."

"No. Some people choose to walk in the Darkness and some are forced to it. For a long while, I chose my path in the choices I made, in the way I thought. Eventually, I cleaned myself up. Figured out who I wanted to be and took the steps I needed to get there. But here's the thing. The Darkness, whether forced on you or chosen, it never lets you go. I fought it. I resisted it. I did everything I could think of to chase it away, but it clings. And eventually, I found out why."

She stared, waiting, but he didn't seem inclined to explain. "Well?"

Harry snorted. "He ain't gonna tell you."

Duncan grinned. "When you think you've got it figured out, Duchess, let me know. And I'll tell you if you're right."

Not good enough. She wanted to know now, damn him. She opened her mouth to argue, but Doom cleared his throat as he approached. "If it pleases you, *Gasan*, I'll show you the way home."

Duncan turned. "How do we know we can trust you?"

"I've known Satrina through many of her lives." His attention returned to her. "The leaders of the thirteen clans have remained loyal to you and Lilith."

She touched Duncan's arm. "Between the three of us—"

George swatted at her hair from his perch on Harry's shoulder.

"—I mean, four of us, we can handle them if they try anything."

"Ah." Doom nodded toward Harry. "I see you have a protector, little one."

Harry opened his mouth, no doubt to put the daemon in his place, but both Duncan and Trina lifted their hands to stay him. "What is it?" Trina asked.

"A minion. They have been standing guard at the bloodtrees, waiting for children to come back to Machon."

"That one came with us . . . except it looked like a cat back home."

Doom smiled. "They have good camouflage when they think it's in their best interest to use it." He motioned in the direction he'd come from. "Should we go?"

Well, if she was supposed to be queen here, she better get her act together. She looked over Doom one more time, measuring the colors of his aura. He had darker hues like Duncan, but she didn't see anything that indicated any malice or deceit toward them. Besides, Kasdeja said she'd find allies here. She nodded. Walked to Doom's side and craned her neck back to look him in the eyes. "There are thirteen clans?"

"The main clans, yes." They started walking toward his men. "There are others, but they're rogue clans. They don't participate in the Grand Council, nor have they guarded your home while you've been away."

"Duchess." Duncan's tone was full of warning.

She waved her hand behind her back. This wasn't the time for his over-protectiveness. She smiled at Doom. "My home?"

"The Citadel." He offered her his arm by holding his elbow out to the side.

She took it, looping her arm with his. "We need a copy of the *Black Book of Daemonology*. I need to find a summoning spell."

"Ah, there's a copy in the great hall. Anything else you may need will be in your library." He strolled her through his men and each tipped his head to her as he passed, but Duncan's gaze at her back, raising the hair on her nape, held her attention. She felt Duncan there. The invisible thread linking them thrummed with tension.

When they reached the highest part of the hill, she gasped. A walled city sprawled below. Houses had been stacked with the precision of a toddler stacking blocks and at the highest part of the hill, a castle towered over it all. A freaking castle.

Doom grinned. "Your home. The Citadel."

J UST. FUCKING. PERFECT.
Who has a house? Not him. His house was ash.
Who was the handsome bastard with *his* woman on his arm? Again, not him.

Who failed to protect her from doing what he damned well knew she didn't ever want to do? Oh, right. *That* would be him. *Fuck.*

The farther ahead she walked, the more he *felt* her. That crazy sense they were linked, somehow strung together, intensified. As did the need to go over there and remind her she belonged to him.

Harry smacked him in the arm and sent a pointed look toward Doom and Trina.

"Relax, pup."

"You need to quit acting like her bodyguard."

"I am her bodyguard."

"You're her mate." Harry brushed his hair out of his face. "Every time you tell her to stick close, or that you'll protect her, or any of that shit, she brushes you off."

Was that true? He tried to think back over the last several days.

"I mean, really, D, does she need your protection?" George had his front paws on Harry's head, those inky eyes watching his every move. "Quit living in the dark ages. Get some perspective."

He shot Harry a side-long glance. She *had* to need him, damn it. He didn't have fuck-all else to offer her.

From a distance, this hadn't looked like more than a shanty town, the way the square houses were stacked haphazardly on top of one another. This wasn't a slum, though. The homes were larger than he first thought, one story built of a glossy black brick. The way they were designed—each turned slightly and stacked above—provided a private entrance for each. The staircases leading up to the homes arched up gracefully, ending in long porches. Blue light radiated from the windows of most of the homes, though some remained dark. Even the paved streets appeared freshly laid, with none of the unevenness or potholes he'd grown used to in London.

He cleared his throat. "How does the town support itself?"

Doom glanced back. "We're a small community. We have very few needs. The bloodtrees provide food, the mountains provide building materials. Some sell services in exchange for favors. Some hire themselves to settle disputes among the thirteen clans. Some choose to work at the Citadel for favors."

Doom led them straight through the center of the town, right up the monstrosity sitting in the middle of it all. From a distance, he'd thought the castle sat on a hill, the way the houses rose in increments, but the ground was level. The Citadel was massive. Made of the same black stone as the other buildings, spires and arches pointed toward the sky like swords. Carvings of cloaked beings, horned creatures, and winged gargoyles decorated the outer arches over doors that rose stories high. Giants could've walked through those doors without bowing their heads. Doom opened them with a slight push.

Inside, flying buttresses arched far overhead, curving down in pillars that stopped two-meters off the floor in upside-down obelisks. Wrought-iron chains dangled from the points holding bowls of blue fire. The great hall went on forever—must've been longer than a football pitch. Between each of the obelisk points the hall widened into vestibules on either side with wide rooms containing wall-to-wall books, the floors covered in thick rugs.

Doom waved to the left. "Historically, the coven has shared with any who brave entering these halls. Once word gets out you are here, daemons will come to pay homage, to ask favors, or with the hope you'll settle disputes."

"Anyone can walk in here?" He didn't like that.

"The Citadel is protected with Magic. Alarms will sound if anyone enters with the intention to harm the *gasan*. Visitors are only permitted on the first floor. The rest of the building is private."

Not all the vestibules held libraries. Some appeared set up for potions—dried herbs hung from the rafters, bottles and jars lined the walls. A cauldron sat in the center. A large labyrinth took up the floor of another—the daemon walking the path cut into the stone floor didn't even glance up at them.

Harry nudged him with his elbow. Pointed up.

Midway between the highest buttresses and where they stood, narrow stone bridges crisscrossed the empty space. Dangling from one, a pentacle spun on a black chain, throwing off the reflected light from the blue-flamed fires.

Doom noticed where they were staring. "Don't worry, the bridges are for those who work here. Your quarters are above."

Good. He didn't like the idea of Trina walking around on those.

In the center of the hall, a huge round fire pit lay in the middle of the floor. He didn't see any fuel in the pit—no wood nor charcoal. The blue flames rising high overhead didn't create any smoke. Long, stone tables surrounded the pit on three sides of the hall. On the fourth side, a table sat higher than the others, raised on a dais. Two thrones sat behind that— the seats far too dainty for a male.

"Here." Doom motioned off to the side, toward a vestibule to the left of the thrones—the room had a thick white rug laid over the floor, the walls covered in glass-encased bookshelves. In the center, there was a table and chairs with a large tome leaning on a book-holder. "*The Black Book of Daemonology*."

Trina headed straight for the book.

"Pup, why don't you—"

"I'll keep an eye on her."

Duncan leaned his hip against the table. He liked his vantage better from here, where he could watch the daemons milling about. Some sat at tables to chat. Others wandered into various vestibules. Many cast curious glances their way, but none approached.

His gaze fixed on Trina. He'd screwed up with her again, but how the hell did he get her to give him a chance as her mate, when she didn't need him?

Doom leaned his hip against the table across from his. "You, my friend, have the look of a male who does not know whether he wants to give his female a tongue lashing"—he grinned—"or a tongue lashing." When he didn't reply, Doom kept talking. "Been there with my female."

"You're mated?" His gaze remained on Trina. She kept turning around to check on him.

He tipped his head left, then right. "Yes, but I have not seen her for a while."

"How does that work?"

"She's human." He shrugged. "I've been stuck here. So if she's reincarnated since I last saw her, she did so on Earth."

"She doesn't mind?" He motioned to Doom. "You know, how you

look?"

"Of course she does." He tugged on one of the curved black horns jutting from his head, fingering the silver hoops pierced through it. "Anu knows she liked me well enough when human, but now that I'm *gallu*, her heart races for altogether different reasons."

Christ, at least Trina didn't fear him.

"Don't suppose there's somewhere we can clean up after she's done there."

"Mm." Doom gave him a sidelong glance. "You looking for efficiency or someplace private?"

Interesting thought. "Where would this private spot be?"

Doom nodded to an arched door across the hall. "Through there, down the steps. You'll find hot springs surrounded by a garden. The Grigori coven used it as a place of meditation and rest from their powers."

"Oh?"

"The garden is bound. Her Magic won't work there." Doom pulled out a ring of keys, selected one, and handed it to Duncan. "Don't scare her."

He took the key. "Scare her? You did see what she's capable of."

"Yes. But she's our *gasan*. If she screams in terror, we must defend her. If we damage her mate, she'll not be pleased. We will all lose, then."

Oh, ho! The balls on this guy. "You wouldn't damage me."

Doom grinned so wide his fangs were visible. "One of these days, for fun, we will fight."

For fun. Duncan held out his hand and Doom shook it. "Deal." He liked Doom. He was his kind of people.

DUNCAN STOOD WITHIN SIGHT, HE was right there and still the string linking them pulled as taut as if he were half a world away. Put her body on high alert, making need pulse through her.

"Are you gonna keep staring at D, or read the damn book?"

"I am read—" She dropped her gaze to the Grimoire to find George sprawled out over the page. His tongue slithered out of his mouth and over the lens of one inky eye.

"You were saying?"

She grit her teeth. "Get your critter off my book."

Harry picked George up and deposited him on his shoulder. "Did you even look up the spell?"

"Yes." She speared her fingers through her hair. "I found the summoning spell. We have Crowley's name. It should be fairly easy." She glanced over the spell one last time. "There isn't anything unusual here."

"You find what you're looking for?"

Duncan's deep voice rolled over her, warming her from the inside out. "Yeah." She repeated what she'd told Harry. "We need to call the coven, and—"

"Already done. Kasdeja will get them here." Duncan folded his arms over his chest while he studied her.

"Oh." Goddess help her, she wasn't ready. The coven had never liked her much. She'd left them to fight the Nephilim while she traveled here. They wouldn't be happy with her. She bit her lip.

"What're you worrying over now?"

The coven. What she would say to them. What they might say to her. How she could find a way to be alone with her mate. How she could make him understand her remaining concerns about being with him. "Nothing."

His gaze bore into hers for a long moment. "Yeah, all right." He gave her a wink before glancing around. He turned to Harry. Sand covered his whole back. "Hey, pup. Doom said he'd show you up to our rooms. Go check it out, yeah?"

"On it."

She brushed her hand over Duncan's backside.

He whirled around, took a step closer. The look on his face . . . . She stood, making her chair scrape across the floor as she backed away. "You're covered in sand. I was just cleaning you off."

He didn't respond. He unbuttoned the first three buttons of his shirt. Deliberately. Slowly.

"What are you doing?" She glanced around at all the other daemons in the main part of the hall. Harry and Doom had left, but they were far from alone. Some of the daemons paused their conversations, taking an interest in what was happening. "They're watching."

"I'm checking on something." He stalked forward the last few steps and her back came up against a wall, stalling her retreat.

"What?"

He took her hand and pressed her palm to his chest. "I think you're looking for a reason to touch me."

"I'm not."

"You are." The little hairs scattered over his chest tickled her fingers. A shiver stole over her skin.

"How's that?"

Perfect. She wanted more. "Don't."

"Don't what? Let you do what you're dying to do?" His fingers twined with hers. "God forbid."

She flattened her other hand against his side, unsure if she did so to touch more of him, or to keep herself from plastering herself up against him. "Dunc, please."

He stooped down to whisper in her ear. "You're making us both suffer. Why?"

She forced herself to meet his gaze. "What if I'm not strong enough? What if I hurt you with my power?" Or the spell on her arm. She had to find a way to get rid of the tattoo.

He pressed her palm to his cheek. "What if I'm strong enough to keep you from ever getting to that point?" His broad shoulders blocked the rest of the room from her view but she had no doubt the other daemons were watching. He was a mountain of a man and it would be so easy to rely on his size alone.

But she used chaos Magic. She knew all too well that the largest, strongest things in the world were made up of the same stuff as the weakest. The smallest. The most fragile. "I'm doing my best to keep you safe, Dunc."

A humorless laugh escaped him. "Twist the knife a little deeper. I'd rather you think me ugly than weak."

"We can't—"

His expression hardened. "I'm not having it. Not anymore."

"Having what?"

"You, pushing me away."

Her breath caught. "You said you wouldn't—"

His grasp tightened on her hand. "We're mated, you and I. I had hoped you wouldn't find me so damn revolting—"

She shook her head. "That's not—"

"—you might get past whatever's keeping you away. But I can see patience isn't going to win out with you." He released her hand. Bowed and hauled her over his shoulder. All the air whooshed from her lungs and she had to suck in a hard breath to shout, "Duncan!"

"Don't make a scene, Duchess." He turned amid the cheers of the other daemons and strode across the room.

Trina flipped the hair out of her eyes and shot them her best bitch face.

The daemons stopped.

Duncan turned a corner and went down several flights of stairs.

"This is uncomfortable, damn it." She wriggled, trying to get into a better position. "You know what I could do to you. Put me down."

"Do it."

The circuitous stairs flying past made her dizzy. She shut her eyes. "I might."

"Go ahead."

"Damn you!"

They went through a door and out into the night air. He shut the door behind him and locked it before setting her down. He put the key far out of her reach on the stone arch surrounding the door.

"Seriously?" She could have that key in three seconds flat.

"Your Magic won't work here." He walked away.

She focused on the stones. On the individual particles making them up. She spread the fingers on her hand as she willed the door to dissolve.

Nothing happened.

"Told you, no Magic here."

"How?" She whirled around.

"Don't think I'll tell you." He looked fierce as hell. "You and I are gonna have a chin wag, but first, I got a surprise for you." Duncan stepped back, revealing a spring surrounded by smooth rocks. Thick steam hovered above and the humidity in the air suggested the water was bathtub hot. She dragged her gaze away to find Duncan half naked. "What are you doing?"

He paused in the process of removing his pants. "Huh. I didn't take you for the prudish sort." He stripped his remaining clothing off.

"I've never been accused of being a prude in my life. You're naked."

"Easier to bathe. I've got sand stuck in places I'm not keen on having sand." He eased into the steaming water with a moan. "You should come in."

"I don't t—"

"You stink, too." He winked, taking the sting out of his comment.

Tempting. She was tired. A little sore. The water looked enticing. He did, too. Right now, though, the water held her rapt attention. Crystal clear beneath the cloud of steam, no sulfur smell or menacing bubbles suggested the water was dangerously hot.

"I'll stay on my side." He waded deeper into the pool where the water rose to his shoulders.

To hell with it.

She wanted a steamy bath and the spring was plenty big enough for them both. Making her way around to the far edge where the steam blocked her view of Duncan, she slipped out of her clothes, grateful for the puffs of vapor keeping her partially concealed, and eased herself down.

Her skin turned to gooseflesh as she sank into the liquid heat. She sighed, tipping her head back and wetting her hair. The water eased away the tension in her muscles. She let her eyelids slide shut, rested back against the smooth rocks, and allowed her mind to wander.

BE LIKE CHARLIE. OPEN. FORGIVING. Don't give up.

Trina looked like a napping water nymph with her dark hair slicked back and all that gorgeous skin on display. He eased up next to her. "Tell me something—"

She jumped, splattering them both.

"Sorry, love." He wiped a hand over his scruff. "Didn't mean to startle you."

Her eyes narrowed into accusing slits. "What happened to staying on your side?"

"Yeah, about that. I, uh, may have stretched the truth a bit." He tried to maintain a somber, apologetic façade, but broke into another grin. He couldn't help it, he had her alone, wet, and naked. "I like to see who I'm chatting with."

She shot him the stink eye before settling back the way she'd been, this time keeping her eyes open.

"Why do you keep pushing me away?"

Her slips parted. "You want to talk about this now? While we're naked?"

"Yeah. From what I've seen so far, you tend to be more honest about things between you and me when you're starkers."

She closed her eyes. "You're . . . you're not what I expected."

You're ugly. Stupid. Useless.

Damn. He'd asked for honesty, but it still stung. Come on, be like Charlie. *Open. Caring. No matter what.* He tucked a strand of hair behind her ear. "Is that such a bad thing?" He leaned in until the individual onyx flecks in her dark brown irises became visible. "I'm not asking for . . ." *Passion? Trust? Love?* He threw away that line of reasoning and settled for,

"Can't you like me a bit, despite me being . . . different?"

A tremulous smile touched the corner of her lips. "Just a bit." She closed her eyes and leaned back again. Some emotion passed over her features he couldn't quite place, but still made his chest ache. "You like stories."

"'S'pose."

"When I was little, I got into trouble all the time. I came into my specialty early—the telepathy, anyway."

Christ, he'd forgotten she could do that.

"I couldn't control it. I heard everything everyone thought. The good and the bad. I couldn't concentrate. I was clumsy as hell. Depressed. Angry. I learned firsthand that people rarely said what they thought."

Christ, he couldn't imagine knowing everyone's unfettered thoughts. No wonder she second-guessed everything he said. "Like what?"

"My fifth grade teacher pretended to want to help whenever I got lost in class . . . and the whole time she worked with me, she was thinking I sucked up too much time. She wanted to focus on the smart kids. Thought they were getting a raw deal." She shrugged. "Everyone has unkind thoughts. And when you're a difficult kid . . . ."

"Not everybody—"

"Everybody." Her gaze met his. "When you fight with Harry, you never have an unkind thought?"

Little shite. "I concede your point, go on with your tale."

Her eyebrows knitted and she waved her hand. "That wasn't the story, just information so you can see where I'm coming from. Okay, so living at Haven House sucked. We didn't go out. We didn't get presents. Clothes were shared. Toys were shared. But this one day, not long after the last of our mothers' funerals—I must have been nine or ten—Rowena gave Nan a break and took all of us out."

The daft bitch must've felt guilty, as she should've. "Where to?"

"She took us to see the Doll Lady." She dipped lower in the pool, wetting her lips. "This old woman with hunched shoulders and all these deep wrinkles. Her knuckles were so gnarled I have no idea how she made the treasures she created. Every kind of doll covered every available space in her living room—porcelain dolls, teddy bears, ragdolls, princesses, and stuffed frogs."

He grinned at her wistful expression. "Sounds like a little girl's fantasy."

"We each got to pick one to keep. Lil got a doll with a porcelain face and purple dress with ruffles, Kat took a sock monkey, Meredith picked a floppy lion, Brenda . . . ."

How the hell did she remember all that? She rattled off the type of stuffy each of the other twelve girls chose in vivid detail. Even after all these years her voice had a note of excitement.

"What about you?" He touched her shoulder, letting his fingers caress down her arm into the warm pool. "Which did you choose?"

"I don't know why no one else saw it, a great big teddy bear sat in the corner." Her lips curved. "As big as me, with tattered ears and glass eyes. His paw pads were real leather and he looked like his arms and legs and butt were weighted. He was perfect."

"What'd you name him?"

"I didn't choose him."

He frowned. "Why the hell not? What did you get? A doll like Lil's? Another stuffy?"

"This little rabbit fell on the floor." Her words came faster. "Nothing more than a yarn head on a Popsicle stick. She'd glued on paper-thin felt ears and googly-eyes and a yellow dress."

He'd seen a rabbit like that in her room back in Haven House—stuck in an empty pot of dirt, its yarn head yellowed with age. "Why would you—?"

"The bunny got knocked to the floor when Lilith took her doll—an accident. Claire and Zoe both stepped on it when they chose their toy— they were so excited to pick out a toy I doubt they even noticed."

An accident of fate . . . kind of like him showing up at Haven House. He clenched his jaw.

"The Doll Lady demanded to know who'd trampled the toy. She said they'd have to put their doll back and take the rabbit."

Just like her chosen mate hadn't work out, and the Watcher sent her him. "What are you trying to say?" His words grew clipped. This little trip down memory lane was leaving him gutted.

"I wanted the teddy." She took a deep breath. "I didn't even touch him." She sat up. "In my head, the other girl's thoughts kept saying to pick something already because I'd ruin whatever I chose, so it didn't matter. Rowena and the Doll Lady, they expected me to take the bear, thinking I'd destroy it and what a shame one of the others had to take the pathetic rabbit while I took something good."

"Why didn't you take the bear?"

"I panicked. I wanted them to like me, to accept me. And I knew they were right. I *would* ruin whatever I took. And the bear was so . . . fucking . . . great, right? Did I want to fuck it up? How bad would I feel when it got ruined? And how bad would it suck when I heard their thoughts saying 'I knew that would happen.'" Her eyes shimmered with unshed tears. "The little rabbit lay by my foot and I picked it up and then I'd already taken it and I knew they wouldn't let me put the rabbit back and the girls, they hated me more. I thought by taking what no one else wanted they'd leave me be, maybe even appreciate me, but instead they believed I wanted to make them look bad. And I thought that if the rabbit got ruined, I wouldn't care as much because the bear would be safe but, you know what? It *didn't* matter. No matter what choice I made, it was the wrong one. No matter what I did, someone got hurt. Something got ruined."

"So what's the moral of the story, Duchess? That I'm the bloody fucking rabbit? The piece of shit everyone else overlooked and shat on and fate tossed your way? Now you're stuck with something you don't want?" He couldn't help the bite in his tone. He'd already played that part once. He'd been Gertie's "better-something-than-nothing."

"You're twisting my words."

"Am I? You told me this long-arse tale about the bear you wanted and the rabbit you got in response to me simple question, 'Why do you keep pushing me away.' I get it. I'm your bloody rabbit." He wiped his hand over his head and turned from her. "Listen to me, I sound like a fucking idiot."

"But that's just it, Duncan. You're not the rabbit. It'd be so much easier if you were. If I didn't care."

He stopped. Thought through the last few minutes. Replayed her last comment in his mind. He wasn't the rabbit. He wasn't the booby prize she'd gotten stuck with.

She wanted him, but . . . what? Didn't *want* to want him? Did she fear what everyone else would say? That they'd look down on her for having a mate like him? That made the victory bitter-sweet, at best. Christ, the coven would arrive soon. *That's* why she was so upset. She feared what they'd think of her saddled with a big, rough-sounding brute like him.

He understood. But he hated it. It fucking hurt. Hurt that she wasn't as proud to have him as her mate as he was to have her. It hurt that he wanted her despite that. Oh, he'd keep his distance once the coven arrived. He got the message. But right now it was just them. He strode through the water and pulled her back against him. "Is that why you kept my handkerchief?"

She tensed.

"Don't understand you." He nuzzled the downy soft skin between her ear and shoulder and with little coaxing she leaned her head to the side in acquiescence. "You can trade that old rag in, you know. Press your face right up against me skin when you want to catch me scent." His hands splayed across her abdomen, pulling her tighter against him and damn, she was soft everywhere. "I don't know if I want to make love to you or spank your arse for twisting us both into knots."

She rubbed her arse against him and his cock took notice. "Do I get a say?"

"No." He nipped her earlobe. She wanted him. Needed him, damn it. Just once he wanted her to say the words. Then he'd hang back. He wouldn't embarrass her. "You're gonna let me love you tonight." His chest squeezed. "And that's gonna be the end of it. Yeah?"

THAT WAS FINE WITH HER. She had no desire to argue with him and she couldn't use her Magic here. For once, she wouldn't have to worry. Maybe they could come back here again. "Dunc . . ."

"You need me."

She shook her head, but leaned all her weight against him. She couldn't help herself, he was so damned big. So strong.

"You do." He turned her around. Cupped her chin. And when her lips parted, he dipped his thumb into her mouth. He fixated on the sight. "Tell me what I want to hear, Duchess."

She closed her lips around him and swirled her tongue against the pad of his thumb before pushing his digit out. His expression darkened. "I need you to hurry." Her nipples brushed his chest, sending a shockwave though her.

"No."

She met his gaze.

"You been making us suffer. Punishing us both. I'm taking my time, and you're going to tell me what I want to hear."

That she needed him, like some old-time Hollywood damsel in distress? "No."

His lips pressed against her ear. "I'm going to make you beg, love."

A shiver swept up her spine. She stepped back, shaking her head. "I don't beg for anyone."

"You will for me." Fierce. That expression returned. The one that made her think she'd pushed him a tad too hard. The one that made her wet. He stalked toward her, forcing her back until she came up against a smooth boulder. He fit his big hands around her waist and lifted her, setting her on top.

Steam rose from her body as her skin broke out in gooseflesh.

He backed away, but held onto one of her ankles. "Let me see you."

See her? He had her bare naked, sitting on a rock. His gaze tracked down her body, over her breasts, her belly. Goddess help her, he wanted to look at her pussy. Her breath caught. Her breasts peaked into hard little points.

"Yeah, you like the idea." His thumb stroked the inside of her ankle. "Don't go shy on me."

Her whole body heated. She'd never allowed anyone to stand there and . . . look. Then again, no one had ever asked before. She bit her lip, leaned back on one arm and spread her legs wide.

"Christ, you're tiny." He shook his head, but his gaze didn't waver. For a moment he swayed and then he stood taller—must have found a ledge to stand on—just the right height to slip himself into her.

Instead, he took himself in hand. She couldn't remember ever seeing anything quite so sexy—that big hand riding over all that rigid flesh—and her inner muscles clenched. His breath came quicker. His chest rising and falling with each shallow breath.

"Show me what you like, how you want me to touch you."

"I don't know—"

"You've never?" His gaze shot up to tangle with hers. Challenging. Calling her a liar.

"Not with someone *watching*."

He grinned. "I'm not *someone*, I'm . . ." *Her mate.* His smile faltered a bit, reminding them both nothing had been settled. "Show me what you want me to do."

Butterflies swarmed in her belly. She slipped her hand down.

A breath shuddered out of him. His reaction alone made desire pool deep inside. She stroked over her closely trimmed curls, used her fingers to part herself, spreading herself wide for his pleasure.

A tremor rolled through him, making the water ripple around his legs.

He liked this, was getting off on watching her. She held herself open, slipping her middle finger over her clit.

"How's it feel?"

"Like lighting shooting through my limbs, electricity pooling in my belly."

She dipped her finger lower, wetting it in the well of her pussy, slicking it, so she could stroke herself off easier. This wasn't anything like masturbating alone. Having his gaze on her. Seeing his breathing change. His expression darkened as she worked herself. "Dunc."

He leaned over her, bracing one hand on the stone near her hip and brushed his mouth over her nipple. "Don't you dare stop, Duchess."

She wanted to drag him closer. To wrap her legs around his hips. To feel all his hard angles and planes against her skin. She wanted his fingers in her. His tongue. His cock. But with one hand supporting her weight and the other on her clit . . . she arched up, high as she could. "Duncan."

"Harder." One word spoken against her nipple. One word that made her belly quiver. Made her inner muscles clench with the need to feel him. His mouth drove her to distraction, light sucks and gentle nips. "Dunc, I need more."

He knelt between her legs, brushing her hand aside. He put his lips to her clit and sucked.

All her muscles locked up tight as her climax shot through her. Her pussy flexed around nothingness. She moaned and let herself fall back against the boulder, her whole body throbbing with each wave of release.

"Good girl."

"I'm not a girl."

He chuckled. "Still in a fighting mood, eh?" His finger slipped inside her and she gasped. That. *That's* what she'd needed two minutes ago. He curled his finger in a "come here" motion, hitting her just right. A low moan tore from her throat and she squirmed.

"I like you like this. Pliant. At my mercy."

She opened her eyes to find him hovering over her. The boulder she lay on curved, leaving her head lower than her chest and the rest of her sprawled out like some ancient pagan sacrifice with her breasts facing the sky.

And her mate wanted to tease. That one damn finger sliding in and out of her body. She started to sit up, but he pushed her back down. "I'm not done."

She stroked her hand over his shoulder, down his arm—the only parts of him she could reach. "I want to touch you."

He winked. "It's not always about what *you* want." He lowered his head, drew a nipple into the heat of his mouth. Stroked her with his tongue. Released her to slide the uneven ends of his teeth over the peak. And all the while that finger slipped in and out, doing what she wanted him to do with his cock. She tried to get one of her feet under her, to at least push against him and gain more friction, but the boulder was smooth and her feet were wet and all she succeeded in doing was sliding down a little.

A second finger joined the first. Her nails dug into the arm he had braced on the boulder. The tension started to build again, winding deep in her belly, making her limbs tingle and burn. He stroked his tongue over her breast again and she felt it in her pussy. Everything inside her strained and she couldn't hide from it. Couldn't curl her body into the pulse and release, all she could do was lie there and accept what he gave.

The tip of a third finger prodded at her entrance.

"Duncan?"

"You're all right. You've taken me cock before. You can take this."

She shook her head but with stubborn persistence that third finger slipped in. "Oh." Eyes wide, staring at the upside down world behind her, she panted. Her nipples tingled and ached. She pressed her free hand to her belly where her muscles quivered with impending release. Tried to shift her hips—to escape, to get more, she couldn't decide.

He twisted his hand and his fingers sank deeper as he curled them up.

She screamed. Her orgasm ripped through her with the force of a flash fire, hot and bright at first, then simmering with a slow burn after.

He pulled her up and turned her over so her forearms rested on the boulder. Behind her, he curved around her, surrounded her as he fit the head of his cock to her entrance. Still, he remembered to keep his weight from her. "Say you want me." He nipped her neck. Soothed over the spot with his tongue. "Tell me."

"Yes." She rocked back against him, all that hard male—thick thighs against hers, pelvis to ass, corded stomach and chest hovering over her curves. "I want you." She pushed back, trying to force him to her will. The broad head caught on her opening. "Please."

Just like last time, he felt impossibly big and as he probed against her, her body refused to open. Her hands fisted. Flexed against the boulder and with every nudge, her nipples scraped against the rock. She shouldn't still be this needy. She'd been expecting him to tease her toward orgasm and then deny her, but he'd made her come twice. Still it wasn't enough.

His big hands cupped her hips, steadying her and he pressed inside. She gasped. Lowered her head to her arms. Lifted to her toes. Too much. Being so absolutely empty one minute and too full the next. "Dunc. . . ."

He forced her back down onto her feet. Flesh to flesh. Full to bursting.

He rested his head on her shoulder. "Never felt anything as good as your well-loved pussy."

They stayed still, her body acclimating to his until need throbbed through her again. She tried to rotate her hips, but he held her still. Slipped one hand down between her legs and stroked her clit. Slowly pumped into her and with each thrust, she slid forward, her nipples grazing the rock below her, sending sparks straight to her pussy.

Her hands fisted. She hung her head. "You're going to make me come again."

"Good. Want to feel all that wet heat clenching around me."

"I want to touch you."

"We all want things we can't have."

"Duncan!"

"Tell me what I want to hear."

Damn him. She bit her lip. Tried to push back to make him increase his pace. Tried to raise up or lower her chest so her nipples weren't dragging against the rock, stimulating her further.

Stronger, he maneuvered her exactly where he wanted her.

"Please."

"Please, what?"

"Please move in me faster. Make love to me. Fuck me, damn it. I need you."

He left her.

She whirled around and before she could say anything, he pulled her up into his arms. Her legs went around his hips of their own accord and cock slipped into her pussy. He clenched his jaw tight. Sweat beaded his brow. "Is that so hard? Saying you need me for something? Anything?"

Already he gave her what she needed. Holding her by the ass, lifting her up, guiding her back down. She'd been a bitch about asking for it. "Dunc, I need you."

"You've got me." He thrust up into her as if to punctuate his point. "You remember you're the one who said you didn't need me." Thrust. "*You* said you're better off alone." Thrust. "*You* said this"—thrust—"couldn't happen again." Thrust. "You." Thrust. "You—"

She kissed him. In part because she needed to. Needed to feel him on and in every part of her and in part because she couldn't hear any more. She wavered. She wanted to be with him. She did need him—not for protection or to take care of her or any of that bullshit. She needed him because he made her feel alive. He made her feel cared for. Loved.

Needed him because she loved him. And that's all she'd ever wanted.

DUNC, I NEED YOU.
Never had he heard sweeter words. He kneaded her arse cheeks with his hands, spreading them every time he lifted her. One of these days, he'd know her there, too. Soon. He wanted to know every part of her, be in every part of her.

Her pussy slid over his cock, clenching around him with his every thrust and she was so damn tight. Fit him like a second skin. Like she'd been made for him. Her breasts dragged across his torso with every thrust, those sweet nipples stabbing into his chest. She tightened her legs, rotating her hips every time their bodies met, driving him insane. Her nails scored his shoulder. Her lips feasted on his. Little moans vibrated through her. She was perfect.

Almost.

Stubborn woman. He shouldn't have to manipulate her to get her to say what he needed to hear.

Her inner muscles quivered, squeezing around him. A hot flush of passion crept over him starting in his loins and sweeping up to his head, making him shudder. He clenched his jaw tight, refusing to submit to his body's demand for release, remaining still in her until he regained control.

She refused to let him. Impatient, her legs constricted around his hips, lifting her body before relaxing to slide back down. She wouldn't let him be gentle, either. Fierce in her quest to please, she made sure he experienced every part of her soft flesh, nipping teeth, biting nails. Uninhibited and demanding, she commanded equal measure as she rode him. Her inner muscles gripped him, clasping, drawing him deeper. Liquid heat poured over him.

He supported her with his arms, holding her above the water, lest she drown while consumed by the orgasm rocking through her. He slowed his rhythm to match the pulsing grip and release of her inner muscles.

She curled herself around him and nipped at his throat. Not hard enough to break skin, but hard enough to send him over the edge. His muscles tensed around her as he thrust into her hard, deep as he could. Chills coursed over his skin as waves of pleasure shuddered through him.

After, she held tight to him. Her face resting against his shoulder. One hand drawing lazy circles on the back of his neck.

"You made me knees weak, Duchess." He pressed a kiss to her cheek. "I thought we were both gonna drown."

"Ah-hem."

Duncan stiffened. Who the hell—?

"I'm not looking." *Doom.*

"You better not, you perv."

"The coven has been spotted. They'll be here within the next fifteen minutes. I'm putting your bags here by the door."

The door slid shut and Duncan sighed. "Guess we'd better get dressed." He set her away from him and they waded to the edge of the pool. She'd gone quiet again. Distant. Hadn't said anything at all since they'd made love.

They got dressed and he watched Trina as she tried to not notice him. The ways she yanked on her clothes, she must be chewing on something, but she didn't appear inclined to share.

"You want to talk about it?"

She shot him a glare as she rubbed her hand over her tattoo. So much for the lingering afterglow.

Maybe not the direct approach, then. He brushed his knuckles across her upper arm. "What's this?"

She shot him a questioning glance and he dropped his gaze to the tattoo wrapping around her upper arm.

Her gaze turned cagey. "Nothing."

The hell it was. The black design had curved symbols that reminded him of the spells he'd seen. "They're words, yeah? Like the ones in the *Black Book of Daemonology*?"

"Witch's rune script." She turned.

He caught hold of her arm.

"You're not going to let it go, are you?" When he shook his head she groaned. "Lilith and I have . . . ." She sighed. "*Had* this ritual. Whenever we'd been apart for a while we'd have a night of drinks and confessions—a fun way to catch up. We went a little round the bend one night—"

He laughed. "Do you even know what it says?"

"Of course I do." She scowled. "It's a spell. Both of our tats are."

"What's Lilith's?"

Her gaze went up, searching the sky. "She wanted love."

"So her wish came true."

She folded her arms over her chest.

"And did yours?"

"Yes." She blinked hard a couple times, as if fighting off tears. Had she cursed herself? Done something to make it impossible for him to claim her?

"Well?"

She pressed her lips together. Looked away. "'During this life, I belong to no man.'"

Relief surged through him. Fuck's sake, he'd been worried she'd done something serious.

Her chin sagged. "I can't believe this. You're laughing." She let out something close to a growl. "I meant it, Duncan. When I performed the spell, I never wanted to be with any man. I have no idea what the spell might do if I try to enter into a real relationship."

"Suits me fine." He pulled his pant leg down over his boot and stood. "Ain't any human men 'round here." He grinned. "Just us daemon males."

He left her behind to think about that.

HE WASN'T A MAN. HE was a daemon male. She'd forgotten they made that distinction—referring to daemons as male and female, while calling humans men and women.

No matter how serious she'd been about the spell, it wouldn't affect Duncan because it wasn't direct to daemons. It hadn't ever occurred to her to include daemons.

She raced into the hall to find Duncan, but slowed as she reached the top of the steps.

The hall echoed with noise as a group of women crowded through the front doors. The coven.

She hadn't seen most of these women more than once since she was seventeen—just the night they'd fought Julius Crowley together. They hadn't liked her much as kids. Though they had been nice enough, all things considered, when she'd seen them last. She came around the table, her stomach knotting, and forced a smile.

At first, they didn't notice her. The women stared at their surroundings, trying to answer their daughters' multitude of questions. She counted thirteen children, so a few of them had multiple kids, because she, Lilith, and Kat didn't have any. The kids, all girls, appeared to range in age from five to early-teens.

She cleared her throat. "Welcome."

As one, they turned her direction. For a heartbeat or two they stared. Someone squealed and the sound acted as a starting pistol of sorts. They all ran toward her, arms extended, shouting all at once so that she couldn't understand what any of them were saying.

The first reached her, her halo of curly red hair giving her away as Rowena's daughter, Kat. "Gaia be blessed, it's good to see you safe!" She gave her a quick hug and stepped back, allowing the others to gather around.

They hugged and patted her. Someone ran her fingers through her damp hair. It was like being in the middle of a multi-armed tornado.

"Oh, the girls," said a gothed-out woman, who wore platform army boots and black lipstick.

"Violet?"

Violet nodded. "Come here, girls."

The children gathered around, wide-eyed.

"This is your Auntie Trina. Remember we told you—"

A little blonde started jumping up and down. "You invited a vampire into your house when you were my age!"

"Mom said you turned Monopoly money into real money and used it to trick Lilith's grandmother once." One of the older girls leaned closer and whispered, "Can you teach me that spell?"

"They all say you have the best April Fool's jokes!" One of the little ones tugged on the hem of her shirt. "Is it April yet?"

Another, the youngest of the lot considering her small stature, held her arms up in a timeless plea to be held.

She picked the child up as she shook her head in answer to the other kid, the lump in her throat making it impossible to speak. All these years she'd thought they hated her because of their unfiltered thoughts from when they were children. She'd never considered that they'd grown up. Never allowed for the possibility that they'd changed. And while she'd harbored resentment for them, they'd told their children about their Auntie Trina.

Goddess bless them. She'd never asked them to, but they'd forgiven her. The only one who hadn't . . . was her. All these years she'd been projecting her own self-loathing and resentment onto others and hiding from them, as if that would protect her.

Augustina had been right, she *had* been lying to herself. She'd put herself into exile with the only person who actually hated her—*her*. The Judgment card made sense now.

She was ruining things with Duncan because she'd never forgiven herself. Because she feared her Magic and a stupid spell that wouldn't even affect him.

Brenda sidled up next to her. "You all right? You're looking a little watery."

"I'm . . . ." She sniffed. Wiped at her eyes. "Happy to see you all."

The next few minutes were full of introductions, but she had no hope of remembering all the little girls' names.

Kat cleared her throat. "Listen, when we were walking up here, we were followed by things like that." She pointed to Harry and George.

"It's the kids." Trina smiled. "The minions follow Harry around, too." She explained about the spell closing the portal and how the minions had been waiting in the grove around the portal for the children to return. "They seem to act as protectors for them."

Zoe shivered, biting down on her lip. "I wonder if they'll follow the girls back home."

"You'll have to let me know. I had to promise to stay here in order to re-open the portal."

Violet reared back. "You're stuck here?"

She nodded. "Well, if Lilith is willing, she can give me a break now and again. One of us has to remain here at all times and I'm okay with it being me." When they stared at her, she shrugged. "I was freaked at first, but it's not so bad. And, you know, now that the portal is open, I'm sure we'll get Netflix and Starbucks soon."

They laughed.

Sherri nudged her and pointed to the other side of the room. "Is that him? The one we summoned?"

Duncan. He leaned against the wall, chatting with Harry, but his gaze never left her. "Yeah."

Meredith hummed in her throat. "Mm. He that big everywhere?"

A rash of giggles broke out and Trina's cheeks flared with heat.

"Never mind that," Zoe said, flipping her blond hair over her shoulder. "Does he know how to use it?"

Claire shook her head. "Okay, I admit it. I'm jealous. I want one. The next summoning is for me." A playful argument broke out over who would be next to meet their mate. Rowena had kept a tight leash on the coven, not allowing them to date or have relationships. All the children were the result of artificial insemination, not love. She imagined they were all ready to get on with their lives and find their mates.

"Where's Lilith? I keep expecting her to walk in, but . . . ."

All at once, they said, "James." Several rolled their eyes.

"James what?"

"He's making her wait for half an hour . . . to make sure nothing happens to us before he lets her in."

He was still worried she'd hurt Lilith. She pulled a face. "Why half an hour?"

Kat grinned. "She told him if he ever wanted to have sex again, she wasn't waiting more than thirty minutes."

As if on cue, she heard James bellow, "Lilith!" The door swung open and her friend marched in, James stalking in behind her. "It hasn't been half an hour."

"It'll take me thirty seconds to cross the room, you over-protective ass."

Lilith looked . . . normal. Healthy. Mad as a wet hornet, but she couldn't blame her. She started walking toward her before she'd even made the decision to take the risk.

Two more strides and Lilith started running. "Look at you!"

"Me? You almost look human." She opened her arms.

"No hugging!"

Trina stuck her tongue out at James. "Fuck off." She hugged her friend. "It's so good to see you."

Lilith rocked her from side to side. "You have no idea. I love James to death but . . . ." She let out a growl. *He's been making me crazy!*

"I can hear you again!"

Still hugging they jumped up and down, laughing. Everything was back to normal.

"I think I figured everything out. We talked to the Watcher and—" Trina started to pull away and something tugged her skin. She didn't *feel* right. "What the hell?" She tried to take a step back at the same time Lilith did, but they stuck. Panic ripped through her with white-hot intensity, heating her face and making her hair stand on end. She tried to lift her arms from Lilith's back but her skin was . . . fused to her. Her skin looked like cheese pulling away from a pizza box, stringy and tacky. All along her temple, cheek, neck, and down the front of her torso she *felt* the pulling and stretching. Pain lanced through her, originating everywhere Lilith touched.

Lilith chanted, "Oh, gods. Oh, gods. Oh, gods."

Strong hands grabbed her shoulders and hauled her back at the same time James reached Lilith. The men pulled them apart and she stared at

Lilith. The World crossed by Death. A sacrifice to get close to her goal.

Duncan turned her around and ran his hands down her face. Her arms. "You all right, Duchess? Anything hurt?"

Am I whole? Did I melt? Her heart thundered in her chest. She touched her cheek. Ran her hands down her clothes, but everything felt fine. "How'd you get here so fast?"

Meredith leaned forward. "That one had your back the minute he heard James bellowing at Lilith."

Her gaze locked onto Duncan. "I didn't do that." She turned to the coven. "I would never do that."

"No one's blaming you." His gaze hardened and settled on something over her shoulder. "*No one* is blaming you."

James sighed. "At least neither of you is hurt." He glanced around at the coven. "Anyone have any idea what happened?"

The women shook their heads.

Duncan's hand tightened on her shoulder. "We've been hearing a lot about how the Original has to merge and become one in order to fight the Watcher as an equal."

Lilith's gaze widened. "What?"

Trina grimaced. "I thought it more a metaphor than literal."

"What's got me worried," Duncan said, "is they keep talking about you two merging, but no one's said anything about you going back to being separate women afterward."

"Maybe they don't think we'll survive that long." Trina chewed her lip. She'd thought being stuck here in Machon was the sacrifice she had to make. What if they had to sacrifice themselves? "Or maybe we won't be able to go back to being ourselves."

TRINA INTRODUCED THE COVEN TO Duncan, Harry, George, and Doom, and they'd all sat around the tables in the great hall. The children hanging out and giggling in the corner, their words too soft for the adults to hear.

Duncan had pulled Lilith to the side. She had no idea what the two of them were talking about, but he'd put his hand on her shoulder and stooped down as they strolled toward the table. When he finished talking, Lilith pressed her lips together as if fighting off a laugh. She composed herself. Nodded. Glanced at Trina and winked. *I like him.*

Back off sister, he's mine.

Kat asked. "So what's the plan?"

"We're going to summon Julius Crowley, exorcize the Watcher from him, and destroy the Watcher."

Lilith and Duncan came and sat at the table. He shook his head. "About that. Kasdeja said that without knowing the name of the Watcher, you can't destroy him, but you can imprison him again."

"You'll have to draw him up close to one of the ruins." Doom leaned back in his chair. "A tower will appear once he's close and you can imprison him there."

She glanced at Lilith, who shrugged. "I don't know how we're going to lure him anywhere."

"Kasdeja said you'd know how to turn into the Original—"

Lilith rolled her eyes. "Yeah, we figured that part out, Duncan."

"So, I'm assuming, once merged, you'd know what to do. Thing is, with all this talk of merging, no one is saying anything about being able to separate again."

James scrubbed his hand over his bald head. "So we find another way."

"I don't see this as a problem." Brenda closed her eyes. "If they learned how to unite, they will learn how to go back to being themselves again." When she opened her eyes again, she gave each male a pointed stare. "You worry for nothing."

Trina met Lilith's gaze. *What do you think?*

Brenda's visions are always right.

The oldest of the girls sidled up next to Harry. "Hi. I'm Skye."

He smirked. "Hi, Skye. I'm a twenty-one year-old man stuck in the body of a late-blooming teenage vampire."

Skye's eyes widened and she left.

Everyone stared at him. "What?"

"We're going to fix that." Brenda nodded. "You're going to do great things someday. Be a protector of women, children, and lost souls." She opened her eyes. "And you're going to look like a man when you do so."

Harry went completely still. Eyes wide. Lips parted. He checked his watch but didn't say a thing.

As the coven's seer, Brenda's visions came sporadically, but they were always accurate from what she'd heard. "When? How long does he have to wait?"

A shiver shook Brenda violently. "We have to practice casting as a coven. We'll practice on him."

Duncan's hand came down on the table hard enough to rattle glasses. "No one's 'practicing' fuck all on the lad." He stood, cocked his finger at Trina. "Can I have a word?"

She winked at Harry and joined Duncan away from the table.

"This is a bunch of shite. Tell me you're not encouraging this?" His mouth drew down, worry lines appeared between his brows. He'd folded his arms over his chest, but his whole body vibrated in agitation.

"Brenda's visions are never wrong. If she's seen him as a man in the future . . . then he's going to survive the spell."

"How do you know? Has she ever had visions in Machon before? Have any of you?" His accent grew thicker with every word he spoke. "Your Magic works better here, maybe hers is worse."

"No. But have you considered what Harry wants?"

"You think I haven't?" He kept his voice to a whisper. "You think I don't want the same for him? I'm not taking exception to the idea. I'm taking exception to the method."

She put her hand on her hip. "You'd rather wait for medical science? Yeah, let's leave him looking like a little boy for the next thousand years."

"Christ. Be a little melodramatic while you're at it." He scowled. "This is me lad you're talking about, not some lab rat." Duncan's phone buzzed. "Fuck's sake." He pulled it out of his pocket at the same time that everyone else's phones started buzzing and ringing.

"Duncan—"

"What!" All his focus snapped to the side where Lilith held out her phone. "I think this is for you."

Trina had a text from Anonymous Caller: **Scott Mason requests your presence**. An address followed.

"Where the hell is Nogales, Arizona?" Duncan asked.

Violet looked up. "Down near the Mexican border. My phone says someone named Scott Mason wants to see you there."

"Mine, too." Trina put her phone back in her pocket, lifting her brow at Duncan. "You told that guy at RI to say your name if he needed to speak to you."

"I'd forgotten." His hand dragged down his face. "Feels like a lifetime ago." He pointed at Harry. "You and I are going to have a chat about this whole thing when I get back."

Trina took hold of his hand. "Ready?"

"Yeah."

She glanced at Lilith. *Sort Harry out while we're gone.*

All over it. Lilith winked.

She spoke the words to the spell, picturing the red dirt and dry air of Nogales. Between one blink and the next, they were there. They stood on the corner of Arroyo and Oak and after studying the numbers on nearby buildings, she pointed up the street. "We need to go up there."

"Looks like the Nephilim hit this place hard." He withdrew his blade.

All the town's signs were in Spanish even though they were on American soil. The adobe-style homes and brick and plyboard buildings from a bygone era. Half the town had burned, the acrid scent making her nose itch. No one was around, but dozens of alarms rang. An overturned police car sat on the sidewalk near the Gran Mercado, its lights still flashing, siren still whining. "You think he's still alive?"

"Mason? Watchers haven't said otherwise."

They passed a Catholic School. The doors hung wide open, blood smeared across one—as if wounded kids had tried to hold themselves up as they exited.

They stayed to the center of the street, putting space between them and the dark nooks and crannies between buildings. "It's quiet. The Nephilim are noisy."

"Yeah." He nudged her arm with his elbow. "There."

Straight ahead of them, the street dead-ended at the front of a church, a two-story, white-washed adobe structure with several long stone steps leading up to the Spanish-scrolled French doors. One man stood to the side wearing a biohazard suit. Four more lay on the ground, blood a dark contrast to the bright yellow suits they wore. And on the steps, a little boy lay unmoving, covered in blood, on his back, arms outstretched, his head lower than his feet like some satanic sacrifice.

"Goddess bless us."

They approached the scene, slowly, unsure what had happened, unsure what to expect from the remaining human. When a few feet away, Duncan put his arm out, forcing her to stop.

"Mason?"

"Yeah." The guy in the yellow suit stepped forward.

Duncan motioned at the suit. "Don't need that. It's gonna be more hindrance than help."

"How do you—"

"It's not biological." Trina kneeled down by the kid. Nephilim didn't kill him. Gunshots did. "He was human."

"I know." Mason cursed and pulled off the helmet to his suit. "We came in by chopper. Those creatures had swarmed the place—"

"Nephilim." If they insisted on getting involved, they should have the correct information.

"Nephilim." He nodded. "Bodies—" He held his arm out, palm down and slowly rotated from left to right. "Everywhere. Blood and broken glass and . . . ." He sighed. "They hadn't started transforming yet. Took longer this time; I thought they were dead for good."

Duncan re-sheathed his blade. "You saw what I did to the dead on Smyrna. You have to check every one."

Mason nodded. "We were looking for survivors and as we approached the church this kid ran out, arms waving, shouting gibberish."

"He has a harelip." She stood. "He probably had a speech impediment."

"I *know*. Now, I know. I hesitated calling 'no-fire' and Lanscome"—he pointed to one of the dead men—"opened fire." He shook his head. "Soon as we saw the blood we knew. And someone started laughing. Laughing like a fucking lunatic watching a puppet show." He pointed off to the side near a tree. "The Harbinger—that's what they call Crowley— stood there. The Nephilim started to wake."

"That's how you lost your men. Fighting the Nephilim?" He was lucky as hell to have survived.

He shook his head. "He made one of those things again . . . a window . . . a portal . . . and they all got sucked into it."

She stood and walked to the bodies. The position of them—not sprawled out as if they'd been fighting or running—dropped in place as if they'd been standing still. The single gunshots to the head. As if they'd been executed. "What happened?"

"I raised my weapon." He pointed to the tree where Crowley had stood and his mouth turned down. "I saw his fucking eyes, I couldn't miss the shot. I ordered them all to fire."

"Jesus." Duncan met her gaze. "Crowley got to them."

Goddess bless him, Crowley had made him shoot his own men.

"The son of a bitch said, 'No.' That's it. I couldn't fire."

"He's a mesmerist talent, Mason," Duncan said. "It's not your fault."

"He said, 'I am your commanding officer and you will obey my com- mands.'"

Trina tried to call him back from the memory. "Mason."

"He said, 'You will destroy the enemy. Do you understand?' And even though in my head I screamed, 'Fuck you!' I opened my mouth, and said, 'Yes, sir.' We all did."

"Look at me!"

Mason obeyed. Hell, Duncan's shout had made her jump to attention.

"The rules of your reality have changed and you can do one of two things now: Either put the gun to your head and end it, or you walk away with a new perspective—knowing the full ramifications of this new world and use that knowledge to help your people."

"This morning they asked me to head up a new agency focused on . . . this new world."

Duncan folded his arms over his chest. "Explain."

"The government has acknowledged two problems in recent days, one publicly, one privately. The first, the Nephilim—we're losing that war right now."

"That's because you keep feeding their numbers, you idiot. A human, once bit, adds to their army. Quit sending people in after them. Put a sunset-to-sunrise curfew in place. No one stays in public spaces at night—only private property. Let us take care of the rest."

"That's the problem they've acknowledged privately. They've known about daemons since the Gulf War when we started using infrared on a regular basis."

Her jaw damned near hit the floor. She had no idea—but Duncan didn't look surprised at all. He nodded. "And?"

"And, if you're willing to offer us a sign of peace, we'd like to work with you in bringing the Nephilim to an end."

Duncan met Trina's gaze before turning back to Mason. "What constitutes a 'sign of peace'?"

"They had several suggestions . . . but after tonight . . . ." He met Duncan's gaze. "I want Crowley."

"As if I can hand him over on a silver platter? Maybe you haven't—"

"Duncan!" She glanced at Mason. "We need to discuss this for a moment."

Mason motioned for them to step away.

She pulled Duncan out of hearing distance. "Look, we're going to summon Crowley. We'll have him in a day or two."

"He's a mesmerist."

"We're going to exorcize the Watcher from him."

He scowled. "He needs to die before he causes anyone else harm."

"I agree." She stuck her finger out and poked him in the chest. "Quit arguing and listen."

He huffed out a sigh.

"One way or another, Crowley's going to die. What if we put a blind-fold on the son of a bitch and hand him over? Give the humans their peace offering, a sense that they have control . . . he still dies. It's done. Cake baked and eaten, too."

He kissed his teeth, glancing over his shoulder. "He's a slippery bastard. Don't trust him."

She glanced over her shoulder. "Mason?"

"Crowley. He never could keep his damn trap shut. He'll find a way to stir the pot."

Trina smiled. "You're forgetting I have Chaos Magic. I can get into his head, scramble things up enough to make him incoherent."

He tipped his head to the side, bottom lip poking out in that thoughtful expression that meant he was considering her idea. "Not bad, Duchess. All right."

They headed back to Mason, and Duncan said, "You have a deal. After talking things over, I realize we could have him to you within a week."

A week?

"Maybe sooner."

Ah, he wanted to pad their time.

"In exchange," Duncan continued, "I want the ability to hand-pick a couple of the daemons who'll become your advisors."

"Advisors?" Mason scoffed. Then stared at the tree where Crowley had been. "You give me Crowley, it's a deal."

They shook hands.

Trina waited while Mason gave Duncan his contact details and a sense of calm washed over her. Everything would be all right. Not the same as before, not by any means, but maybe better. Right now, Harry was being aged. The coven was together and stronger than ever. They had a deal with the humans and a plan for both Crowley and the Watcher possessing him. She just needed to get Duncan alone long enough to apologize to him.

Yeah, everything was starting to look up.

CHAPTER 29

Machon

AS SOON AS THEY RETURNED to the Citadel, Duncan rotated his shoulders and cracked his neck. He was tired as hell and they still had a Watcher to fight. Somehow, he didn't expect it to be half as easy as the coven did.

"I should go find James and fill him in on the deal we made." He opened his eyes to find a room full of daemons watching them.

Sort of. Some wouldn't meet his gaze. Others smiled hesitantly, as if they were all waiting for something. Lilith shoved a young guy forward. He tripped over his own feet, straightened, and glanced at his watch.

His gaze narrowed on the handsome lad. Blond hair, electric-blue eyes. Something about him . . . .

George came bounding across the floor, crawled straight up the guy's leg as if he had tiny suckers on the bottom of his feet, over his chest and around his broad shoulders where he perched himself. Like he did with . . . .

"Harry?"

"Figured we'd get it over with while you were gone. Less drama."

Jesus. His throat grew thick and his eyes stung. This must be what it felt like when you realized your kid had grown up and didn't need you any-more. He cleared his throat, forced the emotions away and made himself smile. "Glad to see you outgrew that awkward stage."

Nervous laughter rolled through the hall.

Christ. He didn't want to embarrass the lad. And he sure as hell didn't need to know how fucking hurt he felt. Everybody seemed to be pushing him away. "I'm glad it worked." He slapped him on the back, knowing a hug would trigger Harry. Hell, a hug would make him cry like a baby all over the lad. "Congratulations."

Everyone started talking at once, their attention turned to their own conversations.

Harry scratched George under the chin. "You sure you're not pissed?"

"'Course not, pup." He couldn't even look at him. "Now that it's done, I can see I worried for nothing."

One of the women called Harry away and the lad left him standing there alone.

A hand curled around his shoulder and Trina walked around his side. "He looks good, right?"

Good? The lad looked like he should be on the cover of GQ. "Yeah. He'll be a hit with the ladies for sure." He turned and left the keep, rubbing his chest as he went.

"Dunc?"

He kept walking. He'd be damned if anyone would see him tearing up. That'd be a hell of a way to show her how fucking strong he was.

"Duncan."

"I'm not mad." He waved her away. "Just need some air."

Instead of stopping, the sound of her footsteps got closer as she picked up her pace.

"Jesus, Trina. Let me be a minute."

The footsteps disappeared.

She appeared right in front of him, forcing him to stop. Her eyes widened. "Oh, Dunc." She wrapped him in her arms.

"Something in me eye, is all. I'm fine."

"Quit trying to hide from me. You're upset. I didn't think you'd be upset once you saw him and knew he was okay."

"I'm not. He looks good. The coven did good." His voice cracked and he tried to pull away. She clung like moss to stone.

"Damn you." With nowhere to go, he gave up. Pulled her up tight in his arms and buried his face in her hair to hide his shame.

She patted him. Stroked his neck and cooed silly crap in his ear. Daft woman. "Tell me what's wrong."

He shrugged. "It's stupid."

"Tell me anyway."

"He's grown up. He's damn near as big as me and what if I didn't teach him right? What if I didn't tell him everything he needs to know? He's scarred, you know, from what he's been through. What if I didn't help him enough to keep him from turning bad?"

"He'd never disappoint you, Duncan. You must know that."

No, Harry would never disappoint him. He'd have to dust the lad if he did. "He doesn't need me no more."

"That's bullshit. He's always going to need you. He can't talk to his own father. When he meets his first girl, he's going to want advice. He'll come to you. When he has his first fight, he's gonna come to you. When he tries to find work or buy a house or any of a million other things, he's still gonna come to you."

"Which is why this is stupid."

She pulled away enough to wipe his tears away with his own handkerchief and grinned. "Duncan, you're experiencing what every parent on the planet . . . well, on our planet at least, experiences when their kids grow up and leave." She searched his face. "Can I tell you a secret?"

"Sure."

"Lilith said, when they did the transformation, they made him state his name—"

"When did she tell you this?" They hadn't spoken since they'd come back.

"We have our link back. She told me telepathically." She cupped his face in her hands. "He gave them the name Harrison Cayce Sinclair."

Jesus. The tears started all over again and this time he laughed. "I'm a fucking watering pot."

She hugged him. "He's lucky to have a man that loves him so much."

"I'm all right." He sniffed. Wiped his eyes. "Thank you."

"Can I talk to you about something else?" She pulled away.

"Yeah."

"When the coven came, I realized that Augustina was right." She tipped her head back to look at the sky and her eyes reflected the starlight. "I kept telling myself they were still the way they used to be as kids. Still angry and resentful of all the trouble I caused."

What was she trying to tell him? "So you're not worried anymore they'll think less of you for having me as a mate."

Her gaze shot to his. "What? I never said that."

"You implied—"

She frowned. "I'm not telling you anymore stories, Duncan. You're horrible at figuring out the moral. I implied that they always thought I ruined everything I've been given."

His gaze narrowed. "And . . . you're worried that . . . "

"That I'll hurt you, you crazy person." She paced away. "I'm scared I'll hurt you and I care too much to let that happen."

"You're hurting me more by pushing me away, love."

"I hadn't thought of that." She bit her lip. "I do want to be with you."

She was coming around. It wasn't a declaration of love, but at least she'd admitted to wanting him. If he let her have her space, she'd be his soon. "Come on, Duchess. Let's go back in before Harry starts worrying."

CHAPTER 30

DUNCAN TIPPED HIS CHAIR BACK on its rear legs, half listening as James, Harry, and Doom chatted. Everything was starting to fall into place. Harry got his wish—he looked his age. Trina and the coven were getting along. She had her link back with Lilith. She finally admitted she wanted to be with him.

She'd wandered off a while ago and with a little luck, right about now she'd be walking into her room . . . their room. He grinned.

"Duncan!" Harry waved a hand in front of his face.

"Sorry, wha—?"

A siren went off, the high-pitched squeal rolling though the building, echoing off the walls.

At the same time an image flashed through his mind. Trina pulling away from a wall. A man with a scar running down the center of his face pulled his fist from her face. She stared at him. At the web tattoo on his neck.

His smile vanished. He glanced around the room, searching for Trina.

Doom stood. "Someone intending harm has entered the building."

"D?"

"When Trina's sleeping, I see her dreams." But she shouldn't be asleep, he'd seen her only a few minutes ago. Was she purposely trying to communicate with him? He stood to better see around the room. "And I'm seeing a web tattoo on a scarred man's neck."

"A Sentry." Harry stood beside him. "She left the hall a few minutes ago, I don't think she's come back."

In the vision, she walked backward, through a doorway, into a hall. Jesus, she was replaying events backward. The bastard must've knocked her out cold. "Which way?"

Harry pointed to the left.

"Come on, Duchess. Give me something more to go on." He headed across the room, pushing daemons out of his way as he went, his attention on the row of arches Harry motioned to. "Where are you?"

She walked backward, through a swirling vortex, out a door, down another corridor that led to the great hall.

"Got her!" He turned toward the archway in the vision.

Two men appeared. One of them had a scar down the front of his face. A web tattoo on his neck. Trina wasn't with them.

Duncan let out a war cry as he withdrew his blade, barreling toward them.

The Sentries looked his way and split up as two more entered the room. They were changing, their heads splitting open, their arms and legs elongating. Black Tamanouses.

Someone screamed.

Conversations stopped to be replaced with the scrape of steel sliding out of sheaths. Tables and chairs overturned as the other daemons and witches realized they were under attack.

"I got your back, D. Dust him." Harry was right behind him.

Duncan reached the slowest of the lot.

He grabbed the bastard before he'd fully transformed, pulling him back into his blade, ashing him without breaking his stride. He had the second son of a bitch in his sights. The fucker was moving fast, trying to transform before he fought. They were strong as hell once they took their true form.

He forced himself faster, reaching out with one hand as he neared. He caught hold of the guy's collar. The daemon turned, slamming his fist into Duncan's windpipe. He held on to the daemon as he went down, dragging the bastard with him.

They rolled and Duncan lost his grip. He gained his feet and stood.

The fucking thing had finished transforming. The Black Tamanous stood twice Duncan's height, each of its four legs ending in sharp, pointed, boney claws. It lifted one of its legs, aiming straight for his chest.

He dove to the side. Got up. Ran toward it again.

Harry had one of the thing's legs grounded as he tried to climb up to its back. George crawled over him, bounding up the body of the Tamanous, biting and clawing at its back.

Duncan slashed at one of the legs but hit more bone than flesh. He barely drew blood.

An orb of fire from one of the witches, slammed into the creature and it reared back. He watched the legs, gauging where they'd come down, hoping the creature would lower itself enough for him to reach the fleshy parts. "Come on, you bastard."

It rolled. Harry went flying. George clung. Duncan waited for the right moment and jumped on top as its back hit the ground. It wriggled around, trying to put the flames out and Duncan held on. Slammed his blade into its soft belly. Dragged the blade through its flesh, eviscerating it.

Thick black blood oozed out of the gaping wound. The smell was atrocious.

"George!" Harry ran around the side, found George and pulled him out from underneath the creature. The minion stuck out his forked tongue and licked his cheek.

Duncan glanced around. The other two Black Tamanouses were dead. Doom pushed through the crowd, wiping his blade on his pants leg.

"There's a portal down the hall." Duncan pointed toward the arch he'd seen in the vision. "Trina walked through it and the Sentries were on the other side. Where does it go?"

Doom drew his brows down and he started to shake his head. "The coven has portals all over Machon going to different locations. The one in this building leads to the coven's quarters in London."

The coven's quarters? Shit. He meant the Vampiric Council Chambers.

James strode over, blades drawn and dripping black blood. To Doom, he said, "The Vampiric Council took over the coven's quarters centuries ago after the clearances."

Doom held his hands out. "I didn't know."

Fuck's sake. There was no way he could've known. "Doesn't matter. What matters is that they have Trina." He headed for the arch, but Harry stopped him.

"You can't barge in there. As soon as someone triggers the alarm, the whole place will lock down. They'll just go room to room, cutting all of you down. Believe me, I tried to escape that place more times than I can count."

"I can't abandon her."

"I'm not saying that. We need a plan, though."

Harry was right. When he'd gone to rescue the lad, the place had been locked down tight as Fort Knox. "I know where the control room is. I watched them open the gates to that damn pit they had you in." He shook his head. "But I don't know how all the controls work."

Harry grinned. "Give me five minutes in that room before you go barging in. I'll make sure the doors open and close when *you* need them to."

Duncan nodded. "All right. Come on, we'll go to the control room with you, make sure you're in, then we fight."

He strode down the hall to the door he'd seen in the vision, opened it, walked across the room to the portal. He glanced back at James and Doom and found the hall crowded with daemons and witches. He, Trina, and Harry weren't going it alone anymore. They had friends now. The Council would pay.

He went through the portal.

CHAPTER 31

TRINA CAME TO IN DEGREES. She didn't move at first, just listened. The room—wherever she was, was quiet. She lay on something cold and hard, maybe the ground or a table. The air had a slight musty odor, as if this room didn't get much air circulation.

Her head ached, but she didn't think she'd sustained any major injury. She opened her eyes a sliver.

"Don't try to use your Magic yet, witch." A female voice.

She froze.

"I'm a prisoner, too. In the next cell. I can't harm you. The Sentries aren't here."

She opened her eyes all the way and glanced around as she sat up. The room was dark, but she saw well enough. Silver bars surrounded the five-by-five-foot cell she was in. A woman sat in the corner of the cell next to her.

Dark-skinned. Thin. Beautiful. Her pale brown eyes were striking against her skin tone.

"I'm Adia."

"Trina." Her brows furrowed. "Why do you think I'm a witch?"

"They put a collar on you to prevent you from using your Magic." She smiled, revealing a jumble of teeth. For such a beautiful woman, she should have had braces long ago. "But there's a secret to those."

She touched the collar at her neck. It felt similar to the one Rowena gave her long ago. "Oh?"

"I used to be friends with the old coven. You look similar to Satrina. She once told me those chokers don't activate until the witch tries to use Magic. In other words, you have one shot at getting out of your cell."

"Got it." She stood and scanned the bars for weak spots. Maybe the hinges.

"Someone's coming."

Trina backed up against the wall, as far from the bars as she could get as footsteps approached. The man who came around the corner didn't look threatening at all. Thin, narrow . . . almost pretty with his long white hair and pale skin.

He held his hands behind his back and studied her. "I'd like to ask a favor, witch."

"I don't do favors for assholes that lock me up."

"It's a formality until we get to know one another better." He waved to the bars. "Once you agree to right the wrong you did in your last incarnation, I'll let you go."

Her gaze sidled to Adia, who shook her head slightly.

"What 'wrong' are you talking about?"

"My wife and I tried to help the old coven. We tried to prevent you from leaving here and pursuing a male named Julius Crowley to the Colonies. Had we succeeded . . . the old coven would never have been decimated."

She folded her arms over her chest. Interesting. She had no way of knowing if what he said was true or not. She was leaning toward "not."

"How did you try to keep us here? By imprisoning us?"

The corner of his lips curved. "They would've lived."

"So what wrong did we commit as we were fighting for our freedom?"

"*You*. You cast against my wife. Threw her against a wall and now she's . . . damaged. From what I've garnered from modern medical texts, I believe she had a stroke when her head hit the wall."

Shit.

He grabbed hold of the bars, his cultured façade burning away with the heat of his anger and she re-evaluated her initial impression. He *was* dangerous. Crazy dangerous. "You will cure her or you will rot in this cell." He nodded to the other woman. "Ask her. She's been here five years now. She'll be here forever if I have anything to say about it."

Adia's lip curled. "I think your time ruling here is coming to an end, *mwanaharamu*." She spit on the floor. "*The Gasan* is here." She nodded to Trina. "It's time for us women to be in control again."

He looked at Trina, tipped his head toward Adia. "The things she's done would curdle your blood, witch. Things that have never been allowed under any daemon regime." He stepped away from the bars. "We'll see how you're feeling in a few days of no Magic. No blood."

Her stomach clenched at the mention of blood. She'd need to feed soon. "I won't be here that long." She lifted her chin. "Duncan will come for me."

His lips quirked. "He's as bad as she is." His chin jerked to Adia. "We know all about Duncan Sinclair, don't we, Adia?"

Adia's mouth turned down. Her nostrils flared. Hands fisted. Trina couldn't tell if the reaction was to Leopold, or Duncan's name.

Leopold wandered closer to the bars. "Did he tell you he killed his family?"

She swallowed, trying to dislodge the tightness in her throat.

"Oh, yes. They say he wandered home one night after a fight and beat his wife and son to death."

He came around the side of her cell, and she backed away. "He wouldn't." Not Duncan.

"No? He killed his father 'cause the old man beat his mother senseless." He put his hands through the bars and rested his elbows on the cross beam. "Duncan killed him, and then the stupid brute turned into him. He *did* murder his family. I saw the place after he left. Blood smeared the walls. The floor. He *crushed* them. Only a man full of jealousy and hatred could do something like that. And you think he's coming for you? If I were you, I'd start praying that he *doesn't*. You're far safer with us." He left the room.

Her gaze didn't leave the spot she'd last seen the male. "Duncan wouldn't do that to his family."

"While I hate to agree with the *mwanaharamu*, I do remember the rumors back then, after his transformation. You should be cautious around that one."

Neophytes did horrible things trying to feed the first time. Hell, she'd tried to attack Duncan when he'd transformed her. "*Right* after transformation?"

Adia pressed her lips together. "Nah. He came here first, went through Guardian training. But a couple weeks after his release, Leopold had to relocate him. Sent him up to Glasgow for decades because there were wanted posters with his face all through London."

No. He was too controlled. Too . . . gentle. Except when he fought, and then he was fierce.

Duncan was innocent. He had to be.

"We should go now, before the *mwanaharamu* comes back."

"What's that mean?"

"Bastard. Leopold is a bastard, if not by birth, then by deed."

"And Gasan?"

Her lips curved. "Queen."

She met Adia's gaze.

"We've been under patriarchal rule for too long. Things are bad for us when the males rule."

"What did you do, Adia? Why are you here?"

"I loved someone I'm not allowed to love under the *mwanaharamu's* rule."

She nodded. Adia must have fallen for a human. She couldn't fault her for that. "Where is he now?"

"Dead." Her lips trembled and she pressed them into a thin line. "They had him hunted and killed like a rabid dog after they dragged me here."

"What will you do if you get free?"

Her light-brown eyes blazed with fury. "I will hunt *them* down like rabid dogs. I will take pleasure in watching their bodies crumble to ash at the end of my blade. I will avenge my lover."

"All right. I'll help you get out of here."

She took a closer look at the door to her cell and reassessed the hinges and the lock. If she had one shot, she'd better go for the smallest—the lock. Old, with a large hole for a large key. She peeked inside and caught a glimpse of the locking mechanism. "Wish me luck."

"Oh, I do. I want out of here as much as you."

She closed her eyes and pulled energy from the Earth, let it pool inside of her. When she was full to bursting, she focused on the lock and released it all.

The lock burst apart into millions of particles at the same time she was thrown back against the wall. She fell to the ground in a heap and moaned. Fucking choker. She felt the stones with her fingers. One was cracked.

"Are you all right? Your lock is open. The keys to my cell are on the wall." Adia stood, her hands wrapped around the bars, her face pressed between. "Hurry before anyone returns."

T HE ROOM WAS EMPTY. SMALL. Lit with torches. There were two doors. "I think it's this way."

Duncan walked across the room, opened the door and glanced both ways. "Three doors down." He motioned Harry to go to the right, but his gaze lingered on the long hallway to the left. Where the hell were the Sentries? He turned back to Harry and the lad was gone, lost somewhere amid the crowd of daemons following them.

He pushed his way through. "Harry?"

Sounds of a scuffle directed him to a room farther along the hall; he turned the corner as Harry ashed a Sentry.

Harry stood and grinned. "Five minutes, all right?" He sat in front of the computer, setting his knife next to the keyboard.

"Yeah." This room wasn't much larger than the last. Monitors covered one whole wall—some showed infrared heat signatures, others the regular images of security cams. Vampires couldn't be photographed, but the infrared picked up their heat—they showed up as dark blue, whereas humans showed as bright reds and oranges.

Harry's hands tapped across the keyboard. "I'm in." He did a few more keystrokes and all the monitors turned to infrared images. "There." He pointed to a monitor in the center. The Council chambers. Each of the chairs showed a faint heat image. A dark purple or blue person-shaped blurp on the screen.

He pointed to another screen that showed several forms crowded into a hallway. "And here are our allies." The witches showed up bright orange and red, but the rest of the daemons didn't look any different from the council.

"We're going to need a signal, so you know it's us."

"One fist, straight up in the air."

"Yeah, okay."

He turned to the others, but James was already relaying the information.

"How do I get to the Chambers from here?"

Harry enlarged a map on his screen. "Left out this door. Right two halls down. Then the first left."

Duncan nodded and turned to go. "Stay safe." He followed Harry's direction and came straight to the vestibule outside the Council Chambers. As he reached for the door, an alarm sounded and a solid steel blockade dropped over all the entrances, blocking access to the doors.

He glanced back at the other daemons. "That must've been Harry." He hoped to hell it was Harry.

"That's it!" Adia pointed to a door down the hall. "The elevator's just through there."

They were almost free. She pulled at the choker around her throat. Adia hadn't been able to get it off. It required a special key.

An alarm sounded and she covered her ears.

Sheets of steel dropped over the doors.

"Shit." Someone must have noticed they were gone. All the doors were covered, locked.

"The control room." Adia started back down the hallway they'd just traveled. "Come on. I know where it is."

Duncan raised his fist as he strode to the double door. The steel blockade lifted.

James drew his blades. "All right, Sinclair, we got your back. Lead on."

He strode in to find half the Council rising from their seats. "Don't get up." He jumped up on the large, oval, iridescent table. The whole damn Council was here.

Someone cleared a throat.

Duncan turned toward the sound as he unsheathed his blade. His gaze lit on Leopold. "You have something of mine, you fucking cu—"

James elbowed him.

"So, the last of the Guardians have decided to grace us with their presence." Leopold sat back in his chair. Smiled.

Duncan took a steadying breath. He'd be better able to help Trina if he stayed calm.

"No Sentries?" James' gaze traveled the chamber. "Who came up with that idea?"

"Me." Leopold scoffed. "Who do you think?"

James shrugged. "Julius?"

Leopold laughed. "You think he controls my mind? Don't be absurd."

Duncan exchanged a glance with James. "Julius is a mesmerist. The idea isn't that farfetched."

"Julius isn't a concern." Leopold's hand shook when he threaded it through his hair. "Not for me."

Duncan snorted. "No, I suppose the Watcher keeps him pretty quiet."

A smirk curved his lips. "Ah, you figured it out, did you?" Leo lifted one brow. "Took long enough."

James tsked. Pointed his blade at a council member with a graying goatee. "You stay right where you are, Diego."

"He's started Armageddon." Duncan glanced around at the other Council members. "The Watcher this prick made a deal with." He waved his blade at Leopold. "Tell them. Tell them what happens when all the humans are dead."

"Don't be over-dramatic. Everything's under control." Leo's gaze darted to something behind him and James. "You brought humans with you?"

He grinned. "Not humans. Witches. Got a whole coven of them."

"They're dead." His gaze traveled from Council member to Council member. "They were dead." Leopold burst out of his seat, fists hammering the table. "Where are the rest?"

Duncan glanced behind him. Kat, Brenda, and a few others were here, but not the whole coven.

Kat lifted her chin. "Preparing."

"For what?" Diego asked.

"War," James said.

Murmurs ran through the Council chambers.

"It's time to choose sides." Duncan turned a slow circle. "The Watcher cannot be allowed to decimate humankind. Balance is required in all things. Join us."

"You're suggesting suicide." Diego shook his head. "The Watcher will dust you all."

"We have the Original."

Leopold smiled. "Do you?"

Bastard. "I will as soon as I ash you."

"You and what army?"

Duncan spread his arms wide. "I got everything I need right here."

Leopold stood. "So do I." His gaze flicked to the side and he nodded.

The lights flickered out.

Duncan pulled Kat flush to his back. Immediately, James and Doom and a few others, pulled the witches to the center and backed against them so they were surrounded and protected.

The witches must be terrified, they weren't battle-hardened. The room was pitch-black. The Council rose from their seats and the table shifted as they climbed on to get closer.

"Capture the witches," Leopold ordered. "Destroy the rest."

Doom growled.

Something snarled back.

An orb of blue light lit the chamber—courtesy of one of the witches—revealing vampires splitting off copies and filling the room, a gargoyle-ish creature rose above the others, flapping great leathery wings, the whooshing the only sound heard past the witches' thundering hearts and labored breathing.

The changeling opened its spindly-toothed mouth to unleash an ear-piercing screech.

Brenda screamed.

The light orb fizzled out.

The first Council member attacked and Duncan's hands snapped out, grabbing both the daemon's hand and the knife he held. With a quick jerk of his arm the blade rent through the bastard's neck. He was ash before he clocked onto what had happened.

Magic lit the room as the coven took offensive shots with orbs of electricity and fire.

Duncan's attention zeroed in on Leopold. He appeared adamant to stay out of the fight, sidling toward the exit while he let the others take the hits for him. Duncan headed his way.

A big son of a bitch stepped in front of Duncan—Iram was his name—blocking Leopold from his view. A mane of shaggy red hair framed a thick jaw, straight patriarchal nose, and dull brown eyes.

Duncan swung without breaking stride, thinking to lay him flat and keep after Leopold.

That didn't happen.

Iram didn't even flinch. He did, however, growl. A meaty fist connected with Duncan's jaw, sending him sprawling.

Pulling himself up, he touched his jaw gingerly, regarding his opponent. In the background, Leopold paused, no doubt lured by seeing him get trounced.

Fine. Leo wasn't going anywhere. They were all locked in. He just hoped no one else got to him before he did. "What kinda talent are you?" He rose, padding closer with fists up, just like in the old days.

Iram didn't respond.

"Strong silent type, eh?" He faked a couple punches to gauge his adversary.

Iram dodged the blows like a well-practiced boxer. No fear crossed his eyes. No adrenalin rush made him shake. Nothing.

He continued to circle, chatting as he did. "Changeling. Must be with a mug like that."

"Fuck off, Sinclair."

Duncan feigned right and threw a left hook to his neck. Iram staggered back. "Even the little guy gets lucky," Duncan sneered.

Iram dropped his knife and tackled him. Oversized hands gripped Duncan's head, bashed it back into the hard ground. *Fuck.* He reeled from the blow. Iram had him pinned, unable to pull his arms back far enough to get a solid hit, incapable of reaching his blade.

Iram lifted his head again. Stars burst behind his eyes as his skull slammed to the floor. He got hold of the larger man's head. Pressed his thumbs to his eyes.

Something rammed into Iram, throwing him clear of Duncan. Whatever it was got his hand, too. He cupped it close, glancing down. The whole back of his hand had been burned, the skin red and blistering. One of the witches must've blasted Iram. He glanced at the shadowy area behind him where Iram had disappeared, but nothing moved.

The whole room had erupted into a kill-or-be-killed brawl. Kat mouthed, "Sorry," before a Council member tackled her. Leopold still stood against the wall, still watching.

A growl came from the shadows behind him.

Shit.

He swung around as massive black paws swiped at him, knocking him back to the ground. A large black bear lumbered closer.

Duncan back-peddled across the floor, putting distance between him and Iram. His mind raced through his kindred, searching for the right fit.

Ah, yes. White fur engulfed him as he took on the form of a polar bear. Iram roared.

Duncan charged. Both reared on their hind legs, paws slashing, claws tearing. They toppled on their sides, each vying for a dominant position.

Iram gained the top position, his claws sinking into Duncan's shoulder.

But he outweighed Iram in this form. He was taller, stronger and far more determined. He shook off Iram and attacked again, this time settling his claws into his neck and ripping flesh and fur.

The large wound forced Iram to shift back to daemon form. Duncan swiped again with one of his massive paws, leaving deep lacerations across Iram's chest. One last blow proved too much. Iram dissolved to ash.

He shifted back into his true form in time to see Leo squeeze through a hole that had been blown into the wall.

Fucking coven.

MATED DAEMONS HAD ALWAYS BEEN the bane of Leopold's existence. They'd do anything, even kill themselves, trying to protect the other. The Watchers had tricked him into sending the Original's mate to her. And now the Watcher inside Crowley had insisted that he be here in his true form. The bastard had known Sinclair would come for his mate. Brilliant.

Leopold hid in the shadows, waiting for Duncan. The big dunce wouldn't stop until he'd found his mate and he had no chance at taking Duncan on himself. Not one-on-one.

Misha, another Council member, darted past with the red-headed witch in close pursuit.

Leopold unleashed his talent on the witch, letting the tendrils of his talent settle around her like a mantle, searching for her desire. Most desired fame, love, wealth, or sex. They were easy illusions to project. The witch's desire took shape into a tall, muscled male. Sandy-blond curly hair formed over a youthful face.

The doppelgänger turned and Leopold stepped back, shaking his head as he peered into Julius Crowley's face.

Impossible.

His mind raced. What had they called the witch? Her name was Kat; Katherine? Was she Katherine the Great?

After all these years the two of them were still causing problems and trying to oust him. He met the Crowley-double's gaze. "Transform her. Then destroy her." It was the only way to ensure she never reincarnated again.

Now for Duncan, the simple-minded fool. Should he project Trina's image? Make him think he'd found her? No. Mated or not, he knew how to twist Sinclair into knots. He needed him rattled. Distracted.

TRINA FOLLOWED ADIA DOWN ANOTHER corridor. The place was like a damned maze. Old. Dark. Winding. She glanced into each room as they passed, half-expecting something to jump out.

"We're almost there, *Gasan.*"

"Wait." She backed up a couple paces. Surely, she hadn't seen what she thought she'd seen.

There. Kat was pinned up against the wall by a male. His mouth on her neck. A blade in his hand.

She ran straight into the room. "Get off her!" She ripped him away from Kat and jumped on him. Slammed her fist down onto his face.

Adia shouted, "Look out!"

She glanced up as Adia rammed a wrought-iron candleholder down on his head with enough force to split his skull. She did it again. And again. And—

"Stop!" Her stomach rolled as she crawled off him. His skull was crushed. "That's him. Crowley." After everything they'd gone through . . . that was it? He was dead?

Adia threw the candlestick to the floor. "Don't think so. Leopold can project his enemy's deepest desires in order to distract them."

"What?"

"It's his talent." Adia pointed at Crowley. "That thing didn't fight us. Didn't know it should. It was created for one purpose." She motioned behind her. "To distract her."

Kat was slumped on the floor, her neck splayed wide, blood pooling between her breasts.

"Kat!" She ran over, knelt down and covered her neck with her hand. "Will she transform?"

"If she doesn't bleed out first." Adia pressed her lips into a thin line, glanced toward the door. "Stay here. I'll find blood."

D UNCAN ENTERED THE CORRIDOR. WHERE had the bloody bastard run off to?

Three-quarters of the way down the hall a little lad came into view. A wall sconce flickered, lighting his mop of blond hair.

The lad turned his direction. Smiled. Waved. Disappeared through a door.

Recognition slammed through him. "Charlie?" He meant to call out the question, but his name came out a broken whisper.

Spurned into motion by the emptiness of the hallway, he ran to the door he'd seen the lad go in. He slowed as he neared, fearing the harshness of disappointment but needing to know. Taking a steadying breath, he entered the room.

The little boy grinned. "Hi, Papa."

Charlie. Duncan fell to his knees.

Crystal-blue eyes stared back above a pert nose sprinkled with fairy kisses. His full mouth curved up into a welcoming smile.

"Is that you?" He half expected his hand to go right through the lad, but baby-fine silky hair greeted him. "How?"

"Been waiting, Papa."

The child propelled himself toward Duncan, wrapping his chubby limbs around him. He inhaled but Charlie no longer smelled of dirt and puppies. He'd always loved that about Charlie—that he smelled of the outdoors.

Shaking himself from his stupor, he engulfed his son in a bear hug. He kept touching him, stroking his soft hair and reassuring himself Charlie was indeed a physical being.

His son. All this time Charlie had been here? Unchanged? He didn't have a heartbeat. But he didn't sound older. If he'd been around all this time, wouldn't he have aged on the inside like Harry?

And how? He'd seen their flat. The blood smeared over the walls as if someone had tried painting the place in it. As soon as he'd opened the door, the scent of decay had rolled over him, twisting his stomach. Flies had clung to the walls, bred in the festering remains of an uneaten dinner still sitting out on the table. He'd never questioned if they'd survived.

But his boy was here. Holding him. "Where you been, Papa?"

"I'm sorry, Charlie. I didn't know. Let me look at ya." He pulled away, touched the lad's chubby cheeks. Ran his hands down his little arms. He could barely see him. Everything blurred. A shaky laugh burst from him and he wiped the tears from his eyes. "My God, I can't believe this."

The lad peered over Duncan's shoulder. "Look, Mummy."

Every muscle in his body tensed. Gertie? He supposed if Charlie had survived, she could've have, too.

He gathered his son close and rose to his feet. He wouldn't allow her to belittle him in front of the lad. Not anymore.

TRINA HAD SAT THERE WITH Kat for so long, she started to doubt whether Adia would return. She had both hands covering the wound in Kat's neck, but she lay too still. Too quiet. She couldn't feel a pulse anymore, but if she was transforming, she wouldn't have a heart anymore, right? She wouldn't be like her and Lilith. She'd be a true vampire. She'd lose her Magic over time and gain the same talent that had been used to transform her.

Footsteps ran down the hall toward them and she tensed.

Adia burst into the room, four bags of blood clutched in her arms. She motioned "Come here" as she came closer. "There's fighting. The Council and others. We should try to get farther away before she wakes."

Duncan.

Adia helped her get Kat up and together they carried her down the hall.

"Are the doors still blocked?"

"Yes." Adia stumbled. Righted herself. "Sorry. I will take us to the control room. We can barricade ourselves inside, if need be."

That sounded like a good plan. The noise of battle drew closer. Shouting. Fists pounding skin. Furniture crashing and skidding across the floors.

"Here. This is it."

The door stood open. They went inside.

Adia pointed to the far wall where keys of various sizes and shapes hung from a pegboard. They took two more steps in and froze as a big, blond male sitting at the controls came into view, his fingers flying over the keys as he watched various monitors.

"Harry?"

"Hey, Lopez." His head lifted and he started to smile, but when his gaze found them, his whole body stiffened. "You."

George bristled at the change in his mood.

Adia's brows came together. "Do I know you?"

"You're my originator."

"Impossible." She laughed. "I have specific tastes and while handsome, you don't qualify."

"I know your tastes, Adia." His voice shook. He stood. "Every twisted nuance. I can assure you I did fit your requirements."

Her nostrils flared. "Harry?"

Trina's gaze darted between the two of them, dread souring her stomach. "You know each other."

He glanced at his watch, pulled his blade, and when he lifted his face again, his lips had curled into an ugly sneer. His eyes blazed. "You're never hurting anyone again. Tonight, you're ash."

Adia let go of Kat, sending Trina toppling to the ground from the other woman's weight. Adia bolted out the door. Harry leapt over her and Kat and followed.

No, no, no! She'd trusted that bitch! She started to get up, but she couldn't leave Kat, not when she could wake up at any moment. She needed Duncan. She needed her damned Magic.

Her gaze locked onto the pegboard of neatly labeled keys. She scanned over the board, touching this one and that one. Found a set that said: collars. *Yes!*

She bowed her head, reaching around to fit it to the lock. The collar came off.

Duncan was here somewhere. She closed her eyes and opened her mind. Let her consciousness follow the thread that linked her to Duncan. And as she did so, she discovered it was a familiar path. One she'd traveled before. One she almost knew by heart.

The connection wasn't the best. She couldn't quite make out his thoughts, but she saw what he was seeing.

A sweet little toe-head with bright blue eyes. And a woman. A beautiful one.

"GERTIE." SHE WAS STILL AS beautiful as ever. Too beautiful, maybe. She had the perfect face of one of those porcelain dolls Trina had talked about earlier. Each of her features symmetrical and dainty, which gave her a fragile, untouchable aura.

She smiled.

His eyes narrowed. He didn't think her lips *could* curve in that direction.

"Duncan, my love, I've missed you." She ran over and embraced him.

It was as though someone dumped a bucket of ice water on him.

None of this was real.

She wasn't Gertie. Not even the Gertie from the night they first met. Gertie wasn't sweet. She didn't smile. She wouldn't miss him. She'd never called him "My love."

His eyes closed against the heartbreaking truth. This lad wasn't Charlie.

It was a lie.

His arms tightened around the boy as if by sheer will he might make Charlie real. Maybe he should take what he could have. For a time, he stood frozen, thinking maybe this was enough.

Duncan, they're not real. Leopold is a projector.

Trina. He closed his eyes for a moment and he felt his mate as if she stood right here with him.

Don't trust them, baby. He's coming for you.

He eased his grip on Charlie and instead held his knife a little tighter.

Duncan sucked in a much needed breath and forced a smile. "Step back, Gertie. Let me see ya, love."

She's not real!

Would she hear him if he thought back to her? *I know, but I need him to show himself.*

Gertie obeyed without question. Smiling.

He eyed the happy Gertie doppelgänger and gave the Charlie doppelgänger a squeeze before setting him down.

A boot scraped the stone floor behind him.

Duncan turned to find Leo sneaking up on him, knife in hand. "You miscalculated, Leo."

"How so?"

Don't turn your back on those two!

He backed away, trying to keep Leopold and the doppelgängers in sight.

"Gertie was a real bitch." He nodded to the doppelgänger. "Always been convinced her face would shatter if her lips ever stretched into a smile."

Charlie edged over and curved his arm around Duncan's thigh, just like the real Charlie used to do. Jesus, Leopold was a bastard.

"She's improved." Leopold motioned to Gertie. "How's that bad? You can have it all."

"I already do."

"Papa?" Jesus, the Charlie doppelgänger sounded so much like his son it made his chest seize.

You have to hurry, Dunc. Harry took off and I can't leave Kat. She's hurt.

Duncan forced himself to ignore the lad hanging onto his leg.

"You're sure it's not him?" Leopold's gaze flicked to Charlie.

He damned near stopped breathing.

Leo shrugged. "Stab him and find out." If a doppelgänger he wouldn't fall to ash. But if he was real . . . .

Duncan's gaze returned to the lad who looked so much like Charlie, then back to Leopold's smug face.

Cold rage boiled through him. Never had he felt such unconditional animosity toward another being. "How 'bout I destroy you, and we'll see if he sticks around."

Out the corner of his eye, Duncan caught furtive movement from Gertie. He glanced over as she threw a blade in his direction.

I've got you, baby.

His hand lifted. Heat wound through his arm to his hand, like electricity shooting through him.

The knife changed course, crashing into a large, oval scrying mirror, shattering it. Glass still tinkled to the floor when he regained control and hurled his knife.

The blade went through a bit of flesh in her arm, pinning her to the wall.

Leopold gasped. "How?"

A little warning next time, Duchess? He flexed his fingers, trying to rid himself of the residual tingling. "How did you know what they looked like?"

Leopold didn't reply, his gaze shifting between the knife in Gertie's arm and the knife lying amid the broken glass.

The dumb shite would never figure it out.

He repeated his question.

"Had to be done." Leopold's gaze jerked to his. "Your loyalty would've been compromised. They'd have always come first."

"That's why you killed them?" Out of every explanation he'd imagined, this wasn't anywhere on the list. "You said if I became a Guardian, you'd take care of them."

"And I did. I went to that stinking hovel of yours and gave your boy his deepest desire—his father. Little lad didn't even fight when my projection put its blade to his throat."

Oh, God. He didn't just kill them. Leopold projected *him* and killed them. No wonder everyone in his old neighborhood thought he'd done it.

"Did you think you'd go to work every night and come home in the morning to play Daddy? You always were stupid."

Duncan charged, knocking Leopold to the floor. He cocked his arm back and punched him. Again. Again. The skin on his knuckles split, leaving his hand throbbing.

The skin on Leo's face split. Leo thrashed against him with weak, unpracticed blows.

"You're a fucking cunt." He raised his fist.

White hot fire lanced into Duncan's back. Too late, he remembered Charlie.

He hadn't been watching the lad. He scrambled up and turned.

Charlie stood there with wide, innocent eyes; the look of a youth caught with his hand in the cookie jar. His hands were empty but deep, midnight lacerations streaked his palms. Duncan's attention flashed to Gertie still pinned to the wall with his knife, to the broken shards of mirror on the floor. Christ, if the lad had picked up the blade, Duncan would've been ash.

Leo scrambled to his feet. Disappeared through the door.

Duncan dove for Leopold's blade. Before he could pursue, Leopold reappeared, arm lifted over his shoulder, his fingertips gripping the blade of a Guardian knife.

His arm cocked back even as Duncan did the same with Leo's blade. They released their weapons at the same time.

Duncan's hand stayed extended in front of him and that same sense of electricity coursed down his arms.

Leo's blade went wide.

Duncan's didn't.

He got one last glimpse of Charlie before the boy dissolved into ash.

Go get your son, Dunc. He needs you. I need you.

IMAGES FLASHED THROUGH DUNCAN'S MIND as he ran from the room. He paused in the hallway, trying to get his bearings—where he was, compared to where he needed to be.

He saw a woman from behind bars, dark skin, pale-brown eyes. She'd tricked Trina, made her think they were on the same side. They helped each other escape but when they'd reached the control room . . . .

Harry flashed in his vision. Those blue eyes widening. Narrowing. His whole face twisted into something ugly and vengeful.

Christ. The control room was down the hall to his left and Harry had chased her out the door to the right.

James said they're doing one last sweep. Everyone is keeping an eye out for Harry.

Got it.

I need to stay with Kat until she's finished feeding, then I'm headed your way.

I've got this. You take care of Kat.

He felt her hesitation. Damn. How much had she seen? What he'd seen, or did she have access to his thoughts, too? Had she accessed his memories of the abuse? Did she think she needed to stay with him because he wasn't strong enough to finish this?

The sound of voices echoed on the stone as he neared a four-way hallway.

A woman. Adia. "I still want you, Harry."

"Goddamn it to hell." Harry's voice. "Fight me."

Duncan turned down the hall to his left, heading for the first door.

"You're lucky you didn't hit my minion, you bitch."

Harry's voice was quieter that time. He'd gone the wrong way. He turned around.

Adia laughed and the sound sent a shiver down his spine. Where the fuck were they?

"Disappointed?" Harry's voice shook. "I may be young, but I've been trained by the best. Now show yourself. You owe me." His voice edged up in volume, echoing off the walls.

Back at the four-way split, Duncan went to the right.

"Oh, I do owe you, dear boy. You've been alive all this time? Remember what I told you would happen if you ever denied me?"

"I never denied you."

"You're denying me now."

Shite. Wrong way again. He ran back to the four-way.

"I will have you, or I will destroy everyone you've ever loved."

Jesus, she was crazy. Her voice kept edging up higher, bouncing off the stone walls and making it impossible to find them.

"I'm not a boy anymore. You don't frighten me."

There. Duncan's gaze zeroed in on a door and he broke into a sprint.

"I will frighten you. You'll never see me coming."

He burst into the room as the woman faded from sight. Harry was pinned to the wall, a Guardian blade sticking out of his chest. George was curled around his neck.

No. That wasn't Harry. That blade would've ashed Harry. It was a copy. Jesus. For years now he'd thought the whole damn Council had taken Harry, but it'd been a woman. His gaze traveled the room. The big bed. The chains.

His stomach roiled. "Christ, Harry." He forced himself to look at the lad—the copy. "Where are you?"

"Go away." The copy disappeared. George dropped to the floor and padded out of the room.

The hell with that. He followed the minion, down the hall and into a different room. George slowed as he entered. Slunk forward, making gurgling noises as he approached. Harry was in the corner, his big frame huddled against the wall, knees pulled up, eyes closed, struggling for breath. Each wheezing inhale sounded painful. His hands opened and closed at his sides reflexively.

Shite. This was a bad attack.

He knelt down in front of Harry. "Breathe, lad. We've done this before." It was all in his mind. He wasn't even sure if, as vampires, they needed to breathe. They didn't have organs, there were no lungs in their bodies, but he also knew from experience that if he couldn't breathe, his body panicked and went through all the same torment as a human body.

Harry scrambled up, leaning his back against the wall as he did. "I'm . . . fine."

Bullshite. He could barely get the words out. "Eyes on me." He took a step closer, ready to block the lad if he tried to run.

"Not—" He choked. Closed his eyes. His whole chest heaved in effort with the next breath, his collar bone stuck out under his skin. His veins thick, bulging. "Doin' this."

"Yeah, we are." He grabbed the lad behind the head, pressed his forehead to his and drew in a slow, deep breath. "Like that, yeah?"

Harry tried to shake his head, but Duncan wasn't allowing it.

"Concentrate on my voice. Slow in. Slow out."

The lad's hands fisted, came down hard on his shoulders. Harry wasn't so little now, his hits hurt. "You . . . saw."

"Yeah." Three hundred years walking the earth. Three hundred years of life experience and never had he felt so inept. So unable to come up with satisfactory words. "Doesn't matter, pup. Doesn't change nothing."

"Every . . . thing."

"Breathe, damn you. Quit fighting it." He inhaled slowly as if he could breathe for the lad. "Whatever you're feeling, let it out. Cry. Scream. I won't think any less of you."

"Never . . . ." His chest locked up. A shudder ran through him hard enough to shake them both. The exhale was too shallow. "Let true emotion . . . show."

Duncan reared back. Jesus, he'd taught him that. Like his father had taught him the same damn thing. "It's a lie."

"You . . . don't lie."

"Sometimes." Shite. "That's a lie I tell myself. I think what I meant was that we never let our enemies see our true emotions. But around the people you love . . . I'd never hold it against you, pup. Not ever. I cry. Fuck's sake, a few hours ago I cried all over Trina. So you let it out, lad. No sense holding on to poison."

Harry's whole body shook. "Can't."

His hand tightened on the back of the kid's head. "Let it out, damn you."

A shout erupted from Harry, the likes of which Duncan had never heard. It lifted the hair at the back of his neck. Made his gut twist. Made tears pool in his own eyes. The pure anguish and hurt and anger that poured from the lad was more than anyone should bear. But the kid's eyes remained dry.

"Good, lad." He'd gotten the air out from his body, at least. That was always his problem, getting the air out before he drew another breath. "You look at me now and I'll tell you the truth."

Harry's eyes shifted up. They were so close he couldn't see more than a blur of features.

"Everybody gets screwed at some point in life. There's no shame in it. It's the way it is."

"Not you."

"Yes. Yes, me, too. Damn it. Hell, I didn't even know how much I got fucked over until tonight."

"Tell me."

"I've been working three hundred years for the man that killed me wife and son."

"What?"

"Leopold's a projector. He projected me and went after me family. Killed them, and everyone in me old neighborhood thought I did it."

"Yeah, but I got fucked over by a—"

"Woman? Me wife used to beat me."

Harry reared back, this time hard enough to pull free from Duncan's grasp.

He shrugged. "See, me father used to beat the hell out of me mum. Told meself I'd never do the same. And me wife, Gertie, that woman hated me. She was nice enough at first. Beautiful. Something happened after she got pregnant, though. Wake me up by kicking me in the head. Drop hot soup in me lap. Bashed me in the face with those damn pans of hers more than once as I was coming around a corner. She was too small to take me head-on, but she had a million ways of getting to me when I wasn't looking." He kissed his teeth. "Never told anyone that." Duncan slid down the wall to sit, motioned for Harry to do the same. "Kind of cathartic, you know?" He shrugged. "Why don't you have a go?"

CHAPTER 32

BACK AT THE CITADEL, TRINA waited for Lilith to enter Kat's room. As soon as she entered, Trina closed the door and leaned against it.

"What happened?" Lilith's gaze darted between the two of them.

Craziness, that's what. She motioned to Kat. "You want to tell your high priestess what happened, or should I?"

"I'm sorry." Kat's eyes widened and she shook her head. "I would never do anything to hurt the coven."

Trina waved toward Kat. "I happened to walk past a room and saw Kat pinned up against the wall by a man. Crowley."

Tears trailed down Kat's cheeks. "You don't understand."

"Leopold has a projection talent—he projects his victim's *deepest desires* to distract them."

For a moment, Lilith stared at her. Then she gasped and swung around to Kat. "Katherine O'Hickey what are you thinking?"

She started to cry in earnest.

Trina had zero patience. "Yes. Tell me what was running through your head. I got stuck saving your sorry little ass while leaving my mate and his son to the mercy of our enemies. Enemies you're cavorting with."

"No."

"If anything happens to Duncan or Harry, I will cut you to pieces, do you hear me?"

"He's my mate!" Kat shouted the confession before slipping to the floor and crying harder. "I didn't ask for him to be my mate, but he is. And maybe it's because I'm a healer. Maybe I . . . ."

"Oh, gods." Lilith turned from Kat and looked at Trina. *If he is her mate . . . .*

Trina shook her head. *She can't possibly know if he's her mate. He's possessed by a Watcher, which means the other Watchers can't see Crowley. They wouldn't have heard any summons she made.*

Lilith's gaze narrowed on Kat. "How do you know?"

"I tried straight summoning first, but the Watchers never responded." Kat shrugged. "Claire used dream Magic. She asked the goddess to lead me to my mate on the Astral."

Lilith nodded to Trina. *Her story adds up. Before you came home from the Navy, I went to get my Grimoire from Kat. She had bruises all over her. Rowena beat the hell out of her because she didn't want to kill vampires. She told me about the dream and her mate.*

Trina deflated. She'd do damn near anything for Duncan. But she and Lilith had both been blessed with good males. Steady. Strong. *Sane.*

Lilith turned back to Kat. "The day you told me about the dream, you said you didn't know his name."

"I didn't, not then. But on Samhain, when Mother tried to force you to do Magic for him . . . ."

"Shit." Lilith shook her head. "Of course. Crowley was there." *The whole coven knows what he looks like. I can't imagine how they'll react.*

"He tried to kill you that night." Trina paced across the floor. "He's in league with a Watcher. They're calling him the Harbinger back on Earth because he's released Nephilim—"

Kat stood and her chin tipped up. "He's not. I don't think he ever was. I saw him on the astral and he's . . . in bad shape. The Watcher is torturing him."

"He's been possessed for a long time, honey." Lilith led her over to a chair and had her sit. "I mean, he wiped out the old coven."

Trina sat on the windowsill. "He's been possessed for at least three hundred years. That's got to mess with a person. He's probably crazy as hell."

"He's my mate." Yeah, it always came back to that little fact. Mates were difficult to refuse.

Lilith held her hands up. *I can't imagine being without James.*

I know. I can feel Duncan when he's not with me. I don't feel right until he's with me again.

Lilith shrugged. "She's an amazing healer. Maybe she could—"

"I can." Kat jumped at the opportunity. "Give him to me. I can heal any damage that's been done to his mind. I can. I'll prove to you he's still good."

"No," Trina moaned out the word. "No, no." She spiked her hands through her hair. "Mason." *Oh, Lil, I screwed up again!* "Duncan and I made a deal with the humans. We agreed to give them Crowley."

Lilith scrunched her face. "What?"

"You can't." Kat grabbed her arm. "Please. He's the Tanin'iver. You'll suffer as much as me if he dies."

This time both she and Lilith stared at Kat. "What?"

"It's in the *Black Book of Daemonology*." She hugged herself.

Lilith met her gaze. "Get the book."

Trina spell-traveled to the great hall, grabbed the book and returned.

Kat waved her hand at the book. "I don't remember the page. Look up The Original, and at the bottom of the page is a 'see also Tanin'iver' and 'see also Blind Dragon.'"

Trina did as she asked and found the page. There were only a couple sentences there. "Says the Original created him from a lost soul and gave him the title Tanin'iver. Then, the Tanin'iver married Lilith and Samael."

James' first name.

Duncan's middle name.

Kat took the book from her, and flipped through some pages. "Under Blind Dragon, which is his other title, it says that when Lilith was punished, both Samael and Tanin'iver were also destroyed."

"Why?"

"Samael had bitten Lilith, so his blood flowed through her veins. And she had created a body for Tanin'iver, so her Magic flowed through his. When the goddess punished her, the spell split her soul in two, and it also affected the two of them."

"Samael's soul must have split, too, hence our mates."

"The point is, that the Tanin'iver brought you to your mates. The Tanin'iver is the symbol of your bond. Even now, neither of you would've found your mates if Crowley hadn't been stirring the pot."

Lilith propped her hand on her hip. "I summoned my mate because Nan was beating me for arguing with her about daemon kind."

"For being sympathetic to them. For insisting they had mates. Why do you think that pissed her off so much? Because a vampire named Crowley was hanging around Haven House demanding information about the girls within. That's why Nan beat you and why Rowena cursed you with the dybbuk." She pointed to Trina. "Why she made you wear that choker. If you destroy Crowley, you may destroy your bond with your mates."

"We don't know that." But could they take the risk? She looked at Lilith. "What are we going to do now?"

Lilith sat on the edge of the bed and took a deep breath. "We're going to stall for time, that's what. We'll move forward with our plan."

Kat took a step closer. "But—"

Lilith held up her hand. "We summon Crowley and take care of the Watcher. And Kat is going to take Crowley to her home."

Trina scoffed. "What if he's dangerous?"

Kat squared her shoulders. "I can handle him. If he's beyond help, I'll bring him back and you can give him to the humans. I promise."

Shit. This was going to be a disaster.

Lilith sighed. *We'll need to find a way to get the humans to imprison him without killing him if he affects our bonding with our mates.*

The U.S. military does not negotiate.

Lilith sighed. *How much time do we have to deliver to the humans?*

A week.

"What are we supposed to tell our males?" Lilith shrugged. "That he got away?"

Trina closed her eyes. They needed a plan. "Okay, Kat, you spell-travel Crowley to your place—I'll show you how—but you stay here. Wait until everything is done. Make sure the males see you here. Then go. No one will be the wiser that you have him."

I hate the idea of lying to James. Lilith bit her lip.

Are you kidding? Duncan made the deal with Mason because I suggested it. She glanced at Kat. "Sorry. I didn't know. All I could think about was how he mesmerized m— We can't do this. What if he mesmerizes Kat?" *And she's going to lose her Magic. I'm not even sure how to tell her that.*

Don't tell her yet. We have time. Lilith shook her head. *It'll take time before her Vampiric talent replaces her Magic. Hopefully, she'll have healed her mate and we'll have everything figured out by then.*

"Mother cast over our minds when I was still a kid. You can't read my thoughts. He can't get into my head."

She looked at Lilith. *Which means I can't tell for sure if she's telling us the truth. What happens if she's as bad as her mother?*

Kat? She's a healer, for crying out loud. "The real problem will be finding another peace offering for the humans if he turns out to be okay."

They talked for a few more minutes and then left to let Kat rest. In the hallway, Lilith stopped and faced her. "Want to tell me what's going on with you and Duncan?"

"Nothing."

Her brows crept up. "Well, that is a problem, isn't it?"

Trina propped her hands on her hips. "You don't know what it's like,

Lil. You have control of your Magic. But mine . . . it's better since I've been in Machon—"

"I think it'll keep getting better the longer you're here."

"—but what if I hurt him? I've had a couple near misses with him already and—"

Lilith frowned. "What happened?"

"I sort of shot him."

Her friend gaped.

"Then I almost killed him when he was transforming me. And later I threw him up against the wall." Tears welled in her eyes. "I love him, but I don't want to hurt him."

"Don't do that! You can't cry because I can't hug you."

She laughed. And cried harder. "I can't help it."

"Look at me."

She forced her gaze to meet Lil's. "I know how to fix this."

"You do?"

"Yeah. I've been thinking about it, since I summoned him, and because of what you almost did to James."

Her gaze narrowed. "How did you summon Duncan?"

"I summoned the Original's mate to Haven House. Mine was already with me, so it stood to reason that yours would be the one to arrive at Haven House." She grinned. "Come on."

CHAPTER 33

THEY WAITED WHILE THE NEPHILIM dusted the two Sentries guarding their destination. Julius watched without emotion. After the horrendous things he'd seen—that Azazel had forced him to do—the last two nights, seeing a couple of Sentries destroyed was nothing. Had Leopold really thought Sentries would stop Azazel?

They went through the gates, into an old abandoned townhome and straight into the basement. There was another door, one that led to more stairs. The air grew danker with each step. Like the rat he was, Leopold had run back to his nesting grounds after his failure with Sinclair.

Though far below ground, in the ancient sewers of London, Leopold's bolt hole was luxurious. The curved stone walls were the only hint of the past. The floors were covered in thick rugs. Large, ornate furniture decorated the space, giving it more the aura of a mansion than an underground cistern.

Azazel had full control of Julius' body and he didn't resist. He was far too curious what the fallen angel had to say. Besides, Leopold was one of the people he wouldn't mind watching suffer.

Leopold walked into the room, pausing partway across. His spine stiffened and he spun around. His icy eyes widened.

"You can't think I didn't know where you lived."

"Why are you here?" Leopold's gaze shifted behind Julius, where the Nephilim paced.

His lips stretched as Azazel smiled. "I thought I'd leave you a gift."

Leopold swallowed, his Adam's apple bobbing with the motion.

"Quite benevolent of me considering you failed today." They strolled to the center of the room, running their hand along the back of a plush couch.

"L-l-leo?" A woman's voice called from the other room. His wife. Azazel's revulsion shuddered though him.

"Sinclair used Magic. I'd have been in a better position from here, but you insisted *I* go. You put me in harm's way. I'm lucky to be alive."

"Duncan was right, you are a prissy little cunt, aren't you?" This time Julius mouth curved from his own amusement. "You let Satrina get away. You owe me."

"Bullshit. I got you that body." He pointed to Julius. "That was my part of the deal. But you, you haven't destroyed the coven. Two guardians still live."

"Three guardians still live—if you count this one." Their hand twisted, pointing at himself. "And the coven will die soon. They plan to summon my host and exorcize me from this prison at long last."

Praise Jesus, it was about fucking time. He needed to make plans—the information he had on Azazel and his activities would be useful for the coven.

"You will come to my tower in a week's time. Alone or with a different body, I care not."

Leopold shook his head. "I held up my end of the bargain. You didn't. If you get stuck in one of those towers again, it's your own damned problem."

"No, it's *our* problem. You promised me freedom. There were no conditions. No provisions. Just freedom. If you do not hold up your end of the bargain, you're ash."

Leopold shook his head. "I can't control the Nephilim and they're everywhere." His gaze darted to the creatures by the door. "They'll tear me apart if I go outside."

Julius' mouth spread in a smile he didn't feel. "These Nephilim will protect you and make sure you get to my tower in a week's time."

"Why a week? This is ridiculous. Fight her now."

"The exorcism will leave me weak and I will not risk failure. You will release me in a week's time after she's exorcised me and then I will destroy her."

Leopold's jaw tightened, ticking out his irritation. "And what of that one." He motioned to Julius. "What if they get hold of him? He'll tell them everything."

"No. We have no reason to fear my host. I have some gifts for him, too."

Gifts? Jesus fucking Christ he didn't like the sound of that. Not considering the gifts he'd left Leopold.

"If my host survives the exorcism, he won't remember anything about our time together."

Leopold scoffed. "Memory spells aren't permanent."

They rarely lasted more than a few days.

"Which is why my second gift is a curse. With each rising sun my host will be overpowered with the urge to destroy himself."

The darkness inside Julius tightened into a sickening knot.

Leopold snorted. "His Vampiric survival instinct won't allow suicide."

Azazel laughed. "Yes. It will be interesting to see how long he can fight the impulse. With his survival instinct set against my suicide curse he should experience a slow, agonizing demise should those he protects not kill him first." Azazel took a menacing step closer to Leopold. "I've considered everything, including those things you do not wish to draw attention to . . . such as that pathetic wife of yours. You *will* obey me."

CHAPTER 34

GODDESS HELP HER. ELEPHANT-SIZED BUTTERFLIES were stomping around her innards, wreaking havoc on her good intentions. She'd been pacing the hall outside her and Duncan's rooms for the last fifteen minutes. He was in there, she could feel him.

She just wasn't sure what to say. Or how to say it. Now that she had the Magic issue worked out, how did she go about setting everything to rights with him? He hadn't come looking for her when he returned with Harry, which worried her. Claire and Violet had seen him come in and taken him to Kat so she could heal the stab wound on his back . . . but he hadn't even asked about her.

The door to their room opened and Duncan stuck his head out. "Are you about finished wearing grooves in the floor?"

Time was up. She swallowed hard and went into the room. Walked to the window and back to the door.

He caught hold of her arm. "Look, Duchess—"

"No." She dug the necklace she and Lilith had spellcast out of her pocket. "I need you to wear this."

The stone—dark green with red blotches—hung from a silver chain. He stared, but didn't take it.

"Please?"

With a sigh, he took it and put it on. "Now—"

She held up her hand. "You're going to have to wait. I'm sick over this and I need to get this out before I lose my nerve."

"Go on, then." He folded his arms over his chest.

"Lilith and I made that, not the rock of course. . . . Okay we didn't *make* it, we spellcast it so you and James—she's giving one to him—will be protected from our Magic. Negative spells, at least. I don't know why I didn't think of it before. I—"

"'Cause you were wearing yourself out over it, that's why."

"Maybe. But now we don't have to worry about that anymore and I wanted to see if I've screwed things up too badly. If maybe you're willing to give this another go."

His head tipped to the side. "Another go?"

She'd finally talked to Lilith and told her everything—about her Magic and Trevor and disappearing. Lilith hadn't even flinched. She'd been sympathetic. If she was going to be honest with Duncan, she had to do so now before all her fears came back. "The guy that I thought the Watchers sent to me . . . Trevor. I killed him."

"I know."

He knew? "I didn't mean to."

His lips curved. "I know that, too."

"How?"

"Whenever you're asleep, I see your nightmares."

Trina wet her lips. All this time…he knew. He knew and he was still here.

"What I'd like to know is how much you saw when you popped into me head."

"Just what you saw and heard. I knew you didn't kill your family. I didn't realize your wife was so beautiful." Magazine-cover gorgeous. She smoothed her hands down her tee-shirt.

"I realized a few things tonight, too." He held up a finger. "One. What you did, barging into me head—"

"I'm so sorry. I didn't know what else to do, I needed you. I won't ever—"

"Yeah, you will." He stepped closer. "I think it comes as natural as breathing to you."

She swallowed. "I haven't done that for years. I don't have to—"

"You do." He gripped her chin between his fingers, forcing her to meet his gaze. "It's part of the reason you hid yourself away. You've been lying to yourself, you can't be around people all the time and always be on guard."

Tears pricked her eyes. "I didn't ask to be like this. Maybe, if we ask the coven they can—"

"No." He took a step closer.

She backed away.

"No one is changing a goddamn thing about you. You have that gift for a reason, did you ever think of that?" He came closer. Let go of her chin to hold up two fingers. "Two. The idea of you seeing in me head scares the shite out of me."

"Duncan. We can figure this out." Now that she'd figured out how to protect him from her spells, she couldn't lose him now.

He lifted the stone. "I'll wear this bloody thing as long as you want me to on one condition. You let go and be yourself with me."

"What?"

"All or nothing. Right now, Duchess. Make your choice. Either we do this all the way, or we both fuck off." He stalked forward again and her back came up against the wall. "I'm exhausted worrying about what you'll think of me when you finally slip up and end up in me mind. You're exhausted worrying about always being on guard to protect me from your Magic and keeping your shields up so you don't slip into me head. We can't go on like this. So all or nothing."

What would it be like? To just let go? Part of her wanted to jump at the opportunity before he came to his senses, but she loved him too much to not warn him. "I'm not sure you know what you're asking me. What if—?"

"Oh, I understand." He pulled her toward the over-sized armchair by the window, sat, and tugged her down over him so she straddled his legs. "I'm driving meself nuts, worrying about what'll happen once you're in here." He hit his head with the heel of his hand. "Do me a favor and just get it out of the way so *I* can relax, too."

"Just tell me."

"I'll shade it. Make a muck of it." He pulled her hands up to his face and kissed her palms. "After the talk I had with Harry . . . I just want it over with. Be like pulling the Band Aid off all at once. Yeah?"

Trina chewed her lip, unsure who was more afraid, him or her. She had no idea what she'd find in his mind. No clue what he may have thought about her in the past. What if she discovered he loved Gertie or Satrina more than he could ever love her?

He pulled her closer, until her forehead rested on his.

"I don't have to touch you, Dunc."

"Yeah, well, I need you to."

Her lips curved and she closed her eyes and reached out to him.

Gertie was a gorgeous woman who liked to sneak into the fights her father arranged at one of his warehouses. Well-dressed, she stood out among those who gathered to bet on the fights. She shouldn't have been there. Not in Cheapside.

Not at a fight. Her presence made him curious and he'd already been enamored of her fair looks.

After his victory, Duncan wound through the crowd to her side. They flirted and he lured her back to his place, to his bed. When she left in the morning he didn't expect to ever see her again, recognizing the one night stand for what it was. But three months later she returned. Pregnant and disowned, she didn't know where to go or what to do. Duncan married her.

As time went on Gertie changed. No longer the flirting, adventurous spirit from the night they met. She became mean-spirited, angry, and cruel. At first he thought her temper might be due to the pregnancy, but she became worse, not better after she gave birth to Charlie.

When Gertie yelled and screamed and cursed he took her berating at face value. Everything was his fault. He'd ruined her life. Was too stupid, too useless to provide adequately for them.

He doted on their son, when she refused. He withstood her punches and slaps as if he did indeed deserve them.

The abuse sickened Trina, she ached for Duncan. For Charlie. Now his worry she'd find him lacking made sense.

Gertie had.

Duncan had dyed his son's diaper purple, just like he'd told her. She smiled at his laughter when he hung the cloth to dry. But when he turned around, Gertie's beautiful face twisted in rage, visible for a flash before being blocked out by the large cast iron pot she wielded.

Trina tightened her hold on Duncan, grateful that he'd demanded she cuddle close. She'd asked him once if he'd broken his nose in a fight, and he'd said, "Of a sort."

"Jesus, Gertie." Duncan grabbed the freshly dyed nappy and put it to his ruined nose to stem the flow of blood. "You tryin' to make me hit you?"

"Yes! They say you killed a man with one blow. I've heard them talking about you in the streets. Hit me like you did him, put me out of my misery."

He stared. Mute. A hot flush assailing his already throbbing face. "It—" He coughed. "It's so bad, then, marriage to me?"

"Yes." Her reply was empathetic. Absolute. "I'm not meant for this." Her hand opened, encompassing everything around them. The little run-down flat. Duncan. Charlie. "If you have any sense in that thick skull of yours, do this for me."

His throat burned. "I'm going out."

"Duncan!"

He kissed his baby's cheek, pausing to wipe the smear of blood from Charlie's face. He grabbed a heavy sack, the metal items within clanging together as he set-

tled the bag on his shoulder and strode from the room.

"You're a coward." Gertie's sobs followed him through the narrow hall and down the rickety stairs.

That's how he knew her so well. He had to constantly guard his temper around Gertie, just like she had to constantly guard her temper around everyone else. If he'd ever hit Gertie, he probably would've killed her. She smoothed her thumb over his eyebrow. "Thank you."

"For what?"

"Sharing." She shrugged.

"You don't . . . ." He stared out the window. "Think less of me?"

Why would she think less of him? She reached out to him again and got the answer. He still believed some of the things Gertie used to say.

She forced him to look at her. "Never." She spread her hands on his chest, her thumbs stroking over his nipples, making his breath hitch. "You're the strongest male I've ever known. A ruthless fighter. An amazing lover. I'm lucky to have you for my mate."

"Say that again."

"I'm lucky—"

"Nah, the last two words."

"My mate." She grinned. "I love my mate."

"Do you now?" His lips twitched. "You planning on showing me how much?"

"Yeah." Her smile faded. "Every single night." It was a vow. "You'll never be my better-something-than-nothing."

He pressed his thumb to the corner of her mouth. "What am I then?"

"My something beautiful."

His eyes darkened and his grip tightened on her. "Good. 'Cause you're mine."

She leaned in and pressed her lips to his. "I need you."

S HE'D FINALLY DECIDED SHE WANTED to be his.
   "Clothes, Duchess."

Their clothing disappeared, leaving them skin-to-skin. She nipped his lip, rubbed her breasts against his chest. "I can't wait."

No. Waiting wasn't an option. Not this time. She lifted up and he fit himself to her opening. As always, her body resisted at first. "Damn it, Dunc."

He grinned. Fit his hands to the curves of her hips and pressed her down. Her body submitted. She turned her face to his neck and nipped him. Wrapped herself around him, pressing closer.

"Christ, I love that." The way she fussed when he entered her—the way she held onto him seeking solace from the very stretch she'd demanded. The way she cursed him and cuddled into him at the same time. The way she bit him in retaliation when he pushed past her tight entrance. The way she tried to wrap herself around him, pressing every part of her to every part of him as if trying to distract herself from the intensity—he couldn't imagine what it was like for her, but for him he damned near saw stars with that first thrust. Those breathy sighs and moans whispering over his skin.

"What?"

"You." He pulled out until just the head of his cock rested inside of her before thrusting back in. "That."

Her lips parted. Eyes closed. Her hands flexed at the back of his neck. "Again."

Yes. Again. He'd never get tired of this. Never. Christ, that was good. Her ragged breath heated his ear. Her nails dug into his shoulders. She rotated her hips each time she sank down on his length, as if trying to get him as deep as possible.

He stood, taking her with him, took two steps to the bed and lay her down. Her legs remained around his hips, his cock still buried inside her. Her hair spread out around her face. He hooked one of her legs over his arm and leaned over her, careful not to put his weight on her. He drew her nipple into his mouth, drawing on the tight bud.

"Oh." Her hands twisted in the sheets. She bucked against him. "Oh, Dunc."

Reaching between them, he stroked her off. Clenched his jaw as she tightened around him, as her release pulsed through her. He thrust into her once, twice more and his orgasm raced through him, setting off fireworks behind his eyes. "Christ, I love you."

CHAPTER 35

DUNCAN STOOD WITH JAMES ON a rise overlooking where the Grigori coven had gathered in a stone circle outside the walls of the Citadel. The children were at the keep, safely tucked away should anything go wrong out here.

Trina walked with Lilith around the perimeter of the Circle. Kat knelt near the center, carving a pentacle into the dirt. From what he understood, once they summoned Julius he'd be bound inside the symbol.

The rest of the coven stood in groups of two or three as they chatted. They were nervous. They milled about, wringing their hands and tugging their hair.

"Hurts like hell." James glanced at him. "Summoning."

"Good. Maybe that'll keep Crowley from trying to mesmerize the coven."

"None of them will look him in the eyes. They know better. They remember."

Harry joined them, George pacing across his shoulders—he had a bigger perch now. "Kat told me they're keeping the spell simple. No embellishments."

Duncan glanced at him. It was going to take him a while to get used to seeing Harry as an adult and hearing him speak with such a deep voice. "Been talking to her a lot, have you?"

He shrugged. "She couldn't sleep last night. Neither could I." He nodded toward the Circle. "They're bringing Crowley in, separating him from the Watcher, and then banishing the Watcher."

Trina had said the same. Said they'd reviewed the binding spell several times, weeding out any potential problems. The less room for misinterpretation from the universe, the better.

Still, his nerve endings burned, making his skin crawl. "None of this *feels* right. I don't like not being able to get to Trina once the circle is cast."

James nodded, his hand scrubbing over his shaved head.

The perpetually-full moon hovered above the horizon, casting Machon in brilliant red light. He checked his watch: 3:06 AM, back home. It was time.

Trina cast the circle, locking the coven inside the protective seal. As long as none of them broke the outer boundary, neither Crowley nor the Watcher could harm anyone.

Lilith started the spell and the coven joined in, "Tanin'iver, Julius Elisha Crowley, I summon thee. To obey all commands made by me. For this we ask or something more, so mote it be, we do implore."

"Something isn't right."

The coven spoke as one, chanting the spell in increasing speed until the words blurred together.

Something more? "Blood-y hell. They're in trouble." He started down the hill waving to the other daemons to do the same.

"What?" James jogged behind him. "Why?"

"Why'd they allow the possibility of 'more'? They're bringing in a Watcher."

His gaze locked onto the electric blue seal separating him from the coven. "Stop!"

A CHANTING SUMMONS POUNDED THROUGH JULIUS' mind, making his body jerk. The chorus grew louder, became consuming, battering all other thoughts away until he chanted along. The words spilled out faster, building in intensity along with a strange, insistent, pulling sensation. They filled his mind, spilled out of his mouth. "I summon thee. To obey all commands made by me. For this we ask or something more, so mote it be, we do implore."

Azazel took command of their body, cocking his head to the side. "More, indeed." A laugh rolled through him, despite the pain rending his body.

It is time, host. I'm so grateful to the coven for freeing me, I think I'll bring them a gift.

Jesus, the summoning spell, it was pulling him apart. Julius' mouth opened on a scream, but Azazel didn't allow any sound to come out.

TRINA FOCUSED ON THE SUMMONING circle, trying to ignore the males shouting for their attention. She couldn't make out their words anyway. They couldn't stop now.

The hair at the base of her neck stood on end. The air shimmered over the pentacle. Crowley appeared, locked into the pentacle.

He was laughing.

His khakis and white button-down shirt were almost unrecognizable due to the amount of blood covering him. The stuff was caked on his hands, his face. What had he done?

Damn it, he shouldn't be laughing. Summoning should leave the daemon in agony, immobilizing him and stripping him of any power he had. She'd expected screaming, not laughing.

She exchanged a glance with Lilith. The other witches were doing the same, all doubtless wondering: What did we miss?

Crowley spun his hand in a whirling motion.

The air outside the pentacle began to shimmer. A deep foreboding settled among them as a small black dot appeared mid-air. He pointed, making sure they all saw.

Their voices died as the dot began to grow, changing into a round, black doorway.

Wind whipped through their protected space. "He can't harm us," she shouted. "Not here."

A Nephilim stepped through, covered in blood much the same as Julius. Then another.

Another.

A dozen more.

Like the start of a rain shower, the first couple drops, fast turned into a deluge. Snarling, Nephilim began filling the circle. The witches backed away.

"It's all in the intention, little witch." Julius grinned, the voice coming out of him far too deep, too loud to be his. "I called them forth with the intention of aiding you on your request for . . . something more."

"Hurry." Lilith's voice rose above the animalistic grunts of the Nephilim. "Separate them so we can bind the Watcher before he can do anything more."

Trina nodded in full agreement. As one they began Psalm 91—the exorcism prayer.

SLOWLY, AZAZEL WAS BEING TORN from Julius, his larger form being pulled through his pores, stretching his skin apart. His vision blackened, but Azazel didn't allow him to lose consciousness.

I know you'll miss me, host. But I've left my gifts—something to remind you of me. Have fun.

His mouth opened on another scream as he dropped to his knees. With one final, wrenching pop, the Watcher was free.

Julius Crowley slumped to the ground like an old, discarded jacket. He had to get up. He needed to warn the coven. He needed to tell them Azazel's name.

HAD ANYONE ELSE BEEN RECEIVING the exorcism they performed, Trina would've been moved to compassion, but not for Crowley. No, this daemon didn't look the least bit innocent covered in blood, surrounded by Nephilim. She had too much history with the bastard for even the slightest twinge of sympathy. How could Kat possibly accept him as her mate?

Nephilim crowded in the center of the protected space, blocking him from her view. As more arrived, they pushed the rest closer to the coven.

The Watcher's twisted, skeletal form rose above them all. Gigantic. Unstoppable.

"Hold your ground," she shouted. The coven was rattled. They couldn't see the Watcher, but they saw Crowley drop to the ground, they knew he was free.

"No harm can come to us in the circle," Lilith reminded them.

As one, the coven moved several feet in from the outer line of the circle. "Trina."

She whirled around. Duncan stood on the other side of the shield. "If things go south, you come to me." She found no give in his steady gaze, only confident assurance. James stood to his left, Harry, Doom, and the rest behind them. Ready. Armed. Waiting.

A siren roared in the distance and more daemons ran to the circle.

She nodded before turning back to their unwelcomed guests.

"Focus, ladies." Lilith had to shout over the increasing noise. The Nephilim never stilled, shifting, moving, and making guttural, animal-like grunts.

She pulled herself together, concentrating on the banishing.

"Watcher, we bind thee," Lilith's voice blended with Trina's. The coven began adding their voices, their power to the spell. She reached out for Lilith's hand. They needed to merge into the Original now . . . but Lilith's hand wasn't there.

Nephilim pushed them apart. Shoulder-to-shoulder, back to front, they separated her and Lilith with their sheer number. "Lilith!"

They filled every available space, pushing her back.

Suddenly she realized what the Watcher had done. The Nephilim would keep pushing them back until they broke the protected circle.

And without that, all bets were off.

She set her feet hard against the ground, bracing herself against their surging force. They strained against her. She shoved back but it was like pushing against a brick wall.

"Surround the circle." James gave the command.

"Protect the coven," Duncan ordered.

Shouts of affirmation sounded off as daemons moved to do as commanded.

The stench of dried blood on the unclean bodies of the Nephilim made her gag as they pressed up against her. They were caked with the stuff. It covered their skin, matted their hair. Their glowing red eyes bored into hers, promising destruction.

Nephilim thrust against her, snarling, hissing, and gnashing their teeth. The Magic preventing the creatures from fulfilling their bloodlust also prevented the coven from destroying them.

Her feet slipped back.

"Watcher, we bind thee." Their voices trembled as the reality of this insurmountable failure began to register in its entirety. They couldn't stop the Nephilim from filling the space. They forced the women back, the words of the spell muffled by the rising animalistic noise filling the circle. "Grigori, we bind thee to your tower."

The Nephilim surged, forcing Trina back. Her heel passed one of the stones bordering the circle.

"Watcher we . . ." Her words faded, replaced by her scream of denial. "No."

The shield went down.

CHAPTER 36

DUNCAN GRABBED TRINA, THRUSTING HER behind him. Somewhere, James surely did the same with Lilith. Now they just had to get the women together.

The whole place erupted into chaos. He stabbed the Nephilim coming at him, backing away. They had to get to the rise. James said he'd bring Lilith there.

Shouts clashed with the growling snarls coming from the Nephilim. Orbs of fire and electricity lit the sky as witches defended themselves. Swords and blades slashed through the air, punctuated by the burst and rain of ash.

Splinters of black stone erupted in front of him courtesy of Trina, skewering the onslaught of Nephilim. The creatures, despite being impaled, grabbed at nearby daemons.

He backed farther, but it was slow going. Daemons ran toward the coven's stone circle to join the fight, hindering their progress.

A Nephilim lurched past him and grabbed Trina. Duncan wrenched her away from it. Ran it through with his blade. He backed away, forcing her behind him as he fought.

Defended.

Destroyed.

A vampire, an air-walker, rose over the crowd, slashing his blade at those below, geysers of ash spouting up in his wake.

Still more Nephilim arrived, pushing through the portal the Watcher had made. Their number legion, an army of amoral undead with no purpose but to destroy.

Something knocked the air-walker out of the sky. Duncan turned and ducked, pulling Trina under the shelter of his body as the air-walker flew past, landing in a heap several yards behind them.

"What the hell?"

"The Watcher swatted him. I'm keeping an eye on him." She sent another wall of spiked rock into Nephilim. "I need to get to Lilith to bind him to the tower."

"Up to the rise, Duchess."

They fought their way back. Violet joined his side, blasting the Nephilim with orbs of fire. He pushed her behind him with Trina before slashing through one. He kicked another away, stabbing a third with his knife.

There were too many.

TRINA LOOKED BEHIND HER. THEY were almost to the rise. James and Lilith stood at the top, waiting. "I see her." She ran straight up to Lilith. "Don't resist this time." *Resistance brought pain.*

Lilith nodded and Trina wrapped her arms around her friend.

CHAPTER 37

THE COVEN CLOSED RANKS IN front of Duncan, slowing the Nephilim, giving him a chance to check on Trina. The women were already together, had already begun melding. Growing. Changing.

Doom led more daemons to where they were, guarding them while they were vulnerable.

His chest seized as the individual women, as his mate and her friend faded. Jesus, he hoped they'd be able to transform back as easy as they united. They changed in shape, growing larger until they blocked out the light of the mammoth moon.

"Duncan!"

He swung around as Nephilim breached the coven's ranks. Daemons ran past him and the fight started anew. Doom tossed him a sword.

"Thanks." The sword had a design cut down the center to reveal the wood beneath the silver blade—a larger version of a Guardian knife. He rammed it through a Nephilim and it exploded into ash. Better. Much better.

A tandem roar filled the atmosphere. Everything stopped. Even the Nephilim paused, their animal instincts forcing their attention to the larger predator.

The Original stalked forward, her two heads high above the battle atop long serpentine necks. Iridescent scales, a rainbow of night colors, shone in the moonlight as she roared her battle cry. Minions swarmed the battlefield, brought to heal by her call. Foe and friend alike dodged her claws and her swinging, spiked tail. Fire blasted from her mouths.

"Bloody hell." A heavy leg stomped by. A scale was missing. "I'll be damned." *Always did like that table.*

He followed her, cutting down Nephilim who got too close. Dragon or not, he was bloody well protecting his mate's back.

An explosion rocked the area, throwing Duncan from his feet. The Original protected him from the worst of the blast. He struggled back to his feet, saw Kat nearby and helped her up. The other coven members appeared shaken but fine.

"What was that?" Kat asked.

"I don't know." Duncan glanced around. "The Wayward Watcher? Crowley?"

Shite. Where was Crowley? He had a clear line of sight to the stone circle. The summoning circle was empty. "Crowley got away."

Kat brushed her hair away from her face. "One thing at a time. First we deal with the Watcher."

The dust didn't have time to settle before the debris from the explosion started shaking, shifting, dragging back the way it came as if being pulled by magnetic force. Everything gathered at a single point, building on itself. Bits of wood, rock, and dirt fused around the invisible form of the Watcher, forming armor around its ethereal bulk. "Yeah. That'd be the Watcher."

A hodgepodge of rubble made up the creature's hide. Splintered wood and jagged rock moved with the Watcher as his avatar took the first ground-shaking steps. Seven heads moved in all directions, some low, others high as the Watcher's avatar searched out prey. Flames leapt from one mouth, another spewed filth. Nothing visible came from another, but as the head breathed out daemons and Nephilim alike fell to the ash-covered ground in agony, pustules bubbling on the surface of their skin. They writhed, screaming, clawing at their flesh.

Duncan backed away from the infected group and found himself next to James.

"He took the form of the Beast from Revelation—Annobapeste."

"Got a thing for Armageddon, that one." He nodded toward their mates. "They'll get him."

She was closer now, slowed by the daemons at her feet, but steadily marching toward Annobapeste.

Another head descended and the creature's muck-encrusted jaws parted, loosing a host of winged insects unlike anything he'd ever seen. They attacked everything in sight, landing on each quarry before tormenting their victims with stingers and teeth. The swarm rounded, coming straight for them.

"Shite."

IT WASN'T AS BAD AS Trina had expected. Her thoughts remained her own. She felt her own limbs cocooned within the larger form around them.

What the hell is that? Lilith asked.

Don't care. Ruins of a tower lay in the distance. *You see where we need to push him?*

Yeah.

She opened her mouth, blasting Annobapeste with pure blue flame and the head Lilith controlled joined in.

The creature reared back, its multiple heads shrieking in outrage as the Watcher's avatar ignited like kindling.

She pressed on and the Watcher retreated farther though its seven heads still struck, biting, gnashing, and spewing foulness over their own avatar. There was no pain. She couldn't feel the scratches and gouges the Watcher left behind.

Lilith spread their wings, making them appear even larger as they advanced. *He's tiring.*

His strikes declined in strength as the flames licked over its arborous frame. Dirt, muck, and rocks crumbled from the Watcher's blazing armament.

Ram him. We're almost there.

They ran and her chest collided with the Watcher, forcing him back, his whip-like tails flirting with the border of the ruins.

One of his heads turned, as if becoming aware of his jeopardy and he leapt against them in a desperate attempt to avoid the threat of imprisonment.

She and Lilith's heads descended, growling, roaring. The jaws of both opened and they sank their teeth into the Watcher's grime-encrusted armor.

Pull him apart, Lil.

They raised the writhing creature high in the air before they pulled in opposite directions, ripping the avatar asunder.

Remnants of timber and shrubs along with a mixture of dirt and stones plummeted to the battlefield. The Watcher sagged to the ground. Struggled to get up.

Trina clamped down on his leg and together they dragged the Watcher closer to the ruins.

He's letting us do this.

Lilith was right, he was. He'd put on a show, displayed his power, but he was allowing them to imprison him. Why?

The ground rumbled and split apart under the ruins, leaving a gaping hole.

Some unseen force lifted the Watcher, tugging it out from their grasp and she released him. Watched as he was sucked down into the hole.

He didn't fight. Didn't struggle. The bastard was smirking.

Over the edge he dropped and the ground rumbled anew as his tower rose. Bit by bit, the structure lifted from the ground, rising until it loomed over Machon.

He thinks he'll get free again.

Never.

CHAPTER 38

DUNCAN PAUSED, HANDS ON HIS thighs as he fought to catch his breath.

The battle was done. Some Nephilim had escaped back through the portal before it had closed. The rest were ash beneath their feet. Minions pounced through the ash, killing off the remainder of the flying insects the Watcher had released. The Original was safe. The Watcher imprisoned, all that was left was to see if Trina and Lilith could unmerge.

She was having trouble, she'd lain herself down, panting with effort.

James ran over to him. "They hurt?"

"Don't think so." If what they'd done was anything like shifting, they were safe and sound far beneath the gouges and wounds on the dragon's flesh. "First shift is hard. It's one thing to pull armor over yourself when you're fighting for your life, another to let it go when everything in you wants to hold on." He wandered closer, between her heads and James followed. "Come on, Duchess. Quit resisting; it just causes pain. You don't need the avatar anymore. Relax."

He put his hands on her snout and they stopped struggling.

A quick glance showed James trying to soothe Lilith as well.

"Close your eyes. Breathe deep. Let go."

Her eyes fixed on him before sliding shut. A big huff sent steam curling out of her nostrils. After a few minutes, she started to shrink in on herself.

"They're doing it." James dragged his hand over his head. As the dragon avatar shrank, they followed. Their mates were in there somewhere.

Faster now, the bulk of her melted away. Blue light shimmered around her and then the women were there. Trina's gaze locked on his and she ran to him. Jumped up and plastered herself against him, wrapping her legs around his hips. "You look like hell, Dunc."

He laughed. "Yeah, well, while you two were playing with avatars, I was down here fighting in the muck."

"Look."

From their vantage, it looked as if the Nephilim were gone. "I wonder if we might be lucky enough that he brought them all here."

"He didn't." Brenda stood nearby. "We have a long fight ahead, but I no longer see the total destruction I saw before. Armageddon will have to wait."

"What about Crowley?" Duncan asked. "Is he still alive? Is he still in Machon?"

Brenda closed her eyes. She was quiet for a long time. When she opened her eyes, her gaze narrowed on Trina's. "It's murky."

"But he's alive?"

She nodded. "He is."

And free. *Shite.*

"Kat!" Trina raised her voice and waved. "Everything okay?"

The redhead gave her a thumb's up. "I'm gonna head back."

Harry had heard the exchange and altered his course to walk back with Kat. George rode his shoulder, taking swipes at her hair whenever she got close enough. Harry glanced at his watch.

"That's interesting."

"What?" Trina raised her brow.

He pulled her back flush to him and wrapped his arms around her. "He avoids all the other women."

"Maybe he likes her because she doesn't have any expectations of him."

They watched the two for a while. Then his gaze shifted to the daemons lingering about. The coven had survived. As had Doom. They'd been lucky. They still needed to find Crowley so they could hand him over to the humans, but now that he was free from the Watcher, that shouldn't be too difficult. Not as difficult as getting rid of the Nephilim back home.

"I figured it out." She pulled away to look at him. "I know why we can't leave the Darkness."

"Oh?"

"So we can guide the others stuck in the Darkness." She leaned in, pulling him down so she could press her lips to his. "Just like when you helped us unmerge."

Duncan grinned. "Yeah. You see? It's like I'm always telling you, Duchess: It's all in your perspective."

"I think you might be right." She pulled away and framed his face in her hands. "In this light, even covered in dirt and ash and blood, you're the most attractive male I've ever laid eyes on."

He laughed. "Only a woman in love could be so damned blind." Duncan Sinclair hugged his female tighter and laughed some more.

He did so because he was happy.

He did so because he only had three rules:

Always let those you love see how you really feel.

Fuck the job . . . do what's right.

Always love.

It was that simple.

AUTHOR BIO

CARA CRESCENT CURRENTLY LIVES IN the Pacific Northwest with her children and three overly dramatic ferrets. When not writing, you can usually find her curled up with a book, engrossed in a movie or playing video games with her best friend.

Please visit her on the web at **www.caracrescent.com**

BOOKS BY CARA CRESCENT

The Last Marine
The Beacon
Don't Let Me Forget You